Moonlit COLORADO

I0835875

MOONLIT COLORADO (Hart County Series Book 2)

Ebook Cover Photography: Regina Wamba

Cover Design (Ebook and Print): Angela Haddon

Produced by Diana Road Books

HART COUNTY BOOK 2

HANNAH SHIELD

Prologue

Grace, Last Year

I was in the kitchen, staring into a glass of water, when Emma came in. I startled and looked up.

"Don't mind me," Emma said. "I'm on a quest for sugar. I heard a rumor about chocolate in the pantry, and I figured I'd better get to the bottom of that before the kids beat me to it."

I smiled, setting aside my glass. "I'll be your wingwoman. Chocolate is exactly what I need."

We went into the pantry to search the shelves. Yet I couldn't take my eyes off the garish bruises on Emma's neck, making any interest in food vanish from my stomach.

"How are you doing?" I asked.

"Getting better every day," she said softly, with a cringe that showed she was still in pain.

She had almost died a couple of days ago. And the thought of what she'd gone through, who had hurt her... It was too much to take. Someone we'd all trusted had tried to silence Emma permanently to stop her from revealing some dark secrets. And here Emma was, smiling as we looked for sugary snacks.

Talk about brave.

And then she asked how *I* was doing, which made me feel even worse. "Me? I'm fine. I have nothing to complain about. I was incredibly lucky."

But as we spoke, a tear slipped down my cheek. Because I had trusted the person who hurt Emma, too. I hadn't seen this coming.

I should have seen it.

"I'm so glad you're all right," I said. If my brother had lost the woman he loved, it would've destroyed him.

Emma put her hand on my arm. "Thanks. You'll be all right too."

I sighed and nodded. Even though I wasn't sure I believed that.

Emma and Ashford had each other, and I was grateful for it. Someday, Emma was going to be an amazing stepmom to Maisie, my niece. But they were the exception that proved the rule.

Love was too much of a risk.

There was no way I'd ever be able to trust someone with my heart.

ONE

Dane

I'D ALWAYS LOVED MOUNTAINS. As a child, those had been my favorite vacations. Skiing in Zermatt, Park City, or Banff. I would stare out the window as the plane descended, watching the shapes below turn into jagged peaks and deep valleys. All of it blanketed with a thick layer of white.

And later, when the mountains had been in Afghanistan, their beauty had been equal even though I'd otherwise been surrounded by danger.

Well, maybe vacations with my family weren't entirely safe either. Just for different reasons.

"Mr. Knightly? We'll be landing shortly. May I take your glass?"

Sharon, the flight attendant, hovered by my seat. I smiled at her and nodded. I hadn't been drinking the bourbon anyway, though it was a Pappy Van Winkle 23 year Family Reserve.

Wasn't the bourbon's fault. It was everything else on my mind.

As we descended onto the private airstrip, I studied the mountains outside my window, and the pressure seemed to lift. I was finally here in Colorado. I took a photo of the view and sent it off via text.

A minute later, a wi-fi call came in, and I answered it, unable to hold back my grin.

"You asshole," Ashford said. "You said you weren't coming."

"True, but I know how much you love surprises." *So* not true. Ashford hated to be caught off guard. I'd learned that when we served together. But my schedule had been chaotic lately.

"First of all, fuck you. Second, it's about time, man. Can't wait to see you."

"I know, there were some false starts there for a while." A pang of guilt went through my stomach, like sudden turbulence.

Ashford had been through some tough times last year, and at first, he hadn't even told me about it. My friend had a bad habit of keeping his troubles to himself.

But I was the same way, wasn't I?

Earlier this year, I bought a ski resort in Ashford's home county on behalf of my family's company, Knightly Global. Unfortunately, other things had always seemed to interfere with my attempts to visit in the months since. My mom's health issues had worsened. I'd assumed I couldn't make it for the hotel's grand opening this weekend.

"But I'm here now, about to touch down in your home state," I said. "Finally. How's the family?"

"Doing great. Busy as always, especially with the wedding planning."

"Do you and Emma have a date set?"

"I was hoping it would be this fall, but now we're looking at winter."

"Can't wait to hear all about it. You free tonight?"

"I'd make you take us out for an expensive dinner, except we're in Hartley visiting Emma's family. We'll be back in Silver Ridge on Saturday. Unless you want to come out here and meet us? You'd be welcome."

"Nah, no worries. Saturday is perfect. I've got this grand-opening party nonsense on Friday to deal with. I thought about sending you tickets to the masquerade ball, but—"

"Hell no. You won't catch me near that. But if you need anything, Callum is around. Same with Grace. I could let them know you're in town."

"No need to bother them." Though I had to admit, I was curious about Ashford's younger sister. I'd met his brothers when we were all in the service, but I'd never met Grace. The last picture I'd seen of her was way outdated. She'd been a teenager with braces. How old would she be now? Late twenties?

She's your buddy's little sister, I told myself. *Off limits. That's what she is, regardless of what she looks like.*

"I'd better go," I said into the phone. "Enjoy Hartley. By the time you get back to Silver Ridge, I'll be running the place."

Ashford grunted. "I have no doubt. Don't get into too much trouble."

"We'll see." Chuckling, I pocketed my phone.

The plane's exit door opened, and Sharon went to grab my bag. I stepped in front of her to reach for it. "I've got it. It's heavy."

"At least let me get your jacket."

I let her slip my blazer onto my arms. After brushing invisible lint from my lapels, she flipped her French braid over her shoulder, giving me the same meaningful look she'd been aiming my way the whole flight. "Anything else I can do for you, Mr. Knightly? Anything at all? We'll be on the ground here for several hours."

I was not interested in the *anything* she was offering. But still, I threw her a wink. "Better not. I've got a drive ahead of me."

She leaned in and whispered, "I could make that drive a lot more entertaining for you."

"Tempting. But I can't." Also, I wasn't going to get busy in the backseat of a rented car. Though my reputation, which I'd earned in my younger and more reckless days, might suggest otherwise.

It was still September, but temperatures were already dipping. Despite the chill, I undid another button of my shirt. I'd already ditched the tie. A few snowflakes whirled around me as I jogged down the stairs and toward the waiting SUV. The driver opened the door for me, but I stopped to shake his hand. "Eddie, right?"

"Yes, Mr. Knightly."

"Dane is fine." I slid into the backseat. A sea of dark leather, low lighting, and glinting glass from the small bar.

"Of course, Mr. Knightly. You'll be happy to know the cabin is equipped with extra oxygen to offset the effects of the altitude."

I laughed. "Let me guess. My assistant Margot's request?"

"I'm not sure, sir. We should be in Silver Ridge in about an hour."

A diplomatic response, and probably all I was likely to get. But that was fine. Margot could be heavy-handed, but she tried to take care of me. And she was the *only* person I'd allow that kind of mothering from. Aside from my own mom. But...

Damn it, there was that guilt again, twisting my insides, and it was worse than useless. Mom's nurses were the best money could buy. More than that, they were kind to her. And Margot was in New York too, if anything came up. Margot had been the one to convince me to make the trip this weekend.

If your mother could speak her own mind right now, she'd tell you to get your butt to Colorado and make the most of it.

I settled into my seat and worked on my laptop, finishing up some work I'd started on the plane. But I paused to admire the view as we drove. First it was wide-open expanses of terrain with faraway ranges creating a backdrop for pastures with grazing cattle. Later, a creek ran along the highway, with the occasional bridge leading to a quaint cabin. Eventually the scenery changed again as we entered Hart County. Soaring mountain peaks in the distance, meadows of swaying grasses, and beyond, dense woods of evergreens.

And everywhere I looked, golden and red fall colors added drama. So different from autumn in Manhattan, which had its own unique grandeur and beauty.

The road kept curving and climbing. The town seemed to

appear out of nowhere, emerging from the trees. A few people on Main Street turned and watched the SUV glide by. The tinted windows were probably unusual around here.

Silver Ridge, Colorado, was straight out of a postcard. A long-lost vision of an idyllic small town. My buddy Ashford had grown up here, but he could've chosen to settle anywhere. He'd chosen to call Silver Ridge home. And to me, that meant something. Sure, cash could buy a luxurious apartment or sprawling mansion just about anywhere. But money didn't make those places feel like *home*.

We followed the road out of the main town and up into the foothills, which kept on ascending toward rocky peaks. The SUV passed a sign for the Silver Ridge Ski Resort, following along a paved driveway as we approached a sprawling complex of buildings amid aspen groves. We parked in front of reception.

It was my first time seeing the resort in person. *My* resort, now. The place didn't disappoint.

The exterior of the newly finished hotel was rough stone and timber, with accents of oil-rubbed bronze. Grander than anything I'd seen down on Main Street, but it still had that western vibe.

I patted Eddie's shoulder, handing him some bills for his tip. "Thanks, man. Appreciate it." I was sure Margot had already arranged for gratuity, but cash was always better.

As I got out, a man in a suit and tie stepped out of the sliding lobby doors. "Mr. Knightly," he said. "Honored to finally meet you in person. I'm Tobin."

The hotel manager. "Of course, Tobin. I remember you from the video conference." I'd already introduced myself to the staff, virtually at least.

He beamed. "Can I offer you a tour of your property? Or if you'd prefer, your suite is—"

"I'll head to my suite, thanks." I strode toward the entrance, carrying my own bag, and Tobin rushed to follow me. "Ask your team if they're free for dinner tonight," I said. "My treat. So I can say hello properly."

"Of course, sir. I would've planned something special if I'd known, but as it is..."

"I know. I've got you scrambling."

"Not at all. We're adjusting. Did you want to go over the final details for the party tomorrow night as well? Or—"

"Margot can handle that. She'll pass on anything I need to know. You've got her number."

He laughed. "Oh, yes. I certainly do."

We took the elevator to the top floor, where there were only two doors. The manager stopped at one and swiped my key. "If you don't mind my asking, Mr. Knightly, how long are you staying? Margot said she wasn't sure."

"That's because I haven't decided yet." That depended on a lot of things. I took the key and stepped inside.

"If there's anything else—"

"I'll be sure to let you know." I gave him my most amiable grin.

Then I swung the door shut, dropped my bag by my feet, and blew out a heavy breath.

Across the room, the curtains were open, revealing a bank of windows that overlooked the resort. A panorama of mountains expanded across the horizon. There were only a few streaks of white on the ski runs so far, hints of the heavier snowpack that would develop as the season got going.

Gorgeous.

Margot had been right. Coming here had been the right move. I just had to make the trip worth it.

A quick tour of the suite revealed more bedrooms than I needed. A kitchen already stocked with basics. Way too much space for one man, but I didn't mind spreading out.

A tuxedo in a garment bag lay on my bed, along with a black mask for the masquerade ball and a note in Margot's handwriting. She was thousands of miles away, but that never stopped her from having things *just so*. One of the reasons I trusted her so much.

The party won't be that bad. Try to enjoy it.
-M

I grunted skeptically, hung the garment bag in the closet, and tossed the mask onto the dresser to deal with tomorrow.

This trip was an investment for the company, sure, but also a chance to see Ashford and meet his daughter and fiancée. The guy was my closest friend in the world, yet I hadn't seen him in person in *years*. There were a lot of reasons for that, some of them nobody's fault.

But...mostly my fault. I wasn't the type to make excuses.

Hard to believe a man in his thirties with my kind of net worth was stuck in a job he hated. If I had thought serving my country and then making my own fortune would earn my father's respect, I'd been wrong. I would never have joined Knightly Global if it wasn't my mom's greatest wish that I reconcile with my father and brother. As if the three of us working together would transform us into a happy family unit. Ha. But I was *trying*. For her.

Even if this job felt like a straight jacket in the form of a tailored suit.

The moment I'd heard this ski resort needed a new owner and an infusion of cash to finish building the hotel, I'd known it was perfect. This was the first project I'd had in a while that I actually cared about. It wasn't really the resort. It was this town. The hope of maybe finding a sliver of the meaning Ashford had in his life here. If I was stuck working for Knightly Global, then I needed something like this or I would lose my fucking mind.

And I'd known that Mom would love Silver Ridge too. At some point I wanted to bring her out here. If I could get Dad to agree.

Good thing I was nothing if not persistent.

When I truly wanted something, it was only a matter of time until I found a way to have it.

TWO

Grace

I LOOKED at the stacks of books on my kitchen counter. Then at the undersized cardboard box in my arms. Then back at the books.

"They're not going to fit," Callum said.

"They are too."

I set the box on the counter. Adjusting my glasses on my nose, I planned my attack. Nestled a book inside. Then another. Taking my time. Callum watched over my shoulder.

"Quit being so stubborn," he said. "Just grab another box. The garage is full of them."

"No kidding." But those were all moving boxes, and I was sick of looking at them.

Niko wandered shirtless into the kitchen. "Hey, Cal. Grace, you look busy." He was one of Callum's roommates.

Oops. Make that one of *my* roommates. Because I now lived with my brother and three other overbearing firefighters instead of in my cute little bungalow by *myself*.

Exactly why I was annoyed at those stupid moving boxes.

Until the summer, I'd rented the same house for years. My pride and joy. My landlord and I had made an oral agreement that

I'd buy the place from him when I had the downpayment saved up, and in the meantime, I'd made all sorts of improvements.

Then my landlord had sold the house out from under me for a far higher asking price than I could afford. And because we'd been going month-to-month on my rent instead of bothering to keep the lease paperwork current, I got kicked out. There was nothing I could do.

I had trusted that man to keep his word. Big mistake.

I should've known better.

My brother Ashford had offered me his spare room. But Ashford had my seven-year-old niece, a golden retriever, and a fiancée to take care of. He didn't need to be worrying about me too.

With no other affordable units available, I'd had no choice but to move in with Callum and his buddies, all of whom treated me like their baby sister. As if I didn't have enough big brothers already. And the amount of food they ate. It was *astonishing*. They'd demolished a lasagna last night like a school of piranhas. I shivered just thinking about it.

At least they were good at dishes. Firefighters knew how to keep a place clean.

"Need help?" Niko asked me.

Callum shook his head. "Don't get involved, man. She doesn't want help. She's on an organizing tear."

"I'm just trying to knock out my to-do list," I said, arranging the books like Jenga pieces. "I'm taking these to Silver Linings to drop them off with Piper. Then I have Zoom meetings this afternoon with my online clients, and a planning meeting for the next fundraiser for the children's center. So don't wait up."

"Gracie, most people mean something different when they say *don't wait up*," Callum said as he rummaged in the pantry for food. "To normal humans, it means they're out having fun." Callum tossed Niko a protein bar, then ripped into one for himself.

"Don't be mean. Planning meetings can be fun."

"You're cute." Callum grabbed me around the shoulders and smacked a kiss on the top of my head. I pushed him away.

"Don't you have somewhere better to be?" I asked. "Like saving a cat from a tree? Serving your community?"

Callum shrugged. "More like serving beers. I've got a shift at Hearthstone." He and his buddies all had other gigs, since there weren't many full-time spots with Silver Ridge FD.

"But I'll bring back potato skins for you," my brother added.

My annoyance disappeared. "I love their potato skins."

"Yeah, I *know*."

"Thank you." I made my hands into a heart shape, then stuck out my tongue.

Laughing, Callum grabbed his keys and phone, spun on his heel, and jogged toward the door.

Niko turned to me. "I think you're fun, Grace."

"Stay away from my little sister," Callum shouted from somewhere near the back door.

I just rolled my eyes, because that was *so* not necessary. Niko was a sweet guy, the type to give you his last dime *and* the last ice cream bar. Easy on the eyes too. But I had no intention of getting romantic with anyone, firefighters or otherwise.

New living arrangements aside, my life was straightforward. *Boring*. And that was the way I liked it.

Because boring was *safe*.

✧

Twenty minutes later, I made my way toward Silver Linings Coffee with my cardboard box of books. Sometimes, I felt like I singlehandedly kept Piper's used books shelves stocked. But it was a sacrifice I was willing to make.

My glasses started sliding down my nose. Praying they wouldn't fall and get scratched on the concrete, I shifted the heavy weight of the box to one arm and popped my glasses back up my nose with my finger. Then I reached for the door to the coffee shop.

It was an elegant balancing act. I *totally* had this.

Just as that triumphant thought ran through my mind, I yanked the door open and went inside.

Then I crashed into something very tall and very solid. The books went sprawling across the tile floor. My glasses almost followed, slipping back down to the very tip of my nose. I looked over them at the man who stood in front of me. A man who had a coffee-colored stain the size of Greenland on his cream-colored sweater.

"Well, shit," he muttered.

"Oh my gosh. I'm so sorry."

He glanced down at his ruined sweater and shrugged. "No worries. Are you okay?"

Shoving my glasses into place, I lunged for some napkins from a nearby counter. "I'm fine, but you're not. The coffee here is extra hot. And from the looks of it, you dumped an extra large all over yourself. Or rather, *I* did."

He laughed softly, taking the napkins from me to dab at his sweater. "It's all good. My fault too. I didn't see you coming."

"I hope that's not a comment about me being short."

"Wouldn't dream of it."

I glanced up at him, then had to keep on going. A little further.

I'd just joked about me being short. But this man was *tall.*

Dark lashes rimmed his steely gray eyes. His wavy brown hair was short on the sides, tousled on top. The sleeves of his sweater were pushed up, revealing tanned, veiny forearms.

Yikes.

The guy threw the wet napkins and his now empty coffee cup in the trash, and then knelt on the floor beside me. "Let me help you with these." He picked up a fallen book. "*Advanced Techniques for QuickBooks*. Looks like a gripping read."

"Scintillating. But not as good as this one. It's a beach read, alright." I reached for my copy of *Bookkeeping Pitfalls and How to Avoid Them* and held it up.

"Sounds like a bestseller." His long fingers grazed mine as he handed the books to me. The man exuded the kind of confidence that came from a well-developed ego, the kind that the giant brown stain on his front couldn't put a dent in.

He had to be a tourist. Probably a rich one to boot.

His type usually marched around town like they owned the place. Yet instead of being furious that I'd run into him, he seemed amused.

Meanwhile, a few new coffee splatters just blended in to the old, oversized sweatshirt I was wearing over my favorite pair of faded jeans. No harm, no foul.

He finished helping me stack my books in the box, then picked it up, balancing the whole thing on one arm like it was easy. "How about I buy myself another coffee, and I can get you one too," he said. "Just to show there's no hard feelings."

His head tilted as he waited for my answer, his smile going lopsided. Despite his air of wealth, there was something disarming about him. Rugged, too. Like if I held his hand in mine, I'd find it rough instead of soft.

Heat prickled as a blush rose in my cheeks, and flutters cascaded through my belly.

Oh, no. Nope. *Stop that.*

Thankfully, Piper came to my rescue. "I saw the accident!" She handed the new guy a fresh cup of whatever he'd ordered. "On the house. I'd replace your shirt too, but..."

"No, it's fine." The man laughed again, smooth and deep. "This sweater isn't my favorite anyway." He glanced at me, which I saw from the corner of my eye. But I carried my box of books over to the counter, putting my back to him and hoping he would go away.

I usually prided myself on being direct. But that man had me all kinds of flustered. I held my breath until I heard the door jingle again.

Piper came around to the other side of the counter behind the register. "You okay?"

"Is he gone?" I whispered.

"Mr. Hunky McHandsome? Yeah, he's gone. Why? He didn't seem mad about the spill."

I exhaled. I'd been rude to the guy, just turning my back on him that way, but he'd seemed confident enough to shrug it off. He probably charmed every woman he met. He'd forget about me the moment I was out of sight.

"He offered to buy me a coffee."

"Is that bad?"

"Not on the surface. But his smile was too nice, and he was way too polite. Serious red flags."

"Very suspicious. I'll put him on my blacklist. No more coffee for that guy. Unless you spill it on him."

We both laughed.

Yes, I was exaggerating. But Piper understood. There was a certain type of man who seemed perfect when you first met him, only to crush your heart, put it through a meat grinder, and throw it out with yesterday's compost.

Once, I might've fallen for that kind of thing. But now I knew better.

Piper waved her hand. "Anyway, forget about Hunky McHandsome. I have much more exciting news."

I shook off my depressing thoughts. "I've got all the excitement I can handle. The fall festival is this weekend. And look at this amazing haul of books I just brought in."

She made a face, shoving the box to the far end of the counter. "Sadly, your used financial books don't tend to fly off the shelves."

"Hey now, there's some historical fiction and biographies in there too."

"Be still my heart. By the way, how are your firefighter bros?" She grabbed a peanut butter cookie from her display case, breaking it in half and handing me the other.

"Only one of them is *my* bro. And they're actually okay as roommates."

"The views are probably nice with all those muscles."

"Gross. That's my brother."

"Not Callum. He's practically my brother too. I meant the other three."

"Not interested."

"Sure, but you can look. However, I recognize that you, Grace O'Neal, are the kind of woman who enjoys a hefty serving of brains with her brawn. You need a touch of elegance."

I gestured at myself, baggy sweatshirt, messy hair and all. "The very picture of elegance, right here."

"All the more reason that you need a glamorous night out. And I do *not* mean the fall festival." Piper reached into the pocket of her apron and produced two tickets, each decorated with a stylized picture of a mask. She glanced around to see who was listening, but the coffee shop was experiencing a rare lull.

"You and I are going to the VIP grand-opening party tomorrow night for the new hotel at the ski resort."

"*What*? How on earth did you get tickets?"

Pretty much everyone in Silver Ridge had heard about the grand opening of the new hotel. There had been some kind of drama about the ski resort's finances, and my brother Ashford's friend from the Army, Dane Knightly, had swooped in to buy them out. Or his family's company had swooped in. Something like that.

Ashford had always spoken highly of Dane. Yet the man had never made a single trip to Silver Ridge, either before or after buying the resort. Knightly wasn't even planning to attend the grand opening.

Piper shrugged. "Hanson Barker provided the tickets. I'm going with him, and he had an extra for you."

"The mayor's son? You broke our no-dating pact for Handy-dandy Barker? The former king of shop class?" Famous for making a bong shaped like a huge penis. Poor Mrs. Barker had been president of the PTA back then, and at the fine arts festival, I'd never forget the shade of purple that she'd turned when she saw her son's creation.

Piper hushed me, giggling. "Give the man a break. High school was a long time ago. Hanson is a nice guy. He only got tickets because of his mother's position, and he wisely chose me to share them with. Besides, my pact with you is about not dating." Her eyebrows wiggled. "Not about sex."

"You're having sex with Handy-dandy?" I deadpanned.

She got a mischievous glint in her eyes and leaned in. "No, we're friends. But who knows. I might get lucky tomorrow night. Because I'm going to that party, dressed to the nines. And you're coming with me. I deserve this night out, and I won't apologize for it."

Piper had been my best friend since we were kids. She'd lived in the house across the street. She and I had gone to college together in Fort Collins, where we'd had plenty of wild times. Usually because Piper egged me on. We'd been a team. If one of us drank, the other stayed sober. We'd been there for each other no matter what. Looked out for each other. Ride or die.

Now that her ex-husband had left Silver Ridge, she was a single mom. Thank goodness her older brother Teller, the chief of police, was around for her son Ollie. Of course, my brothers and our friends stepped in and helped with Ollie whenever they could. But it still wasn't right for Piper's ex to leave her in the lurch like that.

Surprising? No. But so not right. Piper had dubbed our friend group the Lonely Harts club for a reason.

"You do deserve it," I said.

"But so do you. When was the last time you did something truly for yourself?" She paused. Like she really expected an answer.

I didn't have one.

I sighed. "I guess you'll need someone to keep an eye on you."

Piper pumped her fist in the air. "Yes!"

I took the ticket from her hand and my eyes traced the looping script. "I don't have anything to wear, though. It says black tie."

"Leave that to me. I have some of the dresses from our sorority days."

"You still have those?" I'd cleaned out my closet years ago with a more practical eye.

"Didn't know when I might need to attend a movie premiere."

"There are no movie premieres in Silver Ridge."

"There were no black-tie masquerade balls either. Until now." She reached across the counter and pulled me into a hug. "This is going to be epic. I promise, tomorrow night will be unforgettable."

I didn't know if I liked the sounds of that. So far in my life, the most indelible moments tended to coincide with loss and heartbreak.

THREE

Grace

"Are you ready yet?" Piper knocked at my bedroom door. "Hurry it up in there. Or at least let me in."

"Just a sec." I ran my fingers through my hair one last time, then smoothed my hands down the sides of my dress, enjoying the silky glide of the fabric under my fingers.

Here goes nothing.

I opened my bedroom door and stepped out. "What do you think?"

Piper's red lips broke into a huge grin. "It's a good thing we have a firefighter on the premises, because you are *smoking*."

"Shush." I put my finger over my lips. Niko and Darius were out, but Connor was playing video games in his room. Thank goodness Callum had another shift at Hearthstone Brewing tonight, like he had yesterday. "I don't want to make this into a whole thing," I said.

And if any of the guys saw me in this dress, it *would* be a thing.

Piper looked sleek and sophisticated in the purple gown she was wearing. If anything, it was on the conservative side. She had given *me* the racy red number with mesh cut-outs along the sides, placed in exactly the right spots so that I couldn't wear underwear.

In our town, a nice sweater and leather boots were considered formal wear. Maybe with a hat or a shawl thrown in. Silver Ridge was far from high fashion, and I liked it that way.

"You look amazing, and you know it."

Piper fussed over me, arranged my hair and smoothed out the straps of the dress. She'd twisted her blond hair into an elaborate updo. With her in low heels and me in stilettos, we were nearly the same height. I hardly ever wore makeup, but I'd used black eyeliner and mascara along with a rosy color on my cheeks and lips.

She pulled off my glasses. "Except these will not do."

"What? How am I supposed to see?"

"Wear your contacts. You look beautiful in your glasses, but it'll be hard to wear a mask to the masquerade ball if those frames are blocking your face."

I glared. She laughed.

"You're so much like Ashford when you scowl like that. Not nearly as scary though."

"Oh, quiet." I wasn't a fan of my contacts. They dried out my eyes. But she did have a point about the mask.

"Don't mess up the mascara," she called out as I traipsed to the bathroom. "It's perfection!"

"You are so demanding."

"Love you too, babe."

A few minutes later, my contacts were in. Piper handed me a slim black mask with long pieces of ribbon to tie it into place. Piper had a matching one, though hers was purple.

A wave of uncertainty hit me. "Are you sure we have to do this?" I asked.

"Stop. You used to get like this every Friday night before we went out in college, and guess who'd be dancing on the tables by the end of the night?"

"I have no memory of that."

She winked. "Exactly."

Handy-dandy, aka Hanson, texted when his truck pulled up

outside. We dashed out to meet him and jumped into the warm cabin, Piper in the front and me in the back. It was cold tonight, but neither of us had wanted to bother with coat checks.

"You two look hot." Hanson propped his arm on the back of the seat and turned to look at me, then whistled. "Damn, O'Neal. Who knew your usual clothes were hiding all of...*that*. Nice work."

"Um, thanks?"

Piper smirked at me. "*Relax*," she whispered.

I squirmed the whole drive up to the resort. The place was lit up like daytime, with a long stream of cars at the valet line.

In the lobby, we joined a crowd of elegantly dressed people waiting to show their tickets. Rustic iron chandeliers glowed overhead with a warm, flattering light. A fire roared in a massive, double-sided fireplace, and a string quartet played instrumental arrangements of popular songs.

It was like I'd been thrust into a scene from a movie or transported into a parallel reality. Like I wasn't in Silver Ridge anymore.

I thought I recognized a few locals, but most everyone here seemed unfamiliar. Which made me think of that guy at the coffee shop yesterday morning. His gray eyes and megawatt smile. Or rather, think of him yet again, as I'd been doing off and on since we crashed into each other at Silver Linings.

I found myself scanning the people around me for his broad shoulders and dark hair. My chest tightened with anticipation, wondering if he'd be here. Maybe he'd arrived in town especially for this party.

But he was exactly the type of man I should stay away from. Smooth and charming and inevitably untrustworthy. *Dangerous*. Maybe not physically, since I'd been taking self-defense classes with Ashford at his martial arts school. I had moves. But I couldn't take the chance of believing some guy's pretty words and thinking they meant more than they did.

"Piper," I said, turning to face her. "Do you—"

I glanced back and forth, but I didn't see her or Hanson anywhere in the sea of people. Too many women had purple dresses. Had she gone into the party without me? I didn't want to go in and turn over my ticket until I found her.

The colors of the masks started to blur. Someone bumped into me. The energy of the room was suddenly too much. Overwhelming.

Then I saw a sign, like a beacon leading me out of the fog.

Restrooms.

The door of the ladies' room swung closed, cutting off the noise in the lobby. Maybe this was a cowardly exit to take, but I just needed a few minutes to get my head together. And text Piper so I could figure out where she was.

I took my phone from my clutch—something else I'd borrowed from Piper—and jotted out a text, receiving a quick response.

ME

Where are you? Lost you

PIPER

I lost you too! We're inside. At the bar, then going to dance in the next room over. Come find us?

Will soon. Bathroom

Should I come get you? I will

No, I'm okay. Promise.

I set the purse on the counter and rested my hands on either side of one of the sinks, staring into the mirror. I didn't look like myself with the mask on, so I pulled at the tie and took it off. With each moment that passed, I felt less sure of myself.

What am I even doing here?

This wasn't college. I wasn't twenty anymore. Twenty-eight felt like a different lifetime compared to our college days.

I stiffened when the door swung open and a woman in a strapless black dress walked inside. Her mask was far more elaborate than mine. Glittery red, with large jewels set around the edges of the mask and downy, red-dyed feathers. It didn't look like a homemade craft project either.

She tugged off the mask as she approached the other sink. Her eyes were bloodshot. Her hands shook, and her chest moved rapidly with shallow breaths.

My own breath hitched in sympathy. "Are you all right?" I asked.

She inhaled sharply, head turning. Then her features smoothed out, and she tried to smile, though tightness remained at the corners of her mouth. "Didn't realize someone was already hiding in here."

I almost denied it, but I was totally hiding. "I guess it's that kind of night."

"Ain't that the truth."

She was probably in her twenties, like me, but she looked tired. Exhausted, even. Which didn't fit with her perfect makeup or the diamond drop earrings hanging from her earlobes. Her waist was cinched tight, and her breasts nearly spilled from the top of her dress. But the most memorable thing about her was her hair. It was a vivid red that glowed in the bathroom lights. My hair had red tones to it, but hers was like neon.

Ms. Scarlet, I thought, since I didn't know her name. She was beautiful. But she did *not* seem happy to be here.

Ms. Scarlet washed her hands. Then opened her purse and glanced inside, closing it quickly before she froze, as if she'd gotten lost in thought.

"Are you sure you're okay?" I asked. Maybe I was being too nosy, but it was obvious she was anxious.

She opened her mouth, pausing for a long time, before saying, "My date stood me up."

"I'm sorry. That stinks. Do you need a ticket to the party?" I reached for my purse.

You're just looking for an excuse to bail, a scolding voice said in my mind. But if this woman needed the ticket more than me, Piper would understand. I could bum around in the lobby listening to the string quartet until Piper and Hanson were ready to go.

"That's nice of you, but I'm covered." She licked her lips. "Just not sure I feel like staying. I haven't decided yet."

"You can still have a good time without a date," I pointed out.

"Yeah. But have you ever felt like you're just...questioning everything?"

I sighed. "Oh, wow. I've definitely been there. I told my friend I'd have fun tonight, but instead I'm hiding in the bathroom."

I'd come to this party for Piper, but part of me had agreed to it because I did want a night for *me*. Just like Piper had said yesterday when she'd talked me into this.

Ms. Scarlet's gaze had gone distant, like she was lost in her head again. In a way, it gave me courage. It was always easier for me to step out of my comfort zone if I was doing it for someone else.

"How about this," I said. "We both put our masks back on, go into that party, and have a good night."

I made the first move, picking up my mask and tying it on. But one of the ribbons snapped away from the mask, and the whole thing fell off.

"Dang it," I muttered. "You're kidding me."

Ms. Scarlet stared at the broken black mask in my hand. Her gaze moved to the door. To me again.

Then she nodded once, like she'd made some decision.

"Take this one." She picked up her bejeweled mask and held it out.

"I can't do that. This looks expensive."

"Not everything that shines is a real diamond."

"Unlike your earrings?"

"Oh sweetheart, those are *definitely* fake." She smiled, and her hands weren't shaking anymore. Her eyes were brighter too. "Hold still. I'll tie it for you."

"But—"

She was already behind me, placing the mask over my face. "You're doing me a favor. Your mask breaking was as clear a sign as I'm likely to get. This isn't my night. I should just cut my losses and go."

"Do you have a ride?"

"I'll figure it out." She shrugged as she secured the ties. "You should get to the party. Have fun. It's liberating to wear a mask. You can be whoever you want, even if it's just for a night."

Just for a night. I did like that idea.

"Would you take my number though?" I asked. "In case you need a ride later or…anything?"

"I'll be fine. You're helping me out already."

I didn't see how. But if I was making her feel better, that was a win. Right?

Ms. Scarlet held onto my shoulders and gently steered me toward the exit. But just as I opened the door, she said, "Wait a second. You forgot your purse."

"Oh. Thanks. That would've been bad." I took it from her hand. "Have a safe night, okay?"

She flinched, such a small movement I almost missed it. "That's what I'm hoping for."

We both left the bathroom, dodging a cluster of women just heading in. Then I watched, still bewildered, as Ms. Scarlet turned a corner and disappeared. I hoped she would be all right.

That had been *really* strange.

Yet the glittery red mask gave me a new burst of confidence. I could pretend, for one exciting night, that I wasn't some nerdy bookkeeper with an abysmal dating history and zero trust in the male species.

Tonight was about feeling good in my skin and nothing else.

Ready or not, here I come.

FOUR

Dane

JUST AS I finished knotting my bowtie, my phone buzzed with an incoming text.

MARGOT

You're late to the party.

ME

How the hell do you know that?

My spies are everywhere.

The hotel manager just called me in a panic, wondering where you are. I told him you probably looked in the mirror and lost track of time.

Ouch. A palpable hit.

Accurate though.

I grinned at my phone.

Margot had been my assistant for years, since back when I'd been running my own company. But I had known her for longer than that. Her son had served with me and Ashford, and he'd died in an insurgent attack in Kandahar. After I came home, I got to know her and eventually, after I left active duty, wound up hiring her to work for me. When I joined the family business two years ago, I insisted on bringing her with me.

Margot was one of the few people I trusted completely. She never let me get away with anything.

ME

What would I do without you, M?

MARGOT

I suppose you would try to manage.

Make sure you look presentable at the VIP event tonight.

I always look extremely presentable.

Because you spend so much time in front of the mirror.

Ha ha. I'm heading down now.

It was true that I'd lost track of time. But only because I wasn't looking forward to this idiotic party. Which had been my brother Kipling's idea, not mine. I didn't give a shit about impressing the company's VIP clients and business associates, who Kip had flown in to enjoy the changing fall colors and complimentary room service. If he'd wanted to glad-hand the VIPs, he could've shown up in Silver Ridge himself.

He'd fought me every step of the way on buying this resort. And now, he wanted to take over and treat this project like it was his?

Never mind. I didn't want my brother here. That was exactly why I'd come to Colorado. For a break from Kip and my father.

Since taking a stroll around Main Street yesterday, I'd been keeping busy. Working out in the hotel gym. Meeting with the hotel's staff, taking a tour of the property I'd purchased, plus keeping up with my usual duties as a Knightly Global Properties executive. But at the same time, my mind had been engaged in more pleasant pursuits. Remembering shiny auburn hair twirled into a messy bun. Two bright eyes behind oversized plastic-framed glasses.

The woman at the coffee shop yesterday morning. Damn, she had been adorable.

Was she a bookkeeper? That would explain the selection of books in that box she'd been carrying. I did love a good spreadsheet.

She was clearly a local. She'd gotten shy around me, and that had only stoked my interest.

I wondered if I'd see her again. In a town this small, the chances were high. Yet I hadn't spotted her when I took a long run down to Main Street this morning and stopped at Silver Linings Coffee again. The woman behind the register had been someone different, not the tall blond from yesterday. But I had noticed *Advanced Techniques for QuickBooks* on the used books shelf.

The book was now sitting upstairs on the dresser in my bedroom, an impulse buy that I couldn't even explain.

I spent a couple of moments checking myself over in the mirror. More than presentable.

When I got downstairs, Tobin the hotel manager found me immediately. Either Margot had told him I was on my way down, or he had some kind of tracker on me.

"Mr. Knightly, may I introduce you to Mayor Barker?"

Instead of one massive ballroom, the party was set up in various rooms to show off the hotel's event facilities. It created a more intimate feeling, one space flowing into the next through archways. As if this were a private mansion rather than a corporate-owned complex. The staff had done well.

I chatted with the mayor, a woman in her sixties with an impressive handshake. Then greeted some of the other VIPs as Tobin ushered me around like I was a dish of party favors. I had no problem talking to people, but I hated wasting time. When it came to business, I preferred numbers and logistics and strategy.

Data. If I made phone calls or held meetings, it was for a clear purpose. That was why I tracked down lucrative investment opportunities for my father's company, rather than squeezing money from potential investors like my brother did.

When and if I entered a negotiation, I was the guy who closed the deal. Meaningless small talk made me want to jump off the highest point of the nearest ski lift.

As soon as I could, I slipped away from Tobin and made my way to the bar. It was set up in a square shape with the bartenders in the middle. "Bourbon," I said, pointing at the bottle I wanted. "Neat." While he poured, I glanced around at the masked party-goers, realizing the benefit of a masquerade. Hardly anyone here would know who I was. I might actually be able to enjoy myself.

That was when I saw her.

A woman in an elaborate red mask stepped up to the bar. Her dress hugged her curves like a Porsche on a mountain road. Her hair was a mixture of golden and auburn strands, which fell in waves around her shoulders. She rested her elbows on the bar top with her purse clutched in her hands. Ordered a glass of wine.

Something about her pulled at me. A familiarity. But the mask and the dress threw me off. Same with the makeup.

I was about to approach when a heavyset older man with a blue mask stormed up to her and grabbed her by the shoulder. "You were supposed to wait for me in the lobby."

Her mouth opened in a shocked O.

Instantly, I straightened up, my instincts prickling with awareness.

"Excuse me?" she said. "You must have me confused with someone else."

The man tugged on her shoulder, trying to pull her toward him. "I don't know what kind of game you're playing, but this isn't what we agreed."

"I have no idea what you're talking about."

As she spoke, I was already striding toward them, squeezing my bourbon glass with fury burning in my gut.

I stopped close to her, though I didn't touch her. What I really wanted to do was shove this prick out the door and ban him from my hotel. I didn't give a fuck who he was or what he assumed, whether he was one of Kip's VIPs or otherwise. If she hadn't given permission, then he shouldn't have had his hands on her that way. Period.

But causing a scene on my third day in Silver Ridge was the last thing I needed.

"There you are, gorgeous," I murmured softly. "I've been looking for you everywhere." I angled my body away from the prick and winked at her.

She looked up at me. Amber eyes, and again, I was struck with deja vu. Her brows tightened in confusion and suspicion. I wouldn't have blamed her for not trusting me, since I was the second man within a few minutes who'd approached her.

Go with it, I mouthed silently. Her pretty eyes widened.

"This is *your* date?"

Slowly, I swiveled my head to glare at the man in the blue mask. My anger flared back to life. But when I spoke, I managed to keep my tone even and calm. "Exactly. So unless you want me to break every one of those fingers, you'd better take your hand off of her." I grinned, showing my teeth. It was not a friendly smile. Unless you could call a shark's smile friendly.

"But she's wearing the mask," he muttered. I didn't move, and the guy finally got the message. His hand lifted, and he stumbled back a step. "I'm... My mistake."

I kept my gaze on him as he slunk away.

Then I turned back to the woman. "Did he hurt you?" I narrowed my eyes, studying her shoulder.

"No." Her voice was small. Fragile. But she cleared her throat and said the word again, more confidently. "No, he was just some asshole who thought I was someone else."

"He mentioned your mask."

She touched the feathered edge. "I got it from a stranger. This has been a really weird night. First I couldn't find my friend, and then there was this woman in the bathroom who gave me this mask, and now *you*. Seriously. Weird, weird night."

The lights in the ballroom were dimmed, but I could still see a pretty pink blush spread over her pale skin. It crept up from her breasts, across her neck, and into her cheeks. The urge to touch her skin, find out if it was hot, made my fingers twitch.

She went to untie the mask, but I brushed her wrist with my fingers to stop her. "The guy's gone now, so you might as well keep it. Unless you want to be the rebel without a mask at a masquerade. I could get behind that."

"Not ready to rebel just yet. I'd better pace myself."

I grinned, but warmly this time.

Leaving the mask in place, she picked up her glass of wine. "Anyways, thanks. I really should go find my friend."

"But I just declared you my date. We ought to stick together, at least for a bit." If the man in the blue mask bothered her again, or even looked her way, I'd throw him out of here myself. But there was something about her, and I was still trying to figure it out.

"He caught me by surprise," she said. "I'll be ready next time. These heels are very sharp."

I laughed. "If you take those heels off, you'll catch him by surprise for sure. He won't see you coming."

Her mouth twisted with amusement. "Is that a comment about me being short?"

All at once, it hit me.

The girl from the coffee shop. *Advanced Techniques in Quick-Books*. So much about her was different tonight, including those heels that made her a whole lot taller. But it was her.

Now I *couldn't* let her go yet. She was far too intriguing. "Stay here a few minutes. Drink your glass of wine. Then if you like, I can buy you another."

"I shouldn't."

"But this is the second time I've run into you in two days, and if I'm being honest, I already can't stop thinking about the first."

Her gaze flew to mine. It was noisy in here, but I didn't miss her quick intake of breath. She blushed again and took a hefty sip of her wine, then set it on the bar. She wasn't walking away, though.

Instead, she slid her phone from her purse. Her thumbs moved over the lower half of the screen, and it looked like she was texting someone. Maybe that friend she'd mentioned.

"I didn't think you recognized me," she said as she put her phone away.

"Is that why you made the same joke?"

"Maybe. It was an experiment."

"So you recognized me too?"

"Yes."

"How?"

"Your voice and hair." She faced the bar instead of me, but I felt her attention sweep down my frame to my Berluti dress shoes and back up my Tom Ford tux. "Your body. You're fairly memorable."

Fuck.

That body was flooding with endorphins. Her assessment had made all the cells in my body want to stand up and salute.

I rested my elbow on the bar, edging as close as I dared, and took a sip of bourbon. "You do look different tonight."

She huffed an exhale. "*Very* different. I doubt my own brothers would recognize me."

"I disagree. It's that Clark Kent/Superman thing. There's no way Lois wouldn't have recognized him without the glasses."

Another sip of wine. "I'm Superman in this scenario?"

"Why not? Heroes come in all shapes, sizes, and genders. I rescued you earlier. Next time, you can rescue me."

"What if I don't get there fast enough?"

"I'll stall them until you arrive."

She cracked a smile, and that felt like more of a victory than buying this entire resort.

"You're far more beautiful than Superman, though," I said. "With or without the glasses."

That blush again. Irresistible. "You're coming on a little strong."

"Am I?" My voice was husky and low. It was an involuntary reaction to the chemicals running through my veins. Some of it was good old-fashioned attraction, but it wasn't enough that she was pretty. It was the whole package. This woman stoked my curiosity more than anyone else had in a while. "Spend the evening with me."

She shook her head. "I don't know you."

"Not yet," I reasoned. "Spend an hour with me, then."

Those amber eyes widened again. "You *are* forward. I'm not leaving here with you."

"Not what I meant," I said smoothly. "I'm new to Silver Ridge. I don't know anyone here. Take pity on a guy."

"You don't seem like the type to need pity."

"But I *am* in need of rescue." I held out my hands to either side of me. "Here I am, dateless, friendless. Just a guy, asking a girl for some hot tips on how to manage my spreadsheets. Bookkeeping pitfalls and how to avoid them."

Her laugh started out small. She was trying to keep it in. But then it burst out with a joyful, musical sound. "You're extremely persistent."

"You have no idea."

"Okay. An hour."

"That'll do. For a start." I clinked my drink glass against hers.

FIVE

Grace

"WHAT'S YOUR NAME?" he asked.

My fingertip traced the rim of my wine glass. "I'm not ready to tell you that yet."

"Do you have a boyfriend?"

Another laugh snuck out of me. "My gosh, you don't let up."

"I'm taking that as a no. I'm not seeing anyone either, in case you were wondering."

"I wasn't."

He smirked like he knew that wasn't true.

I'd never been around a man with such an intense presence. From the moment I'd heard him speak tonight and seen those broad shoulders, the thick, dark hair, I'd known it was him. The man I'd spilled coffee on yesterday. Who now wanted to "spend the evening with me."

Who even said things like that in real life?

Yet here I was, standing beside him at the bar instead of finding Piper. I'd texted where I was, but that I was okay for now. She and Hanson were dancing in some other room.

This night really was surreal. Like something out of a dream.

"How about you call me Lois," he said. "I'll call you Clark. Or Superman. Whichever."

I barked a laugh. *That* was why I'd stayed. He kept disarming me with his sense of humor. And the way he looked at me...like I was some work of art that he wanted to study and understand and protect.

It was concerning how much I liked that. But we were just talking. No harm in that.

"I'm not calling you Lois," I said. And I certainly wasn't going to call him Mr. Hunky McHandsome, as Piper had called him yesterday. "You be Mr. Black, since you're in all black." His tux, his shirt, bowtie, and mask were all silky and dark as midnight. "I'll be..." I thought of the woman in the bathroom. "Ms. Red."

"Intriguing. And fitting. I like it."

I played with the stem of my wine glass. "I don't know the name of the woman who gave me this mask. In my head, I called her Ms. Scarlet because she had bright red hair. She said her date stood her up, but I wonder if it was that guy in the blue mask. Maybe she wanted to get away from him."

If so, I couldn't blame her. No wonder she'd said I was doing her a favor. I didn't look much like her, but the mask plus the shades of red in my hair had been enough to distract her creep of a date so she could make her getaway. I was a touch annoyed that she hadn't told me her plan. She might've thought I'd refuse.

Whatever that had been about, I hoped her night had improved.

Mr. Black frowned. "If you're concerned, I can let security know to keep an eye out for her. And blue mask guy. He shouldn't have touched you the way he did. I could have him thrown out."

I shook my head. "Ms. Scarlet left, and I doubt the blue mask man will bother me again. You make it sound like you're important around here."

"Kind of." He smirked again, but didn't elaborate.

He was probably one of the VIPs who flew in just for this party. As I'd suspected earlier. That would explain his confidence.

My first impression of him yesterday, *rich tourist*, hadn't been wrong. He wore that tux like he was born in it.

Maybe he even knew Dane Knightly.

He finished off the liquor in his glass and lifted his finger at the bartender for another. "I hate these kinds of events. I'd rather be analyzing financials. Or reading a book." He aimed his crooked grin at me. "Or chatting with a friend in a coffee shop."

"I thought you didn't have any friends in town."

"I didn't *exactly* say that. I didn't have friends at this party, but now..." He gestured at me.

"We're strangers, not friends."

"You're tough. But that's even better. I like when I have to earn it." The rasp in his voice, combined with the heat in his eyes, traveled down my spine like a caress.

"You're not earning anything." But I couldn't stop smiling, no matter how much I tried to rein myself in.

He was the kind of man I should stay far away from. Yet I wasn't walking away. Maybe it was the mask, like Ms. Scarlet had said. A chance to be someone else for one night.

Ms. Red.

I'd done Ms. Scarlet a favor, but perhaps she'd done me a favor too. Without knowing it.

The bartender arrived with his fresh glass, and Mr. Black took several folded bills from his pocket and passed them over. "You're a local, right?" he asked me. "Tell me. What do the Silver Ridge locals think of this place? The ski resort and the hotel."

I spun to face the room, resting my elbows on the bar top behind me. "It's mixed. The first ski runs opened on the mountain a few years ago. People were excited. But as the resort has expanded, everything's gotten more expensive. Seems more like a place for tourists than for us. Especially with this new hotel."

"Huh." His eyebrows drew together. "The resort has a new owner though. He probably wants to make the locals happy too."

"Dane Knightly?"

Mr. Black's eyes sparkled. "Yes. Knightly. What do you think of him?"

"Do you know him?"

"We've crossed paths before."

I didn't want to badmouth Ashford's best friend. But the man hadn't even come to his own grand opening. He had better things to do. "Knightly has never bothered to visit Silver Ridge. Hard to make the locals happy when you have no clue who they really are or what's important to them."

Mr. Black's lips pressed into a line. His gaze was assessing. "You're absolutely right."

The wine had made my limbs feel warm and languid. Throw in the mask I was wearing, and it served to loosen my tongue. "I'm sure Dane Knightly is a nice enough person. For a rich guy. It's fine to have money. But the wealthy tend to lose touch of what it's like for everyone else." I glanced at him. "No offense."

He chuckled. "You assume I'm rich?"

I pointed at...well, all of him.

"Fair enough," he said. "Life is easier with money. No denying it. But it can't fix everything."

"It fixes a lot."

He sipped his drink. "If someone handed you a million dollars tomorrow, tax free, what would you buy first?"

"That's easy. I'd pay off my student debts. Pay for my brother's wedding and honeymoon. Buy a big playhouse for my niece."

"That's generous. But what about something indulgent, just for you? The first time my bank account was flush with money I'd earned, I bought myself a vintage Rolex MilSub 5517. A thing of beauty, craftsmanship, and engineering. Just because I could."

He stretched out his arm, showing off the watch. Without even thinking, I reached out and stroked the smooth metal, catching his wrist at the same time. He was so warm.

I pulled my hand back and looked up at him, realizing he'd been staring at me. His eyes had darkened, pupils swallowing most of the gray.

I tugged my lower lip between my teeth. "A cheeseboard."

"Pardon?"

"That's what I would buy."

He lowered his arm and stuck his hand in his pants pocket. "A cheeseboard? That's it?"

"A really fancy one!" I defended. "With artisan cheeses and prosciutto and fresh, handmade bread. And fruit and olives and tiny pickles, arranged like it's a work of art and not just food."

His grin was awfully big. "You're adorable."

"Don't laugh."

"I'm not laughing at you. I love a good cheeseboard."

My face heated. I wished I didn't like the way he looked at me so much. Warnings kept shooting off in my brain like emergency flares. *Mayday. Don't trust him.*

But I didn't have to trust him with my heart. It was just a conversation. A little flirting. One strange, unlikely evening spent together at a party. I was a Silver Ridge girl, and he was from... somewhere else. New York or Chicago or LA.

He would leave town soon, and I couldn't imagine I'd ever see him again.

We talked about our favorite foods and books. And then college football, which I followed because *brothers*. We talked about things that were personal but also not, and our banter flowed easily. The man was clearly intelligent. Smart enough to steer around the things I didn't want to discuss, like our real lives and identities.

I skipped the second glass of wine. But I leaned into his arm, feeling his solid bulk up against me. It was distracting enough to feel his body through the layers of his shirt and jacket. But those few times we touched skin to skin, electricity sparked between us. His fingers grazing my ear when he fixed the strap of my mask. My touch on his wrist again to check his watch, even though I could've looked at my phone.

Far more than an hour had passed.

"My friend is probably looking for me," I said. Though we

hadn't left the bar area, so Piper could've found me if she'd been so inclined. "I should go."

"I don't want tonight to end yet. And I don't think you do either."

"Maybe. So far it's been fun."

"It has. I like you, Ms. Red. I think you like me too."

"You have a lot of opinions about what's going on in my head."

"Am I wrong?"

"No," I admitted. "You're not wrong."

His fingertips nudged the underside of my chin, urging me to tip my head. Putting me in the perfect position to lower his mouth to mine if he'd wanted to.

"Come upstairs to my suite."

Liquid heat ignited in my veins. "For what?" I asked before mentally kicking myself. I knew *for what.* But even though we'd been talking and flirting and touching for almost two hours, I still hadn't been expecting his invitation.

He laughed softly. "For whatever you like. I'd love for you to spend the night with me."

Air. I needed air. Every breath I took was infused with his scent.

It took a long time, far too long, to drag the words out of me. "I can't."

"You *can* do whatever you want. That's the question. Do you *want* me to take you upstairs and worship you until the sun comes up?"

"Uuurghm." The sound I made was embarrassing. Nowhere near sexy. Yet for some reason, it made the wicked glint in his eyes flare even brighter.

He knew exactly what he was doing to me, and he liked it.

"I would love to see how far down your body that pretty blush goes," he murmured.

I couldn't think. My brain wasn't working. But the rest of me wanted to strip down right here and let him do whatever he wanted. Which was madness. I didn't know what kind of sexual superpower he had, what kind of pheromones were mixed into his cologne, but he was dangerous alright.

Tonight, though? I was Ms. Red. And Ms. Red kind of liked the idea of dangerous. Wanted excitement and passion. Things that I normally stayed far away from and didn't allow myself. When else would I have this chance?

For one night, I didn't have to be Grace O'Neal.

I'd made my decision, but I could still hardly believe it as I said, "I have to find Piper first. To tell her where I'm going."

His smile unfolded like a piece of silk. "I'll come with you. I'll give her my name and contact info so she knows you're safe."

"*No*. I'll tell her your room number. That's enough." I didn't want the temptation to ever contact him again or give him a way to contact me. This was just about tonight. "I'll meet you upstairs. What room is it?"

"701. Top floor."

Nerves and anticipation fizzed beneath my skin. *I can't believe I'm doing this.*

"I'll head up and order us a bottle of champagne." He stroked the back of his hand down my cheek. "I'd love to take off that mask and kiss you right here, but I'm going to save it until we're alone. That way, I won't have to stop."

"Okay," I breathed.

He pressed a keycard into my palm. "I'll be waiting." He turned and walked toward the lobby.

My heart thumped like crazy while my hand squeezed the card he'd given me. The key to his room. No, not just a room. His *suite*. Where he was heading up now to wait for me to join him. *For sex.*

"701," I repeated to myself. I had the absurd thought that I was going to forget the number. "701." The top floor. Like a penthouse or presidential suite or something?

Opening the flap of my purse, I tucked the keycard inside and took out my phone to text Piper.

ME

Meet me in the lobby? Need you asap

PIPER

Of course. U ok?

Yes, but need to talk to you. NOW

I put my phone away and wove around partygoers on my way to the exit. The same way Mr. Black had gone a few minutes ago, though I didn't see him when I emerged in the cooler air of the lobby. He must've gone straight to the elevators and up to his room.

Maybe he was taking off his jacket right now, unknotting his bowtie. Rolling up his sleeves and ordering a bottle of champagne with two glasses.

I wondered what he'd feel like. I could already imagine his large, rough hands on my body. His tongue in my mouth. His cock pushing inside me, filling me while he held me down on the bed.

Oh my lord.

"Miss?"

I jumped at the gruff sound of a male voice behind me, my hand pressing to my throat in surprise. "Yes?"

This man wore a boxy suit and a hard expression. His head was shaved bald, his skin pale, and his goatee was a mix of black and silver. He wore a mask, but didn't look like a party guest. More like a bouncer. Or private security, except there was something cruel in the twist of his mouth and the lines around his eyes.

"Where did you get the red mask?"

"Why does it matter?" I sputtered.

"Answer the question."

"I found it."

"Where?"

"None of your business." I untied the mask and took it off, lifting my chin defiantly. Something told me not to mention Ms.

Scarlet. Just how many men were looking for her tonight? And *why*?

A soft hand rested on my shoulder. “Grace, what’s up? You okay?”

It was Piper. I looked back to meet her gaze. “No, I’m not. This guy is—” When I turned to face him again, all I saw was his broad back walking away.

“Was he bothering you?”

“I...I don’t know.”

“You look way too pale. What’s going on?” Piper took me by the wrist and pulled me over to a padded bench by the wall. “Sit. Tell me what happened.”

“I’m not sure where to start.” But I was pretty certain Ms. Scarlet had been escaping more than just a bad date tonight.

“Sweetie, you’re shivering. Do you want to head home? Hanson said he’s okay with leaving whenever.”

I had that keycard in my purse. An incredibly sexy man was waiting for me in his suite upstairs. A man I’d been about to spend the night with, even though I knew almost nothing about him.

What the hell had I been thinking?

“Yeah, I’m ready to go home.” I just wanted to put this entire strange night behind me.

This wasn’t some fantasy. This was real life. With real danger and consequences.

I knew far too much about both already.

SIX

Dane

I WOKE to a bucket of melted ice, an unopened champagne bottle, and a very lonely bed.

"Fuck," I said, staring at the ceiling.

That hadn't been a bad dream. Ms. Red hadn't shown. She'd ghosted me. Dashed off like Cinderella about to turn into a pumpkin.

I was sprawled on the mattress, shirtless but still wearing my tuxedo pants for some reason. Maybe because I'd stayed up until the wee hours, sipping mini-bar whiskey and hoping my girl might show, before I finally gave up and passed out. Now I had a mild hangover to show for it.

One-night stands weren't a typical thing for me. I liked taking my time to get to know someone. But I'd never met anyone that sparked my interest the way she did, and I'd really wanted to spend more time with her. To show her a great time. I wouldn't have minded if one night turned into several, at least for as long as I stayed in Silver Ridge.

I liked her. Simple as that.

Maybe I should've expected this. She'd been skittish. But what exactly had gone wrong? Had she simply gotten cold feet? Was it something I did?

I'd even called down to the front desk to see if she'd left a message for me, or if anything strange had happened. Such as an alien abduction of the gorgeous woman in the red dress and elaborate mask. *Nothing.*

My phone buzzed on the nightstand, and I threw a pillow at it. If it was Kip hoping for a report on his VIP guests, he was shit out of luck.

I padded out to the kitchen, where I stuck the champagne in the fridge and downed some pain relievers for my headache along with a bottle of water. After a shower and a shave, I figured I should check my messages. My mood lifted when I saw Ashford had written.

ASHFORD

Back from Hartley. How was the party?

ME

I'm hungover.

The good kind or the shitty kind?

The latter. A pretty girl ditched me.

My condolences. Bright sunlight and the loud screams of children will fix you right up. Fall festival in the square today. Want to join us?

I can't think of anything better.

Except, of course, breakfast in bed and an uninhibited round of morning sex with Ms. Red. But since that wasn't going to happen...

ASHFORD

Meet us at Silver Linings on Main. Half an hour? They have breakfast burritos.

Perfect. Breakfast is on me.

Which made me laugh as I thought of my first visit to Silver Linings and my ruined sweater. Those wide amber eyes behind her glasses. That blush. Hell. I wanted to find her. At the very least to ensure she'd made it safely home last night.

Maybe Ashford knew her. It wasn't that big a town.

After putting on jeans and a long-sleeved Henley, I grabbed the gift bag I'd brought for Ashford's daughter, then lined up for the shuttle that took hotel guests down to Main Street. The hotel had a Range Rover for me to use if I needed it, but this morning I preferred blending in and hearing what people were saying.

I was still thinking about what Ms. Red had said last night. That I didn't know what the people of Silver Ridge were about. I wanted to find out. And the first step toward getting there was listening. Especially since Ms. Red herself wasn't going to give me that insider scoop.

Taking a seat at the back of the shuttle and pulling my ball cap down, I watched the other guests file on from the corner of my eye. Some were VIPs from the party last night. Thankfully they didn't recognize me. I overheard some comments about the party and the resort grounds, all of them vaguely positive. In other words, unhelpful.

Once we got to Main Street, I tipped the driver and stepped out into the sunshine. The town was bustling this Saturday morning, and the air was bracing and clean. It did make me feel better. I was about to see my closest friend for the first time in years, and that was something to celebrate.

I strolled toward Silver Linings with one hand in my jeans pocket and the small gift bag swinging at my side.

When I was about half a block away, I spotted Ashford, a pretty brunette, and a golden retriever cross the street. They tied the dog to a railing.

A grin broke over my expression like the sunrise.

By the time I reached the coffee shop, Ashford and Emma had already gone inside. The retriever's tail wagged and she shuffled excitedly on her paws as I approached. "You must be Stella. I've heard all about you." She barked happily, and I took a moment to rub her sides. "I can't stay long, though. Gotta say hi to your owners."

Once I got inside, Emma was looking over the used bookshelves while Ashford stood just behind her, their fingers casually tangled together. He glanced over as I walked toward them, his smile growing to match mine.

"Dane! Holy shit, you're actually here. In the flesh."

"I know. It's taken way too long." I pulled him into a back-slapping hug, then flicked his bearded chin. "You look scruffy as hell."

"You look tired as shit. How's the hangover?"

"What hangover?" I hugged him again.

This. This was why I'd come to Silver Ridge. I'd obsessed enough about Ms. Red for one morning. I didn't intend to think about my family woes either. For now, I was going to put everything else out of my mind and focus on my best friend.

"Dane, this is Emma." Ashford put a hand on her back, looking down at her with the pure adoration of a guy who'd found exactly what he needed.

"You're every bit as beautiful as Ashford described you."

He smacked my arm. "Don't hit on my fiancée."

"Me? I would never." I grinned mischievously.

"It's great to finally meet you, Dane." Emma opened her arms, so I gave her a hug too.

"Likewise. I would've sent you both tickets to the party last night if you hadn't been in Hartley. But Ashford would rather go back to boot camp than attend a stuffy black-tie party full of strangers."

Emma laughed. "It's like you know him or something."

"I would've braved the rich assholes if you'd wanted to go, baby," Ashford said to her. Emma kissed him on the nose, and I felt a pang of longing that I played off by rolling my eyes.

Ashford had meaning in his life. Exactly what I was missing.

Ashford was far richer than me when it came to the things that counted most.

We got into the line waiting to order. "Where's Maisie?" I asked, holding up the gift bag I'd brought with me. "I've got a present for her."

"Buying your way in as usual," my buddy joked.

"Not gonna lie. I'm hoping for honorary uncle status."

"Maisie is already at the festival with Grace," Emma said. "They're helping out at the kids' craft table. We're supposed to meet them. Oh, I can't forget about Grace's order. She wants an autumn spice latte."

"Then I'll be happy to get it for her. Breakfast is my treat." As we neared the register, I noted that the tall blond was once again not working today.

I almost asked Ashford and Emma if they knew anyone matching Ms. Red's description. Hair a mix of gold and auburn, eyes that glowed when she smiled. A tendency to blush adorably and study up on spreadsheets.

Damn it, this was getting pathetic.

"What do you think of your investment so far?" Ashford asked. "I heard they'd finished construction on the new hotel finally, but I haven't been up there."

"We were waiting for you to give us the insider tour," Emma added with a cheerful smile.

"It would be my pleasure. I think the hotel looks great, not that I had much to do with that part. I was just thrilled we could step in and get the project finished. But now that I'm here, I plan to get to know the town better. It doesn't seem like the previous owners of the resort thought about how the property would fit into Silver Ridge, so that's something I want to focus on."

"If you want honest opinions, I'll introduce you to Dixie Haines," Ashford said. "She's president of the local business association. But she doesn't hold back what she's thinking."

"Exactly what I need."

"Then I'll make it happen. But remember, you asked for it."

I laughed. "I'd love to get involved with the local charities too."

"Grace can help you there," Emma said. "She does a ton of volunteer work."

"Then I look forward to meeting her. What about your brother, Ashford? How's Callum?"

"Cal's at the festival too, but he's on duty. Sort of."

I'd met Callum a couple times in our Army days. I knew he was a volunteer firefighter. I hadn't seen him in years, but Ashford dropped details here and there about his siblings. When it came to Grace, Ashford's love for his sister was always clear, but I had no idea what she did for work.

I'd also met the oldest O'Neal brother, Grayden, though I certainly didn't expect Grayden to turn up here in Silver Ridge. Ashford and his other siblings had no contact with him. A difficult relationship with a brother was something I could understand.

Our backgrounds were different aside from our military service, but there were certain things that Ashford and I got about one another without needing to explain. Exactly why his friendship meant so much to me.

We left Silver Linings with a tray of drinks and a bag of food. Outside, Stella pranced with excitement as Emma untied her leash. "Hold on," I said. "I've got something for you too, Stella." Dipping into my pocket, I pulled out the dog treat I'd bought at the counter. I'd already checked with Emma on which kind Stella liked. Stella gobbled it from my hand, licking her chops.

"You *are* a kiss-up," Ashford muttered.

"Can't help it if I have a way with the ladies. You might want to take some notes."

He flashed me his middle finger, and we both laughed. Fuck, this was fun. The day couldn't be more beautiful, and I was here with my best friend and his family. I had no reason to complain.

We set out for the festival, which was being held in the square across from town hall. Meanwhile, I wolfed down a breakfast burrito to absorb the last of the alcohol in my system.

The sidewalks bustled with happy families going the same direction as us. Kids kicked up fallen leaves and jumped in piles of them. The aspens that dotted Main Street were a mix of golden yellow and fiery orange-red. A few blocks ahead, in the square, crowds of people meandered around the white tents set up for the festival.

"You'll have to come for dinner at our place soon," Ashford said.

"I'd love to. I'll return the favor, but at a restaurant. My hotel suite has a kitchen, but you don't want my cooking."

"Trust me, dude, I remember. How's your mom been doing?"

My smile faltered. "Pretty much the same as the last couple months." I focused on the peaks of the white festival tents. "She would love Silver Ridge. I'm hoping to get her out here at some point. If I can make it work."

Emma's blue eyes were sympathetic. "Your mom isn't well?"

"She has early-onset Alzheimer's. Diagnosed a couple of years ago. It's progressed quickly."

Emma touched my elbow. "Oh, Dane. I'm so sorry."

"Thank you." Whenever I thought about my mom, about how much she'd lost already and how little the treatments were working, it made a furious ache build in my throat and my chest. Money, power, connections—none of that mattered when you were sick and there was no cure and, on the worst days, you couldn't even recall your own name.

"Let us know if we can help. We'd love to meet her." Ashford rested a hand briefly between my shoulder blades. A show of solidarity, and it meant a lot.

"I did offer to fly you and your family out to see me in Manhattan. More than once."

My friend shrugged. "Even you aren't worth that hassle."

"Good to know how much I really mean to you."

We'd reached the festival. At the entrance, we exchanged cash for some tickets, then dove right into the midst of small-town autumn charm. Booths selling spiced apple cider and cider donuts. Lawn games with pumpkin-shaped balls and beanbags. The scents of barbecue and tacos wafted over from the food trucks.

Ashford pointed at a fire engine parked on the street, where kids swarmed around firefighters in full gear. "Callum's over there somewhere. They're letting the kids pretend to drive and honk the horn. If Maisie hasn't stopped by already, I have no doubt that's on our agenda for later."

"I wouldn't miss it. I've always wanted to sit in the jump seat."

"Bet Cal will even let you wear the helmet."

Suddenly a streak of long hair and bright colors ran toward us. "Daddy, Emma! Stella! You're here!"

Maisie collided with Ashford, who picked her up and tossed her into the air. His daughter screamed in delight. When he set her down, Maisie got a hug from Emma and took Stella's leash.

"Where's Aunt Grace?" Ashford asked. "You were supposed to stay with her."

"She's still helping some kids at the craft table. I'm seven, Daddy. I don't need anyone to hold my hand."

Then Maisie noticed me and took a few steps to the side, ducking behind Emma.

"Maisie, this is my friend," her dad said. "Remember I told you he was coming to see us?"

"Hi. I'm Dane." I tried not to look scary, but it didn't seem to be working. Before I could say anything more, someone else called out Maisie's name, waving and jogging toward us.

"There's Grace," Ashford said. "She must've gotten a reprieve from craft duty."

"Maisie, I asked you to wait for me." Grace reached us, pushing her auburn hair back from her face and adjusting her glasses.

Fuck. Me.

I could barely make out the shape of her under her baggy sweater and jeans. But I didn't need to. Her sexy dress last night had accentuated that hourglass shape and practically burned it into my memory.

Ms. Red was Grace O'Neal. Ashford's little sister.

Then she looked over at me, doing a double take.

SEVEN

Grace

No. No, this couldn't be happening.

Mr. Black could not be Dane Knightly. There had to be some mistake.

Ashford beckoned me over. "Grace, this is Dane Knightly. He came to town for the hotel grand opening. Dane, this is my sister."

I did my best to lock down my expression. "Hello," I choked out.

Dane lifted his chin at me. "Good morning." All sexy and gruff. His eyes were full of questions that I didn't want to answer. Much less answer them in front of my brother.

Gah, I needed to act normal, which wasn't easy when I was ready to yell at the man. I'd asked him last night if he knew Dane Knightly, and he'd lied to me.

The *hell*.

Emma glanced back and forth between us. "Have you two met before?"

Dane opened his mouth.

"We met at Silver Linings," I blurted. "I spilled coffee on him. Had no idea who he was." I stared at him, begging silently for him not to add any more. I assumed Dane had some sense of self-preservation, but what did I know? He'd been pretty uninhibited with his words last night.

Tingles ran through me, goosebumps raising all over my skin.

After I'd left the party, I'd stayed at Piper's. I hadn't breathed a word about Mr. Black or how I'd almost accepted his offer to spend the night with him. I'd been hoping the man would leave town soon, and I'd never have to see him again. As if the last evening had been some weird dream. I could go back to my regular, small-town life and pretend the masquerade ball hadn't happened.

Not so much.

Dane's questioning gaze lingered another second. "Good to officially meet you, Grace."

He held out his hand. The contact was just as electric as it had been last night. When I pulled my hand away, my palm slid against his, and I tried to hide my shiver.

"You too," I said, teeth clenched. Less than twelve hours ago, I'd been ready to head up to his room to get those hands all over me. "Ashford, why didn't you tell me Dane was in town? I thought he wasn't coming to the grand opening."

Ashford shrugged and took a swig of his coffee. "It's impossible to get this guy to nail down his plans. I didn't even know until a couple of days ago."

"My fault entirely," Dane said.

I felt a blush spread up my neck and into my cheeks. Should I say that I'd been at the party too? Would that make it more obvious that I'd seen him there, or less?

Dane held out a cardboard tray of drinks. "I believe you ordered an autumn spice latte."

Change of subject. Okay. Yes.

"I did." I took the coffee, careful not to brush his fingers. I'd had enough of that. "Thanks. I'll be sure to drink it far away from you. Because of, you know, running into you the other day." I snapped my mouth closed to stop my rambling.

Dane turned and held out another drink to my niece. "This one's a hot cocoa, Maisie, and I believe it has your name on it."

While Ashford and Dane chatted with Maisie, Emma sidled over to me. "Are you okay? You're jumpy this morning."

I drank a hefty gulp of latte, and it burned the roof of my mouth. "Got worried when I couldn't find Maisie by the craft tables."

Emma and I watched my niece, who already had a thin mustache of chocolate above her lip from the cocoa.

If my brother had said something to me about Dane being in town, then *maybe* I would've guessed his identity. Maybe I wouldn't have talked shit about Dane Knightly *to his face*. And he'd just stood there and let me do it. Encouraged me to spout my opinions. About him. About his hotel.

Oh, crap. Dane hadn't known I was Ashford's little sister, right? Had he been playing some kind of game with me? Though I couldn't imagine why. Not unless Dane secretly wanted Ashford to kill him, because I had my doubts about the reasonableness of Ashford's reaction if he'd found out.

I had to make sure that Ashford *didn't* find out. If only because I couldn't take the sheer embarrassment.

Dane knelt on the grass, ignoring the dampness, and held out a gift bag to Maisie. "I brought you something from New York. That's where I'm from."

"Really?" Maisie thrust her cocoa into Emma's free hand and reached for the gift bag. Digging inside, she pulled out a snow globe of the Manhattan skyline.

"Wow," she whispered. "This is *amazing*."

Dane glanced up at me. My skin went hot again.

Maisie shook it, marveling as the specks of white swirled inside.

"If you wind it up here, it plays 'New York, New York,'" he said, pointing.

She looked up at me. "Will you help me with the music, Aunt Grace?"

I cleared my throat. "Of course."

I set down my coffee and helped Maisie wind the little piece of metal at the back of the globe, feeling Dane's gaze on me the entire time. The melody started faintly, not easy to hear over the noise of the festival. Maisie held the globe to her ear and a wide grin bloomed on her face.

Then I made the mistake of glancing at Dane again, who was still down on one knee in the grass. His eyebrows lifted slightly when our eyes locked, and the corner of his mouth curved.

I blinked and looked away, grabbing my coffee.

"Mr. Dane, do you live in one of those buildings?" Maisie asked, pointing at the snow globe.

"The buildings in there are pretty small. Not sure I'd fit."

Maisie giggled. "In one of the real ones."

"I don't live in any of these, no. But I do have an apartment in a tall building. It's near Central Park."

"I've read a book about Central Park."

"Dane sent that to you for Christmas a few years back," Ashford said.

Dane stood, brushing off his knee. "You like that book, Maisie?"

"It's the best! And this snow globe is too. Thank you!"

"You're very welcome."

"Dane seems like a charmer," Emma whispered in my ear.

Oh, she had no idea.

We helped Maisie pack up her snow globe. Then my niece asked, "Is it time for the pumpkin patch now? Please please please?"

"Okay, monkey." Ashford ruffled her hair. "*But* you have to hold someone's hand. Seven is not old enough to be free range."

Maisie held onto my hand, and we all walked through the festival toward the pumpkin patch. The whole way, I felt the warmth of Dane's gaze on my back. I could only stomach half my latte before tossing it into a trash can.

Near the entrance to the pumpkin patch, we ran into Piper and her son Ollie. As soon as Ashford introduced Dane, Piper winced. "I assume you recovered from the coffee incident?" Piper asked him. She had recognized him from the coffee shop, just as I'd known she would.

"I did. Though I don't think my sweater will be as lucky."

"We had no idea you're Ashford's Army friend." Piper tapped my arm. "Isn't that hilarious, Grace?"

"So hilarious," I said through gritted teeth.

Thank God Piper hadn't met him at the party last night. Because then I'd have to make her lie to my brothers for me. She would do it, of course, but it wouldn't feel right. I hated lying.

Also, Piper and I were both pretty terrible at it.

The kids ran through the rows of pumpkins, and the minutes ticked by with agonizing slowness. But my determination grew. I had to talk to him. We had to sort this out, and then we were going to pretend last night had *never happened*.

The first moment that nobody else was watching, I grabbed the sleeve of Dane's Henley and pulled him behind an apple cider booth.

"Please tell me you didn't know," I hissed.

Dane leaned one shoulder against the red wooden siding of the booth. "Of course I didn't know."

"You swear?"

"I wouldn't have hit on you if I knew you were Ashford's sister." He seemed like he was telling the truth, though I'd met guys who could make a girl believe anything. "You've grown up a lot compared to the old photos of you Ashford showed me."

He didn't even try to hide it when his gaze slid down the length of me. I crossed my arms.

"You look *nothing* like the photos Ashford has of you." The snapshots of him in the Army had been in combat helmets or wraparound sunglasses. Not tuxedos and sexily tousled hair. "You weren't supposed to be in Silver Ridge at all."

"There are plenty of current pictures of me online. I'm not a fixture of the New York gossip pages, but I've been there a time or two."

"Why would I spend my time googling my brother's friend?"

Dane glanced at a group of teenagers walking by. When they were gone, he said, "I'm more interested in what happened to you last night. You were going to come up, then you disappeared. Why'd you ghost me?"

Ugh. I'd known he would ask that. I gripped the skin between my eyes. "I realized I was making a mistake. It's a good thing I did. Otherwise we'd have a lot more to hide from my brother."

"You make a habit of doing things your brothers don't know about?"

"Do you make a habit of talking about yourself in the third person? You tricked me into gossiping about you last night."

He smirked. "I thought that was cute. And I welcomed your opinion. I can take it."

"But I didn't know who I was really talking to."

"Neither did I."

"Clearly you preferred it that way. You invited me to your hotel room an hour after you'd met me, and you didn't even know my name."

"Longer than an hour, but okay. Are you saying I'm easy? Very judgmental."

"But true."

He edged closer, his dark-gray eyes going even darker. "You said yes to me. You wanted me."

My chest went tight, and my stomach swooped like I'd taken a spin on a tire swing. "I wasn't acting like myself last night."

"Then it's too bad I didn't kiss you. Guess that was my one chance."

"And there's not going to be another one."

His mouth was inches from mine. I shouldn't have looked, but I did. His lips were full, the lower one thicker than the top. I wondered how he kissed. Probably dominant and commanding and bossy as hell.

I pivoted and got myself out of there.

I'd wanted him last night. There was no denying it. Thank goodness I'd thought better of it.

Never happened, I repeated to myself.

Nothing had happened between us. And nothing ever would.

EIGHT

Dane

"Dane, are you listening?" My brother Kip scoffed. "I don't think he's even listening."

I sat forward in the desk chair. I was in the office of my hotel suite. "I'm listening. Not my fault that you're boring the hell out of me."

Actually, I hadn't been listening at all. I'd been thinking about Grace O'Neal. Ashford's sister. Practically all I'd done for the past few days. Certainly hadn't been doing much that was useful.

"Dane," my father warned.

"I'm all ears."

There was a brief pause, and Kip went on. "As I was saying, it sounds like the grand-opening party last weekend went well. But several of our clients had hoped to speak with you there, and they couldn't find you. I invited the most important people from our network on the assumption that you would do your part. These people are very important to our business."

Your business, I thought, since Kip's guests were all bankers and potential investors in *other* projects. Ones I had nothing to do with. But the Silver Ridge resort was small potatoes in the world of Knightly Global.

"Yes, Kip, I know the meaning of VIP."

"Like the Penningtons. I'm close to getting their buy-in on the property development in the Bahamas, and I need you to make them feel special. They're at the ski resort for one more day."

"Then I'll be sure Tobin sends them some free spa treatments and comps their dinner tonight."

"Tobin? Who's Tobin?"

I gripped the skin between my eyes. "The hotel manager. And you claim *I'm* not paying attention."

"The Penningtons can get free shit anywhere. You're supposed to be offering a personal touch."

"That sounds like a *you* problem. If you'd wanted to *personally touch* them, you should've flown out here yourself. I'm not interested."

Kip made a choking sound.

"Boys, that's enough," my father said. "Dane is going to take this seriously and see that our guests have a good time at the resort. Because he knows how much is riding on the success of this pet project of his. Correct?"

My jaw clenched. "Yes. I do."

"I've given you six months, Dane. If I don't like the results at the end of that period, we sell and then you go where *I* say."

"I know."

Because, at the end of the day, I didn't really own the resort. Knightly Global did. My father would get to make the final call. And if it wasn't for the massive cloud of guilt hanging over my head when it came to my mother, I wouldn't be working for him at all.

"We must present a united front," my father said. "We're a family. You both need to act like it."

I held back my sarcastic comments. My brother tried complaining for a bit longer, but soon we were off the phone. I tossed my device onto the desk, and it skidded so far it fell onto the plush carpet.

Then it started ringing again.

Bending over, I picked up the phone and answered it. "Hey, Margot. Warning you, I'm in a shitty mood. Just got off the phone with Dad and Kip."

"We're in the same boat then. I just heard from your father's assistant."

I groaned. "What now?"

"He wants to know your plus-one for Kip and Bristol's wedding."

"That's weeks away!"

"Dane, you seem to have no grasp for how formal events are planned. Calligraphic place cards take time."

"I don't even know what the word calligraphic means. Nor do I ever want to. But when you talk to Dad's assistant next, check on the scheduling for Kip's surgery to remove the stick up his ass. I have to think that would improve the wedding night for his fiancée."

Margot snickered. "Shush. You're going to get us both into trouble. Why don't you think of a memorable toast for the reception instead."

"Why? I'm not the best man. I was saved from that privilege." Not like Kip would want me planning his bachelor's getaway. I'd been able to skip all that crap. Dad hadn't been happy about it, since he wanted to present the fiction that the Knightlys were a *united front*. But there were a few things Kip and I did agree on.

"You're his big brother. Have a toast ready. Your father will expect it, even if nobody else does."

That was the truth. At least I could rely on Margot to speak it.

Kip had been raised as my brother, though by blood he was my cousin. We were only a few months apart in age. His mother, my mom's sister, had passed when he was a baby, and his father had never been in the picture. My parents had never made a secret of any of it.

But from the time we'd been kids, Kip had a monster-sized chip on his shoulder. Especially when it came to my father. As if he had to prove he was more worthy of the Knightly name than me.

I recalled the memorable Easter egg hunt hosted by one of the exclusive clubs my parents were members of. Kip walked in on me in a storage closet with one of my senior high school classmates. A girl who also happened to be the daughter of the president of the club. Kip tattled on me, and Dad actually told him to mind his own business, while later pulling me aside to lecture me about my recklessness.

Which, okay. Fair.

But Kip didn't seem to understand that this competition between us was one-sided. I wasn't vying to take my father's place at the head of Knightly Global. Kip could have it. I was there to do what my mom had always wanted. What she'd *begged* me to do, back when she was still sharp enough to debate philosophy with me and out-bluff any of us at the poker table.

I owed it to Mom to keep trying to be a part of this family, no matter how infuriating Kip and my father could be.

"A warning, though," Margot added. "If you don't have a plus-one, I believe there are plans to set you up with the maid of honor."

The bride's sister, Ainsley Harcourt. And also, coincidentally, the girl I'd been caught in the storage closet with at that long ago Easter egg hunt. Ainsley was great, but it wasn't happening.

"Please tell me you snuffed that out."

"I'm trying to plant seeds with your father's staff to dissuade him. You know how it is. But I don't think you need me to fight your battles anyway, soldier. You could make my life easier and pick a plus-one of your own."

"Why do I need a plus-one at all?"

"That's above my pay grade."

I didn't want to think about it right now. "I'd better go. I have dinner plans."

"A date?" she asked hopefully.

"No, dinner with Ashford and his family."

"Oh, that sounds lovely. Doesn't he have a sister?"

"He has a sister."

"A pretty one?"

I smiled into the phone. "Very pretty."

"Is she free on the day of Kip's wedding?"

I barked a laugh. While I would've been happy to bring Grace as my date, it was even less likely than Kip removing that stick. "She doesn't care for me."

"What did you do?"

"*Me*? You have no faith in me at all."

"I have faith, Dane Knightly, but I've also known you a long time."

I leaned back in my chair. "Then you know that these days, I'm very strategic and careful about what I do." With one glaring exception, working for my father, but that wasn't the issue. "I'll get back to you on the plus-one."

I was about to say goodbye, but then I remembered something else, and a fresh wave of guilt hit me. I'd almost forgotten.

"The birthday flowers—" I started.

"All set. I'll drop by to deliver them myself next Friday."

"Thank you, Margot."

It should've been me delivering flowers on Mom's birthday. But now that I'd made it to Silver Ridge, I knew I couldn't leave yet. No matter how bad a son that made me. "That means a lot. She loves you."

"I love her too. She's an incredible woman."

She was, once, I thought, and then banished that cruel sentiment from my mind.

My mother was still the same woman I'd admired for my entire life. The people who loved her remembered how incredible she was. *I* remembered.

✧

Ashford and Emma lived in a huge blue stucco building that doubled as their place of business. He taught martial arts classes, while Emma offered music lessons. I texted that I was outside, and Emma came down to open the door for me. I'd driven the Range Rover this time instead of taking the hotel shuttle. I was carrying precious cargo.

"Whoa, what did you bring? That box is huge."

"I told Ashford I'd bring the appetizers. Picked this up from the resort's kitchen on my way out."

Emma held the door wide for me. "Benefits of owning a hotel, right? My aunt and uncle own one too, in Hartley, except they also do most of the cooking."

"I'd love to check it out sometime."

"Definitely. So, are you going to be in Silver Ridge long-term? Or..."

"I'm a New Yorker, born and bred. But I'd like to make this an extended visit. Depending on how things are going back home."

Emma nodded. "I hope you can stick around Colorado for a while. Ashford's so thrilled that you're here."

It meant a lot to me to hear that. Especially coming from the woman who had changed so much in my friend's life. Used to be, when I spoke to Ashford, he sounded like he was barely holding together as a single dad. After Emma came into his life, he wasn't half as grumpy.

There was a couple who should be getting married. My brother and Bristol? Their engagement was more a business arrangement than anything else. They'd announced it out of the blue earlier in the year. I hadn't even known they were dating.

I would be damned before I'd let my father try to push the same thing onto me and Ainsley.

We started up the stairs. "Maisie can't stop talking about you," Emma went on. "Get ready. She already has plans for you when you get upstairs."

"I can't wait. Uncle status, here I come."

"You've made a big impression on her. I can say that much."

At least I was getting things right with Maisie, if not with her aunt Grace.

After our run-in at the fall festival, I was determined to be on good behavior with her. No more propositioning Ashford's little sister. I did have a habit of going after things I wanted, but I would never risk my friendship with Ashford unless I had serious intentions toward her. And Grace...she'd said it herself. We didn't know each other. If I hurt her, Ashford wouldn't forgive me. I wouldn't forgive myself.

But that didn't mean I couldn't be *nice* to her. That wasn't a crime, was it?

"Grace and Callum are coming tonight?" I asked, very innocently.

"That's the plan. Dixie is already here. Ready to bestow her wisdom upon you."

"Good. I'm ready for it."

Inside the apartment, Ashford was talking to an older woman with chin-length white hair. "Dane, get over here. Dixie, this is who I've been telling you about. Dane Knightly."

I had to dip my chin to look down. The woman was tiny. "Pleased to meet you, Ms. Haines."

She squinted up at me. "So you're the new owner of the resort. Ashford tells me you're looking to connect with local business owners."

I slid past her and set the box I was carrying on the kitchen counter. "I want the ski resort to be a thriving part of Silver Ridge. I think we could be doing a lot more for our local community."

"Because it's good for your bottom line?" Dixie asked.

I heard the skepticism in her tone, and I understood it. "It's more than that. It's the right thing to do."

"I like that answer." Dixie pointed at the kitchen table. "Sit with me a while."

"Yes, ma'am." I exchanged a smile with Ashford. I felt like I'd just been invited to dine with the godfather. Wouldn't have been surprised if Dixie said she'd help me, but that I'd be called upon to do a favor for her later.

And of course, I would do it. I wasn't stupid.

Dixie gave me an insider view of the Silver Ridge business landscape until Maisie came racing into the kitchen with Stella. "Mr. Dane! You're here! Will you color with me? Emma printed some pictures of New York, and now I'm making my own skyline."

"Duty calls," I said to Dixie. "Your advice is invaluable, truly. Can we continue this conversation later?"

"No need to flatter me. *Much.* I wouldn't dream of standing in the way of a girl and her art."

I thanked her again, and Dixie waved me away.

Maisie and I sat on the floor of the living room to color. Stella came to check things out, probably because she could smell the treat I'd brought for her. She scarfed down the biscuit and then settled on her cushion nearby to nap.

Ashford's younger brother Callum showed up shortly after and joined our coloring party for a few minutes. "I heard you were bringing food tonight," Callum said. "So I brought drinks." He held up a paper bag with the neck of a liquor bottle inside. "Interested?"

"Absolutely. I'm in."

"I'll pour in the kitchen."

"Perfect. I'll be there in a few. Gotta finish coloring the Empire State Building."

Callum laughed. "Serious work you're doing there. You'll need a drink when you're finished for sure." He got up and headed into the kitchen.

It was so easy to be around Ashford's family. Unlike visits with my family, when it was like walking through a minefield where everyone was wearing bespoke clothing. I could relax here. Let down my guard. It felt really fucking good.

But I kept glancing at the door, wondering when Grace would arrive.

"What do you think?" I asked Maisie, pointing at the skyscraper I'd been filling in.

"Hmm." She touched her chin. "Needs more purple." She reached over to help me out, because clearly I needed to keep working on my architectural design style. But Ashford's daughter knew what she liked, and that was a valuable skill.

"I wouldn't be surprised if you're running the world someday, little miss," I said to her.

She nodded sagely. "I know."

The door to the apartment opened. "Maisie, I brought some new crafts for you." Grace appeared holding a paper grocery bag in her arms, and stopped in her tracks when she saw me.

My smile was involuntary. I got up and took the bag from her hands. "We meet again."

"I didn't know you'd be here."

"It's like you're not happy to see me."

Grace looked over at Maisie, who was still busy coloring on the floor. "Seems I can't get away from you," Grace muttered.

"And why would you want to get away from the handsome Mr. Knightly?" Dixie asked, walking toward us from the kitchen. The lady had impressive hearing.

Grace's cheeks pinked. "You'd think Dane would stay away from *me*. Since I scalded him with hot coffee the first time we met."

"She loves bringing that up. Like she's warning me it might happen again. It's a good thing I have thick skin."

Dixie patted my shoulder. "Hot beverages aside, you'd hardly need protection from Grace. Everybody in Silver Ridge knows she's a doll. Sweetest, most selfless woman in town." Dixie winked. "Aside from yours truly."

I laughed, and I saw Grace holding back a smile.

"Sounds like Ms. O'Neal can do no wrong," I said.

"I say, we all need to do a little wrong sometimes. Life is a bore otherwise." Dixie tapped my bicep. "I suspect you're a man who knows what I mean. See if you can talk Grace into joining in."

"Oh believe me, I've tried."

Grace's eyes bugged behind Dixie's back, and she made a slashing motion over her throat. But Dixie assumed I was kidding. She was laughing along with me. "He's a wily one, Grace."

Maisie looked up from her coloring. "Dixie, what's wily mean?"

"It means smart enough to be dangerous, and dangerous enough to be a heck of a lot of fun."

Grace muttered something like, "*Exactly my problem.*"

"Am I wily?" Maisie asked.

"You certainly are. Ready for some snacks? There's quite the spread in the kitchen." Dixie coaxed Maisie toward the promise of food, and I hung back a moment with Grace, pausing to set her bag of craft supplies on the coffee table.

"How's your week been?" I asked. "Haven't seen you since the festival."

Grace spun to face me. "Don't act so innocent," she whispered. "You have to quit dropping hints about...the other night. Dixie thinks it's a joke, but someone else will catch on. I think Emma already suspects something."

I stuck my hands in my pockets. "I'm not going to tell anyone. Besides, nothing happened, right? There's nothing to tell."

"Exactly. Nothing."

"You don't need to worry about me causing problems for you. I'm harmless."

"I don't believe *that* for a second."

A grin tugged at my lips. "Are you hungry?" I gestured toward the kitchen.

She crossed her arms over her stomach. "Kind of."

"Then you should eat."

Grace sighed. "Wait. I wanted to say thanks for being so great with Maisie. Looks like you were coloring with her just now. And the snow globe was really sweet."

"She's a wonderful kid."

"She really is."

We found the others gathered around the kitchen table, where they'd set out the appetizers. Emma gave Grace a quick hug, and Ashford handed her a plate. "Wondered when you'd get here, Gracie," Ashford said. "Dane brought like ten kinds of cheese. You're going to be in heaven. Look at all this."

"Oh, do you like cheese, Grace?" I asked, keeping my tone neutral.

Her jaw dropped for a moment before she shut it, staring at the platter.

I'd ordered the restaurant's fanciest cheeseboard, then made a few requests of my own. There were local and imported cheeses, nuts, stewed and dried fruits, house-made crackers, thinly sliced prosciutto. Plus three different kinds of olives *and* the tiny pickles she'd mentioned the other night at the party.

"This looks amazing," she said. "Thank you."

"Pleasure's all mine."

When she glanced at me, I gave her my most boyish grin.

I didn't intend to pursue Ashford's sister. But I still wanted Grace to like me, and I had no shame about trying to make that happen.

NINE

Grace

When I pulled into the community center parking lot, it was still mostly empty. In another hour, this place would be packed. In Silver Ridge, community bingo was always a hot ticket. It could get pretty wild sometimes. Especially when Dixie brought a batch of her homemade rum runners or margaritas.

But this afternoon, I'd brought backup.

Chief Teller Landry waited beside his Silver Ridge PD vehicle, arms crossed over his uniform as he studied his phone. As soon as I turned my engine off, he tucked his phone into his back pocket and headed toward me. I was dressed in my own uniform, in a way. Worn-in jeans, pale lavender sweater, glasses, hair pulled back in a messy ponytail.

Teller stopped in front of me, hands on his hips and his expression grave. "Here I am. Reporting for duty."

I laughed. "It won't be that bad. I promise."

"Well, if I make my officers do this, I should make appearances myself."

I opened my trunk. "Except I know you'd rather be just about anywhere else than calling out bingo numbers."

He grunted. "We all have to make sacrifices."

Teller helped me unload. Inside, I set my things down against the wall. "We can grab the extra-long folding table from the storage room to get started," I said. "We'll set up the microphone and the ball cage here beneath the windows. Then we just need the rest of the tables and folding chairs. Oh, and the concessions, but Mrs. Stuckey has the money box for that." I racked my brain for what else I might be forgetting.

"What about the bingo cards?" Teller asked.

I snapped my fingers. "Those are important. And they're still in my car. You make an excellent assistant, Chief."

"A man does like to feel useful."

I ran out to the car to get the stack of cards and a fresh box of mini-pencils. When I returned, Teller had already carried several folding tables from the storage room.

The community center was one of my comfort zones. It smelled familiar, like dusty old books and pine cleaner. As a little girl, I'd taken ballet lessons here. The center had also hosted prom my senior year because the high school gym got flooded. I'd made some fond memories here. Many included Teller, since he was Piper's older brother and had been close to my older brothers growing up.

"Anything new and exciting to report from the world of law enforcement?" I asked.

"Thankfully no. It's been quiet. With all the activity at that hotel grand opening last weekend, I stepped up patrols in case the out-of-towners caused any problems. But it proved unnecessary."

"Oh?" I bent over to unfold another table, which also conveniently hid my expression. Teller's mention of the party brought Dane to the forefront of my mind, and I had no idea what my face was doing in response, but it was *something*. "There weren't any issues at the hotel party?"

"The resort is the sheriff's jurisdiction, but I didn't hear reports of anything. Which is good. I don't like disruptions in my town."

Dane was a disruption, alright. But not so much in our town as in my own mind.

I hadn't seen Dane in the last week. And trust me, I'd been watching for him, torn between anticipation and dread. Every time I was around the man, I got flustered.

Heck, even when I *thought* of him it was difficult to keep my composure.

He'd brought that elaborate cheeseboard to Ashford's house for me. Because *I* was the ridiculous person who'd said I would get myself a fancy cheeseboard if I suddenly struck it rich. If I was being extra cynical, I might assume Dane had some nefarious ulterior motive. But my gut told me that it had been a peace offering. A kind gesture, given simply because Dane liked making people happy. Ashford had always been the same way.

Of course, my brother didn't have nearly unlimited funds available. Unlike Dane Knightly.

A couple of days ago, I had given in to the urge to google him. That was how I figured out he's an actual billionaire. He had been telling the truth about the gossip columns, too.

Jealousy had surged in my stomach, taking me by surprise, as I saw those pictures of him with elegant Manhattan socialites.

I'd suspected he was the playboy type. Of course he was. He was a handsome, rich man in his thirties who traveled the world. Silver Ridge was just a stopover for him. He could go anywhere and have anything he wanted.

But I had maybe stared at those pictures of him a little too long, feeling a secret satisfaction that he'd wanted a night with *me*.

It was better for all of us that it hadn't actually happened, but...I could still fantasize about what-ifs. That was harmless.

Only me and my vibrator would know.

What I really needed to do was stop thinking about him and focus on my usual life. Like helping run bingo, something I did about once a month and always enjoyed, even if it wouldn't be a rich jet setter's idea of fun.

This was the real Grace O'Neal. Community events and volunteer work and triple-checking spreadsheets. Not evening gowns or glamorous dates worthy of a New York gossip rag.

Teller and I went back to the storage room for more folding tables. "I wanted to ask how you've been lately," Teller said softly. "I heard from Piper that you moved in with Callum."

"Just for financial reasons. My former landlord decided to sell the house I was renting, and Callum and his roommates had a space available. I'm trying to save up to buy my own place."

"It must be comforting to have your family close. Now that Ashford has Emma, the dynamic is different. I want to make sure you know I consider you family too. If there's anything you might need."

Teller had always been serious, even when we were kids. He was twelve years older than me. A decade older than his sister. Back in the day, Piper's big brother had intimidated the heck out of me. Which only increased when he became a Green Beret, serving until he was wounded. He still had that same gruff manner, only honed by maturity.

It used to surprise me that a wild child like Piper could have such a straight-laced sibling. But it was probably good for her to have someone as grounded as Teller. He was great with her son Ollie, too.

"Thanks," I said. "I promise, the only thing I need right now is help getting the room ready before the bingo crowds descend."

I also needed a distraction from a certain billionaire hotel owner, but I had no intention of mentioning that to Teller.

Unfortunately, he brought up that very subject in the next breath. "Wanted to ask you about something, though. Dane Knightly. I know he's close with Ashford. Have you spent much time with him yet?"

I paid extra attention to a stack of chairs. "He came to Ashford's for dinner. I think he's been busy with the hotel."

Teller hummed thoughtfully. "I figure I should introduce myself at some point. Make sure he knows he can't do whatever he wants here. I'm aware that he served with Ashford, but rich types like Knightly tend to act like they own everything they see."

"I don't think Dane is like that."

"Maybe not. But after that drama last year and the other new elements Ashford has brought to Silver Ridge, I have a reason to be concerned."

"You mean Ayla Maxwell? You're not a fan?"

Now, it was Teller's turn to seem uncomfortable. "I don't know anything about her music," he said testily. He scratched at the long scar on his cheek. "Just that my officers have to work overtime to keep her safe when she decides to grace us with her presence. I don't have the funding to babysit celebrities."

I smiled. "Especially a pop star who's considered one of the sexiest women in the world?"

Teller's expression barely changed, but there was a flicker in his eyes, and for *him* that gave away plenty. "She's...memorable, I suppose."

Hmm. Interesting.

I could've kept teasing the chief about his crush on Ashford's much younger sister-in-law, but I decided to show mercy. We had work to do.

Half an hour later, the room was all set up and filling with bingo regulars. I waved at Dixie, who was at the concession table pouring a pitcher of something that looked suspiciously like sangria. We weren't supposed to be serving alcohol here, but it was impossible to rein Dixie in.

Thankfully, the chief didn't notice. He was currently surrounded by white-haired ladies. I heard several mentions of granddaughters that they wanted to introduce to the very single police chief. The man kept glancing over at me like he hoped I might save him.

Nope, I wanted nothing to do with that.

We were just about to get started when there was a new swirl of excitement, and heads swiveled toward the door. Whispers spread about the newcomer who'd just walked in. I turned.

And my stomach swooped like I was suddenly on a roller coaster.

Dane was rocking black jeans that hugged his strong thighs

and the long lines of his legs. His shoulders filled out a dark-gray flannel that matched his eyes. Not that different from the clothing that most men around Silver Ridge favored, yet Dane made it look almost as good as his tailored black tuxedo.

Instantly, my heart rate picked up, and blood rushed to my face. What in the world was he doing here?

I watched as he went over to the concession table to say hello to Dixie. She didn't act remotely surprised to see him. Dixie said something to him, pointing in my direction, and he turned around, his eyes locking on me as he smiled.

My chest went tight.

"Should we get started?" Teller whispered, touching my arm. "Gotta be honest, Grace, I'd rather this not run any later than it has to."

I turned to face him, forcing a smile. "Yep. You're right, sorry." I nearly fumbled the microphone, and it let out a high-pitched screech that had everyone cringing. I swore I saw Dane laughing from the corner of my eye.

"Hi everyone, welcome! The game tonight benefits the new Silver Ridge Children's Toy Library, so please don't forget your donations." I picked up the donation jar to start it passing around. "And I know you're all as excited as I am that our very own Chief Landry will be reading out the numbers tonight, so let's give him a round of applause."

Relax, I told myself. *Dane isn't staring at you*.

Ugh, he was staring at me.

I tried to focus on the bingo game, but it was nearly impossible. Whispers spread from the corner where Dane was sitting and talking quietly to the grandmas around him. They fussed over him, giggling at whatever he was saying. Couldn't he turn that charm off for a few minutes? Did he need that much attention?

When it was time for a break, I bustled around at the front table and tried to look busy. But then a shadow fell over me, and a deep voice said, "Evening, Ms. O'Neal."

I glanced up into steel-gray eyes. I composed my face into a polite smile. "Hello."

Dane held out the donation jar. "I was told to return this to you."

"Thanks." My voice cracked, and I cleared my throat. The donation jar nearly slipped from my hands, and it plunked roughly on the table, bills jostling inside. "I didn't know bingo was your thing."

"I didn't either. But Dixie invited me, and when I heard you were in charge, that sealed the deal. I wanted to see you."

Oh lordy. Heat flooded my face.

Why was I like this? If there had been a vaccine against Dane Knightly's charms, I would've been first in line for the injection.

Teller stepped over and hovered protectively at my side. "Knightly, right? We haven't met yet. Chief Landry."

"Good to meet you, Chief. I've heard about you from Ashford."

Teller grunted. "Likewise. Enjoying bingo?"

"Sure. I'm mostly here for Grace, though. I have a favor to ask her."

I opened my mouth, but Teller spoke before I could. "She's a bit busy at the moment."

"I'm a patient man. I can wait until later."

"She might have other plans. I'd be happy to chat with you instead. Let you know how we do things around here."

Okay, this was ridiculous. Dane and Teller were eyeing each other, puffing their chests, and talking about me like I wasn't even here. They were throwing off so much testosterone it was hard to breathe.

"We can talk after bingo," I said to Dane, resting my hand on Teller's arm and trying to nudge him back. *Stand down.*

Dane's eyes zeroed in on the spot where I was touching Teller. "Works for me."

I let out a breath when Dane returned to his seat.

Teller leaned in to speak quietly in my ear. "Are you having any issues with him? You seemed uncomfortable. Like I said, some wealthy men think they can have everything they see. I know he's your brother's friend, but if you need me to have a chat with Knightly about boundaries—"

"No. Dane is alright. I've just had a lot on my mind."

"I thought you said earlier that you were fine."

"I *am*, and I would love if you stopped interrogating me and called some bingo numbers."

Teller raised a skeptical eyebrow.

As we resumed the bingo game, my mind went back to the favor Dane had mentioned. Did it have something to do with Ashford? Maybe Dane wanted to buy a nice gift for Ashford and Emma's wedding and needed my advice.

Teller seemed to have the routine down, so I grabbed the donation jar to count out the funds. There were the usual small bills and a couple of checks. But I stopped when I pulled out a folded stack of crisp bills.

They were all hundreds. A *lot* of them.

By the time I finished double-checking my math, that stack of bills alone came to five thousand dollars, more than enough to cover the rest of the funding for the toy library. And I knew exactly who must've put these in the jar.

When I looked up and glanced in Dane's direction, he was studying his bingo card.

"Hey, Grace," Teller murmured. The microphone dangled from his hand, and he was staring intently at me. "Mrs. Stuckey has a bingo."

I jumped up. Crap, I hadn't even heard her yell it out. "Whoops, sorry. Got a little distracted. Bring your card up, Mrs. Stuckey."

Teller eyed me like he could guess where my mind had been. But what was I supposed to do?

Any time Dane Knightly appeared, I wasn't able to focus on anything else.

TEN
Grace

AFTER BINGO ENDED and the prizes were distributed, we usually had a bunch of people chip in to help break down the tables and chairs and clean everything up.

Today, Dane was among them. He and Teller seemed to have an unspoken competition going for who could carry more tables at once. Then I was about to make a trip outside to load up my car, but the two men grabbed everything and did it for me.

At least they were efficient.

Finally, the space was clear and most of the participants had trickled outside. Dane waited for me over by the exit door.

"Want me to stick around?" Teller asked quietly.

"I really don't. You have better things to do."

"Better than looking out for family? I disagree."

I smiled and said, "*Go*," giving Teller a push toward the door. I had little chance of moving his bulky frame if he'd really intended to stay, but he did as I asked, up-nodding at Dane as he passed.

Dane narrowed his eyes as his gaze flicked between me and Teller. Which, now that I thought about it, was one of the few times I'd seen Dane portray anything except complete confidence.

Could he really be jealous? About *me*?

"I need to lock up," I said, pulling the keys from my pocket.

We stepped outside, and I closed the door. Teller's SUV slowly pulled out of the parking lot, and he gave me a final wave as he left.

Dane leaned against the brick exterior of the building as he watched me lock up. "What's the story with you and the police chief?"

"He's Piper's older brother. They lived across the street when we were kids. He's protective."

"But is that because you and he..."

"Teller and I are friends." I stuck the keys in my pocket and crossed my arms. "Why do you care so much?"

Dane's lips quirked. "Just curious. Looking out for my best friend's little sister."

I lifted my eyebrow skeptically, and he shrugged.

"That was a very generous donation you gave to the toy library," I said.

"There were a lot of donations. You don't know which was mine."

"Yeah, I do. Nobody else in Silver Ridge would stick thousands of dollars in that jar."

"Cash donations are anonymous, so you can't be sure."

"I'm *sure*. But you deserve to get credit. They'll be able to fund the whole toy library project with that money. The Hart County Children's Center will be thrilled."

He tilted his head, his smile growing. "Then why do you sound angry?"

"I'm not!" Fine, I did sound angry. "You're just...infuriating."

"Because of an anonymous donation?"

"No, because I don't know how to act around you!" I confessed.

Whoops. I hadn't meant for that to come out.

"Believe it or not, I don't entirely know how to act around you either," he said. "It's been awkward between us the last couple times we saw one another. I'd like to get to know you better. As a friend."

"You said you needed a favor."

"I do. A friendly favor."

My mouth quirked, wanting to smile, even though I was still frustrated. "Are you going to tell me what it is?"

"Take a walk with me, and I will." Another grin.

Ugh, it was useless fighting him.

He'd compared me to Superman the night of the party. But Dane Knightly's lopsided smile was my kryptonite.

"There are woods behind the center," I said. "With a creek winding through the trees."

"Sounds beautiful."

We walked in that direction. I had to admit, it was a lovely day for it. The sun was just now sinking, leaving a deeper chill in the air that made goosebumps rise on my skin beneath my sweater. But it wasn't unpleasant. Now that it was early October, the fall colors were really popping. Maroon, yellow gold, and vivid red.

We stopped in the middle of a wooden bridge that crossed the small creek. Fallen leaves floated and eddied in the crystal-clear water. Polished stones lay beneath.

Dane rested his elbows on the railing, gazing down. "Reminds me a little of Central Park."

"Is it pretty this time of year?"

He turned his smile on me again. "It is. You've never been?"

I shook my head and glanced back down at the water. "Except for a road trip to Wyoming with Piper once, I've never even left the state." Dane was looking at me, so I searched for something to say to fill the quiet. "This is Aspen Creek. It starts all the way up near your ski resort and winds down here through the town."

"Gorgeous."

"The summer after third grade, Piper and I tried to hike all the way to the source of the creek." I laughed, remembering that day. "They had to send sheriff's deputies on ATVs to find us. Our brothers were so pissed."

Dane's smile softened. "I got lost in Central Park once. Totally my fault. I decided to search for dinosaur bones. My mother was terrified."

"I bet."

"Once she found me, she grounded me for a week. Spanked my butt too for scaring her so much."

"Did you behave better after that?"

"I wish I could say I did, for my mom's sake. But no. Not really."

That, I did believe.

He angled his body to face me. Even if we'd had more space between us, it would've been impossible to ignore the man. "I'd like you to be my official guide to Silver Ridge," he said. "Help me get to know the town the way you do. The people."

"That's the favor you want? Why me?"

"Because everyone here adores you. You know the insider secrets. Like where this creek begins. You're plugged into the pulse of the town."

"What about Dixie or Ashford."

"Dixie is a fantastic lady, but she's a steamroller. And as much as I love Ashford, he's the town grump. I need a guide with a more...diplomatic touch. I need *you*."

I looked off into the trees, just for a break from the relentless pull I felt toward him. "I'm pretty busy as it is."

"I could hire you. Name your price."

"I like my job. I don't need a new one."

"Donations in your name to whatever charities you want."

"You're bribing me?"

"I'm not above it. I'll beg, if that's what it takes. You wanna see a man brought low? I'll get on the ground if I have to."

Laughter bubbled in my chest. "You're ridiculous."

"You haven't even seen ridiculous yet." He dropped to his knees in front of me, lower lip pushing out in a pout.

"Get up. Someone's going to see you."

"Not until you say yes."

"Fine, *yes*. Just get up." I didn't need rumors spreading about Dane Knightly begging me for something on his knees. The gossips would have us engaged and pregnant in no time. Ashford would *love* that.

But Dane was a friend of the family. That was reason enough for me to help him out. I would've done the same for plenty of other people. Had nothing to do with the fact that he was extremely easy on the eyes, made me laugh, and knew how to talk me into *anything*, apparently.

"I can be your guide to Silver Ridge. As a friendly favor, and nothing more than that."

He stood up. "Wasn't asking for anything more."

"Good."

"Are you busy tonight? We can get started. I'll buy you dinner."

"Anyone ever told you you're incredibly pushy?"

"Yes," he said simply.

I huffed another laugh.

"You drove here, right?" he asked. "How about we head to your place to drop your car off. Then we can get something to eat. Whatever spot is your favorite."

I sighed, giving up. "Okay. You win."

"That's what I like to hear."

"You claim Dixie is a steamroller? She's nothing compared to you."

He smiled.

✧

As I drove toward my place, I still wasn't exactly sure what had just happened.

I had agreed to be Dane's guide to Silver Ridge and to have dinner with him. We would have to spend a lot more time together. I had no idea how that man was so convincing. He was so persuasive it was unnerving.

I had a reputation around town for being easy to get along with, but I was no pushover. Anybody who ever worked with me knew I had a stubborn streak, which my brothers could attest to. But that didn't seem to apply to Dane. It seemed like my life wouldn't go back to boring until Dane finally got tired of Silver Ridge and left town.

You were right, Dixie. The man is wily.

I would have to be careful with this one. Otherwise he would talk me into any number of questionable situations.

The worst part was that I might enjoy every second of it. I had to keep some emotional distance.

I parked in front of my house and got out. Dane's SUV hadn't caught up to me yet, and I wanted to make this quick. Otherwise, I had no doubt he would follow me inside and introduce himself to my roommates. I could only imagine his reaction when he found out I was living with four burly firefighters, only one of whom was related to me. I didn't need a repeat of the testosterone showdown he'd had with Teller.

Even if I enjoyed it a *tiny* bit when Dane made it obvious he was attracted to me. I was only human.

Grabbing the box of bingo equipment in my trunk, along with the donation money, I made a beeline toward my front door. Luckily I didn't spot Callum's truck or the vehicles belonging to the other guys.

I was putting my key in the lock when the door pushed open on its own. Had one of the guys forgotten to close and lock it earlier?

Then I noticed the splinters in the frame.

Someone had forced the door open. Oh, God.

I pushed the door wider, and my entire body went cold at what I saw inside.

ELEVEN

Dane

I PULLED up to the curb outside Grace's house. She'd just gone inside.

Her place was half a mile from Main Street, a one-story ranch with mature trees growing around it. It looked nice, but not exactly what I would've expected for Grace. It was nondescript. Grace had an indefinable, special quality about her, even when she was dressed casually. A spark that naturally drew my eye. But maybe she hadn't lived here long, and she hadn't had the chance to put her own personal mark on it yet.

She'd left the door open, which I figured was an invitation for me to follow her inside. I made my way up the front walkway with a grin on my face, still feeling triumphant that she'd agreed to have dinner with me and be my guide to her hometown. It was all platonic, of course, but I had every intention of enjoying her company.

I'd also been relieved to hear she and the police chief were no more than friends. I had no claim to Grace, and I couldn't be more than friends with her either. But she seemed to bring out a possessive streak in me that I'd never experienced with anyone else.

Then the hairs on my arms started to prickle, and my smile faded in an instant.

Grace was standing just inside the doorway, not moving.

I jogged the last few steps to reach her. "Hey, what's—Oh, *shit.*"

The living room was a disaster area. Cushions thrown off the couch, lamps knocked sideways. The kitchen was visible through an archway, and the drawers and cabinets were all open, contents strewn everywhere.

"Grace, you need to get out of this house. Whoever did this could still be here." I put my hand on her shoulder, and that seemed to wake her back up.

"My bedroom!" She slipped out of my grasp. *Shit.* The girl was fast.

I rushed after her, catching up to her in the hallway. My fingers closed around her wrist to keep her from going into the bedroom. "Did you not hear what I said? We need to get out of here."

She struggled. "Dane, let me go. Some asshole has been in my room."

"Exactly my point." Her bedroom hadn't fared any better than the living room. Her bedding was thrown haphazardly, drawers rifled through. My stomach lurched with anger when I saw broken glass on the carpet.

Whoever had done this to Grace, I wanted to smash every bone in his body the way he had smashed her possessions. But only once I was sure she was safe.

"We're going outside, and we're calling your police chief friend."

"Dane—"

"Nope. I'm not messing around anymore."

Before she could run away from me again, I hoisted her over my shoulder in a fireman's carry. Grace screamed. "Put me down!"

"I will. When we're safely outside."

"What about my roommates? What if someone's hurt?"

From the hall, I quickly glanced in the other doorways, just to make sure nobody was injured and lying unconscious. None of the other rooms had been touched. I didn't see any sign of an intruder, either. But I wasn't going to push our luck.

Once we were outside, I carried Grace to my Range Rover, opened the door, and dropped her into the passenger seat. Then I stood there in the doorway of the SUV to block her exit as I took out my phone. She glared at me.

I dialed 911 and a dispatcher answered. "What's your emergency?"

"There's been a break-in at Grace O'Neal's residence." I glanced at the mailbox and read off the address. "No one injured that we know of. But it's possible the intruder could still be inside the house. Yes. Will do. We're not going anywhere."

I lowered my phone. The dispatcher had asked me to remain on the line, but I would be able to hear if she said anything else. "They're on their way. Are you all right?"

"No, I'm *furious*. My phone is in my purse. I dropped it in the living room. Let me go get it." She tried to push past me. I kept her in place.

"You *should* be furious. But you're staying right here. We need to wait for the authorities to arrive."

"This is my home, Dane. Not yours. I promise you, if I run into the asshole who did this, he's going to be the one fleeing for his life."

I smothered the grin that tried to rise on my lips.

Her glasses had slipped down her nose, and it was so damn cute that it made me want to kiss her forehead. But I had the feeling that would only piss her off more.

The thought of someone going through her things, though, returned me to that simmering state of fury. It shocked me to think anyone would want to cause Grace harm.

"Any idea who would do this? The other bedrooms weren't ransacked. Only yours." It had looked like Grace had several roommates, and I suspected they weren't the female variety given the decor choices in their rooms. I was curious about that, but it could wait until later.

I wanted her gut impression. Because if someone had been bothering her lately, that name would come first to her mind. I liked Grace a lot, and I would be damned if I let someone frighten and intimidate her this way.

She hesitated, averting her eyes. "I'm not sure."

"Give me his name, Grace."

"I don't have any names. I have no idea if it's connected. But—"

A police cruiser roared down the street and stopped behind us. Chief Landry jumped out, along with another officer. I wanted to hear what else Grace was going to say, but Landry charged up to us.

"What happened?" he demanded. His expression hardened when he glanced at me.

She explained what we'd seen inside. While Landry and the other officer went into the house, more vehicles pulled up. Grace's brother Callum and a younger guy wearing a Silver Ridge FD T-shirt jumped out. Callum's head swiveled until he spotted his sister, and he went straight toward us.

"Gracie, what the hell is going on? We were at the fire house. We heard about the 911 call."

Grace hugged her brother. "Someone broke in. Dane was with me when I got here."

"Wasn't clear if the intruder was still in the house," I chimed in. "I took Grace outside and called the police."

The one with shaggy black hair who'd arrived a second after Callum crossed his arms over his chest, glaring at me with suspicion.

Callum exhaled. "This is messed up. I'm gonna call the other guys and let them know."

By the time the police finished checking the house, we had a crowd gathered on the front lawn. Me, Grace, Callum, and their roommates. I wondered when Grace had been planning to mention that she lived with three single men. Sure, her brother was around as well, but from everything I'd heard from Ashford, Callum wasn't a model of responsibility.

I also couldn't help thinking about the fact that nobody else's room had been touched except for Grace's. Did that mean the culprit had been looking for something of hers?

"Dane, what exactly were you doing here with Grace?" Callum asked. His tone was friendly, but there was a hard edge beneath. The other roommates frowned at me, grumbling that they wanted to know the same thing.

Grace rolled her eyes. "All of you calm down. I'm helping Dane with a project."

Chief Landry stepped out onto the grass. "Grace, could I have a word with you?"

I stayed beside her as she crossed the lawn toward the chief. Landry frowned, but he didn't tell me to leave. "Can you explain again what happened?" he asked Grace. "From the beginning. Don't leave anything out."

"There's not much to tell. After bingo, I drove here, and Dane followed me so we could get started on a project I'm going to help him with. But when I arrived, I saw the door was already open. I walked in and found it just like it is now."

She didn't mention the part where I threw her over my shoulder and carried her back outside. Probably for the best.

"The common areas and your bedroom were the only parts of the house that appeared to be affected," Landry said. "The parts of the house you presumably used. Certainly looks like someone was targeting you."

"That's what Dane said too." Grace's skin had gone ashen. I rested my hand on her lower back.

"You'll need to take a look and see if anything is missing," Landry said. "Do you have any idea who would've done this?"

Same thing I'd asked her before. But this time, Grace shook her head emphatically. None of the hesitation I had seen earlier around that question. "No. No idea at all." Her eyes met mine, silently pleading with me not to say anything.

I didn't like it, but I held my tongue. We would be discussing it later. Without a doubt.

"Are you checking for fingerprints?" I asked the chief. "What about doorbell cams at the neighbors' houses?" I hadn't seen one at Grace's. No alarm system of any kind.

The chief fixed me with an annoyed look. "We're following all our usual procedures. This isn't New York City, but believe it or not, I know what I'm doing."

I held up my hands. "Just making sure."

Landry took Grace inside. I almost asked if she wanted me to go with her, but I figured I had ruffled enough feathers for the moment.

"Is there something going on between you and my sister?" Callum asked.

Uh oh.

I turned around, finding Grace's brother and his three buddies glowering at me.

"We're friends. I'm worried about her. Same as you. But if this were my place, I would've had a security system and stronger locks on the doors to keep her safe."

Callum took off his baseball cap and ran his fingers through his hair. "I've always liked you, Knightly. Don't give me a reason not to."

"I've always liked you too, Callum, but I can't really help what you do and don't like."

Grumbling, he pushed past me into the house.

✧

I joined in with the others to help clean the living room and kitchen. When Grace and the officers finished in her room, she walked out into the hallway, looking shellshocked.

"Anything missing?" her brother asked.

Her gaze flew to me, then away. "No, not that I can tell." She rubbed a hand down her opposite arm.

Grace was lying. I couldn't say how I read her so well based on the few interactions we'd had, but I felt it in my gut. Just like she'd lied to Chief Landry earlier. The question was why.

One of the roommates nodded his head toward Grace's room. "You want us to help clean up in there?"

"It's not that bad," she said faintly. "I can handle it."

You shouldn't have to, I wanted to say. But I didn't think pushing her was the right move at the moment. She was upset, and all my protectiveness had reared to the surface. I wanted to put my arms around her and get her somewhere quiet. Somewhere she felt secure enough to talk and tell me what was really going on.

I crossed the room toward her. "I don't think you should stay here tonight," I said softly. "I can get you a room at the hotel."

"There's no need for that," her brother said. Callum pointed a thumb at another of the bedrooms. "Grace can take my room. I'll sleep on the couch."

"Or she could take my bunk," the guy who'd introduced himself as Connor said.

"Or mine," Niko added.

Grace opened her mouth, but Chief Landry spoke over her. "No, I think Knightly has a point. But Grace should stay closer to home. I'll call Piper. Grace, you can stay at my sister's place tonight. She has a security system."

"We're fine here," Callum protested. "I'll head to the damn hardware store right now, get a new lock, and have it installed within the hour. Hell, I'll install a camera outside too. Grace is completely safe."

"Would you all shut up and let me *speak*?"

Every head turned toward the small, flustered woman in the corner.

"I can decide for myself where I want to sleep. I appreciate all the concern, because you're right, my room doesn't seem all that attractive tonight after some creep was in there. But I also need space without all of you fretting over me. I'll go to the hotel."

Her brother tried again to talk her out of it, but Grace wasn't having it. "I'm going to grab my things," she said.

I made a quick call while she packed an overnight bag.

Callum went to help her, then wandered back to the living room and frowned at me as I finished my call with Tobin, my hotel manager. Grace emerged with a bag hanging from her shoulder.

Callum hugged her. "Text me when you're in your hotel room, all right? I love you."

"I love you too."

Her brother glanced at me. "Make sure she has what she needs at the hotel?"

"Planning on it."

I took Grace's bag, along with the stack of books she carried in her arms. We went outside and headed toward my SUV.

It took some convincing, but she was leaving her own car here. She didn't love the idea of being stuck at the resort and needing me to drive her around, but I'd reminded her that the shuttle made several trips to Main Street every day.

I had no intention of sticking her on the shuttle, of course. I would drive her wherever she needed to go tomorrow. But for as much as Grace bent over backwards on behalf of her family and the town, she wasn't so great at accepting help for herself.

I opened the door for her, then stowed her bag and the stack of books in my backseat. It was fully dark by now, way past dinner time. I switched my high beams on to light the road to the mountain.

"You can scream it out if you want," I said. "Now that it's just us."

"*What*?"

I saw her turn toward me from the corner of my eye, but I

remained focused on the road. "A primal yell. Don't you ever do that when you're pissed off?"

"Just scream? Right now?"

"Sure."

She paused. Inhaled. "I'll...think about it."

"All right. I'd prefer you use the car though, if you change your mind. Screaming in the hotel could raise some questions."

"I'll keep that in mind." She chuckled. A half-hearted one, but it was something.

We drove in silence for several minutes, and then she said, "I'll pay you back for the hotel room."

"No, you won't."

"I can afford it. I don't need charity."

"No offense, but I don't need your money. I take care of my friends." I tapped the steering wheel with my thumb. "I do think you should tell Ashford about what happened, though. Before he hears it from someone else."

"Are you going to tell him?"

"Not unless I have your permission. But whenever he hears it, he's going to be worried, and there's nothing you can do about that. He loves you."

She sighed. "Ashford and Emma have been through enough. I don't want to add to it."

"I doubt they'd see it that way."

Ashford had told me about how Emma was hurt last year by someone they'd all trusted. From what I understood, that person had been a friend of Grace's too. I was glad the attacker was dead and wouldn't hurt any of the O'Neals again.

"But you're right," she said. "I'll call Ashford tomorrow. I'm exhausted."

"Let's get you settled and comfortable, then."

When we reached the resort, I parked in my reserved space beside the hotel and grabbed her things from the backseat.

"You plan to read this many books tonight?" I asked.

"I've got my e-reader and laptop in my bag too. Some of it's for work, some of it's for pleasure. And I never know what reading mood I'll be in."

I smiled. "Got it."

We walked together into the lobby. There was a low hum of activity tonight, the sound of people talking and dishes clinking coming from the restaurant. But this was practically dead compared to how busy it had been the night of the grand-opening party. The last time Grace had been here.

Tobin spotted me and came out from behind the desk. "Evening, sir. Here's the extra key you requested. The dinner you ordered should be up in a few."

"Thanks, Tobin. Ms. O'Neal will be staying here a few days. Can you give her your direct number? And take care of anything she asks for?"

"It's one day," Grace corrected, accepting the business card that Tobin handed her. "I'll be out of your hair in the morning."

I shrugged. "We'll see. You might like it so much here you decide to stay longer, and you're welcome to. The owner is a generous guy."

That earned me a faint smile.

I nodded toward the elevators, carrying her bag. The car opened as soon as I pushed the up arrow. We stepped inside, and I waved the keycard to get the elevator moving.

"What room number am I in?" Grace asked.

"701."

She blinked at me. "*Your* room?"

So she remembered. "My suite. It actually has three bedrooms. I'm only using one of them. If you don't feel comfortable, I can make other arrangements. You said you wanted space, but..." I considered my words carefully. "If you need anything while you're here, I'd like to be close enough to anticipate it. Since I have the feeling you won't ask for it yourself."

I expected some kind of pushback. The woman had been skittish around me from the first moment we'd met.

But instead, a hundred pounds of tension seem to melt away from her shoulders. “Thank you. That sounds pretty nice.”

“So you’re willing to trust me? At least for tonight?”

“I guess I am.”

I held out the keycard to my suite. “I did give you one of these already, but I’m assuming you got rid of it.”

She smiled sheepishly. “I left it in the purse I was using that night. The purse belongs to Piper, so it’s at her place. I can get it back for you.”

“Nah, don’t bother. You might as well have access to an extra copy.” I winked. “I’m willing to trust you, too.”

TWELVE

Grace

I COULDN'T BELIEVE I was going up to Dane's suite. I had almost done this a couple of weeks ago. Before I had any idea who he really was.

But the circumstances couldn't have been more different. Now I knew he was my brother's best friend, and also a pretty decent guy. The kind of man who made me feel secure. And I did need a safe place right about now. Because what had happened at my house, the break-in... I didn't know what to think.

He swiped the keycard to get the elevator to bring us to the seventh floor. Dane squeezed my hand and let go of it when we reached the door to 701. It was indeed at the top of the hotel, one of only two doors on this floor.

Dane opened his door for me, and I went in. The decor was similar to the lobby. Granite floors with flecks of shimmery minerals. Elaborate light fixtures. I felt completely out of place. It was a reminder that, even when Dane dressed down, he was an outlier in my usual world.

He carried my bag and my books to a door on the left. I glanced briefly at a full kitchen and a spacious living room before following him. Dane set my things inside the room, then stepped out, leaning against the door frame. "You've got your own bathroom here. My bedroom is on the other side of the suite." He tilted his head in that direction. "Dinner will be up soon."

I crossed my arms over my stomach. "That sounds great, thanks. I think I'll get cleaned up." I felt grimy after being in my bedroom at home, knowing that some stranger had been in there.

I couldn't understand why someone would do that. Invade my home. Not just steal from me, because he *had* taken something, but trash my room too. The cruelty of some people made my head spin. I needed a few minutes alone just to know which way was up.

Maybe my acceptance of Dane's offer was evidence of the fact that I wasn't thinking straight. But I had needed out of that house and away from Callum and the other guys.

If I had stayed, they would've been checking up on me all night. *Everything's fine, Grace*, they would insist. *Just relax. Don't you worry your pretty head.* While at the same time breathing down my neck like they thought I would break. I hated that. As if my being angry or upset made them uncomfortable, and they couldn't handle it.

Right now, I appreciated the fact that Dane hadn't known me since I was a kid. He didn't see me as a little girl with skinned knees crying in the woods and trying to keep up with her older brothers.

Dane was protective too. Clearly. And bossier than nearly anyone I'd ever met. The man had actually thrown me over his shoulder and carried me out of the house earlier. My brothers wouldn't have dared. And *fine*, it had also probably been smart, since the intruder could've been hanging around.

But when I'd told him how pissed I was, Dane had agreed with me instead of placating me. I'd been so *angry*, and even though Dane forced me to leave and call the police, he hadn't told me not to feel what I was feeling. He'd actually risked his eardrums by giving me permission to scream. An unusual offer, and I had been seriously tempted. Not ready to take him up on it. But...tempted.

Something I seemed to feel a lot around Dane Knightly.

I went into the room and closed the door. There was a lock, just like a regular hotel room. I flipped it, not so much because I thought I needed it around Dane, but because I could. It felt good to have that little bit of security there.

Yet it also felt good to know that he was nearby. That anybody who somehow tracked me to the seventh floor of this hotel would have to go through him to reach me.

The room was decorated in neutral colors. Luxe bedding, modern artwork on the walls. A combination of upscale hotel chic and mountain style. A quick trip into the bathroom revealed a similar vibe. The vanity looked like it was made of upcycled barn planks, while the tile was sleek and monochromatic. A stack of thick white towels waited for me on a shelf.

But the very best part was the shower. A huge rain-can shower head sprouted from the ceiling, and there was a steam setting too that I wanted to try.

The first thing I needed to do was text Piper. My friend would probably hear about the break-in from Teller or Callum, and I didn't want her to worry about me.

As for my other brother, I'd tell Ashford what happened tomorrow. He was going to flip, and I couldn't handle that tonight.

A few minutes later, I undressed and stepped beneath the spray. I sighed as the heat and the falling water released the knots between my shoulders. Wow, this was nice.

Made me wonder how fancy the bathroom was over in Dane's bedroom.

He'd probably show you if you asked, a mischievous voice said in my brain. *A nice, personal tour*. But I couldn't get carried away with ideas like that. Dane and I were friends now, and with a man like him, that was by far the wisest course. I had to stay strong.

I switched the water off and forced myself to get out.

After pulling my damp hair back and dressing in comfy sweats and a loose top, I ventured out. Dane was nowhere to be seen, so I assumed he was in his own room. I veered the other direction and went into the kitchen. It was fully stocked. Not just pots and pans and small appliances, but food in the fridge. Maybe that was standard when anyone stayed in the ski resort presidential suite. Or maybe he'd gone down to the market on Main himself and pushed around a shopping cart.

What exactly did a billionaire eat for breakfast, anyway?

I opened the fridge to snoop and found containers of fancy yogurt, cut fruit, cooked chicken breasts and steamed veggies. A carton of organic eggs and a packet wrapped in butcher paper and labeled *bacon*.

"You're welcome to anything you'd like." Dane strolled into the kitchen. "Dinner will be here any minute."

I closed the fridge and spun to face him. "Could I get a glass of water?"

"I have sparkling, and filtered comes from the tap."

I opened cabinets until I found a glass. But Dane took it from me. "I've got it." A buzzing sound filled the suite, coming from the front door. "And that must be dinner," he said.

I peeked at him as he walked toward the door. His butt looked great in those jeans. Just a harmless observation.

A hotel employee pushed the cart into the dining area. I would've been fine with takeout boxes and paper napkins, but the woman laid out a white tablecloth, then placed several dishes covered in metal domes in the center of the dining table. From another shelf on the cart, she brought out plates and silverware, arranging everything like it was a restaurant.

"Perfect," Dane said. "That's all we need. Much appreciated." He passed her a tip on her way out, and then he was back, pulling out a chair for me. "I ordered Italian, since that's what we had at Ashford's place. Assumed that was a safe choice."

"It smells delicious." My stomach rumbled as he uncovered the dishes. One looked like chicken piccata, and the other was pasta with a ragu sauce. Dane sat across from me and served me first. Which, okay, was gracious of him.

I took my first bites with a small groan. "This is *really* good." I took another big bite of chicken and realized his eyes were tracing the movements of my fork. "Aren't you going to eat?" I asked with my mouth full.

"I'm already enjoying this meal."

"You have some kind of kink about watching women eat?"

"I didn't think so. But watching *you* eat? Maybe."

Oh lord. This man.

I put my fork down. "Is that why you brought the cheeseboard to Ashford's last week? To watch me eat it like a weirdo?"

He laughed. "No. I brought it because I knew you would like it. No other reason."

"But *why*? Why was that important to you?"

"Because you were mad at me after the fall festival. I wanted to make up for it."

"That's typical for you? Buying people's affection?"

"Do I have your affection?"

Yes, my traitorous heart responded. Thank goodness I didn't say it out loud.

I barely knew him. Yet it was impossible not to like Dane. And that was aside from the fact that he was one of the most handsome men I'd ever sat across from. Plenty of women would love to be in my shoes.

Plenty of women have been in your shoes, I reminded myself.

"I thought you weren't going to flirt with me anymore."

"Who said that?"

I rolled my eyes. "Maybe you're not capable of it."

"I'm capable. But I think you enjoy when I flirt with you."

"There you go again, telling me what's in my head. It's presumptuous."

"Yet you're not telling me I'm wrong." With that smirk still on his face, he dished twice as much food as he'd given me onto his plate and started to eat. I shouldn't have worried about the man going hungry.

I went back to eating. The food warmed my stomach, and I

glanced around again, my attention drawn back to the luxurious surroundings. "How did you end up buying this hotel, anyway?" I asked.

"Ashford didn't tell you?"

I shook my head. "Not really. Just that you thought it was a good investment. But there must be even better investments in other places."

He finished his last bite and leaned back in his chair. "I'd rather not talk about me tonight. I'd rather hear why you lied to Chief Landry."

I hid my shock by taking a sip of water. "Why do you think I was lying?"

"A hunch. You said nothing was missing from your bedroom, but you looked at me right afterward."

I bit my lip and drummed my fingers against the table. "It might be nothing."

"Tell me so I can help." Dane's tone was gentle, but firm enough to emphasize that he wouldn't back down. "That's why you agreed to come here tonight, isn't it? You're trusting me already. So trust me with this."

This man kept pushing his way into my life. Sticking around even when I tried to avoid him. I still didn't understand exactly why, but if anyone could help me figure this out, it would be him.

Hard as it was to believe, even for me, I did want to trust him. At least with this.

"The red mask was missing from my room."

His brows knitted. "The one you wore at the grand-opening party?"

I nodded. "I hung the mask on the edge of a frame on my wall, but after the break-in, it was gone. I lied to Teller because I didn't want to explain about that night."

"About seeing me there?"

"Yep." And the fact that I almost went up to Dane's suite to spend the night with him. Teller had those interrogation skills. And I was no hardened criminal. Teller would've gotten every last detail out of me. "Besides, it could be a coincidence. I didn't have money in my room or jewelry worth stealing. Maybe the intruder thought the mask was expensive, and that's why he took it."

I thought of what Ms. Scarlet had said to me that night. *Not everything that shines is a real diamond.*

Dane pushed his plate aside and rested his elbows on the table. "You said a stranger gave the mask to you."

"A redhead in the hotel ladies' room. Just before I went into the party."

"Then that VIP in the blue mask thought you were her."

"Right. I assume so. Then later, when I was in the lobby after you went upstairs..."

"What happened?"

Memories from that night flitted through my mind in a hazy blur of music and color. The man in the blue mask grabbing my shoulder. Dane swooping in to my rescue. Flirting with him afterward. His invitation.

Do you want me to take you upstairs and worship you until the sun comes up?

And the way he'd spoken, the intense desire in his eyes—the memory made my breath catch and arousal tingle in all my nerve endings, just like it had weeks ago. I'd thought countless times about that night in the last couple of weeks, but not with the same man sitting right across from me.

My thighs squeezed together.

"What happened in the lobby?" Dane prompted.

I took another sip of cold water. "A man stopped me. A different one. He asked where I got the mask. I think he was looking for the woman I'd met in the bathroom earlier that night. Ms. Scarlet."

"What did he look like?"

I closed my eyes, picturing the man. The hard lines of his mouth and the gleam in his eyes. It made me shiver. "He's white. Has a goatee. And...a mole on his right cheek. His head was shaved. I almost thought he could be security at first, just from the way he carried himself. But then I figured he wouldn't be wearing a mask." I rubbed my eyes beneath my glasses. "Maybe I should've said something to the hotel staff about it. Made a bigger deal of it. But I just..."

I'd wanted to get away from the resort and forget about that night. Forget about sexy Mr. Black and his seventh-floor hotel suite.

From the way Dane was watching me, I figured he could guess that part too.

"The whole night was so strange," I finished. "Now today, Ms. Scarlet's mask goes missing from my room. And the person who took it trashed my bedroom and other parts of my house. It could be connected, but how?"

"I'll give Tobin those descriptions and pull the security footage from the night of the party. See if we can identify the woman who gave you the mask or either of the men who stopped you. And we can find out if any of them are still in Silver Ridge. If they're staying at my hotel, I want to know."

I groaned. "This is a mess. Exactly why I don't like having things to hide. I don't want secrets or mysteries to solve. I wish I never put on that mask."

"The party wouldn't have been nearly as interesting if you hadn't, though."

"That would've been better. If you and I never saw each other there. I prefer to keep my life simple. *Boring*."

"Are you sure about that?"

I drummed my fingers against the tablecloth, looking down at my empty plate.

"The woman I spent time with at the grand-opening party was far from boring," Dane said. "It wasn't about the dress or the heels, though you did look incredible in those."

"I keep telling you, I wasn't acting like the real me that night."

"Your quick wit is the same. Your humor. Your candor. Are you sure you want boring? Or do you just want to feel safe?"

I bristled. "Nothing wrong with wanting to feel safe."

"Not at all. I *want* you to feel safe. I don't blame you, especially with what happened to Emma and Ashford last year. Ashford has also mentioned what your family situation was like when you guys were kids, and—"

"*Don't.*" My entire body flooded with heat, but this was nowhere near pleasant.

He held up his hands. "Shit. Let me back up and try again, because that came out all wrong."

"I'd rather not." I pushed my chair back from the table and stood. My chest heaved as I breathed. "My brother might be your best friend, but don't assume you know *me*. You don't. A few conversations doesn't change that fact."

Dane calmly stared back at me.

Perhaps I was overreacting. I couldn't help it though. The way Dane looked at me, the way he reached into my head and seemed to see the things I didn't want anyone to see...

I felt exposed around him. Right now, it didn't feel remotely good.

I grabbed my plate and glass, intending to rinse the dishes and go to bed. But Dane got up and stopped me, making me set everything back on the table. He held my hands in his.

"I'm sorry," he said. "I was putting words in your mouth, and I shouldn't have. I just want you to know you can talk to me. That has nothing to do with Ashford or the friendship I have with him. But everything to do with the friendship I would like to have with you."

Despite how close we were standing, there was no flirtation in his voice. I believed that he meant it.

"Okay."

"I can get on my knees and grovel."

"I'd rather you didn't." A couple more deep breaths, and I was calm again. I gently pulled my hands from his grip. "I can take care of the dishes."

"No, I want you to relax. Go to bed early."

I almost argued, but I felt strung out. "I appreciate dinner. And the place to stay."

"Of course. If you need anything, you know where to find me. Door at the end of the hall."

Ugh. The last thing I needed to focus on was how close he would be tonight.

As I got ready for bed, I tried to keep my mind blank. I didn't want to think about everything Dane had said. Especially because I suspected he could be right.

What if I didn't want boring at all?

Ever since Dane Knightly had arrived in Silver Ridge, my life had taken a severe turn toward the exciting. Break-ins at my home were *not* my idea of a good time. But I liked being around Dane.

Radical honesty here: I enjoyed his attention. Whenever I was around him, he made me feel...special. *Alive.*

Maybe I needed a little more of Dane's particular brand of excitement. And that thought scared me. Not as much as someone robbing my house, but still.

Dane made me want things I was afraid of having.

THIRTEEN

Dane

THE NEXT MORNING, I stepped onto the elevator at the ground floor and swiped my keycard to head back to the seventh floor. I had a box of pastries and a couple of coffees balanced on top. I would've gone down to Main Street to grab breakfast from Silver Linings, because they had the best coffee in town. Way better than the mediocre stuff we were serving up downstairs in the lobby. I'd already made a mental note to ask where Piper sourced her beans.

But with Grace upstairs, I hadn't wanted to take such a long detour. I also had a feeling that if I drove her into town, she might take off. She could leave whenever she wanted, technically, but I didn't want to give her any excuse to cut our time short.

Especially after that asinine comment I had made last night. I worried she was already looking to make an exit.

Bringing up her childhood and what Ashford had said? Such a bad move. Not surprising she had been pissed about that. My point had seemed valid at the time, but I'd delivered it in exactly the wrong way. Hopefully these chocolate pastries would make up for it.

Also, I did have a thing about watching her eat. Whenever she bit into something delicious, she made this sexy little moan and closed her eyes like she wanted to savor the moment. That noise was turning into my guilty pleasure.

When I reached room 701, I did another balancing act to unlock the door and went inside.

"Dane?" she called out.

"It's me. Brought breakfast."

Her voice had come from the living room, so I headed there. Grace was curled up at one end of the couch, looking so cozy I wanted to snuggle in right beside her. She had her glasses on, her hair in a messy bun on top of her head, and a throw blanket draped over her legs.

"Comfy?" I asked.

"Very, actually. I've been admiring the view." She swept a hand dramatically at the windows and the broad expanse of evergreens, along with swathes of red, orange, and gold from the changing leaves of the aspens. Once the season started, the hotel would offer the full ski-in/ski-out experience.

Grace lifted up her phone. "Also, I've been fielding questions about the break-in yesterday. Which is not as fun. Everyone in town seems to know."

"Small-town rumor mill?"

"Exactly. I need caffeine to deal with all these busybodies."

I set the food and drinks on the coffee table, then pulled sugar packets and creamer from my jeans pockets. Not fancy, but it would do for present purposes. "How do you take it?"

"One sugar, one cream." She held out her hand, but I opened the lid of her coffee myself, doctoring it up and stirring it with a spoon I'd grabbed in my kitchen.

"Here you go."

"Thanks. I could've done it myself."

"Could have. But you didn't have to." I winked and picked up my own coffee cup. "While I was downstairs, I spoke to Tobin."

"The manager, right?"

"You've got it." The man worked long hours, and he'd been doing an excellent job. Another mental note. See about giving

Tobin a raise. "I asked him to pull the security footage from the night of the grand-opening party and look for the three people you described. He said he would have it for us later this afternoon."

"Good." She fiddled with the lid to her coffee cup. "I also texted with Ashford. I told him about the break-in. And where I stayed the night. Well, it started as texting, and then he called all freaked out."

"Ah." I was surprised Ashford hadn't written me, asking for an explanation. "Is he about to storm the ski mountain looking for you?"

"I don't think so. I told him I'm fine and that you're taking care of me."

I smiled. "I hope I am."

"I had my best night of sleep in ages in that cushy bed, and you keep feeding me. You'll spoil me if you're not careful."

"You deserve to be spoiled."

Grace's cheeks turned pink. She sipped her coffee.

"If you're not busy," I said, "I was hoping you would join me for a tour of the resort this morning. I'd like your advice."

"I thought you wanted me to be your guide to Silver Ridge."

"I do. That includes providing a local's perspective on the resort. I'll make it worth your while."

"I'd say you're already doing that." She took a bite of flaky croissant.

I expected Grace to put up more of a fight about the tour of the resort, because she fought me over just about everything. But she was being surprisingly compliant this morning.

So within an hour, we were tucked into a chairlift and riding toward the mid-mountain lodge, which was halfway to the highest point of the resort.

Grace sat with her spine rigid, eyes fixed uphill.

"Do you ski?" I asked. "Snowboard?"

"Never learned. These ski runs weren't here when I was

growing up, but even if there had been anything close by, we couldn't have afforded it."

"Do you want to learn?"

"It's not high on my priorities. I kind of, um, don't love heights."

The wind chose that moment to pick up, causing the lift to rock slightly. Grace cursed and grabbed me with both hands, one fisting my long-sleeved shirt and the other on my thigh.

I put my arm around her, tucking her in closer. "The resort has offered ski school for kids in past years, but do you think families would be interested in a discounted program for locals?" I was partly trying to keep her mind off the drop below us, but I genuinely wanted to know. Skiing was an expensive sport, and I wanted the kids of Silver Ridge to be able to learn if they were interested.

"I think so." Grace's grip on my shirt eased. "You could host day camps in the summers, too."

"I like that."

She shifted so she could look up at me. "I also had some ideas for fundraisers the resort could host for the schools."

I squeezed her shoulder. "Tell me."

Grace shared her ideas as we walked around the mid-mountain lodge, then headed back toward the hotel, taking the hiking trail down the mountainside. It was a perfect day for it. Those aspens we'd seen from my window were now surrounding us with fall colors and picturesque showers of leaves every time the wind shifted.

But the best part was Grace herself. She kept talking, so all I had to do was listen. And admire her.

Damn, she was gorgeous.

She stopped to sip from her water bottle. "Why are you looking at me like that?"

"Just thinking about how beautiful you are."

She rolled her eyes.

"What?" I asked. "It's the truth." *Ashford's sister*, I reminded myself. *Off limits*.

The rational parts of my brain knew those facts, but the rest of me wasn't listening.

I officially had a thing for Grace O'Neal. It was a problem.

We resumed our hike. It was a gentle descent, following switchbacks that curved back and forth.

"You seem like you know your way around a ski mountain," she said. "I assume your family had the money for ski vacations when you were a kid."

"We did. Never had a choice about learning, but for different reasons than you might think. My mom was an Olympic Alpine skier. Medaled three times."

Grace stopped short. "Really? That's amazing."

"My mom *is* pretty amazing. She took up mountaineering as a hobby. That's how she met my dad. They were both at the Everest base camp in Nepal. Neither got to summit because the weather didn't cooperate, but Mom claimed Dad's heart."

"That's so sweet."

I grunted. My father had been good to my mom. No matter how much he and I clashed, I could never forget about that. "Mom had me in her late twenties, and they adopted my brother Kip not long after. The origins of the Knightly Global empire," I said wryly.

"But you didn't always work for your father."

I watched her from the corner of my eye. "Somebody's been on my Wikipedia page."

"Fine, I googled you! Ashford told me some things, but he's not much of a gossip."

"Something I've always liked about him."

"It sounded like it was a big deal, though. When you joined your father's company."

"It was." Dad made it a big deal. Press releases, articles in business magazines, appearances at high-profile events. *The prodigal son returns*. I'd hated every second of it. "I never wanted to work for my father. We've never gotten along. Kip was the ideal, and I was the disappointment." In family photos growing up, Kip looked as perfect as a statue, while my hair had always been messy no matter how much Mom smoothed it down.

"You're hardly a disappointment."

"It's all relative, I guess."

When my father expected me to head to the Ivy League, I only made it through a semester and a half before I was in an Army recruiter's office. Mom had been worried about me, yet she'd also cheered me on.

"When I left for basic training, my father disowned me. Didn't speak to me for years."

"*Seriously*? Even when you were deployed?"

"Yep."

But the Army had been exactly what I needed. Maybe it was strange that I'd found freedom among so much rigid discipline. But I'd had a purpose. Something larger than me that resonated more than making money. And then, when I left the service, I took that drive into starting my own company. Because I certainly didn't have any problem with making money, per se. But I had needed to do it on my own terms. For reasons that spoke to me.

With some friends I'd made during my brief stint in college, I started a health tracker app. Worked my butt off day and night to get us off the ground. When we got the offer from a massive media company to buy us out, it felt like I'd summited Everest myself.

Then our company went public. Once my shares had vested, I used the money to invest in other start-ups. I got really good at picking winners. It all snowballed from there. By my thirty-second birthday, I was a billionaire in my own right.

Then Mom got her diagnosis. And my entire world crashed back to the ground.

"My mother's proud of what I accomplished on my own, but she always wanted me to join Knightly Global. Reconcile with my dad and Kip. I did it for her."

"Is she happy that you're working for the family business now?"

I rolled my tongue against my teeth. "I think so. Yes." I almost told her about my mom's condition, since it was no secret, but something held those words at bay. I had no idea what.

"But are *you* happy?"

I stopped and grinned at her. "Happy right now. I have excellent company."

She pressed her lips together, her amber eyes assessing.

We continued along the trail. "My mom died when I was in middle school," Grace said. "Our dad...none of us were close to him. We haven't heard from him in a very long time."

"Do you want to hear from him?"

"Dad? *No*. He's not someone I want in my life. Even though it makes me really sad to say that."

I nodded because I understood. "Grace, I need to apologize again for what I said last night. Ashford's told me things about your family, but your thoughts and feelings are your own. I would never assume that Ashford speaks for you."

"I know. I was pissed last night, but you were right. It can be hard for me to trust people. Especially men. There are several reasons for that, but my father is one."

"Understandable." Her admission made me want to hunt down and punish anyone who'd taken the shine from her eyes.

Grace crossed her arms. "But my brothers don't make decisions for me. And they don't know everything about me. Not even close."

"If you let me get to know even a fraction of you, I'll consider myself a very lucky man."

"You're flirting again."

"*Am* I?"

I felt gratified when she laughed. I was such a sucker for this woman.

"There's plenty of things Ashford and I don't agree on," she said. "Like Grayden, our oldest brother. You know what happened with him, don't you? You must. You were serving with Ashford when all of that went down."

I nodded. I'd met Grayden a few times through Ashford. Then suddenly he'd been arrested, courtmartialed. Sentenced to prison time and dishonorably discharged. At the time, I'd offered to get outside legal help for his brother, but Ashford had refused.

"Ashford hates talking about him," Grace said. "Callum claims to be indifferent. But sometimes, I think about finding Grayden. I miss him. I wish I knew he was okay."

"I'll find him for you, if that's what you want."

She froze there on the trail, eyes wide. "Are you serious?"

"Of course."

"You say that like it's simple."

"It probably would be. I know investigators. It wouldn't be too hard." All it would take was money and time.

"Why? Why are you so..." She waved a hand at me.

"Why am I what?" I asked.

"You keep doing things for me. Being sweet and generous and making me like you." Her voice dropped to a whisper. "Making me want to believe you're for real."

"You think *that's* bad? Just imagine what you're doing to *me*."

Grace's dark eyelashes fluttered, and it was nearly impossible to suppress the urge to close the distance between us, like we had on the chairlift. She'd been pressed up against me, holding tight to me like the last thing she wanted was to let me go.

I didn't want to scare her, though. I wanted to comfort her. Defend her against anyone or anything that dared to make her feel unsafe. Hold her and protect her like something rare and precious.

I wasn't usually a soft, cuddly guy. But Grace brought that out in me more than any other person I'd met. Maybe because I could sense the strength she held in reserve underneath. Between her femininity and her kindness and the glasses, other people might not see her bravery. But I did.

Courage was pushing yourself to try something new. It was

facing down your fears. Speaking up. Helping others. I'd seen Grace do those things countless times already.

Still, I was surprised when *she* edged closer, placing her palm against my chest. My heart kicked in response, and my cock jumped, swelling up against my fly.

Her voice was thick when she spoke. "You make it very difficult to be good."

"Being good is overrated," I murmured.

"Tell me more about Kip."

My face scrunched up, and I made a frustrated huff. "I thought we were having a moment. You bring up my brother *now*?"

"Better than whatever was just going through your mind," she said.

The woman did have a point. My mind had just been imagining how nice it would be to kiss her breathless, right here on the trail, then strip her and lay her down on a bed of leaves to have my way with her. *Bad boy*.

We started walking downhill again. "Imagine a guy who was born to send a filet mignon back to the private chef on a yacht. That's my brother."

Grace snickered.

"He's getting hitched next week. His bride, Bristol Harcourt, is the daughter of my dad's business partner. It's more of a merger than a marriage. I'm not looking forward to it. I leave on Friday for a long weekend in Manhattan. I'd much rather stick around here."

"A New York wedding sounds glamorous though."

Behind Grace, a breeze made the aspen leaves quake. The air smelled fresh and pure. But she put all of that natural beauty to shame. I had no doubt Kip and Bristol's wedding would be expensive and elaborate, but all the glamor I could need in the world was right here.

I had my impulsive moments. This was one of them.

"Come with me," I said.

Her mouth pursed in a small frown. "Where?"

"To New York for the wedding. Be my plus-one. It'll be a lot more fun if you're with me. You've never been to the city, so I can show you around. You're my guide to Silver Ridge, I'll be your guide to NYC."

"Would I be going as your friend? Or as your date?"

There was a right answer here. A *good behavior* answer.

But that didn't sound very satisfying.

Whenever I analyzed a potential investment, I paid attention to the numbers, but my final decision was always by gut instinct. Everything inside me said that Grace was a good bet.

"I've been trying to be friends with you," I said. "Turns out I'm not that great at it."

Grace bit her lip. "I should probably say no." But she had that glitter in her eyes. I'd seen it before, and I knew what it meant.

"You want to say yes. I can tell."

Grace laughed and shook her head. "I will think about it."

I reached for her hand, lacing our fingers. "And I'll be thinking about all the ways I intend to spoil you when we get to New York."

FOURTEEN
Grace

This man was killing me.

The things he said. And the way he said them. Dane was over the top and completely sincere at the exact same time. How was that even possible?

I had sworn off dating, and then here came my greatest temptation, testing my resolve to within an inch of its life. What I kept wondering was, *why me*? Was this good karma? Had I been a saint in a former life or something? I did try pretty hard to do the right things and give all I could to other people and all that. But come on.

He wanted to take me to New York City. A place I'd been dreaming of visiting ever since I'd seen the skyline in movies and wondered, *Can that really exist*?

Exactly what I kept wondering about Dane.

He held my hand all the way down the trail and as we entered the lobby. I felt everyone's eyes on us. For a girl who was fine disappearing into the background, it was a strange and uncomfortable feeling.

The hotel manager, Tobin, raised a hand and came out from behind the reception desk. "Morning, Ms. O'Neal. How's your stay so far?"

"No complaints."

Tobin glanced between me and Dane, his gaze lingering on where we touched. The manager had questions. *Well, so do I, Tobes. So do I.*

At least Dane wasn't completely perfect. That was the only way I knew for sure that he wasn't a robot designed to be the ultimate lure for straight women. Also, there was the part where he was Ashford's best friend. Another complication, and I didn't know what to do with that either.

"Mr. Knightly, could you step into my office for a moment?" Tobin asked. "I finished that task you gave me."

Right. The security footage Dane had asked him to pull. The reminder of Ms. Scarlet and the break-in at my house yesterday sobered me.

Dane held my hand tighter. "Ms. O'Neal will come with me. We're eager to hear what you found." Tobin dipped his head in a nod, and we followed him to a discreet door just off the reception area. Once we got inside, he went behind his desk and switched on the computer. He turned the monitor so we could see.

"That's him," I said. "The man in the blue mask."

Tobin's screen showed a still image from a security camera. It was full color, but even if it hadn't been, I would've been able to pick the man out of a lineup. Short gray hair and a frame that was heavy around the middle of his tux.

Dane nodded. "Yep, that's the guy. What do you know about him?"

Tobin clasped his hands behind his back. "This is Dirk Lancaster, sir. One of the VIP guests who arrived for the grand opening."

"Is Lancaster still here at the resort?"

"No, he left the morning after the party. I checked him out myself."

"Was he alone?" I asked, thinking of Ms. Scarlet again.

"He was. Lancaster's reservation was for his name only, and I didn't see him leave with anyone else. From the hotel's perspective, his stay was uneventful. He stayed two nights, ordered room service breakfast for one each morning. Nothing else of note. After you asked about him, Mr. Knightly, I ran a quick google search on the man. If I may?" Dane nodded, and Tobin tapped at his keyboard. Another window came up with the search results.

"High net-worth real estate investor," Dane read. "No wonder his name sounded familiar. I assume my brother knows Lancaster, so I'll have to ask Kip about him. What about the other two? The redhead and the bald man who stopped Grace in the lobby later that night?"

Tobin's expression turned sheepish. "There, I have more disappointing news. I wasn't able to find footage of anyone meeting the descriptions you gave me."

What? That didn't make sense. "But they were both here in the lobby."

"Yes, Ms. O'Neal. But it seems there was a glitch with the lobby camera."

"A glitch?" Dane snapped. "How the hell did that happen?"

"I don't know, sir. The staff is looking into it. We regularly delete the security footage on our server to clear up memory. It's possible those files were replaced sooner than expected."

"You're telling me someone deleted them?" Dane asked.

Tobin opened his mouth, hesitating before he spoke. "I can't imagine it was on purpose. I have no idea who would've done that, or why."

None of it made sense to me either. But I also didn't know who would have broken into my house yesterday and taken the red mask. It was bizarre.

"And the woman?" I asked. "She would've stood out. Bright red hair, a low-cut black dress, diamond earrings. Another camera must've caught her at some point when she was coming or going."

"I completely understand your frustration. But I didn't see her on any of the camera footage that we have. Nor do I remember her myself. She didn't match the description of any of our other guests, and given the importance of the grand-opening party, I was paying close attention."

"Not close enough," Dane growled. "I want access to all of the hotel's remaining footage from the night of the party and the morning after. And a full briefing on the resort's security protocols."

Tobin's throat moved as he swallowed. "Of course. I'll have that for you right away."

We went out to the lobby. In a quiet corner beside a deserted sitting area, Dane put his hand on my lower back and pulled me aside. "I'm so sorry about that."

"You didn't know the camera recordings would be important. I certainly didn't think my house was going to get broken into."

"No, but this is my hotel, and that means it's my responsibility. Even the screw-ups."

Dane's fingers moved around to the side of my waist. His touch felt possessive as much as it was comforting, and I probably shouldn't have liked it so much. But I leaned into him. I wanted to put my face against his chest and let him wrap his arms around me. Only the fact that we were in public held me back.

"At least we got Dirk Lancaster's name," Dane said. "I'll ask Kip about him. See what I can find out. Maybe Lancaster knew Ms. Scarlet and can give us her real name."

"Maybe."

But Lancaster couldn't have broken into my house. He'd left Silver Ridge weeks ago. He could've hired someone, but it was hard to imagine what a rich investor would want with that mask. Why *anyone* would want it enough to steal it.

Dane pushed a few strands of hair from my forehead. "Not too late to tell Chief Landry what you held back about the break-in. Someone else in town might've seen Ms. Scarlet. The woman came and went from the resort somehow. She didn't just disappear."

I shook my head. "Maybe when we have something concrete

to tell him. We don't even know for sure if the break-in was connected to the grand-opening party."

"I'll keep working on it. I'm glad you're here instead of that house, though. Until we know what the intruder was really after."

"Aunt Grace, Aunt Grace!"

I jumped away from Dane, his hand falling away from me, just as Maisie dashed across the lobby toward us.

Emma and Ashford were right behind her.

"Crap," I whispered. My brother wore his usual resting grump face, so I had no idea if he'd seen Dane touching me. Of course, as they approached, Dane strolled casually toward them like he didn't have a single thing to hide.

Maisie jumped into my arms, and I gave her a hug, holding her against my hip. "I didn't know you all were coming here today." I glanced over at Emma and my brother. "Quite the surprise."

"We wanted to see Dane's fancy hotel." Maisie turned her big puppy-dog eyes toward him. "You promised we could come whenever we wanted, didn't you? And play outside and have treats?"

Dane laughed. "I do remember saying something along those lines. Of course you guys are welcome. It's great to see you." He reached for Ashford's hand, which turned into a bro-hug. Then he gave a one-armed hug to Emma. "Come on. I'll give you the grand tour, and then we can have some lunch."

Hopefully I could take the opportunity to get my heart rate to slow down. We hadn't been doing anything. Yet I felt like my brother had caught me doing something scandalous with Dane.

Maybe because I wanted to.

✧

"How're you doing with this whole break-in situation?" my brother asked.

We were walking around the lobby atrium while Dane pointed things out to Maisie. My niece held hands with Emma, but she kept gazing up at Dane with awe like he was Santa Clause or a cartoon character come to life.

Girl, I can empathize.

I glanced over at Ashford. "I texted you this morning that I was fine."

"Yeah, and if you lost both legs in a wood chipper and your car broke down on the way to the hospital, you would also say you were fine."

"That's unnecessarily dramatic. And violent, geez."

Ashford nudged my arm affectionately. "My point stands. I wanted to make sure you're okay. Teller said he doesn't have any leads on who broke in and trashed your room."

"The kitchen and bedroom too."

"Exactly. The spaces that you were in."

So Teller had shared that part too.

Ashford tugged my wrist and made us both stop. "Seriously, Grace. Do you have any theories about who would've done that? Because if somebody's been bothering you, I intend to take care of it."

I didn't like keeping things from him. Even though, to be fair, Ashford had kept some pretty major things from me in the past. "You don't have to beat anybody up right now. Or ever, because I don't want you doing something stupid and getting arrested. Dane is helping me look into it."

Ashford's expression did something funny. "That's another thing. Since when are you and Dane so close?"

"I can't hang out with him just because he was your friend first? Are you going to tell me I can't play with your toys next?"

"*Grace*," he warned.

I groaned. Big brothers were the worst sometimes. "Okay, I saw him at the grand-opening party for the hotel a few weeks ago. I came with Piper."

There. It wasn't a secret anymore.

"Why is this the first I'm hearing of it?"

"Because I don't have to tell my older brothers every single thing I do. Dane and I got to talking that night, and then yesterday at bingo he asked me to help him get to know Silver Ridge. We're friends."

Ashford frowned, squinting at me like I was a math problem that wasn't mathing. But I didn't want him to add it all up and realize I was lusting after his buddy.

"Come on," I said, "we're falling behind. You're missing the tour."

We made a thorough circuit of the hotel and grounds, then stopped by the restaurant for some lunch. Maisie had plenty of time to run around outdoors, though they hadn't brought Stella with them. Then Dane said, "Let's head upstairs. I'll show you the view from the top floor of the hotel."

I nearly panicked. I had avoided discussing the fact that I was staying in Dane's suite with him, and it would be obvious once we got upstairs. But apparently, Dane wasn't worried about that. As if he had no idea that Ashford would have strong opinions on the matter.

It's nothing, I told myself. I was a twenty-eight-year-old woman, and it wasn't Ashford's business who I spent the night with. I had slept in a separate room, anyway.

We took the elevator up. Dane swiped his keycard. Inside, Maisie ran straight for the living room, while Ashford immediately got a sour look on his face.

It had taken him all of two seconds to zero in on the open bedroom door where my stack of books sat on the dresser along with my bag.

Thankfully, Ashford kept his observation to himself. For the moment. Probably because Maisie was within earshot. But that grumpy look of his still pissed me off.

While Ashford and Dane went into the kitchen, I took the opposite direction, following Emma into the living room. Maisie had found a sunny spot on the carpet right in front of the windows. Dane had given her an illustrated map of the ski runs, and it looked like she was trying to match the picture to the actual landscape through the window.

"How's the wedding planning?" I asked Emma. "I haven't had an update lately."

My future sister-in-law huffed. "If it were up to Ashford and me, we would have a little party at my aunt and uncle's place in Hartley and call it a day. But no, my parents are all very determined to be there. Of course I want them there, but with my mom living overseas, her dates of availability are limited. And don't even get me started on Ayla's scheduling issues."

"Family. What can ya do."

She laughed more than my little quip warranted. Like she could guess that I was thinking of my brothers. Emma's siblings were around Maisie's age, but she did have several uncles with strong opinions of their own.

"Nice of Dane to give you a place to stay last night," Emma said. "I'm so sorry about the break-in. Must've been scary."

"That kind of thing doesn't happen often in Silver Ridge, that's for sure." Then I grimaced, thinking of what had happened to Emma last year. "I'm sorry. I don't mean to downplay what you went through—"

Emma reached for my hand and squeezed it. "We were talking about you. That's okay, you know. Letting people focus on *you* for once."

I squirmed, because I wasn't so great with being in the spotlight. "Dane has been focusing on me plenty."

"He likes you."

"We're friends."

She tilted her head. "I overheard you saying that to Ashford. But I mean Dane *likes you* likes you. He looks at you like he came to Silver Ridge just to find you."

Blood rushed to my face. My stupid blush always gave me away. I did need some girl talk, though. Piper was my number one, but Emma had become a close second.

"He invited me to New York for his brother's wedding," I whispered. "As his date."

"*What*?" she hissed. Emma grabbed my arm and pulled me a few feet away so Maisie wouldn't hear us. "When is his brother's wedding?"

"Next week."

"You're going, right?"

"I haven't decided. I have responsibilities here."

"Cancel them. If it's volunteer stuff, Piper and I will cover for you. If it's work, then take your laptop. You can do most things your clients need on the computer, can't you?"

"Yeah." Some of my clients weren't even in Silver Ridge. Plus I was pretty well caught up on work. I didn't do things like this, though. Just taking off for a long weekend, obligations be damned.

"You have to go," Emma said.

"The thing is..." Ugh, how did I put this in a way that wouldn't get back to my brother? "If I do, I have no idea what will happen between me and Dane. If you know what I mean. That freaks me out."

Her smile faltered. "You think he'll do something you don't want?"

"*No,*" I whispered, glancing in Maisie's direction. She wasn't listening. "Not at all. It's how much I want *him* that freaks me out. He's always telling me how beautiful I am. He wants to spoil me in New York. Who says things like that?"

Dane was interested in me, sure. He had made that plenty clear. He lived a jet setter lifestyle, though. I thought of those socialites on his arm. The practiced way he used his charm. There was no way he wanted more than a fling with me.

No, for that man, fling was the wrong word. *Liaison.* Much sexier.

Slowly, Emma grinned. "Never mind about liking you. He's crazy obsessed with you."

Maisie chose that moment to get interested in our conversation. "Who's crazy?"

Emma crossed the living room and bent down to tickle her. "Me! I'm crazy about you and your dad."

"I already knew that," Maisie said between giggles.

I smiled as I watched them, but inside, I wondered what the heck I should do. Because there was no way I could go on a trip with Dane without jumping him. I considered myself a strong woman, but I had my limits.

Dane had tested every one of them.

He'd been enticing when he was just a stranger at a masquerade ball. But the thought of going to bed with Dane Knightly, the generous, sophisticated, gorgeous billionaire who seemed to find *me* irresistible... It was enough to make my blood pressure rise to unhealthy levels.

I might not survive the actual sex. Death by orgasm.

But if all he wanted from me was sex, that was a good thing, wasn't it? I wouldn't truly be risking my heart.

If I already knew the end was coming, then it wouldn't break me when he inevitably walked away.

FIFTEEN
Dane

WHILE THE GIRLS went into the living room, Ashford stuck by me in the kitchen. I opened the fridge and took out a few bottles of sparkling water.

"This is a nice place," Ashford said.

My buddy hated small talk as much as I did, and he wasn't nearly as good at it. "You can say whatever it is you want to say. Hit me with it."

He crossed his arms and pushed out his chest. "It's something Callum told me. He thought it was weird that you just happened to be with Grace last night, and then she was so quick to leave with you. He thinks there's something going on with you two."

"Did he ask Grace? Did you?"

"She doesn't like when we get overprotective. That's why I'm asking you. Especially since she spent the night here. And not in some hotel room on another floor, but here in your suite."

"Yes, she did. You're not the only one who's protective."

Ashford's jaw tightened. "Grace told me that you two met at your grand-opening party. Which you didn't bother to tell me."

I tried to keep the surprise off my expression, though I wasn't sure I was successful. But I was glad she'd shared that tidbit with her brother. I didn't want to lie to my friend. "I didn't think it was crucial to tell you." It was true enough. But if he already knew she'd been at the grand opening, then would she mind me sharing the potential tie between that night and the break-in?

She wasn't here for me to ask. So I had to make my own call. Ashford was her brother, and I preferred having him in the loop if this involved her safety.

"But we think the break-in at her place yesterday could've been tied to the grand-opening masquerade," I said.

"*Why*?"

I explained what little we knew. How she believed someone took a red mask from her room, as if they'd gone specifically looking for that item. Then, this security footage "glitch" that had prevented an ID of Ms. Scarlet or the man who'd confronted Grace in the lobby.

"This is a weird situation," Ashford said. "I don't get any of it."

"Neither do I."

"Does Teller Landry know about this lead? He didn't mention it to me."

"Grace didn't mention any of this to the chief, no."

"The hell? Why not?"

"Grace was flustered and upset last night. She only told me the red mask was missing later on, after we'd had dinner. Maybe she needed time to process." There was no way I'd reveal what else she said about her hesitation to tell Landry the truth.

And maybe some small part of me wasn't eager to admit to Ashford that I'd nearly had a one-night stand with his sister.

Ashford pulled out his phone. "I'm calling Teller. He needs to know about this."

"I agree, but don't you think we should pull Grace in as well? She's the actual witness. We should also handle this in the office, since I guess you don't want to hash it out where Maisie can hear."

"Yeah. Good point. I'll get Grace."

I put out a hand. “No, I’ll get her. We can talk in my office. Maybe you can call Landry and explain what’s going on?”

I went to the living room, where Maisie had Emma and Grace sitting on the carpet, playing some kind of game. “Sorry to interrupt,” I said. “Can I pull Grace away for a moment?”

She got up, and we walked over to the kitchen. “What is it?”

“Ashford and I both feel you should tell Chief Landry about the red mask being stolen last night.”

Her eyes went round. “What did you tell Ashford?” she whispered.

I made a calming gesture. “Nothing too personal, I promise. Ashford said you’d already mentioned you were at the grand opening. I shared that the break-in could be connected, and Ashford wants to give those details to Chief Landry. Which was also my advice last night. Are you willing to do that? Ashford’s in my office right now. We can call the chief.”

“Fine, I will. Since it’s not a secret anymore that I was at the party. But I don’t appreciate you teaming up with Ashford and springing this on me.”

“Grace—”

She pushed past me, walking toward the office.

Shit. I didn’t like having her unhappy with me. But I stood by my decision to share more details with Ashford.

I followed her into the office and shut the door. Grace stood stiffly by the desk while Ashford put Chief Landry on speaker. “Teller? Grace is here.”

“Hi, Grace,” the chief said calmly, all business. I gave him some credit for that. “Go ahead. I’m listening.”

She cleared her throat. “I realized that something was missing from my room. A red mask I wore at the hotel grand opening.”

She shared the same story with Teller that she’d told me. Meeting Ms. Scarlet in the ladies’ room, Dirk Lancaster mistaking Grace for someone else, and then the mystery man with the shaved head bothering her. Only the vaguest details about meeting me.

"I tried to get security footage of the two people we haven't been able to identify," I added. "Came up empty-handed."

"Hmm," the chief said. "This woman you call Ms. Scarlet. She had bright red hair, Grace?"

"Yeah. About halfway down her back. She was very beautiful. Unusually so."

The chief hummed again. "Actually, I wonder if this connects to another mystery that came across my desk recently. We got a call a week ago from someone looking for a woman with red hair. The caller said she was his friend, that she'd gone missing. He claimed she'd been in Silver Ridge, though neither of them were locals. Woman was named Nina Jamison. Does that ring any bells?"

I glanced at Ashford and Grace. "No," she said. "Not at all."

"Well, the caller refused to give his name. He was calling from an unregistered number. Burner phone. When my officer asked more questions, the caller hung up. But then we checked around with local hotels."

"Including the ski resort?" I asked.

"No, we didn't get that far up the list. We found a Nina Jamison registered as a guest at a roadside motel. Turned out she never came back to her room a couple of weeks ago. Left some of her belongings behind. The motel owner had taken a photo of her ID when she checked in, since that's his policy."

"But the motel owner didn't report her missing?" Grace asked incredulously.

"He said it wasn't that unusual. She didn't leave anything of value behind. But he sent the photo of her ID to us. Nina had red hair, and I'd say she's...very attractive. Objectively speaking."

Grace arched her eyebrow. "Objectively," she repeated. "But she's no Ayla Maxwell?"

The chief made a choking sound, while Grace and Ashford flashed smiles at one another. I wasn't sure what that was about, but I was grateful for the brief levity, if only because it lightened Grace's mood.

But there was something I had to know.

"When was this Nina Jamison last at her motel room?" I asked.

The chief recited the date.

"That's the same night as the grand-opening masquerade," I said.

"Grace, I'm emailing you the image of Nina Jamison's ID. See if you recognize her."

Grace took out her phone and checked her messages. She sucked in a breath. "It's her. That's Ms. Scarlet. The woman who gave me the red mask."

So it was possible Grace was the last person who'd seen Jamison before she vanished. If that anonymous caller was to be believed.

"And you're *positive* that the intruder yesterday stole that same mask?" the chief asked.

Grace paused a moment, thinking. Then nodded. "I'm sure. Yes. But I have no idea what any of it means."

None of us did. This story had started out strange, and it was only getting more bizarre.

And somehow, Grace was in the middle of it.

SIXTEEN

Dane

We talked to Chief Landry for a few more minutes. After we finished up with the call, Grace went back to the living room. Ashford shut the door behind her.

Then he turned to me, arms crossed over his chest. "Look, I appreciate you looking out for Grace, if that's all this is. But she's my sister."

"I'm aware."

"So I'm obligated to ask. Can I trust you with her?"

Hell, I didn't want to have this conversation. Because the answer was probably, *No, you shouldn't. I'm planning to take her back to New York with me, get her naked, and do whatever filthy things she lets me do to her.*

That probably wouldn't go over well.

"You've known me a long time," I said.

"I have. I've trusted you with my life, and I think you would say the same."

"I would."

Laughter came from the living room, Grace rejoining whatever Emma and Maisie were up to, and the expression on Ashford's face tightened. "That's why this is awkward."

"You're asking for my intentions toward your sister?"

"Yeah, I am, and it's making me fucking uncomfortable. But Grace and Callum and I have had too many people in our lives let us down. I almost lost Emma last year to someone I trusted."

"I know, man. That was terrible."

"And now this break-in? A woman going missing, and Grace being mixed up in it? She acts like nothing gets to her, but she's in a vulnerable place. I appreciate you watching over her. Being her friend. But I will not allow *anyone* else to hurt the women in my family."

I kept my calm, but it wasn't easy. "You think *I* would harm Grace?"

"Of course I don't. If I did, this interaction would be going very differently."

I knew how much Ashford's family meant to him. I'd seen this coming. That was why I'd told myself I wouldn't go after Grace unless I had serious intentions.

I wasn't planning to stay in Silver Ridge forever. My work was elsewhere. My family, such as it was. And Ashford's friendship meant the world to me. The smarter, more cautious thing to do would be to set aside my interest in his sister. To refuse to risk the closest friend that I had.

But if I had met Grace some other way, would I have agreed to stop pursuing her based on what anyone else said?

No, I wouldn't. That wasn't in my DNA.

"When I first met Grace," I said, "I didn't realize she was your sister. Would it have made a difference if I had known? Honestly, I can't say. But I like her."

"And what does that mean, exactly?"

Fuck, he wasn't letting up, was he?

Ashford and I had the kind of friendship where we could tell each other uncomfortable things. Was I disrespecting him by pursuing his sister? Maybe. But I would be disrespecting him a hell of a lot more if I couldn't be honest about it.

"I invited her to come to New York with me for Kip's wedding, and I'm hoping she says yes. What else happens between us is up to her. If you're going to ask me to back off, then we might be at an impasse. Because I don't intend to."

Ashford held my gaze for a long moment. Staring me down.

Then he shook his head. "That's exactly the kind of thing I figured you would say."

"At least I'm consistent."

He scrubbed both hands over his face. "Have you ever dated a woman for longer than a month?"

"No." But Grace wasn't like anyone else. In the last couple of years since Mom's diagnosis, I had been drifting. Grace made me feel grounded.

"Just be careful with her. Please."

"So you're okay with this?" I asked.

"I didn't say that," he growled. "But I know you, and I know Grace. I realize that I can't stop this. But I *will* track you down if you hurt her."

"I would expect nothing less."

Ashford rubbed a hand over his beard. "If Grace is in some kind of danger in Silver Ridge, a trip out of state isn't the worst idea. I'll keep pressing Teller on his investigation into the break-in and this Nina Jamison person. But I have to know Grace is safe."

Ashford wasn't an effusive guy. He kept his feelings close, like I usually did. But his concern was obvious on his face. That of a man who had lost his mom. Lost the mother of his child. And last year, almost lost the woman he loved.

No matter what we disagreed on, this was a point where we saw eye to eye.

"Regardless of what happens between me and Grace, as long as I'm around, I swear I'll do whatever it takes to keep her safe and sound."

I kept the rest of what I was thinking to myself.

Now that I'd acknowledged how much I wanted her, I also knew I'd do whatever it took to make her *mine*.

✧

We joined the others in the living room until it was time for them to head home. After my suite had been so full of life with Ashford and his family, it would be hard to see them go.

Especially since Grace would be leaving with them.

Aside from when I was in the Army, I had lived alone for nearly all of my adult life. The thought of an empty, echoing apartment didn't bother me. Until now. Didn't help that Grace seemed to be having trouble holding eye contact with me, which irked me after we'd made so much progress this morning.

When Grace went to pack up her few belongings in the extra bedroom, I got up and followed her, stopping in the doorway. She'd made the bed and set everything exactly as it had been when she arrived. As if the hotel staff wouldn't have taken care of it.

"Not still mad at me, are you?" I asked.

She closed her bag, zipping it more vigorously than was probably necessary. "Not really. No."

"You feel okay about heading home?"

Grace shrugged. "Callum has the security system and cameras installed. The firefighters will know all my comings and goings. If I thought my roommates were overbearing already..."

At least Callum lived there too. Otherwise, I would've talked her into staying with me for longer. Didn't love the idea of her living with three other single guys.

If it proved necessary, I could make a trip to the firehouse to have a friendly chat with her roommates.

"Are you free for lunch tomorrow?" I asked. "I'd appreciate the lowdown on the Silver Ridge Business Association members."

"Didn't get enough of me between yesterday and today?"

"Are you kidding?" I dropped my voice an octave. "Not nearly enough of you. But you already know that."

A rosy glow crept into her cheeks. My fingers twitched with the urge to touch her.

"I thought some more about your invitation to New York. Your brother's wedding."

"And?"

"I'm still slightly annoyed that you and Ashford were deciding things behind my back. *But...*"

"Yes?"

"I'd like to go with you."

I grinned slowly, reaching to link our fingers. "I thought it would take more convincing."

She rolled her eyes. "Don't make me regret it already." I mimed zipping my lips, and Grace laughed quietly. "Can you give me a list of where we're going, so I can plan what to wear?" she asked.

"You don't need to worry about that. I'll take you shopping when we arrive. And just so we're clear, I'm buying."

"Dane..."

"You would be just as gorgeous if you wear jeans and a sweater to Kip's stuffy wedding events, but I'm guessing you don't agree. I want you to feel good. So I'll pay for whatever you feel like wearing. I'm paying for everything else on the trip too, just so we're clear. That's non-negotiable."

"Fine. But there's something else I want."

"Name it."

Grace's amber eyes lifted, and there was pure fire in them. "I want you to kiss me," she whispered.

Oh, *now* we were talking.

I prowled several steps forward into the room, forcing her to back up. Ashford, Emma, and Maisie were still in the living room, so they couldn't see us. But they weren't that far away. We could hear their voices.

My thumb traced along her jawline to her bottom lip. "At the grand-opening party, I waited to kiss you because I didn't want to have to stop. I've been kicking myself for that ever since. You said I wouldn't get another chance."

Her eyes glinted again, this time with humor. "I'm right most of the time. But not always."

"I'll remember that."

I lowered my mouth to hers, anticipating those last few seconds before contact. Three, two, one.

Damn.

The first taste of her shocked my senses. Like a pure hit of oxygen mixed with caffeine, lighting up my insides.

Her plush lips molded to mine, then moved in sync with me as I deepened the kiss and nudged my tongue into her mouth. She whimpered and grabbed hold of my shirt.

Fuck me, I wished we were alone. I'd pick her up, lay her on that bed, and kiss the hell out of her before undressing her and kissing my way down her body.

Then Maisie said something in the living room, and Emma laughed. Reluctantly, I pulled away by an inch. "They're going to hear us." I didn't care that much if Ashford or Emma caught us, but Grace would mind. Also, I didn't want Maisie to stumble upon us having an inappropriate moment.

She whimpered again. "Yeah. You're right."

"Was that the sort of kiss you wanted?" I asked quietly.

Grace nodded, her eyelids hooded. Her fists released their grip on my shirt. "Good enough."

"I thought it was slightly better than *good enough*."

"Good enough for me to know I want more."

Ah. I liked the sound of that. I reached out to squeeze her hip. "Plenty more where that came from."

"Next weekend? While we're on the trip?"

"Absolutely."

Grace licked her lips, the deep pink fading from her cheeks. She shivered like she was shaking off the haze our kiss had induced. "But there's something that's non-negotiable for me. Whatever this *thing* is between us, it ends when we get back from New York."

I couldn't help the scowl that darkened my face. "Hell no.

The trip will only be five days." I already knew five days wouldn't be enough with her.

Her brows lifted in a challenge. "Non-negotiable," she said again. "We have fun together in New York, and then we end it as friends. I go back to my regular life. And you go back to yours."

I exhaled, considering. Ashford wouldn't appreciate me bedding his sister and then dropping her. Nor did I want to. I wanted to see where this could go. More of that spark between us. Of the way I felt around her. Just *more.*

So...I would have to convince her she wanted more with me, too.

"All right," I said. "If that's really what you want."

"It's for the best." She went onto her toes to peck me on the cheek. Then she grabbed her bag.

"I'll be counting the days until our trip," I said.

"Me too." She smiled, and it took all my willpower not to crush my mouth to hers again, slam her bedroom door closed, and lock it.

Patience, I told myself.

Grace didn't take me seriously yet. Didn't really trust me. So I would have to earn it.

She had no idea just how persuasive I could be.

SEVENTEEN

Grace

"MR. KNIGHTLY. Wonderful to see you again. Anything I can get you before takeoff?"

The flight attendant smiled at him. Then she glanced at me, and her smile didn't seem quite so sincere.

Dane waited for me to sit by the window, then took the seat beside me. "Two glasses of champagne. Thank you, Sharon. You have Dom on board, right? A 1985?"

"Of course." She eyed my messy hair and glasses before she went to the galley.

Believe me, hon, I thought. *I barely know what I'm doing here either.*

Dane reached over to fasten my seatbelt and then laced our fingers together. "Comfortable?" he asked.

"Perfect. But champagne for breakfast is more indulgent than my typical menu." I wasn't counting the rare brunch mimosa with Piper.

"We'll have coffee afterward. But I'm in the mood to celebrate." He picked up my hand and kissed the back of it.

I'd never even been in first class before. But here I was, on a private plane about to jet off to Manhattan with the sexiest man in existence. Somebody pinch me.

How was this my life?

That morning, Dane had picked me up before sunrise in his Range Rover. I'd been careful to disarm the security system at my house. We'd already had a false alarm a couple of days ago, and I didn't want a repeat of that. Four grumpy, exhausted volunteer firefighters who'd been up all night on a call, and then I woke them mid-morning. Oops.

The alarm system had made a big difference to my peace of mind, though. Especially since we still had no leads on whoever had broken in to the house.

But not so great for my peace of mind? The growing frustration whenever I was with Dane and he didn't kiss me. He hadn't since that day in his hotel suite last weekend.

I had been dreaming of that kiss. It hadn't even lasted that long, but it had been the best kiss I'd ever experienced. A tease of what was to come.

Yes, I was the one who'd insisted that our fling last only as long as this trip. But I hadn't expected him to take that rule so literally. Nearly every day this week, he had stopped by my house to say hello. Or met me for lunch or coffee. Always to discuss ideas for the resort or hear my insights into the local community. We'd had a few meetings with local business leaders too. Every time, he'd kept things G-rated. But Dane had this way of looking at me that fired me up without a single touch. Like he was imagining all the filthy things he wanted to do to me that would scandalize the town if they knew.

Lordy, he was giving me *that look* right now.

If we didn't get to the liaison soon, I might spontaneously combust before I even got to enjoy the shopping and sightseeing.

Sharon walked over carrying a tray. She set a flute next to my seat and one by Dane's. "Enjoy."

"Thanks." He smiled at her. "Once we're in the air, we'll have breakfast. Coffee and pastries. And whatever else Grace would like."

"Yes, sir." Sharon aimed a death-glare at me before she left.

"She doesn't like me," I whispered.

"What? Why wouldn't she like you?"

"Because I'm with you. You knew her name. Did you and she ever..."

"No. But I like that you're jealous. It's cute."

"I'm not jealous."

"Sure. And I'm not jealous about those firefighters you live with."

I opened my mouth and nothing came out for several seconds. "No reason to be jealous."

"You don't have one either." Dane picked up his glass and clinked it against mine. "To our long weekend. It will be infinitely better having you with me."

"Cheers. Thank you for bringing me." I took a sip. "You could kiss me if you want. Since we're on the trip now. Technically."

Dane smiled, but he didn't take my not-so-subtle hint. Instead his leg pressed against mine as we sipped more of the champagne. The bubbles and citrusy flavor tickled my tongue. Not as good as a kiss from him, but close.

Sharon collected the glasses for takeoff. As the plane accelerated down the runway, I grabbed Dane's arm.

"First time flying, right?" he asked.

I nodded, my response stuck in my throat. He put his arm around me and held me tight against him. I was relieved that he didn't laugh. Seemed ridiculous, since I'd had three brothers in the Army who were deployed overseas. But they'd always been eager to come home.

"Takeoff and landing are the noisy, bumpy parts," Dane said. "But you've got this."

Once we'd reached altitude and the flight smoothed out, my breathing relaxed. Sharon brought coffee and an assortment of danishes, croissants, and hearty bread with butter. *So* good. Then Dane ordered smoked salmon and an omelet with goat cheese and roasted tomatoes, holding out his fork to give me a bite of each one and giving me fiery-hot looks whenever the fork disappeared into my mouth.

Yikes.

After eating, I used the wi-fi to check my messages. Piper had written.

PIPER

Did you leave yet? I must know all.

ME

We just took off. Had champagne and breakfast.

I snapped a picture of the dishes, which Sharon hadn't picked up yet, and sent it to my friend. This was already my best vacation ever. Made me wonder, with a delicious, turned-on shiver, how much better it would get. Five whole days to look forward to.

It was also nice to get some time away from home. My brothers had been even more overbearing than usual lately, especially since Teller hadn't discovered any new leads about the break-in or about Nina Jamison.

If possible, I didn't want to think about that stuff this weekend. I wanted an escape, however brief, from my life in Silver Ridge.

PIPER

I am DYING. Have so much fun. Text me everything!

WAIT don't text me. I expect you to be having too much hot sex for that. Just enjoy it and tell me later. 💦

I snickered, and Dane looked over. "What's so funny?"

I put my phone away. "Nothing. What's on the agenda when we land?"

Dane's arm draped around me again, making me snuggle into his side. "We arrive at Teterboro Airport. It's in New Jersey. We'll drive into the city from there. I was thinking we'd shop first. Margot made us some appointments at places she thought you'd like." He pulled out his phone. "Take a look and let me know which strikes your fancy."

"An appointment? I've never had an appointment to buy clothes." I glanced at the list of different boutiques on his screen.

He'd told me a lot about his assistant Margot, and I'd looked her up online. She was in her fifties, a Black woman with a pixie hairstyle and a confident smile in her work profile photo. Margot gave every indication of being a whip-smart lady. I was looking forward to meeting her, and I was grateful that she'd been thinking of what I might like. But these boutiques seemed expensive. The pictures alone were intimidating.

"I thought we'd just go to H&M or something. I've been to the one in Denver, and they had a lot of great stuff."

He tilted his head. "You *are* cute."

I nudged him. "Quit. Clothes don't have to cost a fortune for me to feel good in them."

"If you don't find anything you like in these shops, we can go to a chain. But you have to give them a chance."

"Alright." This whole weekend was about doing something different. Something *exciting*. Piper would tell me to go with it.

He leaned closer, his nose brushing against mine. "Good. This weekend, you're going to have *anything* you want. I mean anything. Name it, and it's yours."

My skin flushed. "Just like that?"

"Just like that. Except for one thing."

"Only one?" I joked.

"Yep." He brought his thumb to my lower lip. "No kissing until we're back at my place later."

I pulled back and gave him an incredulous look. "No kissing?"

"Not until we're at my apartment. Next time we kiss, we're ending up naked."

Arousal bloomed between my legs. "Maybe I'll kiss *you*."

"Then I'll have to take you in the bathroom over there. And that's not how I envisioned our first time together."

"You've been envisioning it?"

"Fuck yes, I have. Several times a day."

Desire flooded my body and throbbed in my clit. I wasn't usually the kind of girl to follow a man into an airplane bathroom for a naughty rendezvous. But Dane had me tempted.

Bonus points because Sharon the flight attendant would know exactly what we were doing. She kept glancing back and aiming razor-sharp looks at me.

But I could wait. I'd waited long enough already, hadn't I? I hadn't had sex in... It was a bad sign that I couldn't even remember.

"The rehearsal dinner is tonight?" I asked.

He grimaced. "Yeah. I can't skip this one. A lot of people from Knightly Global will be there. The bride's family too." He rubbed a hand over his chin. "My father has some ridiculous plan about setting me up with the maid of honor, Ainsley. She's the bride's sister. I made it clear I wasn't interested, and I doubt Ainsley is either. But I wanted to give you a heads-up because somebody might say something about it. She and I had a very brief thing back in high school."

All the pastries and champagne turned to acid in my stomach.

His *ex* was going to be there? Ainsley probably looked just like those other socialites I'd seen in the gossip columns with Dane. Elegant and effortless and perfect. "So I'm, like, a decoy date?"

"I asked you to come with me because I want to spend time with you."

I shrugged. "It's not a big deal." It was *so* a big deal. "But you could've told me before. I'm guessing your father won't be happy that I'm there."

"Hey." He tucked a finger under my chin. "Since I met you, you're the only woman I've wanted." His voice was low and hypnotic. "It's up to you where this weekend takes us. But have no doubt—I want *you* in my bed. Tonight and every night that you'll let me have you."

Dane's words set off a flood of heat in my belly. I could hardly breathe. "That's what I want too. For this trip I mean."

"I don't care what my father and brother think. You're here because *I* want you to be. Okay?"

I nodded.

But the knowledge that his family might already dislike me was a splash of cold water. Maybe it shouldn't have mattered. Not like we were actually dating. But it was a reminder that, for all Dane had shared with me, there was far more I didn't know about him and his life. Women like Ainsley belonged in his world. I didn't. Not really.

After this weekend, I doubted anything like this would ever happen to me again, so I had to soak up every minute of the good parts. Because when it was over, I'd be living on these memories for a long time.

EIGHTEEN

Grace

"Oh my goodness," I breathed, craning my neck.

Dane's driver had picked us up in a luxury SUV from the airport, and now we were driving into the heart of Manhattan. Downtown Denver had skyscrapers and an old warehouse district, but this was on another scale altogether.

"You like it?" Dane asked.

"I *love* it," I breathed.

There was just *so much*. So many cars, so many people. Gorgeous Gothic architecture and tall, futuristic spires and bridges spanning the water. Trees wearing their vivid fall colors. Sensory overload.

"The shop you liked best on the list is in SoHo. So that's where we're heading."

Dane kept pointing out landmarks along the way, explaining how Manhattan was laid out on a grid and which area was which, but I was too distracted to pay attention to which avenue we were on. I could worry about navigation later. I didn't want to miss a single tiny detail outside my window.

SoHo was all charming brick buildings, narrow streets, and shoppers filling the sidewalks wearing far edgier outfits than me. I thought I looked good though. I'd worn my favorite jeans, leather boots that I reserved for special occasions, and an untucked white Oxford shirt. Classic and simple.

I'd blow-dried my hair and left it down, but now I was second-guessing my choice to wear my glasses. Of course, my contacts would've been killing me in the dry air of the plane. Dane didn't seem to have a problem with how I looked, though. He kept touching me and giving me that pure-sex grin.

Dane's driver Ben pulled into an alley, and someone popped out of nowhere to open the door for us. "Right this way, Ms. O'Neal." A few people on the sidewalk stopped to watch us. One even lifted her phone to take a picture like we were famous.

My head was spinning already.

I realized I had left my purse in the back of the SUV, but then Dane was there, wrapping his arm around my waist and handing me my clutch. He steered me inside the boutique, and the noise of the street faded instantly.

The store was modern and beautiful, full of sunlight that made the white walls and pale wood floor glow. Upbeat music played. I saw lots of pastel colors, which had appealed to me in the online pictures.

Then a well-dressed woman appeared in front of us. "Mr. Knightly, Ms. O'Neal. Welcome. I'm Lisa. We've got everything set up for you. Come on back."

"How did you ever get used to this?" I murmured to Dane as we followed her. "Everyone knowing your name."

"Everyone knows your name in Silver Ridge."

"That's completely different."

He squeezed my shoulder reassuringly. "Is it though? Anyone can figure out your name. But far fewer actually know the real you." I glanced over at him, and a bittersweet expression had blanketed his features.

I wondered how many people Dane let in enough to truly know him.

That was when I realized there was nobody else here. We had the entire store to ourselves. "Did you rent this place out?"

"I assume so. Margot took care of it."

Lisa took us to a cozy area near the back of the store, where a rack of clothes waited, along with two cushy chairs and a table with more champagne. If I kept drinking champagne every time it was offered to me, I'd get very drunk very soon. And I already felt semi-drunk just from how surreal this day was.

"I pulled some pieces in your size that I think you'll love, Ms. O'Neal," Lisa said. "But feel free to take a look around the store as well. Have fun. Please let me know when you need me." She winked and smiled before disappearing.

Dane brought his lips to my ear. "Two rules. First, if you see anything that interests you, try it on. Even if you don't think you'd want to buy it. Second, no looking at price tags."

"I can't not look."

"But you'll enjoy this more if you don't. You trust me, right?" He pressed a soft kiss just behind my ear. I assumed a kiss there didn't count under his "no kissing" prohibition. But given how kiss-starved I'd been this week, I still nearly melted into the floor. Good thing he had his arm around my waist.

"This is not the kind of thing that happens to me," I said breathily.

"It does when you're with me."

✧

I took a while picking through the items Lisa had put on the rack. I could admit to being skeptical at first. But there were a ton of cute things that fit my style and personality, except they happened to be made of the softest, most gorgeous fabrics ever invented. The designs leaned toward colder weather, since it was fall, and that was exactly what I needed for both New York and Colorado weather.

I was supposed to be shopping for this trip though, not for my future dream wardrobe back home. I needed something for tonight's rehearsal dinner, which would be at an uber-upscale restaurant. Then the wedding tomorrow and a brunch on Sunday.

Luckily, I was a woman with a business mindset. I knew how to set productivity goals and accomplish them.

Pretty soon, I had a stack of *nos* and a stack of *maybes*. Dane hung back, arms crossed as he watched me and gave the occasional opinion, but mostly he let me do my thing. Lisa transferred my *maybes* to the dressing room. Then she disappeared again.

I started trying things on. There were even shoes here to pair with the outfits, all of them in my size.

But the only mirror was outside in the sitting area, where Dane was. Clearly a conspiracy. But I could work with it.

Before I stepped out, I gave into temptation and checked the price tag on the dress I was wearing.

Holy crap, I mouthed.

I really shouldn't have looked. I couldn't let Dane buy this for me.

"How's it going?" Dane called out.

"Um, not bad." I pushed aside the thick curtain and emerged in a pale pink shift dress and white ankle boots. Very brunchy. The dress hugged all my curves in the ideal spots, while also creating a subtly modern silhouette. I thought so, anyway. I was no fashion expert.

Dane stood up from his chair. "Very nice."

"You don't think it's...too much?" I twisted back and forth in front of the mirror.

His reflection gave me a wry look. "You looked at the price tag, didn't you?"

"I couldn't help it!"

Dane laughed. "Just for that, I'm definitely buying this dress for you. It looks great, and I promise it's in my budget. But from now on, no more looking."

"Fine. You should be trying on clothes too. Then I wouldn't feel so on display."

"Since when is you being on display a bad thing? But also, there's the issue that this boutique has only women's clothing. *I* don't need a dress for the wedding."

"How about a cream-colored sweater, with or without a giant coffee stain on it?"

His smile dazzled me. "I'll consider it. What about this dress? Tell me the truth. Do *you* like it?"

Something about the sexy beat of the music, the flattering lighting, and the *New York* of it all made me daring. I did a little spin. "I guess I look good."

"That's an understatement."

I glanced around for Lisa, but she was still nowhere to be seen. "Just to let you know, I taste even better."

He made a growly sound, his hands going to my waist. "I know you do. I can't wait to find out *all* the different ways you taste." Dane dipped his head and nipped at my earlobe. "Now try on something else and show me."

The gentle yet commanding tone of his voice danced up and down my spine.

I tried on more outfits. Some I liked, some I didn't. Dane leaned casually against the mirror in his dark jeans and black button-down, his gaze locked on me every time I emerged from the dressing room.

Having his attention was like a drug. Like I'd already had way too much champagne. I could squint and almost pretend Dane was my boyfriend instead of my hookup-date for the weekend. And let's face it, him watching me try on clothes was *very* boyfriendy.

Good thing I wasn't in the market for one of those, because this man was ruining me for all future dates.

"How's it going in there?" he asked.

I hadn't come out of the dressing room in a while. But I needed something special for the wedding itself, and the other dresses Lisa had chosen just weren't *me*. "I need to look for a dress for the wedding. I don't love any of these."

"Hold on a sec," Dane said. "There's one more."

I peeked out from behind the curtain. He grabbed a dress hanging on the rack. I hadn't seen this one before. It was pastel blue. I adored the color, but the shape was a *statement*.

"It's pretty. Did Lisa bring that over?"

He shrugged. "Try it. See what you think."

The dress had a slinky inner lining that was cool against my skin as I pulled it up. The zipper was impossible for me to close the last few inches, so I slipped my feet into a pair of stilettos, came out, and turned around. "Zip me the rest of the way?"

Dane's long fingers ghosted over my skin.

I looked up, and my lips closed on a gasp when I saw my reflection. Holy cow.

The dress was strapless, pushing my breasts way higher than I'd imagined possible. The bodice exaggerated my hourglass shape, and the skirt flared out in ruffles, ending just below my knee. The designer stiletto heels were icing on the ruffled cake.

I had never in my life felt so beautiful.

Dane's eyes darkened as he stood behind me in the mirror. He fitted his hands to either side of my waist. "Thoughts? Is this a yes?"

My chest felt funny and tight, but it wasn't the dress's fault. "Did you pick this for me?"

"Yeah. I don't think I did half bad."

I had no words.

So I spun around, wrapped my arms around his neck, and pulled him down to kiss me.

Dane rumbled out a moan as he held my waist, walking me backward until I was against a wall. I felt the smile on his lips. Dane's fingers slid into my hair, and he cradled the back of my head as he took over, his tongue gliding into my mouth. *Finally*. I had been aching to have his lips on mine again.

When he broke the kiss, we were both panting. "I guess that means you like the dress."

"It's the best dress ever."

"Best dress for the best girl." His thumb stroked my chin. "Except you broke my rule about no kissing."

"I'm more of a rebel than either of us thought."

Dane's grin widened, turning wicked. He lifted his hand and ran his thumb along my lower lip. "I told you what would happen the next time we kissed. You would end up naked. You've put me in a difficult position, because you look too pretty in this dress to take it off just yet."

"I'll make it up to you later."

"Oh, you will. I'm going to punish you for this."

I sucked in a breath, liking that idea far more than I'd expected. "Promise?"

He reached down to lift the hem of my dress. His warm hand caressed my thigh. My lungs stopped working altogether as his fingers traced upward until they brushed the crotch of my panties, and a desperate sound snuck out of my throat.

"*Dane*," I gasped.

"Or I could take you into the dressing room right now," he whispered.

Heat raced along my skin. "We really shouldn't."

"But do you want to?"

Did I?

My body said yes. But the more sensible parts of me won out. I just hoped Dane wouldn't be mad. He wouldn't, right?

I shook my head. "Not here."

"Then we won't." He kissed my nose, stroking my thigh once more before his hand withdrew.

"I'm sorry."

"Hey, do not be sorry." He touched my chin again. "I don't mind hearing no. Besides, Lisa would probably blacklist us from this store, and I'd like to bring you back here on your next trip to New York."

NINETEEN

Dane

We spent the rest of the afternoon shopping at the other boutiques on Margot's list. I loved watching Grace show off in front of the mirror. Even better that she was doing it as much for herself as for me.

Damn, she was gorgeous.

I'd been on good behavior all week leading up to our trip. But after that kiss Grace laid on me while wearing that sexy-as-hell blue dress, I had just about reached the end of my patience. I really had been tempted to pick her up, carry her into the dressing room, and make good on my threat to get her naked then and there. But Grace was wiser than me, making sure we'd still be welcome at that boutique.

It was probably ridiculous to already be thinking about future trips to New York with her. But I couldn't help where my mind went.

At the second shop, I made sure a pizza was waiting for us. I fed Grace bites of the best pizza in the country while she tried on fancy dresses for the wedding.

Was it a smart idea to risk getting tomato sauce on expensive gowns? Maybe not, but I liked to live dangerously. I wanted to buy her everything she tried on, anyway. Even though Grace was all kinds of picky about what she agreed to let me get for her.

But she found plenty she liked. My black card got a workout, and every time I waved it over the card reader, I got a thrill that Grace was letting me do something special for her. Plus, the longer I could avoid thinking about the actual wedding events and seeing my family, the better.

Then she surprised me by picking a tie for me at the last boutique, which carried menswear, and paying for it herself. "So you have something to remember this trip," she said.

That wasn't going to be an issue. But I appreciated the gesture more than I could express. "Thank you."

By the time we were finished and the back of the SUV was full of shopping bags, I was beyond worked up. In the elevator on the way up to my apartment, my mind was going all sorts of dirty places. I had told the doorman to send up our things later. Right now, I had to get my hands on her.

I pulled her in front of me in the elevator, wrapping my arms around her middle. "Are you ready for me?" I murmured.

"I've been ready for a while now." She gave me a cute little smirk over her shoulder. While I had been growing more desperate all afternoon, she had been getting more bold. "What are you going to do to me first?"

"Mmmm." I had been pondering that exact question. I'd been picturing my first time with Grace all week. Which was a unique form of self torture, and had resulted in plenty of solo orgasms, all of them unsatisfying. "Depends. Do you want me to be sweet and gentle this first time?" I massaged her hip with a firm but easy touch, then dropped a soft kiss to her neck, showing her just how sweet I could be.

"That does sound nice." She turned her head, eyes glinting. "But I thought you promised to punish me. "

Desire poured through my veins, heady as bourbon and equally intoxicating. *Fuck.*

She was ready for me, but now I wondered if I was entirely

ready for Grace O'Neal. For the spell of infatuation she was already putting me under.

The elevator doors opened on my floor. I pressed my lips to her ear. "I think you're hiding a bad girl behind those glasses and the books on spreadsheets."

"I don't know," she said innocently. "Spreading some sheets is exactly what I was just thinking of."

I laughed and grabbed her hand, fishing for my keys in my pocket. She had to rush to keep up with my long strides. Somehow I got the key in the lock, and then we were inside and I pressed her up against my closed door. I tossed my keys to the floor behind me and took her purse from her, tossing that to the floor as well.

Then I held her face in my palms and kissed her. My tongue stroked into her mouth, and my hands started to wander, moving down the curves I had been eyeing all afternoon. "I've been watching you model different outfits for the last several hours, but I never got to see the good parts. So the first thing I want is to watch you take off all your clothes. Show off how pretty you are for me wearing nothing at all."

Grace bit her lip, gazing up at me.

Then a throat cleared primly behind us.

Grace yelped, and I cursed under my breath, tipping my head back in frustration. *Why now*? Then I discreetly adjusted myself, thankful my shirt was untucked, and turned around.

"Apologies," Margot said. "I texted that I was on my way."

"I was distracted."

"I can see that." Margot's expression didn't change except for some lines appearing around her eyes, and I knew she was laughing at me inside.

I was thirty-five years old and had no reason to be embarrassed about being caught with a beautiful woman, but Margot was such a mom. Even more than my *own* mother had ever been.

Grace came out from behind me, holding out her hand. "I'm

guessing you're Margot. That wasn't the way I would normally introduce myself."

Margot laughed. "I had my moments back in my day. I hate to interrupt, but I'm afraid we are in a time crunch."

I ran my fingers through my hair, still trying to get my heart rate under control. "I thought we had another couple hours until the rehearsal dinner at least."

"Try forty-five minutes. That's why I'm here. Thought we'd share a ride downtown." No wonder she was in a black dress and heels. To work, Margot usually wore one of her trademark pantsuits.

"How environmental of you." I smiled, even as my guts twisted, knowing my father was somehow behind this. Margot looked out for me, but this was a bit much even for her.

"I guess I'd better get cleaned up for dinner then," Grace said. Her cheeks had turned pink. She glanced around. "If you could just point me in the direction of a shower, and I'll need my suitcase..."

I rested a hand on her lower back and guided her to my bedroom and the en-suite bathroom. "There are bathrobes in the closet. Toiletries in the cabinets."

"This is your room?" she asked.

"Yes. I hoped you'd stay here with me. Unless you'd prefer the guest room."

"No. Your room is...good. Your...bed."

I tugged her closer. "You're not getting shy on me, are you?"

She traced her fingers down the buttons of my shirt. "Trying not to."

"Are you going to wear your new blue dress tonight?"

"I was planning on it. Are you going to wear your new tie?"

"I am. But I was thinking about some other uses I might have for that tie later on. When we're alone."

Grace sucked in a breath, eyes flaring with interest. "That so?"

"I also had ideas about joining you in the shower," I said, "but

I guess we'll have to save that for later too. I should've kept better track of time. I'm sorry about that."

"Margot handled it well."

"She's a professional."

Grace played with the collar of my shirt. "Has she walked in on you in an intimate position with someone before?"

"Actually, that was the first time."

"Okay."

"I've never asked her to make appointments for me to take someone shopping before, either."

A tiny, satisfied smile played across Grace's lips. "Good. I really had fun today. It was amazing."

"Good. You deserved it."

"You keep saying that."

"It's still true." I kissed her on the mouth. Slow. Sensual. But not taking things any further because we couldn't. Not yet. No matter how much I wanted to.

"Good," Grace whispered again when I pulled back, her focus going hazy, and I chuckled.

"One of us needs to stop saying *good*."

She nodded. "Until later. Then, I wouldn't mind hearing about how good I'm being."

I growled, my grip tightening on her again. Dammit, I wanted her right now. Wanted to skip this stupid rehearsal dinner altogether and spend the rest of today doing far more pleasurable things.

Maybe it was wise Margot had shown up after all.

"I'll bring in your suitcase and your new clothes in a few minutes." I forced myself to take a few steps back from her, even though it was the last thing I wanted to do. "Let's get through this dinner," I said. "And then the rest of the night is ours."

When I got back to the living room, Margot said, "I called downstairs to have all your things brought up immediately. Should be here any minute."

"Thank you. But I'm a big boy. I don't need you to manage me. No matter what my father claims."

"You think I wanted to bother you? Your father's assistant made it clear, in no uncertain terms, that I had to make sure you were on time tonight."

"Of course he did."

"Your absence at the other wedding activities this week has been noted."

"I was absent because I was *working*. The Silver Ridge project is important to me. Dad already lectured me about how it had better be profitable, and I'm not going to put my entire life on hold just because Kip is getting married."

She held up her hands. "You and me both. But you know how your father is."

"Yeah, I do." Everything was about loyalty. And I never managed to show enough.

There was a knock at the door. I opened it a bit roughly, making the guy outside jump. "Your bags, Mr. Knightly?"

"Yeah. Thanks." I shoved a generous tip at him. Hopefully that made up for my shitty mood.

Grabbing Grace's suitcase and the garment bag with her new clothes, I excused myself and carried them into my bedroom. The shower was running, the bathroom door not quite closed. Like an invitation. And did I ever want to accept it.

But my conversation with Margot wasn't finished, and I preferred to get this over with while Grace wouldn't overhear.

I went out to the great room again, and Margot was in the kitchen fiddling with my coffee maker. As soon as I walked in, she handed me a shot of espresso. I downed it and said, "Thank you."

She went to make one for herself, sticking a fresh pod into the coffee maker. It was some hard-to-find European model Margot had ordered for me for my last birthday. Because she knew me. She cared.

I had very few people in my corner in Manhattan these days, but I had Margot, and thank goodness for that.

"Sorry I grumped at you," I said. I went to pour a glass of water from the fridge.

"Already forgotten. There's something else I wanted to share with you in person. You asked me to find out more about Dirk Lancaster."

I snapped to attention. "Yes? Did you locate him?"

Since I'd first heard that name from Tobin the hotel manager almost a week ago, I'd been pestering Kip for info on Lancaster. The man in the blue mask. My brother had conveniently ignored my calls and messages. Margot had tracked down Lancaster's business number, but the man hadn't responded either.

"Lancaster's assistant kept claiming he was unavailable," Margot said, "and I finally learned he left the country a few days ago for a vacation in Fiji."

"*Fiji*?"

She shrugged. "Apparently, the trip had been planned ages ago, but who knows. Since Kip's assistant wasn't helpful either, I decided to look up Lancaster in the Knightly Global system myself. He committed recently to a significant investment in your brother's pet project in the Bahamas."

"So Kip does know him."

She nodded. "And your brother's calendar showed he had dinner with Lancaster two weeks ago."

Which would've been *after* the masquerade ball.

"Technically, I shouldn't have been accessing Kip's personal calendar," Margot said, "but if he insists on being mysterious about Lancaster, then I had to resort to more extreme measures."

"I assume you didn't leave traces on the system?"

Margot smiled thinly. "I'm much too careful for that, dear." Of course she was. Good thing I had the woman working for *me*. "I passed everything I have on Lancaster to your investigator, Warren Crenshaw. He'll be able to find out more for you on Lancaster's business dealings and travel."

"Thank you. I can talk to Kip about Lancaster too at some point this weekend, and I'll be sure not to give away your spying."

She nodded. "I'd rather avoid the ire of your brother. If I can help it."

I wanted to say Kip wouldn't dare harass someone so close to me, but who was I kidding? Kip was a coward when it came to striking directly, but he could still make Margot's life difficult.

"What about Nina Jamison? Anything?"

We had already concluded that her name might be fake, since Margot hadn't been able to find anything about a Nina Jamison matching the redhead in the photo Chief Landry had shared. No social media, credit history, nothing. Ms. Scarlet was apparently a ghost.

Margot shook her head. "Afraid not. But the investigator will work on finding her too. Hopefully he'll have more luck."

I cast a glance toward my bedroom door, making sure it remained closed. "And the other matter I asked you to look into?"

"Grace's eldest brother? Aside from Grayden O'Neal's military discharge and incarceration record, I didn't find much. He was released from prison several years ago, but I wasn't able to tell where he went afterward. Should I get Warren involved?"

"Send him the info. Just to see if we can find O'Neal, but tell Warren no contact yet." I needed to know for sure if Grace wanted her brother in her life again. And there was the fact that Ashford would want the exact opposite, but...yeah. I would deal with that later.

"One other thing, Dane. I saw Izzy this morning. Gave her your love."

The espresso churned in my stomach. "I was planning to visit Mom tomorrow. How did she seem?"

Margot paused. "It wasn't the best day for her today. Tomorrow's a new one."

True. But I hated that I actually felt *relief*, knowing I hadn't missed one of Mom's rare moments of clarity while I'd been out with Grace.

"Has Kip taken Bristol to see Mom this week?" I asked. "Or at all?"

"Not that I'm aware of. The nurses didn't mention any other recent visitors. Aside from your father, of course."

I muttered a curse, but a resigned one. I couldn't believe my brother had failed to take his fiancée to see our mother during the week of his wedding. Not like Mom could come to any of the festivities. But Kip owed it to Mom to at least *try* making her a part of it.

"Maybe they'll stop by and visit your mother tomorrow before the ceremony," Margot said. "You might run into them."

I huffed a laugh with zero humor. "One big, happy family."

Margot sipped her espresso. "And Grace? Are you bringing her with you to see Izzy tomorrow as well?"

Shit, I hadn't even considered that. "Not sure. Grace might prefer to hit a museum or sightsee instead while I take care of the visit with Mom."

"You really think Grace would prefer that?"

"She already has to deal with Dad and Kip. I can't subject her to all the Knightly family issues. She's here to get her mind *off* of bullshit like that. To have fun."

"Grace doesn't seem like the type to want only fun."

"Well, maybe that's what *I* want for her," I snapped.

Margot frowned like she was disappointed in me. Couldn't blame her. I was being an asshole.

"I need to get ready," I said, knowing I was avoiding the issue. But I didn't have the energy to untangle it.

"Please do." Margot checked her watch. "Thirty-five minutes."

"Yeah, yeah," I muttered as I walked away.

I hadn't told Grace about my mom's diagnosis at all yet, and I couldn't even say *why*. Maybe because, when I was with Grace, I actually felt like happiness was a simple thing that I could reach out and hold. Something I might be able to keep.

But my mother's illness was a reminder that nothing was guaranteed.

I could fight for everything I wanted and still lose it.

TWENTY

Dane

I DECIDED to get ready in the guest room, just because I didn't want to get distracted by being undressed around Grace. I trusted her to have some discretion, but I was running low on willpower at the moment, even with Margot, a.k.a. Super Mom, in my apartment.

I made quick work of it, washing off and styling my hair. While I was knotting my new tie, someone knocked on the guest room door. There was no shouting afterward about how I was late, so I figured it wasn't Margot.

"You can come in, gorgeous," I said.

Grace pushed the door open and stepped inside. "Already calling me gorgeous? You don't know how I look yet."

I turned and smiled. "I made an educated guess."

She had her blue dress on, her hair smoothed back into a high ponytail, and she had worn just enough makeup to accentuate her features rather than hiding them.

I whistled. "You are something else. New York City doesn't know what it's in for tonight."

She rolled her eyes like she didn't believe me. "I'm trying to decide if I should wear my glasses or not."

I went back to knotting my tie. "Whatever you're more comfortable with."

"Somehow I knew you would say that. Glasses, then. I kind of hate contacts." She lifted her chin defiantly.

I finished with my tie and walked over to her, running my hands along her sides as soon as I was close enough. "If I could have my way, you would be wearing your glasses and nothing else. But then I would really have to watch you around the other men there tonight. They'll try to steal you from me. It'll be tough enough as it is with you in that dress."

"You're absurd," she said, but she was smiling.

"Can I kiss you? Or will you get mad about me ruining your makeup?"

She gave me a firm kiss on the lips. "I didn't put any lipstick on yet. But Margot already gave her five-minute warning, so..."

"Hell. Then I'd better make this quick." I pulled her to me and kissed her more thoroughly, holding nothing back this time. Getting a shot of the taste of her, because I was going to need that to get me through this party.

When I pulled away, she was breathless.

I put my hands on her bare shoulders. "Thank you for coming with me to this. I promise I'll get us out of there as soon as I can."

"I doubt it will be that bad."

"Just remember that my brother and my dad have issues with *me*. It has nothing to do with you."

She shrugged one shoulder. "I'm no stranger to family discord. My big brothers weren't always nice to their baby sister. I can handle it."

I knew she could, but I felt a sudden jolt of uncertainty. I hoped this wasn't a mistake, subjecting Grace to this crowd. I had only been thinking of myself when I'd invited her. Selfishly wanting her beside me. I also wanted Grace to agree to keep seeing me after this. But showing her exactly how much Dad and Kip despised me might not be the best way to go about it.

"The car is waiting downstairs," Margot called out. "Let's go, children."

"It'll be fine," Grace whispered to me.

I tucked her hair behind her ear. "I'm supposed to be spoiling you this weekend, and here you are reassuring me. You shouldn't have to do that. But thank you."

"I'm happy to. I'm tougher than I look."

That was something I *really* liked about her.

I thought about passing on what Margot had shared about Dirk Lancaster. But there wasn't much to tell. Things would be tense enough tonight as it was without reminding Grace of the break-in at her house.

Grace was tough, but I still wanted to shield her from the bad things. To be her safe place for as long as I could.

✧

As we walked into the restaurant, exactly on time, I resolved to focus on Grace tonight. Which was no hardship. I kept my arm around her as we waded into the fray. Acquaintances and business associates eyed Grace curiously and asked me how I had been, making small talk about the wedding. I steered her through the gauntlet as quickly as possible.

"You're the only interesting thing here," I murmured. "We should sneak out the back."

"You haven't even seen your brother yet. Is your family that scary? You don't want me to meet them?" She sounded like she was joking, but I saw a flicker of insecurity in her pretty face, and I felt like an ass.

I spotted my brother and his fiancée across the room. "Of course I want you to meet them."

"If Kip isn't nice to you, I'll put him in a headlock. I learned it from Ashford." Grace winked at me, and I laughed so loud that some stuffy woman in pearls took a step away from me.

"You're my hero, gorgeous." But if anybody said a cross word to *her*, my good behavior was going to be out the window, and I wasn't kidding.

We made our way toward them. Not just Kip and Bristol, but my father and the bride's family too. The Harcourts.

"Dad," I said.

"Dane," my father said stiffly. "Good to see you, son."

Translation: *It's about time you got here, you ingrate*. But too many people were looking on for him to say what he was really thinking. So I forged ahead.

"Dad, everyone, this is Grace O'Neal. Grace, my father Dennis Knightly. My brother Kip. His fiancée Bristol." I rattled off the names of the others. Grace's mouth tightened when I introduced her to Ainsley, the maid of honor who my father had been conspiring for me to date.

"You're from that little town in Colorado Dane's been hiding away in?" Bristol asked, disdain dripping from her words like the diamonds she was wearing.

Every cell in my body clenched as I frowned at my brother, warning him with my eyes that his fiancée better back the hell off.

Grace interlaced her fingers with mine. "I wouldn't say Dane's been hiding. He's charmed the whole place. And trust me, coming from a little town in Colorado, I *definitely* know charming."

Then my father actually cracked an almost-smile. "That does sound like Dane." The bride's father chuckled, and Ainsley's laugh was genuine.

It hadn't exactly been a compliment coming from my dad, but Grace had managed to defuse the tension in a few seconds flat. She was impressive, alright.

And thank God the introductions were over. As soon as there was a break in conversation, I pulled Grace toward the bar. We both needed a drink.

"You were right," I said softly. "You handled my family just fine."

"Something I learned from my brothers. Never show fear. It works well on mean girls too."

"What about bankers and businessmen? I should bring you along next time I'm closing a deal. Bet we'd make a great team."

She laughed. "At the very least, I could check your math."

"Another invaluable skill. You're a woman of many talents."

And I was dangerously close to falling under her spell. Grace had no idea what she was doing to me.

When it was time for dinner, we sat at a long table with my family and the wedding party. Because we Knightlys had to present a united front. The best man was there too, one of Kip's buddies from college. I tried not to engage in conversation with anyone else, which left me free to flirt with my date. I slowly teased my fingers up Grace's thigh beneath her dress until she stopped my hand with a glare.

When dessert came, I pushed back from the table. "Be right back. Bathroom break."

"No problem. I'm going to need to focus on this beauty, anyway." Grace dug into the dessert, some layered thing with lots of chocolate and cream.

I leaned in and said, "Don't eat it all until I'm back. I want to watch you enjoy it."

She gave me the sexiest side-eye I'd ever seen.

Nobody else was in the bathroom. I zipped up just as the door swung open.

I glanced back. My brother had just walked inside. "Did you bring a date from Colorado just to piss off Dad?" Kip asked.

"Hello to you too." I went around him to reach the sinks.

Kip appeared behind me in the mirror. "Not going to answer my question?"

I scowled. "It was a stupid question. Seems like you're trying to pick a fight with me."

"I'm just trying to understand the things you do. You joined the company to make Dad like you more, and yet you can't resist defying him every chance you get."

"Why do you care?"

"I'm wondering why you don't just quit."

Ah. So that was what this was about.

Grabbing a folded towel to dry my hands, I spun and faced my brother. "You'd love that, wouldn't you? If I quit."

My little brother crossed his arms, thinking he had me on the ropes. "You'd probably love it too. Go back to that town in Colorado that you were so insistent on investing in."

Maybe he did have a point there. "But I didn't join the company for Dad's approval. I joined it for Mom. I don't expect you to understand that."

"Screw you. I love our mother."

"Yeah? When's the last time you went to visit her? Have you taken Bristol to see her, since Mom can't come to the wedding?"

"Mom probably won't even know who we are. What's the point?"

I had sworn a long time ago that I'd never hit my brother, but he was really pushing me. I needed to change the subject before I lost control.

And there was something else I needed to talk to him about, anyway. I'd been planning to wait until he wasn't in the middle of wedding stuff, but *he* had started this conversation. Not me.

"Dirk Lancaster," I said, without preamble. Kip gave me the reaction I wanted. He tried to hide it, but he flinched.

"What about him?"

"I left you voicemails and messages about the man. Lancaster caused a scene at the grand-opening masquerade in Silver Ridge. He put his hand on Grace, and it pissed me the hell off."

"Yes, and Dirk recognized you. He says you threatened him. He complained to me, and we're lucky he's still willing to do business with us at all."

"Fuck him and his business. I want him to answer some questions for me."

"What questions?"

"For starters, does he know a woman called Nina Jamison

who was at the party that night? I didn't see her, but I'm told she was very striking. Memorable. And she may have arranged to meet Lancaster there. I think Lancaster mistook Grace for her."

Another flinch. Like Kip knew exactly who I was talking about.

"Do *you* know Nina?" I asked. "Or whatever her name really is."

He snapped out of wherever his mind had gone. "I don't have a clue what you're talking about. Why should I care about any of this?"

"Because somebody broke into Grace's home last week. Trashed her room and stole something. I have reason to believe Nina Jamison or Dirk Lancaster could have information about it."

He shrugged. "All I know is that Lancaster has invested a heck of a lot of money in our developments."

"Then give his money back. I don't care. I want to know why someone went after Grace."

Kip snorted. "Don't be shortsighted just because the man offended your flavor of the week."

My jaw clenched tight. So did my fists. "Do not speak about Grace that way."

"You're a joke, you know that? You go looking for authenticity in some nowhere town, but what else do you expect to bring back except a gold digger?"

I lunged, grabbing Kip by the shirt. A button popped. The bathroom door swung open at the same moment. "Dane, that's enough," Dad said.

Hell.

I let go, and Kip scrambled back from me, trying to smooth down his tie. "Asshole," he muttered, then stormed out of the bathroom. Leaving just Dad and me.

Dad flipped the lock, because apparently the well-appointed men's room of this Michelin-rated restaurant was now an extension of Knightly Global. Who knew?

"I expect you and your brother to get along," Dad said.

"Unless Kip gets a personality transplant, I don't see us becoming best friends."

"You don't have to be close. But people have been asking me why you're not the best man in his wedding. You're not even in the wedding party. How do you think that looks?"

"Are you kidding? Kip doesn't want me anywhere near him. He's up to something. I'd keep a close eye on him if I were you."

"I don't have a need for your advice, Dane. I just need you to act like you respect this family."

"I don't respect this family?" I seethed. "When's the last time Kip visited Mom? He acts like she's already gone."

My father betrayed his first hint of emotion. But it disappeared fast. Whenever I'd tried to discuss her illness and prognosis with him, he shut me out. And right now was no different.

"Kip is doing what he's supposed to. He's found a partner in life, and believe me when I say nothing is more important. Your mother..." He cleared his throat. "Your mother is the best thing that ever happened to me. If you would do the same, you'd be far better off."

"If you're going to push Ainsley Harcourt on me—"

"No, I'm not. I just remembered that you used to like her, so I thought it was a possibility. Given her family background, she would be a good match. Don't paint me as an evil villain just because I expect you to grow up and be serious."

Incredible that he didn't count my military service or business success as *serious*. As if I'd just been wasting my time until joining his company.

"Look," Dad said. "Kip's marriage has business implications as well as personal ones. We're in negotiations with Harcourt Hotels for an ownership stake in their holdings. As part of that deal, we would bring our hotel properties under their brand. Including the Silver Ridge resort. You're part of our executive team, so they need to see you're an asset instead of a liability."

An inferno of *fuck you* raged inside me. I wanted to smash my hand against the wall like some punk teenager. The fury of the powerless.

My father and his bullshit. My mother's illness. Problems that all the money in the world couldn't fix. It all made me feel so damn powerless, and I couldn't stand it.

"Sure, Dad. I'll be a team player," I said instead.

"Thank you. You'd better get back to your date. She seems like a pleasant girl." He washed his hands, undid the lock, and left the bathroom.

I almost laughed. What a concession. Grace was the brightest light to appear in my life for a long time. Since Mom's diagnosis. Maybe since before then.

Is this really what Mom would want, though? I asked myself. *Me working for Knightly Global and being miserable?*

I didn't know anymore. But I'd be damned before I turned my back on her and acted like she didn't matter anymore the way Kip had.

TWENTY-ONE

Grace

After Dane left to go to the bathroom, his brother got up with a determined expression and followed. Which seemed like a bad sign.

Then Bristol came and sat right next to me in Dane's seat, and I knew for sure that was a bad sign. Everyone else at the table was already mingling or over at the bar except for her, me, and Ainsley.

"Dane seems smitten with you," Bristol said. "It's so cute. You're not his usual type though."

Really? We're doing this? You would've thought the bride would have better things to do on the eve of her wedding.

I returned her smile with an equally sardonic one. "I like him too."

"I would assume so. Dane has that magic touch when it comes to women. Isn't that right, Ainsley?" She looked over at her sister across the table. "You and Dane had a thing too."

Ainsley picked up her glass of red wine and sipped it instead of answering.

Then Bristol looked over at me, pretending to be shocked. "Oops. You probably didn't know that."

Annoyance started to build, inching up my throat. But I kept my tone civil. "I did. Dane told me." I dipped my spoon into my dessert.

She was getting to me, and I hated it.

"Did he tell you that his father wants him and Ainsley to get back together?"

"Bristol, stop," Ainsley said. "Don't be a bitch."

She gasped. "Such harsh language. Grace is going to get a bad impression of us."

"Don't be fooled by the glasses and small-town accent," I said evenly. "I have claws." I waggled my pink fingernails at her to emphasize the point.

"Is that supposed to scare me?"

"Just letting you know. If you think this small-town girl doesn't have a hell of a lot of fight in her, you would be wrong. And trust me, I'm not afraid to fight dirty, either." I smiled and took another bite of chocolatey cake. "But I'd much rather be sweet."

Bristol dropped her sugary veneer altogether. "You're very impressed with yourself for someone who will be gone in a week. Dane will get tired of you in no time. And then you'll be back to nowheresville where you belong." She got up and strode away, smile already back in place as she went to greet the occupants of another table.

Then I glanced over at Ainsley and found her lifting her glass toward me. "I should apologize for my sister. But if she wasn't so awful, I would've missed your comebacks. Seriously entertaining."

"At least *someone* was laughing." I was trying not to be jealous of this girl, given her history with Dane. I had no right to be. But I still didn't like the thought of her touching him.

Maybe I was a bit more attached to him than I'd wanted to admit.

Earlier he'd mentioned us visiting New York again, but had that just been a throwaway comment? Did I want it to mean something more?

"My sister was right about one thing though. Dane really likes you. He never acts this way about a woman, not that I've seen."

I took another careful bite of dessert. "Sounds like you know him pretty well."

"I used to. But please retract those claws, because I promise I'm no threat."

I raised my eyebrows at her.

Like Bristol, Ainsley had jet-black hair, but her features were less angular than her sister's. Her eyes were kind instead of cruel. She got up and rounded the table, coming to sit beside me so she could lower her voice. "Dane and I were friends back in high school. And more than that for a while, but it was nothing. That was practically a million years ago. Our fathers might have other ideas about setting us up, but... How can I put this? Dane's really not my type."

"But he has such a magic touch with the ladies."

I was glad when she laughed. "Maybe. But I prefer men who let me take the lead. Dane is way too bossy for me."

Now, I was the one who laughed. "He's definitely bossy. Luckily, I don't mind it." In fact, I enjoyed Dane's bossiness. That man knew how to push all my buttons. In the good way.

"Then it sounds like a match. Which is obvious to everyone else in the room when they see the way he looks at you. That's why Bristol feels threatened."

An unpleasant thought raked down my spine. "She doesn't have a thing for him, does she?"

"Oh, no. Not even close. But Bristol likes to be the center of attention, and she wants to run Knightly Global with Kip, especially once our fathers agree on this little hotel partnership they've been negotiating. Dane is already a threat to that, and you're a new factor in the mix."

"I have no interest in Knightly Global. I really am a small-town girl. Dane and I aren't officially together, and when this trip is over, we're going back to just friends."

"You can tell yourself that, but Dane might have other ideas." Ainsley had such a disarming look on her face that I couldn't help but smile.

An hour ago, I'd been bracing myself to meet Dane's ex, but I actually kind of liked her.

"Hey," I said, dropping my voice to a whisper. "Is Dane and Kip's mother here tonight? I assumed she would be, but he hasn't introduced me. I didn't ask him because I didn't want to bring up an awkward subject, given his relationship with his dad. But..." I trailed off when I saw the uncomfortable expression on Ainsley's face.

"Dane didn't tell you about Isadora?"

I set down my spoon, no longer interested in the rest of my dessert. "Didn't tell me what?"

✧

When Dane didn't come back to the table, I went to look for him.

Dane's mom was sick. Ainsley hadn't given me all the details, saying that I should ask Dane for the full story. But he'd had plenty of chances to tell me. He'd chosen not to. I was trying not to overreact about it, but I did want to know why.

I passed by the restrooms, listening for voices. There was no sign of Dane or his brother. But when I glanced up a nearby staircase, I saw the back of a man ascending the stairs.

It wasn't Dane, though. Or Kip. This man wore a boxy suit and had a shaved head.

Instantly, my pulse raced into overdrive.

It seemed impossible, but he reminded me of the man who'd stopped me in the lobby the night of the masquerade. What on earth could that guy be doing *here*? Not just thousands of miles away from Silver Ridge, but at Kip and Bristol's private rehearsal dinner. They'd rented out the whole place. It couldn't be the same man.

But what if it *was*?

I started mounting the stairs. I kept on the balls of my toes so my heels wouldn't clack on the wood.

If there was any way I could find out that man's identity and how he was connected to Nina Jamison and Dirk Lancaster, I had to take the opportunity. He might know something about Nina's disappearance or the break-in at my house.

I reached the top and looked around the quiet upstairs dining area. The lights were dim. This part of the restaurant wasn't being used, so nobody else was around. I didn't see the man with the shaved head anywhere, either. Had no clue where he'd gone.

Unease suddenly gripped me. Maybe I shouldn't have come up here.

Then I spotted Dane through a set of French doors, standing on a balcony, and my heart seemed to restart, flooding me with relief.

I was probably just on edge because I hadn't been able to find Dane. And here he was. So everything was fine, right? I was being ridiculous.

There was no way that bald man could've been the same creepy guy as in Silver Ridge.

When I stepped out onto the balcony, Dane turned his head. "Hey." It was too dark to see him well. The air was chilly but not uncomfortable. I was a Colorado girl, after all. The sounds of the city surrounded us, filling in the silence.

"You disappeared," I said.

"Sorry about that." Dane's voice was rough. "I needed to clear my head. Didn't mean to abandon you."

"I told you, I'm tougher than I look." I almost asked if he'd seen a man with a shaved head pass by. But Dane shifted so his features stood out in sharper relief in the low light. And I forgot everything else.

"What happened?" I asked.

"I had some words with Kip and then my father. Wasn't pleasant."

"What did they say?"

"I'm not in the mood to repeat it."

I'd never seen him like this before. Dane was always steady, as if nothing could touch him down deep. This was the man who'd tossed me over his shoulder when I was freaking out about the break-in at my house. Who'd handled Dirk Lancaster so easily when the man grabbed me at the party. Who didn't even flinch when Callum and his firefighter friends *and* Teller Landry had all been staring him down.

But right now, Dane's eyes were two dark pools of shadow. His mouth cut a hard line across his face, and his knuckles turned white with how hard he gripped the railing. He looked like a man who was struggling to keep his control.

"I'd much rather kiss you," he said.

"Then you should do it."

Dane spun me and pressed me up against the balcony railing. His mouth slanted down on mine, hot and demanding from the get-go. Like he was desperate for this. And I was right there with him. His tongue pushed past my lips, and I sucked on it, making him groan.

His hands were rough, sliding over the soft fabric of my dress to squeeze my curves. His thumb found the hard point of my nipple and circled it, flicking and teasing until I was panting.

He started tugging up the skirt of my dress. Distantly, I knew the fact that we were in public. I'd seen someone aside from us come upstairs. But that person had gone somewhere else, and I could barely recall why that mattered, much less remember what I had been thinking about before.

That was the thing about Dane. He could sweep me away with a look, with a few words, no matter where we were. I'd said no to him earlier at the boutique, but that resistance was gone.

I took pride in my inner strength. But I was nowhere near strong enough to resist Dane Knightly.

His fingers caressed their way up my inner thigh as he kept

kissing me. Hypnotizing me with the movements of his tongue and lips against mine.

Then his thumb brushed across the crotch of my panties for the second time that day. Dane broke the kiss, his forehead resting against mine. His hand was still under my dress, and his fingertip pressed right against my clit. I couldn't help the sound I made in response. The city sounds drowned me out, but just barely.

"Someone could see." Anyone could walk out on this balcony at any moment. Or spot us through the French doors.

"If anyone comes up here, I'll just stop touching you and let your dress fall back into place. You can tell me no, but I don't think you want to. I feel how wet you are already." Dane's voice was guttural. Drenched with need. "I want to know what sounds you make when you come, gorgeous."

I shivered all over. I felt that same need, tingles of arousal blooming in my lower belly and between my legs where he was touching me. But I wasn't *completely* unaware. If anything, Dane's presence in front of me and the city around us stood out more clearly. Like all my senses had been turned up in volume.

I tipped my head back and shivered again. He kissed my throat. At the same time, his fingertip stroked back and forth over the crotch of my panties. Just enough teasing pressure to make me need so much more.

"Look at me," he demanded.

I did. The way he devoured me with his eyes—I'd experienced that before. But not with so much need radiating from him. This was a dark and dangerous side of Dane I'd only glimpsed a few times. But I'd never had such a clear sense of him before. The suit and tie, the polished shoes and the Rolex. None of that conveyed the wildness that was inside him.

It scared me a little. But I craved it even more.

"Tell me yes," he said.

I nodded. Yes. I wanted this.

I wanted what he'd started a few hours ago, after I first tried on this dress.

Two of his fingertips pushed aside the damp fabric of my panties and, after circling my opening a few times, slowly pushed inside me. My hands scrambled behind me to hold on to the railing. That sensation of being filled, especially by a man like *him*, took my breath away. And it was only his fingers, not his cock.

But if he unbuttoned and unzipped his fly, pushed my dress all the way up, and took me right here, I had the feeling I'd let him.

His fingers stroked in and out of me, then switched to stimulating my clit. His eyes didn't look away from mine, seeming to pin me in place. He didn't act like this wasn't affecting him though. Every time I whimpered or moaned, he groaned in response. His breaths quickened, nostrils flaring as he breathed.

"You're going to feel so perfect when I fuck you tonight," he murmured.

When Dane kissed me again, his tongue and his fingers moving relentlessly, I felt my orgasm building. There was nothing else except Dane right now. His fierce kiss and the sheer, unfettered desire pouring off of him. I wanted to give him everything he needed, and right now, that seemed to be me.

"*Dane*," I gasped into his mouth. The pleasure hit me all at once. It was a good thing he was kissing me to muffle my shout. Otherwise the whole neighborhood would've heard it. His fingers circled a few more times through my wetness, coaxing aftershocks from my body, until I squeezed my thighs together.

"No more," I whispered.

He pulled his hand away, my skirt falling, and he slowly placed those same two fingers into his mouth to lick them off. "Did you like that?" he asked, low and husky. My glasses had slipped down my nose, so he gently pushed them back up.

"Yeah. Did you?"

Dane turned me to face the balcony railing, held onto my sides, and nudged his hips against me. I felt the hard ridge of his erection even through the layers of ruffles in my skirt. "That's what you do to me. You'll help me with that later?"

"I could do it right here. Anything you want." *What on earth was I saying?* I barely even knew. Thankfully, Dane was thinking more clearly than I was.

He chuckled and said, "When we get home. I don't want us to get arrested. That would *really* be one for the gossip pages."

TWENTY-TWO

Dane

By the time we got back to my apartment, that mixed-up fog of anger and lust had disappeared from my brain. And I realized what a complete asshole I had been.

What had I been thinking?

Leaving Grace alone while I brooded, then mauling her when she found me. She'd noticed something was wrong from the look on my face, and I'd felt this click inside me. Like Grace was the exact answer to the emptiness I'd been feeling.

It wasn't the first time I'd felt that about her. But it was the first time I'd shoved my hand into her panties in public and then didn't allow her a real choice about giving me what I wanted.

Anyone could've caught us on that balcony, which was bad enough. But *Margot* could've seen us. She'd been at the rehearsal dinner, though she'd stuck with other Knightly Global staff and stayed away from my family. If she knew what I'd done, she would've had strong words, and I'd already faced Margot's disapproval once today. Though I deserved it.

"That was a misjudgment on my part," I said when we were inside. "What happened on the balcony. I'm sorry."

Grace smirked, one hand on her hip. "Why are you sorry? I enjoyed it."

I loosened my tie. "But I didn't give you much of a choice."

Grace stepped up to me, still tall in her heels, and grabbed the lapels of my jacket. "I said yes because I wanted to. Having your hands on me on that balcony was the hottest thing that's ever happened to me."

Some of my regret retreated. "It's still possible someone saw. Imagine what your brothers would do to me if they heard. Or if we show up on some gossip website. Ashford's had issues with those in the past."

Just be careful with her, Ashford had said. *Please.*

"I highly doubt that's going to happen."

"I assume you didn't get to finish your dessert, either. I never came back to the table." After our encounter on the balcony, we'd grabbed Grace's purse and left without even saying goodbye to anyone.

"So? We can have dessert here. Can't we?"

"We can. I have cheesecake in the fridge."

"New York cheesecake is high on my dessert agenda for this trip. But I was thinking of something more...metaphorical."

Mmm, I did love that wicked look in her eyes.

I was a bad influence, but Grace brought it out in me even more.

I kissed her, less urgently than on the balcony, just enjoying the taste of her. And it was finally occurring to me that my family obligations were over for tonight, and it would be just us. I could take my time with Grace. Spoil her the way I'd promised instead of being rough and *taking*.

But when I pulled back, her brows had knitted. Like she was thinking serious thoughts.

"What is it?" I asked.

"Why didn't you tell me about your mom being sick?"

Oh, damn it. "I meant to."

"Then why didn't you? I had to hear it from Ainsley, and I felt kind of ridiculous for not knowing. Not that you have to tell me everything. We're not...involved that way."

"No, I should have. That's on me. But it's beyond depressing. That's why I didn't say anything." Exactly like I'd told Margot earlier. I wanted this trip to be fun for Grace.

Lot of fun you're being right now, Knightly, I scolded myself.

"I can handle depressing," she said. "If you want to talk about it, I'm available."

I cupped my hand at her cheek, dragging it down to the side of her neck, feeling her pulse thrum against my palm. She was so sweet. Maybe too sweet for me. Yet that truth only made me want her more.

How many times had I told Grace I wanted the chance to know her, and for her to know me?

"I can tell you the basics." I was going to need whiskey for this, though. Grabbing her hand, I led her into the kitchen and opened my liquor cabinet. "Want a drink?"

"Just ice water."

"I'll grab you a glass. But I need something stronger." I got Grace's ice water, then a finger of whiskey for myself. Then I recalled what she'd said a few minutes ago, and there was a record scratch in my head.

"You were talking to Ainsley?" I asked.

She laughed. "It was fine. Bristol was awful to me, but Ainsley is kind of great. She said nice things about you. And also that you're not her type and she has zero interest in you."

I relaxed momentarily. "Wait, Bristol was awful?"

"Can we not talk about the bride and maid of honor? We will have plenty of wedding drama tomorrow."

This time, it was Grace who took my hand, and we went into the living room. My lights were on timers, so just the floor lamps were on in here, emitting a soft, warm glow. I sat heavily on the couch, and Grace sat on the cushion beside me, kicking off her heels on the way.

But she wasn't close enough. I hauled her right up against me and draped her legs over my lap. "That's better."

"You told me how your mom was an Olympic skier and a

mountain climber," Grace prompted. "And how your mom and dad met at Everest base camp."

Half my whiskey went down in one gulp. A shame, given how expensive it was. "The highlight reel."

"You wanted to focus on the happy parts of her life. Not the hard ones."

"Yes." And I was impressed that Grace understood that. Floored, actually. I'd spoken a little about Mom's decline to Ashford and Emma, but that was different.

Grace was different.

"My mother was diagnosed with early-onset Alzheimer's. She's not doing well. That's why she can't be at the wedding."

"Is she in a care facility?"

Another gulp of whiskey. "No, she lives at home. My parents' apartment here in Manhattan. But she has twenty-four-hour care. Doesn't leave the house much anymore. And I think that's all I can say about it tonight."

My arguments with Kip and my dad were too recent. It was all too raw, and Grace was already seeing more of my flaws than I'd ever intended.

Thankfully, she nodded. "That's okay. If you want, I can take your mind off things."

Interest swirled in my belly and went lower, pushing away the ache. "Oh yeah? I'd like that."

She shifted so that she was straddling me, her hands going to my shoulders. "Today was one of the best days I've ever had."

I squeezed her thigh with the hand that wasn't holding my glass. "Same. Except for the dinner. Wish I could've skipped that part."

"But we wouldn't be here if you hadn't needed a date to the wedding."

"I'm not going to thank Kip for anything."

"You don't have to think about him at all." Grace leaned forward to kiss my cheek, yet her hips also ground against me. A little sweet, a little filthy. Just like Grace herself. My cock thickened against the seam of my pants. "You were amazing to me today," she said. "I have never felt so spoiled or so beautiful in my life." Another light kiss, this one to my jaw.

Then she pushed back, her knees dropping to the carpet as she sank between my spread legs. She reached for the button of my trousers and flicked it open. "I think you deserve to be spoiled some too."

Nngh.

I tipped back the last of my whiskey and set the glass aside. Grace slid my zipper down. Pulled out my cock. I wasn't fully hard yet, but within less than a minute, the soft heat of her mouth had my dick swelling against her tongue. She moaned, and the vibration stimulated me even more.

"*Fuck*," I breathed. "Just like that."

Grace tongued the underside and cradled the tip in her mouth, gazing up at me with her glasses on the tip of her nose like a scandalous librarian. I pulled the tie from her ponytail so her auburn strands fell around her bare shoulders. From the way she was bent over in my lap, her breasts nearly spilled from the top of her strapless dress.

She was the hottest thing I'd ever seen.

When she started bobbing down and hollowing her cheeks on the way up, I realized how close she'd already gotten me. And we couldn't have that. Not yet.

"I want something else now, gorgeous. Since you're being so obliging."

She lifted her head, sucking along the way. My cock wasn't happy when it left the warmth of her mouth. But I tucked myself away, just for the moment.

"Get naked for me."

"You'll have to unzip me." Grace stood and turned around. I grasped the tiny zipper pull and tugged it down until her dress fell and pooled at her feet. She stepped out of it. Her back was bare and elegant, a long swooping curve that ended with the flare of her lower body. She still had her panties on, but they didn't cover much. I got a fantastic eyeful of her round behind.

"Put the heels back on."

Grace narrowed her eyes at me over her shoulder, trying to hide a grin. "You're pushing it."

"Please? Thought it was my turn to get spoiled."

With her back still toward me, she toed into her heels. She'd left them conveniently there on the carpet.

"Turn around, gorgeous."

She did, and I nearly choked on my tongue. She was incredible. There was so much I wanted to touch, and I wanted all of it right now. Standing up, I put my hands on her hips and bent to kiss her. She held on to my shoulders. While Grace was nearly naked, I was still fully dressed aside from my fly being open.

"Didn't you say something earlier about punishing me?" she asked. "I'm wondering when that's going to happen, or if you make promises you can't keep."

I laughed out loud. "I forgot, actually." This had been a really long day. Most of it had been perfect, and it was ending in the best possible way. "How do you feel about having your wrists tied?"

Grace's eyes widened. "I like that idea."

I removed the black-striped tie from my neck. Grace put her arms in front of her. I wrapped the tie around her slender wrists and tied it with a nice little bow. "Now walk over there to the chaise and lie down with your arms above your head." I gestured with my chin.

"All the way over there? I think you just want to ogle me."

"Hell yes, I do."

My tongue traced my lower lip as she walked over to the chaise longue and knelt on top of it. With the bow around her wrists, she looked like the best present I could ever imagine.

Grace was true to her name as she sat and lay back, her body splayed on the lounge with her arms stretched over her head. The heels completed the naughty image, and I tried to sear it into my memory.

"Like this?" she asked teasingly.

My cock jumped, and I pressed the flat of my palm against it. I closed my mouth on a moan. "Yes, baby. You're doing so well for me."

I took my time crossing the room toward her, picking up her glass of ice water as I went. She'd left it on a side table, using a coaster I might add. Always so thoughtful.

I sat beside her on the chaise.

"What are you going to do to me? Should I be worried?"'

"No," I said softly. "I'm going to take very good care of you."

Taking a sip of the ice water, I caught a cube between my teeth and bent over to brush the ice over her nipple.

"That's *cold*!"

Her arms tried to lift, but I reached up to gently hold them down. Smiling wickedly around the ice cube, I circled her nipple a few times until it was a hard peak. Then did the same to the other breast.

"Dane," she whimpered.

I took the half-melted ice from my mouth. "Should I stop?"

"No. But I hate you."

"You're the one who kept asking to be punished."

"I wanted to see what would happen."

"Those are not the words of a woman who prefers her life simple and boring."

She frowned, but there was pure heat in her eyes.

I set the glass aside so I wouldn't knock it over. My fingers brushed the ice cube along her stomach while my cold mouth kissed her neck. She squirmed underneath me. I repositioned so I was straddling her thighs and had better access to everywhere I wanted to kiss and touch. Once my mouth was warmer, I took turns between teasing her with the ice and then warming the same spots with my tongue.

She wasn't complaining anymore. The sounds she was making got my cock harder than it had ever been. Even better than when I'd made her come earlier on the balcony, probably because we were alone and Grace was slowly losing those inhibitions she usually kept wrapped around herself like a shield.

And I wanted that so badly. For her to give herself to me with nothing held back.

The ice got too melty, so I tossed it somewhere on the floor and sucked her nipples with abandon. From the way she was squeezing her thighs and rubbing them together, I guessed she was ready for some more attention there. I was beyond ready too. My own breaths were shallow. Hot. Needy. I kissed my way down her body.

Her panties were skimpy and silky. But I was too damn impatient now. I grabbed the thin fabric in my fists and tore one side to get them off.

"Hey! I liked those."

"I'll buy you more." I held her thighs in my hands, pushing them apart. Then I dove in between her legs and lapped my tongue over her.

"*Oh*," she cried. "Yes. Please." Her hands tangled in my hair, still bound with my tie.

"Arms up," I growled. "I'm still the one in charge."

"Okay. Just don't stop. Please don't stop."

I had no intention. If I had my way, I'd have Grace underneath me accepting all the pleasure I wanted to give her as often as possible. And for a lot longer than just one weekend.

TWENTY-THREE

Grace

IF THIS WAS A PUNISHMENT, then I was going to be rebellious a lot more often.

I was lying here in nothing but my high heels, my legs draped over Dane's shoulders, while he did unbelievable things to me with his mouth.

I had loved going down on him earlier, trying to take his mind off of everything that had been upsetting him. But I certainly had no problem with what we were doing right now.

This man made me feel more alive than anyone else I'd ever been with. I had complained about the ice, but I couldn't believe how much it had excited me. The play of warmth and cold. The little hint of discomfort, followed by so much pleasure.

I didn't completely feel like myself with Dane, but I also felt more like myself than ever before. And no, it didn't make sense to me either. All I could do was lie back and enjoy it.

His tongue pushed inside of me, then went back to flicking over my clit. It was difficult to keep my arms stationary over my head, but also hot that Dane had insisted on it. I really did want to move though, especially as the tension built between my legs, an orgasm rushing up on me fast.

"I'm almost—Dane, I'm—"

He slid two fingers inside me, and I arched my spine as pleasure shot through me, so intense that I spaced out for a moment or two.

When he finally sat back, he was grinning smugly. "Hope none of my neighbors were sleeping. If they were, they're awake now."

"Was I loud?"

He dropped a kiss to my inner thigh. "So loud. I loved it. And the way you clenched around my fingers. Fuck. Guess I found your G spot."

"Is that what that was? Holy cow."

He looked so satisfied with himself, and I wanted to pounce on him and kiss him, but all the energy had drained out of my limbs.

Dane reached over my head to untie my hands, then gently rubbed my wrists as he brought my arms down. "You okay?"

"Mmhmm. Will you take off your clothes now? I want to see you."

He laughed. "In a moment. I'm still admiring you." A flush spread over my skin, and he said, "There it is. There's that pretty blush." Dane bent over to kiss my stomach and my breasts, moving up my body until he was kissing my mouth again, languorous and deep, putting me under a spell again.

His erection pressed into my thigh, and I reached between us into his pants. My hand closed around him, stroking. He moaned into my mouth.

Dane had commented before about the noises I made, but I loved his sounds too. His low growls and rumbles that showed me he was enjoying the moment, even when I thought I was getting all the pleasure.

His mouth broke from mine, and he asked, "What do you want next, gorgeous?"

"I get to choose?"

"Yep. Lady's choice. See, I'm not always demanding. I can be a giver."

Oh, he was a giver all right.

I'd told him today was *one* of my best days ever, but that wasn't exactly accurate. Certain days in my past ranked up there, like holding my niece Maisie for the first time. But today had been *the* best day because Dane had made me feel...cherished. Maybe that was silly and even selfish of me. But I'd felt like the center of his universe for a little while, and even though it was fleeting and not really *true*, it had still been amazing to experience.

I wanted to do the same for him. Spoil him. Show him how much today had meant to me.

I *really* wanted to make him feel good.

"Let me finish what I started earlier," I said. "My mouth on you. But you have to be naked this time."

He hummed, nostrils flaring as he inhaled. "Better undress me then."

Dane stood up, pulling me up by my hands. His steel-gray gaze was like cold fire, igniting in my veins as I started on the top buttons of his shirt. He had such an effect on me.

This was supposed to be about *him*, yet he had desire throbbing between my legs again. My hands were shaking from how much I wanted him.

I pushed his shirt off his shoulders, then tried getting it off his muscled arms. Which actually wasn't that easy because the man wasn't helping *at all*. But it was wild how submissive I felt right now, naked except for my shoes and taking off his clothes while he stared down at me. I hadn't expected this to be my thing, but it was.

Maybe everything Dane Knightly did was my thing.

Finally his shirt was off, his broad chest and shoulders and tan skin exposed. I ran my hands over him and kissed his pecs, then the happy trail that led down into the open fly of his pants. The tip of his cock already jutted out. I slid my tongue around it as I sank to my knees, pulling on his pants at the same time.

"*Grace.*" His voice was strained, revealing how much this was getting to him. I smiled and worked down his boxer briefs.

Suddenly Dane was toeing off his shoes and helping me get rid of the rest of his clothes like he couldn't wait any longer.

He was finally naked. The hair on his thighs tickled my palms. I looked up, marveling at the personification of sex standing over me.

When I took his tip into my mouth, his fingers sank into my hair and tightened, his hips giving a small push to slide his cock in deeper.

Oh, yes. Yes I wanted this so much.

Somehow, Dane turned the blowjob I was giving him into a seductive dance. Lightly thrusting his hips and moving in and out of my mouth as I used my meager range of tricks to drive him wild.

"I'm going to come, Grace. Your mouth is...*ungh*."

I sucked him deeper one more time, and his cock pulsed again and again against my tongue. But I was pretty sure I'd enjoyed that as much as he had.

After, I stood up on wobbly legs. "Come here," Dane said. He picked me up, and I let my heels fall as he carried me to his bedroom. I was suddenly so exhausted that I could barely keep my eyes open. Wasn't even sure what time it was.

He brought me into the bathroom, where I had left my toiletry bag earlier, and he set me on my feet. Dane stood behind me with his arm wrapped around my waist and put toothpaste on my toothbrush.

"I can do that," I said. "I'm not helpless."

He kissed the side of my head. "Just getting a little more spoiling in before bedtime."

Once we were both in his bed and snuggled under the covers, Dane pulled me close and tucked me into his chest. "Thank you for everything today," he murmured.

My eyes were closed. I was comfy and warm and already halfway asleep. "You did so much more for me than I did for you."

"You'd be surprised," he said, just before I drifted off.

✧

I woke up to watery sunlight and Dane snoring quietly beside me.

Yawning, I stretched my arms over my head. I had slept hard and deeply. Couldn't remember the last time I'd been able to turn my brain off that much. No dreams.

But maybe that was the result of two amazing orgasms and the best day ever.

Dane was still out, so I tried not to jostle him as I sat up against the pillows and looked around. I hadn't paid a ton of attention to his bedroom yesterday, between hurrying to get ready and then being half asleep when he carried me in here. Like the rest of his apartment, it was stylish, like a designer had put it together. Lots of dark, neutral colors and masculine furniture. Modern and tasteful, but nothing too daring or personal. It kind of reminded me of Dane's hotel suite in Silver Ridge.

Actually, his apartment didn't fit him that well. Now that I was getting to know Dane better, his adventurousness stood out. Made me wonder if he had just not wanted to spend his time on decorating, or if he didn't really feel at home here.

The California King mattress was an excellent choice, though. I starfished my arms and legs, enjoying the sheer fact of taking up space. This thing was nearly as big as my entire bedroom at home.

Which made me feel a twinge of homesickness. I had texted our family group chat yesterday, letting them know I had arrived in New York. But I missed Maisie. Piper and Emma too. And, *fine*, my brothers. Maybe I would have a chance to make some calls today, depending on what Dane had planned before the wedding ceremony.

Dane lifted his head, his hair adorably messy and his eyes slitted like he had just opened them. "What are you doing all the way over there?"

"Stretching out. This is nice."

"But you're too far away."

I wriggled away even further, and Dane retaliated by reaching under the blankets and grabbing my ankles. I screamed as he pulled me across the bed and started tickling me. He used one arm and the rest of his body to pin me down, and even though I screamed again because I hated being tickled, I loved that feeling of him on top of me. The warm weight of him, making me feel like I knew exactly where I was, right in this moment and nowhere else. I certainly didn't want to be anywhere else.

We were also still naked from last night, so I wasn't surprised when I felt Dane's erection nudging against me.

"Good morning," I said, full of innuendo.

"It's an excellent morning. But it could be even better."

"I think so too." I wrapped my legs around him. Dane went to kiss me, and I turned my head. "Wait, let me go brush my teeth."

"Don't want to. I can't wait that long to kiss you." His mouth claimed mine, and he was right, this was much better. Within seconds, I forgot about my potential morning breath and got lost in him. The way his tongue glided in my mouth and his cock felt heavy between my legs.

We had been building up to this moment for weeks now. Since the night I had almost slept with him before even knowing his name. And now here we were, in his fancy apartment in Manhattan, stretched out in his huge bed, with no more doubts about what either of us wanted. Hours of time and nothing standing in our way.

"You want me?" he asked, already reaching over to his bedside table for a condom. Then my stomach made a growling sound, and he burst out laughing. "Actually, it sounds like what you really want is breakfast."

I swatted his arm with the back of my hand, though I was laughing too. "Pretend you didn't hear that. Breakfast later. I want you now."

"That monster in your stomach sounded pretty insistent."

I pressed the heels of my hands to my eyes. "Dane, please. This is so embarrassing."

He chuckled, getting up and rounding the bed to pull the covers off of me. "I happen to think it's hilarious. But it also proves I'm doing a bad job of taking care of you. Come on. I'm going to feed you." He winked. "You know I love watching you eat."

"Well, at least there's that." Since my growling stomach had ruined the mood, I got up. Dane pulled on a pair of sweatpants, throwing me a T-shirt to wear from his dresser drawer. I made a quick visit to the bathroom and took care of brushing my teeth. Much better.

In the kitchen, Dane started the coffee, then opened the fridge. "Eggs and bacon sound good? Or I could run to the corner and get some pastries."

I peered around him at the fridge shelves. "Oh, cheesecake! Yummy. That's what I want."

"For breakfast?"

"Yep."

He paused, blinking. "You are so damn adorable."

"What? Cheesecake is every bit as healthy as champagne and pastries. Or unhealthy."

He kissed the top of my head. "You're just proving my point. Cheesecake it is. But I'm having eggs."

"I'll make them. Scrambled? Sunny side up?"

"Sunny side. Because I'm in a very sunny mood." He grinned, and I went up on my toes to kiss him.

The cheesecake was to die for. And so good with coffee, which suggested that I should have cheesecake for breakfast a lot more often.

"Should we go back to bed after this?" I asked.

Dane finished the last of his coffee. "That is extremely tempting." Then a furrow appeared between his brows. "It's already ten though. I needed to take care of something this morning."

I licked my fork. "An errand?"

"Not exactly. I'm going to visit my mom. You could come with me, or you could hit a museum instead. There's several you could walk to, or—"

"I would love to go with you. I'd be honored to meet your mom. If you're good with that."

He exhaled and lifted his eyes. I hadn't even realized he was holding his breath. "Definitely. I want you to meet her."

TWENTY-FOUR

Grace

DANE SEEMED nervous as we left the apartment. Well, as close to nervous as he ever got. A wrinkle of worry between his eyes and a tight frown instead of his easy smile.

"I called the nurse while you were in the shower," he said. "It sounds like mom is having a good day. But that's relative, you know? Hard to tell how things will go until we're there."

"I get it."

"Mind if we stop at a bakery on the way? Mom has a weakness for strawberry tarts." A smile reappeared on his gorgeous face. "Kind of like you and your cheesecake. You moaned more eating that than when I had my mouth on you last night."

That was so not true. But he had me grinning as I remembered how much I had enjoyed both experiences. "Never stand between a woman and her dessert."

"Words to live by."

He'd said his parents' place was within walking distance. I expected I would see his father there, and I wasn't looking forward to it.

Mr. Knightly hadn't been rude to me last night. He had laughed at my little joke about Dane being charming. But he hadn't been welcoming either. It didn't matter so much what

Dane's father thought of *me*, though. I cared a lot more about whatever he had said to upset Dane before I found him out on the balcony.

Dane could obviously fight his own battles, but I was starting to feel protective of him. Maybe that was silly when the man was a decorated soldier and richer than I could ever dream of being. But for all his over-the-top confidence, Dane was incredibly kind and generous and intelligent too. It made me angry that his father didn't value him.

How was it possible for anyone to get to know this man and not think the world of him?

At least it was a beautiful day. It was chillier than yesterday, and I wore a coat that Dane had bought me at one of the boutiques. It was off-white and made of wool, both warm and fashionable enough to wear with my gown to the wedding tonight. Dane looked effortlessly handsome with his dark-gray peacoat and a navy cashmere scarf.

We stopped at the bakery, where Dane greeted the woman behind the counter by name, and she grinned so wide when she saw him it was like the sun coming up. She went right to the strawberry tarts in the case. Dane bought four of them, since they were individually sized, and the woman boxed them up.

The building where his parents lived was half a block away. The doorman ushered us in, warmly greeting Dane, and then we were in the elevator and on our way up.

I started fidgeting, but Dane reached for my hand and squeezed it.

I was surprised when he didn't use a key, knocking at the door instead, but it opened up almost that same moment. I assumed the doorman downstairs had called up.

"Morning, Dane!"

"Hey, Mary Beth. Good to see you. This is Grace." After I greeted her, Dane tugged me along by my hand as my head swiveled, amazed that this place was called an apartment at all. It was huge. Beautifully decorated. Yet, unlike Dane's place, it actually felt like people lived here.

When we walked into the kitchen, a woman in an apron exclaimed, "Look who it is!"

She gave him a hug, and Dane introduced her as Rhiannon, their chef.

Rhiannon gasped. "You've brought a young lady home? How exciting. Will you and your girlfriend stay for lunch?"

He smiled, glancing over at me, but he didn't correct her. "Sadly, I don't think we'll have time for lunch. Lots to do before the wedding."

The chef pursed her lips and dropped her voice to a murmur. "I'm just glad I'm not the caterer. Your brother's future wife has been putting them through their paces."

Dane barked a laugh and patted her on the shoulder. "I'm glad you were spared that as well."

Rhiannon gave me a conspiratorial look and dropped her voice. "But if my favorite member of the Knightly family needs a wedding caterer in the future," she said in a mock whisper, "I'd be happy to do it. Just don't tell this one I said he was my favorite."

Oh lordy. I felt my blush getting even worse.

But Dane just laughed again and put his arm around me. "We'll let you know." He asked for some plates and silverware, and Rhiannon went to grab them, along with some linen napkins.

"Shouldn't you tell her that we're not..." I whispered.

He shrugged. "Doesn't do any harm. Let her think what she wants. Easier than explaining our weekend arrangement."

"Good point." It was getting harder for me to explain it even to myself. And the fact that it would be over in just a few days.

Dane was...wow. So much more than I'd imagined he would be.

I wasn't the only one who saw it, either. Everyone we'd met this morning seemed to love him.

I helped carry the plates and napkins, and we went up a grand staircase to the second floor. Again, how was this called an apartment when it was the size of a mansion? I kept bracing myself to run into his father, but there was no sign of the man. Until I saw the photos on the walls upstairs. I recognized Dennis and Kip Knightly from meeting them last night. And there was a younger Dane in all his handsome glory, though his smiles didn't look so bright.

A beautiful blond woman stood beside the Knightly men, her charisma vibrant even through the two-dimensional images.

That had to be Dane's mom. Isadora.

Dane didn't glance at the photos, instead ushering me along. "Mom's wing is this way." We went down a hall, then stepped into a room full of cabinets and shelves holding medical supplies. A woman wearing purple scrubs looked up from organizing the contents of a plastic box and smiled.

"Well, well. You're back in town. We missed you."

"I brought someone special with me. Grace, this is Jasmine Choi. Chief of medicine around here."

"Oh, this man and his flattery." Jasmine's eyes twinkled. "But I'm assuming you know about that, Grace."

I nodded. "Believe me, I do."

"Izzy's in the sitting room. She's in fine form today. You can go on in. I see you've brought her favorite?"

"Yep, and extra for you."

Jasmine shook her head. "You're hell on my blood sugar," she muttered. "Go on."

Dane's hand slid back into mine. He hesitated for a split second, a cloud passing over his features. Then we walked through the doorway into the next room. "Hey, Mom. How are you this morning?"

A woman in her sixties with thick, gray-blond hair sat on the couch. She wore light-blue pants, a turtleneck, and a cardigan draped over her shoulders. She arched one sculpted eyebrow. "I'm all right, but they insist on keeping it colder than a witch's butthole in winter around here."

I snorted a shocked laugh, and Dane grinned. "I'll see about turning up the thermostat. Mom, this is Grace O'Neal. And Grace, this is Isadora Knightly. Izzy to her friends."

She grasped my hand. "I can't promise to remember your name. The old memory isn't what it once was." Her manicured finger tapped against her temple. "But I can promise to try."

"That's all any of us can do, right?" I sat in the chair across from her.

"I like those glasses. They make you look smart. That's good. You'll keep us on our toes."

"I can promise to try," I said, and she laughed, pointing a finger at me.

"A sense of humor too. Thank goodness. Hardly anyone else around here has one of those."

Dane set the tarts and the plates on the coffee table, lowering himself gently onto the couch beside his mom. I mostly stayed quiet as Dane chatted with her. It was hard to tell if she recognized him exactly, but she seemed to be enjoying herself. Especially when he served the tarts.

She continued with her sharp quips too, and I could imagine how this woman had the determination to win Olympic medals and climb mountains. It wasn't fair that a disease was causing Izzy's mind to fail her.

Yet watching Dane with her… It was a whole new side of him that made me admire the man even more.

After an hour, Jasmine came in. "Sorry to break up the party, but Miss Izzy is probably getting tired."

Izzy huffed. "You would think I had important places to be with the schedule they keep me on."

Jasmine chuckled. "Two more minutes." She left the room.

Dane sat forward, elbows on his knees. "Mom, today is Kip's wedding. I don't know if he had a chance to come by and see you lately, but I'm sure he wishes you could be there."

"That sounds nice." She did seem like she was tiring out. Her gaze had started to lose focus.

But after Dane said he loved her and kissed her cheek, she looked straight into his eyes.

"Your brother's been having a terrible time. They've...they've been..."

"You mean *Kip*? Has he been here to see you?" Izzy didn't respond. Dane reached for her hand. "Mom, has Kip been here? Did he say something to you?"

"There's a lady who helps me sometimes. Could you ask her to come in here? I'm tired."

Dane sat back, emotions playing across his face before they vanished. Like he was pulling a mask into place. "Sure, Mom. I'll go get Jasmine." He lifted his chin at me. "We'd better head out."

TWENTY-FIVE

Dane

I LIKED to think I was a logical guy. Not overly driven by emotion. But right now, both my head and my heart were all over the place.

What had my mom meant when she'd mentioned my brother? Had she known what she was saying, or had she been thinking of something from the past? Something entirely unrelated?

It was confusing as hell, and I had no idea what to do with it.

Once we were back on the street, I sucked in two lungfuls of city air. Car exhaust, garbage, cigarettes, and cloying perfume from some woman walking by. Radically different from the clean mountain air of Silver Ridge. Yet familiar enough to ground me.

If Kip was having some kind of difficulty, who did he have to blame but himself?

I put my arm back around Grace, where it belonged. "I thought we'd walk through Central Park. Get some food and have a picnic."

"That sounds great. You can talk about your mom too, if you want."

I massaged the back of her neck. "I'd much rather show you a good time."

"Dane—"

I stopped walking in the middle of the sidewalk, pulling Grace into the shelter of my arms. Somebody cursed as they had to veer around us, but I didn't fucking care. "This is what I need right now. To focus on you." I pressed a kiss to her mouth. "That's the best thing you can give me."

"Okay," she whispered. "I'd love to see Central Park. With you."

"Excellent, because I'm sticking to you the rest of today. There's no getting rid of me. Sorry."

"You have a strange sense of what's a privilege and what's a punishment."

I laughed, steering us in the direction of the park.

We walked the paths aimlessly for a while. It was a perfect fall day. A bite to the air, but a blue sky and sunny.

"The fall colors are so different here than in Silver Ridge," she said.

"Which do you like better?"

"Nothing compares to home."

She was right, but home was a more complicated concept for me.

Grace took pictures of the scenery and sent them to her family and friends in Colorado. I asked someone to take a picture of the two of us, because I hated selfies. Then we got gyros from a cart and I talked Grace into ice cream. "I'm going to gain ten pounds on this trip," she complained.

"I have a workout planned for us later."

"Is that a sex reference?"

"Definitely a sex reference."

She giggled and slid her hand into mine.

While we digested, I picked a shady spot for us to relax beneath a tree. Grace took off her coat, and I hung it on a branch so it wouldn't get dirty. I spread out my peacoat on the ground for us to lie down. We stared up into yellow-orange leaves.

"Mom has good days and bad days," I said. "Today, she was a

lot like herself. But sometimes she's scared and angry. I hate that I can't make it better for her."

Grace turned onto her side to face me, but she didn't say anything. Just waiting for me to go on.

I told her about the early symptoms and Mom's diagnosis. How early-onset Alzheimer's tended to progress more quickly, which had been true in Mom's case. None of it was easy for me to talk about. Especially the way that Mom had seemed to lose the spark that had driven her. Basic things became a struggle. Remembering her past. Remembering her family.

"I can't imagine how hard that must be," Grace said. "For all of you."

"You lost your mother."

"But it happened fast. That was incredibly hard too, but not in the same way. It's something that's not fair about grief. So many people go through similar things, yet for each person it feels unique. No one else can ever fully understand."

I nodded. "My father refuses to talk about it. Refuses to consider relocating her, even though I'm sure Mom would love being near mountains again. She never really liked the city. Only lived here because of him. I'd love to bring her to Silver Ridge. But I can't imagine Dad agreeing."

"You said that you joined Knightly Global for your mom. She wanted you and your dad to reconcile."

"Yes. It was after her diagnosis. After she was already struggling, and I thought if I could make her happy during her moments of clarity, it would be worth it."

"Do you still feel that way?"

"Not sure." I closed my eyes. "Grace, I know it seems like I have my shit together. But I don't."

Fuck. That was maybe the most honest thing I'd ever said to her, or to *anyone*.

"That's a relief. You seem like the perfect man sometimes. I started to wonder if you're a robot."

I opened my eyes and looked at her. "I'm nowhere near perfect."

"Perfect is boring. And it turns out that boring is not my thing at all." Grace shifted so she was lying on top of me. She folded her arms on my chest.

"What *is* your thing?" I lifted my head to nip at her lower lip.

"Mostly...you."

"That's convenient, because you're my thing too."

We kissed until someone roller-bladed by and whistled at us. I was also starting to get hard, and I didn't want to be *that* guy in the park. "Continue this back at my apartment?"

"Yes, please."

Fifteen minutes later, we were stumbling into my place while we kissed and pulled at each other's coats. A quick glance around showed we were definitely alone this time. No surprise visitors.

I pushed off my shoes. Tossed my scarf onto the entryway marble floor. Broke away from her mouth long enough to tug off my sweater, then hers. I put my arms around her hips and lifted her up, sucking on her neck. Her skin was a little salty from our time in the sun. I wanted to lick every inch of her.

Grace tightened her legs around my waist, and I carried her into my bedroom. I was too eager to play games or be subtle.

This morning, it had felt like more layers between us had been stripped away, and I wanted every physical barrier gone between us too. As much as was possible, anyway.

I set her on the bed and undid her jeans, pulling them down. "You're gonna have to help me a little. These are sexy, but they're tight enough to give you denim burn if I'm not careful."

She laughed and wriggled her hips, helping me get the jeans off of her. Mine were far looser and were gone in a few seconds. My boxer briefs went next.

"I'm taking these off myself," she said, pushing down her panties. "Don't want to lose another pair."

I smiled, remembering how I'd gone a little feral on her last night. But I had no regrets. "Happy to take you lingerie shopping anytime for replacements."

"How about you focus on what I'm *not* wearing right now." She had just stripped off her bra. I stretched out over her, skin to skin. A groan rumbled out of me.

"I love buying clothes for you, but you're right. This is your best look by far."

Last night, in the warm, soft glow of the lamp in my living room, Grace had been straight out of an erotic dream. But this afternoon, she was bathed in bright sunlight, and I could see even more details of her. Every dimple and freckle and the exact slope of her curves.

"You're studying me like there'll be a test later."

"I didn't study nearly this hard for tests." No, I only paid this much attention to things I cared about. Things I wanted to understand from every angle.

This was a woman who'd already gotten under my skin more than anyone ever had. Who was sexy and smart and fun. Who had sat next to me during an hour-long visit with my mom and got the imperious Izzy Knightly laughing.

I was a lucky, lucky man.

We made out for a while, our hands exploring while our bodies rubbed together. Such a simple pleasure, but it heightened the heat and the anticipation between us.

Then I nudged her to roll over onto her stomach. "I need to admire the other side of you now."

I kissed my way down her back, paying a visit to every knob of her spine. Her behind was especially cute. Perfectly round in my hands. I rubbed my cock against her butt cheeks, and the moan she made was pornographic.

"I might lose my mind if you make me keep waiting," she said.

"Waiting for what?"

Grace rolled over onto her back inside the cage of my arms. "You know."

"Getting shy again all of a sudden?" I rocked my erection against her belly. "Tell me you want my cock, gorgeous."

"I want it."

"How much?"

She arched up against me. "So badly. I've wanted you since the night of the masquerade ball."

"Then why didn't you come to me that night?"

"I was...scared."

I stopped, straightening my arms so that I could look down at her and see her full expression. "Are you scared now?"

She seemed to be thinking about it, and I was glad for that. Because any doubt or hesitation on her part was the last thing I wanted.

"No," Grace whispered. She reached up and touched my face. "I'm not. You said you'd take care of me. I believe you."

I leaned down to kiss her, wanting to seal those words on her lips.

I grabbed protection and suited up. She was soaking wet. Pushing inside of her was effortless, though she was tight enough to make my head swim with the way she gripped me. She inhaled sharply.

"Good?" I asked.

"Mmhmm. Yes. You're just...a lot."

I grinned. "A lot in a good way?"

"In *all* the good ways. Keep going. I'm ready for more."

"I like you greedy for me."

Once I was deep inside her, I paused and kissed her forehead. I needed a moment to gather my composure. I'd been acting cocky, but this was intense for me too.

I'd felt the sting of rejection when she bailed on me the night of the masquerade. But this was so much better than an anonymous hookup. And in a way, a little scary too. Because of how much this woman already meant to me.

"Fuck me, Dane," Grace murmured. "Please."

"I know, baby. I've got you." I started to move. Slow drags of my cock, then surging back inside.

Grace dug her hands into my hair, legs squeezing my sides. "More," she begged.

"It'll be better if I don't rush."

"No, it'll be better if you give it to me hard. Be rough with me. I won't break."

Damn. Grace's inner bad girl was present and accounted for, and I was here for it.

I put my hips into each thrust. My headboard banged into the wall, and Grace rewarded me with loud moans that just made my blood burn hotter. Tingles gathered at the base of my spine.

My hand reached back to close around one of her ankles, and I lifted her leg up onto my shoulder. I kept up that relentless pace, angling my hips until she gasped and cried out. The sound she made, the tightening of her body. That was all I needed to send me barreling toward my own climax. I pushed as deep inside her as I could go until I was spent.

I collapsed beside her with a groan. Grace rolled onto her side to rest her head on my chest. We lay like that for a while as the beams of sunlight slowly shifted.

Finally, I asked, "What if I told you I'd like to keep seeing you after this weekend?"

She lifted her head to look up at me. "That wasn't our deal."

"So what? I want to negotiate a new one."

"You don't know how long you'll be staying in Silver Ridge."

I grumbled under my breath, not at her but at myself. Because that was true. I wasn't promising her much, was I? "Those are details," I said. "I can figure them out."

"But I have this pact with Piper. We both swore off dating."

I smirked. "You swore off dating? I thought people only did that in movies."

"It's not funny."

I wiped my smirk away. "No, it's not. I'm not laughing. You told me about your trust issues, and I take that very seriously.

Means a lot to me that you've given so much of your trust to me so far. Staying with me after the break-in. This trip." I smoothed my hand over her sex-tangled hair.

"I *want* to trust you."

But... She didn't have to say the rest.

Spending a weekend with me was one thing. Trusting me to take care of her for a few days.

Giving me her heart? That was something entirely different.

I reached out to cradle her face. "And I want to earn it. Let's enjoy the rest of this trip together. I'll work on the details for afterward. Then we can see what happens. Deal?"

Her teeth tugged at her lower lip.

"Deal," she whispered.

TWENTY-SIX
Grace

"HERE WE GO AGAIN," Dane said with a sigh. "The Kip and Bristol show."

We were in the car on our way to the wedding ceremony. "At least they'll be busy the whole time with the event and their guests," I said. "They'll hardly have time to notice we're there."

"Good point."

"I bet we'll even have fun."

"What are we betting?"

I leaned into him and whispered, "If I'm right, you can tie me up again."

He gave me a hot look, shifting against the leather seat.

We'd spent as much of the afternoon as possible naked in his bed. Enjoying each other, napping, snuggling under the covers.

We'd talked about our families too. Both the good memories and the bad. Dane told me stories about his time with Ashford in the Army, things I'd never heard before. It was strange to think of how close Dane had been with my brother before I even knew him. But at the same time, that connection between us was comforting. Like we'd always been destined to meet.

Ugh, I was getting so romantic about this man. It wasn't a good thing.

He'd asked me that afternoon to keep seeing him after this trip was over, but how could that possibly end well?

"You're scowling," Dane said. "What's going through your mind?"

I shook my head, smoothing out my expression. "Nothing."

"You sure?" He studied me.

"Sibling stuff, I guess." That was close enough.

Dane nodded, glancing out the window. "Speaking of siblings, I asked Kip last night about Dirk Lancaster and Nina Jamison. Kip claimed to know nothing, and I'm pretty sure he was lying to me."

"You think Kip knows Nina Jamison?"

"It's a hunch. But it's possible. And then my mom mentioned him today, saying he's having a rough time... Makes me wonder if Kip told Mom some part of it."

"You think Kip would do that? Like, confessing his sins?"

"I don't know. But I have an investigator looking into the different pieces, so I guess we'll find out how it all fits together. Then we'll decide what to do about it."

I was glad that Dane kept saying *we*. I hated to think his brother could be involved in whatever had resulted in someone breaking into my home. But it was clear Dane considered me a part of this, no matter what he learned about Kip. He wasn't going to shut me out.

"What else do you want to do in NYC?" Dane asked. "After the brunch tomorrow, we'll be free. We can do anything you like."

It was bittersweet to think about tomorrow being my final full day here. "Hmm. Maybe some more touristy stuff. Oh, the subway! I want to see what that's like."

"The subway? You really are adorable," Dane said, and I stuck my tongue out at him. He kissed my head. "Alright, subway it is. I will take you any other places you want to go. Even the Circle Line boat tour."

"That too! Thank you."

He kissed me again, lips lingering on mine.

Dane's driver, Ben, pulled into the driveway of a modern tower, all glass and steel and striking architecture. "Your family owns this hotel?" I asked, peering up.

"Yep. Another Knightly Global property. This one's pretty swanky. My father's pride and joy."

"Bristol's family owns hotels too, right?"

"They do. Kip and Bristol had plenty of wedding venues to choose from." Dane leaned into me, speaking against my ear. "Harcourt Hotels has name-brand recognition. But technically, Knightly Global is the bigger enterprise. Choosing this hotel was a compliment to my dad. Kip is all about scoring those brownie points with my father."

We got out and went through the lobby doors, joining other people in evening wear. I was in a slinky, pale-green gown with cap sleeves. Dane wore a tux. Not the one he'd worn to the Silver Ridge hotel grand opening, but another that was equally well-tailored and hugged all his muscles. I'd never known it was possible for a man to be this sexy, but Dane managed it like it wasn't even hard. I had spent an hour making my hair and makeup just right, while he'd spent all of ten minutes getting ready. So not fair.

The ceremony was being held on an outdoor patio way up on the twentieth floor. When we stepped out of the elevator, a server holding flutes of champagne greeted us, along with classical music played by a dozen musicians over by a reflecting pool. Flowers and greenery were everywhere, draped in garlands and placed in dramatic, tall arrangements.

Dane held my hand and steered me through the crowd, greeting people as he went.

"Cutting it close," his father said under his breath when we reached our seats near the front on the groom's side. "The ceremony's about to start."

Dane lifted his champagne flute. "Great to see you too, Dad."

I had to give it to Bristol and Kip's wedding planner. The ceremony was beautiful. The patio overlooked a Manhattan cityscape, with the sun sinking behind us and painting the surrounding buildings in vivid colors. I wasn't a huge fan of the couple, but I couldn't help being affected by the romance of it all. The sweeping music and the heartfelt words of the officiant. Bristol's gorgeous bridal ballgown.

And more than anything, the man beside me, who hadn't let go of my hand once since we'd arrived.

Only one more full day here. Yet as Kip and Bristol exchanged their vows, I wasn't thinking about sightseeing on my final day in NYC. Instead I found myself imagining all the places I wanted to take Dane in Silver Ridge. Little hidden-away hiking trails with breathtaking views. The places Piper and I had played as kids. And of course, I also imagined lots of sex with Dane in his hotel suite overlooking the ski mountain.

I wanted him to be part of my life there. A *real* part.

I didn't want this thing between us to end.

While Dane was called over to pose in some family photos, I took the opportunity to text my best friend. Because after that sudden realization, I was *freaking out*.

ME

Remind me of the general parameters of our no-dating pact?

PIPER

We made it up, girlie. You don't need a loophole if you like him!

Do you like him that much?? 😍

Dane wants us to keep seeing each other.

Then listen to your instincts. Trust yourself. What do YOU want?

Dane interrupted me, resting his hand on my back, and I glanced up in surprise, holding my phone screen against my chest. He looked pensively at my device. "Something wrong?"

"Nope. Finished with the photos?"

"I've officially appeared in photographic evidence that I was here. But my dad demands that I make nice with Mr. Harcourt, father of the bride. It should be just a few minutes, but—"

"Go, I'm fine. I'll top up my champagne and have some of those hors d'oeuvres I saw waiters carrying around."

"But I hate leaving you alone."

"I am *fine*." I gave him a kiss on the cheek, then pushed him gently in the direction of his father. "Besides, I'm in the middle of a text conversation with Piper."

"Say hi for me. I'll be right back."

I had a few appetizers and sipped champagne, walking over to a quieter side of the patio to admire the scenery.

The hotel really was gorgeous. The place sparkled. Not just the lights of the city, which twinkled in a panorama around us, but the inside of the hotel too. I made a quick visit to the ladies' room, then looked for a spot where I could think for a minute or two, away from the wedding festivities.

I found a sitting area that wasn't occupied, off to one side of a quiet hallway, and sat on a sofa. There was a fireplace with a roaring fire. It reminded me of home. Of everything and everyone that I missed back in Silver Ridge.

I still hadn't answered Piper's question.

What did I want?

Dane had said he would head back to Silver Ridge with me after this trip. He still had work to do with the ski resort, and I was still supposed to be his guide to the town.

How would my brothers react if I came back and Dane and I were a couple?

I didn't worry so much about their disapproval. Ashford and Callum both were forgiving. But they worried about me too much. And Dane's friendship meant so much to Ashford. If things didn't work out between me and Dane, would I be causing permanent damage to their friendship?

If things didn't work out, would my *heart* be able to take it?

I had been terrified that I would trust the wrong man, fall for him, and then he'd turn his back on me. Leave the way my father had, or hurt me even worse than that.

But deep down, way in the center of me where I really knew what was true, I believed that Dane wasn't like that. We might not work out, but not because he wasn't trustworthy.

Heaven help me, I wanted Dane to be my boyfriend.

I was about to text Piper back, because I had my answer, and I didn't want to leave her hanging. Then I glanced over, catching movement from the corner of my eye, and every part of me went cold.

The sofa where I sat was partially concealed by the fireplace, so he hadn't seen me. But I'd gotten a good enough look to recognize the man as he walked down the corridor. A shaved head, a salt-and-pepper goatee.

The same man I'd seen last night at the rehearsal dinner. The guy who'd confronted me at the ski resort back in Silver Ridge.

He was here in New York, and this time, I knew I *definitely* wasn't imagining it.

I stood up, quietly crossing the sitting area while keeping myself mostly hidden behind the fireplace. I watched the man's back as he strode down the hall with purpose. Like he had somewhere important to be.

Who the heck was he?

I wasn't going to let him vanish this time. At the very least, I could find out where he was going, and there would be security cameras around here that would catch an image of his face. The police could identify him. Unless the cameras conveniently "glitched" again, like the security cams at the ski resort...

No, I couldn't let that happen. I had to get a picture of the man myself.

I followed as closely as I dared, while still keeping some distance between us. I kept my phone up with the camera ready, which would be an excuse to keep my head down in case the guy looked back. I would look like I was messing around on my phone and not paying him any attention.

The man turned a corner, and I took a few quick steps, hoping to catch up. I was about to peek around to see what he was doing. But then his voice rang out.

"Did you think I wouldn't find you here?"

I froze up against the wall, expecting him to dart out and grab me. My heart thrummed so hard I couldn't make out the individual beats.

Then someone else spoke. A woman. "I don't have time to—"

"You'll make time. You've been avoiding me. Makes me think you have something to hide."

I carefully angled my phone so that just the camera lens edged past the corner. Using my thumb, I snapped several photos. My phone was on silent, so it didn't make any noise.

"I'm just trying to get by, like always," the woman said.

"You do what I tell you to. Right now, I want to know where Nina is."

My hand shook as it held the phone. They had to mean Nina Jamison. I switched the camera setting to video and hit record.

"I don't know. Nobody's seen her in weeks since that ski resort in Colorado."

"But I'll bet she's been in touch with you."

"Seriously, Vincent, I have no idea."

So that was his name. Vincent.

"It's not my fault she slipped away and disappeared," the woman said. "Bother somebody else about that, not me. It's not my problem."

"Not your fucking problem?"

There was a scuffling sound, then a muffled cry. I risked glancing around the corner, still recording with my phone. Vincent had shoved the woman up against the wall. I hadn't seen her at the wedding, but she was dressed in an evening gown, her blond hair up in a twist. His hand was over her mouth, while his other squeezed her roughly by the arm.

"Get this straight, Lexi. If I don't find out where Nina is soon, I'm going to get suspicious that her friends are helping her stay hidden. And what do you think I'll do if I find out you're involved in that?"

Her eyes were wide and terrified. She tried to say something, but her voice was muffled by his hand.

"I'll make sure that pretty face of yours can never be shown in public again. But I can already see that you're not listening. You think it's not your problem. So I'm going to have to show you that it very much *is* your problem." He suddenly wrenched her arm at an angle that made me flinch in sympathy. I saw the agony in her eyes, and I couldn't stop myself from taking a step toward them into the next hallway.

"Stop!" The shout left my lips before I'd even realized I was doing it. "Let her go!"

Vincent went still. His head swiveled in my direction. "Excuse me?"

I lifted my phone, still recording. "I'm filming this, asshole. So you're going to let her go. Right now." My whole body was shaking, but I couldn't just hide behind the corner and watch him hurt her. It wasn't right.

Somebody had to stand up to men like this, and if I stayed silent, what did that say about me?

"What's happening here is none of your concern."

Lexi shook her head, eyes begging me not to do this, but I stood my ground, lifting my chin. "It is now. Leave her alone."

Vincent shoved Lexi, and she went sprawling on the carpet. He turned fully toward me. "You're brave, I'll give you that. But you're also very fucking stupid."

He started toward me. I walked backward, still holding up my phone, then realized that I had to get out of here. Shit. Okay, maybe this hadn't been the best idea.

I pivoted and ran.

A vise-like grip landed on my shoulder, spinning me and pushing me up against the wall so hard I felt my insides rattle.

Vincent was in my face, pure malice bleeding from his gaze. "I remember you. You helped Nina get away that night."

"What? No, I—"

"I'd planned to let that go. But you should've kept your nose where it belonged. Out of my business."

I sucked in a breath to scream. But a blow landed to my chest, robbing my lungs of air. Then Vincent's fist lashed out again, and pain exploded across my nose before my vision went dark.

TWENTY-SEVEN

Dane

THIS SO-CALLED business meeting was a farce. My father didn't actually want me to talk, just to stand here like some kind of show pony.

But you know what? I was going with it.

If I could smile and shake the hand of Kip's new father-in-law and make this all go faster, then I was willing to do it. I could be nice.

I just wanted to get back to Grace so we could enjoy the rest of our evening together.

After my father released me, I went looking for Grace. But she wasn't by the bar or mingling with the other guests at cocktail hour. I tried the dining room, where the staff was still putting the finishing touches on the tables before dinner.

Grace wasn't there either.

But I spotted Ainsley on her phone in a quiet corner of the patio, like she was avoiding her family responsibilities as much as I wanted to. I went over to her. "Enjoying your duties as maid of honor?"

Ainsley put her phone away, rolling her eyes but not bothering to look guilty. "Bristol is always a lot, but on her wedding day? Bridezilla doesn't even cover it. She and Kip are off somewhere, so I made my escape."

I chuckled. "I was just roped into a talk about our fathers' potential hotel deal. The excitement never ends."

"If only our parents would leave us out of it." She crossed her arms over her bridesmaid dress. It was plain black, since Bristol and Kip had gone with a black-and-white theme. "I didn't get the chance to apologize for our fathers' scheming about you and me being an item."

I shrugged. "Par for the course. I didn't let it get to me, and it sounds like you're the same."

She laughed. "I'm just grateful your date didn't hate me over that whole thing. Not like you need my approval, but I like her."

I smiled fondly. "I like Grace too. A lot. I was just looking for her, actually. Last place I can think of to check is the ladies' room. Not exactly my turf, though."

Ainsley set her empty champagne flute on a waiter's passing tray. "I can check the bathroom for you. I'm all for a strategic alliance. Even if it's not the one our fathers were plotting, heaven forbid."

We passed through the maze of wedding guests guzzling free booze and eating hors d'oeuvres.

"Have you noticed all the plotting that Kip and Bristol have been doing lately?" Ainsley said when no one else was in earshot. "It's painful to watch. They think they're so subtle."

I tensed. "What exactly do you think they're up to?"

"Pretty sure it's something to do with the hotel partnership. But more than anything, cutting you and me out of things."

That tracked. Yet I couldn't understand my brother's latest tactics, and I wondered if Ainsley had any insights there. "Do you know a guy named Dirk Lancaster, by any chance? An investor in one of Kip's projects."

We paused by a sitting area just outside the women's restroom. There was no one else here, so it was safe enough to talk. "Lancaster?" Ainsley asked. "Sure. Bristol knew him before Kip did, though. She's the one who introduced them."

Now that was interesting. "What about a woman named Nina Jamison?"

Ainsley looked thoughtful, then shook her head. "That name doesn't ring a bell. Why? Who is she?"

Before I could answer, someone screamed.

Ainsley and I exchanged a concerned glance, then followed the sound down the hall and around the corner. A woman with gray hair was bent over, hovering over someone else lying on the carpet.

"What's going on?" I asked, trying to get a better view.

"I just came out of my hotel room and found her here." The woman stood, and I saw who was lying there.

My heart lurched straight up into my throat.

"Call an ambulance." My voice was harsh and guttural.

"Oh my God," Ainsley said. "Is that *Grace*?"

I knelt beside her. Grace was crumpled on the floor like a rag doll. She had a gash on the bridge of her nose, and blood covered her face. Her glasses were broken. She blinked slowly like she was just coming back to consciousness.

"Dane?"

I'd heard people talk about seeing red, and I had experienced something similar before, but right now I saw fucking black. "Someone call a fucking ambulance," I shouted.

"On it," Ainsley responded.

I couldn't risk moving her. Instead I tried to murmur comforting words, gently holding her down by the shoulders when she tried to get up. "You need to stay right there. Don't move yet." I had to do something about that cut on her nose. Wrenching off my jacket, then my shirt, I tore a piece of the white fabric to hold against her nose.

"Ice!" I shouted. Then I leaned down close to her again, holding the fabric to the cut. She winced. "Grace, who did this?"

"I..."

She seemed confused and in pain. It took everything in me to stay calm and keep my voice relaxed. "Baby, listen to me. Who did this? Who hurt you?"

"Vincent," she choked out. "My phone... I think he took it."

Vincent. I didn't know that name. But whoever he was, when I found him, I'd make him pay.

I lifted her hand and kissed it. "I'm going to fix this. I swear to you."

"It was my fault," she whispered. Tears spilled from her eyes. "I shouldn't have..."

"This was *not* your fault. Erase that thought from your head. You can tell me the rest of what happened later, but for now, just stay still. I've got you."

"Okay. Don't leave." The fear in her voice knifed through me.

"I'm going to stay with you. No matter what. I'm not going anywhere."

Then I straightened and turned around. A small crowd had started to gather around us. "Get the hotel manager and security up here," I yelled at anyone and everyone who was listening. "Someone named Vincent did this. He could still be in the hotel, and I want him found."

"I'm sure you do," Ainsley said quietly. "So do we all. But if you burst a blood vessel, that isn't going to help Grace."

Ainsley probably had a point. But I felt like I was turning inside out.

Within a few minutes, someone with a first-aid kit ran toward us. A member of the hotel staff. He held out an ice pack and a wad of gauze, like this was a simple skinned knee.

"She could have a concussion," I barked. "Where are the damn paramedics?"

Ainsley put her hand on my shoulder. "I'm still on the line with emergency services. They said the ambulance is a couple minutes away. We're going to sort all of this out. Grace will be fine."

But I couldn't stop trembling as waves of rage crashed

through every inch of my body. Someone had hurt her, and I hadn't been there.

I had sworn to Ashford that I would keep his sister safe, and *I hadn't been there.*

I was going to find that piece of shit named Vincent. And I was going to kill him with my bare hands.

✧

I lifted Grace out of the wheelchair and laid her on my bed, making sure the pillows were nice and fluffy.

"How's your pain?" I asked.

"You don't have to ask me about it every five minutes. The pain will get a lot worse if I have to scream out my frustration."

"I certainly don't want that."

"Want to help me work out my frustration in other ways?"

I sat beside her on the mattress as gently as possible. "I might have a tendency to defy authority figures, but you have a concussion. Sex is not on the agenda."

She stuck out her lower lip. "At least kiss me. This is the first time since yesterday we've been alone together, and I'm sick of feeling like an invalid. It sucks."

I stretched out beside Grace and brushed my lips over hers.

"A real kiss," she insisted. "Please?"

"All right, gorgeous. I can't deny you."

Annoyance flashed in her eyes. "I'm hardly gorgeous right now."

The lead weight that had been sitting on my chest since I had found her last night seemed to get even heavier. "Yes, you are."

We had spent all night and much of the morning in the hospital getting her checked out. Grace had a concussion and some bruised ribs. She was lucky that her attacker hadn't broken her nose. But there were bruises spreading out over her beautiful face beneath the bandage. He'd broken her glasses too, but she'd packed a spare set in her bag. Margot had brought them to the hospital.

Our mouths connected again, my lips and my tongue gliding more firmly against hers. But I stopped myself, pulling back sooner than I wanted to.

"The moment you're better, I plan to show you just how irresistible I find you. But for now, I'm going to be gentle. For my sake as much as yours." Because if I added even a little to the pain she'd already been through, I wouldn't be able to forgive myself. "Now, you should get some rest. You're barely keeping your eyes open."

"It's these pain meds. I hate them."

"But your body needs sleep. I'll be right here with you."

She shifted around uncomfortably. "I was thinking about what you said last night. That it's not my fault."

"Because it's *not*."

"I know. I agree with you. After having more time to process what happened, I don't regret trying to help Lexi. But I'm sure she's still in danger. Nina too. That guy, *Vincent*, he was so... *awful*."

In the back of my mind, I couldn't stop repeating every word Grace had told me about what happened. A doom loop. It was going to haunt me. Knowing I had been just a few minutes away with no clue that she'd been in danger.

Grace had been sticking up for some woman she didn't even know. I couldn't get over that. How courageous she was. Vincent had taken her phone, most likely because of the pictures and video she had taken of him.

The same man who'd been in Silver Ridge. Who Grace had apparently seen at the rehearsal dinner, too. Then at Kip's wedding. I mean, what the fuck?

"I know you're worried about those women," I said. "I doubt I've ever met someone with a heart as big as yours. But at the moment, there's nothing that you or I can do."

"Promise you won't keep anything you learn from me. I want to know all of it. Anything you find out."

"Grace—"

"*Promise* me."

"Alright. I promise. If you close your eyes and get some sleep." I brushed a lock of hair from her cheek.

"And I need to tell my brothers. Ashford and Callum will be furious if they hear I was in the hospital and I didn't let them know."

"Taken care of. I texted them last night. *Rest.* That's an order."

"I don't take orders from you." But a yawn obscured the last part of that sentence, and her eyes were already sinking closed. I lay my head on the pillow beside Grace's, smoothing my hand up and down her arm to provide whatever comfort I could.

But inside, I was seething.

NYPD officers had come to the hospital to take our statements. They'd shown up to the hotel as well, but Vincent had gotten away. Same with the woman named Lexi. The police hadn't found a single witness so far who could identify either of them.

Neither Vincent nor Lexi had been on the wedding guest list. And for all the security cameras in my father's hotel, the footage wasn't helping either. Vincent had seemed to know where every camera was and managed to duck his head.

There was a slight possibility that the location of Grace's phone could lead us to the man, but I had no doubt her device was in pieces in a dumpster somewhere not far from the hotel.

There were clearer security images of Lexi, but still no leads on where we might find her.

The detective assigned to the case hadn't even wanted to give me those few details until I'd called in favors from the mayor's office. I hated using my privilege to pull strings that normal people didn't have access to, but for Grace, I would do a lot worse.

All I cared about was finding the man who'd hurt her. Maybe

Vincent was the person who had broken into Grace's home too. The guy seemed to be everywhere, and I had no idea why.

But as soon as we found him, I wanted answers. Like who Nina Jamison really was, why she had disappeared, and why Vincent was so determined to find her.

And what my brother had to do with all this.

At some point in the future, after the police had finished their questioning and Vincent wasn't looking over his shoulder, I was going to make him pay. Didn't matter to me how long it took. I would *not* let him get away with what he had done to Grace.

While Grace napped, I responded to the messages I'd gotten since we left the hospital. I'd been keeping in close touch with Margot. Thank goodness for her, because if she hadn't stepped in to help, I would be going off of zero sleep and zero food. At least I had eaten.

Margot was in her office right now, updating our private investigator and doing anything else she could think of to drum up info for me.

It was more than my family was doing. When Ainsley had suggested she would leave early to check on me and Grace, Bristol had thrown a fit that her maid of honor couldn't leave in the middle of her reception. Kip and Bristol had kept on with their party even though Grace had been attacked.

My dad had stopped by the hospital last night after the reception ended. Predictably, my father protested that he knew nothing about anyone named Vincent, even though the man had turned up at two different properties owned by Knightly Global.

Whether my brother had some connection to Vincent, I didn't know, but I planned to find out. One of the *many* things I was saving for later when I wasn't so damn exhausted.

Finally, I succumbed to my need for sleep. My dreams were not pleasant. Full of images of Grace lying on the floor, bleeding. And me standing beside her, so close yet unable to reach her. *Powerless*.

The buzz of my phone in my pocket woke me. I slipped out

of bed as quietly as possible, glad when Grace continued to sleep peacefully. Closing the door behind me, I answered the call. It was from the doorman downstairs.

"Mr. Knightly, your guests have arrived. Should I send them up?"

"Please do. I appreciate it." I opened my front door and waited there for the elevator. I probably looked ragged. Hadn't shaved, hadn't showered.

I'd contacted Ashford last night, asking him and Callum to come to New York. I'd arranged to fly them on my jet as soon as possible this morning. Grace needed her family close just as much as they deserved to be here in person.

For the first time, I wasn't eager to see my closest friend. But I also *needed* him here. Not for me, but for Grace. And she needed her best friend. Which was why I'd asked Piper to come along too.

When the elevator opened, Ashford and Callum stepped out first. Piper was right behind them. She smiled at me cautiously, while Ashford pulled me in to a hug when he reached me.

"This isn't the way I wanted you to finally visit Manhattan," I said.

Ashford patted my back roughly. "Grace inside?"

"Yeah, she's resting. Come on in."

Ashford pulled back, and Callum stepped toward me next, his expression hard as stone. "Callum," I said. "Thanks for coming."

"I came for my sister, not for you, Knightly. Don't expect me to thank you for the ride on your fancy-ass jet." He brushed past me on his way into my apartment.

Okay, then. Pretty much what I'd expected. But if Callum wanted to take out his anger on me, I could handle it.

Inside, I showed them to the guest rooms to drop off their bags.

"Can I see Grace?" Piper asked.

"Of course. She's in my room asleep, but I'm sure she'd love to see you when she wakes up." I showed Piper to my room, opening the door silently so she could slip inside.

When I returned to the living room, Ashford was sitting on the couch looking like he hadn't slept in a week. And Callum was glowering at me. "Grace is sleeping in your bedroom?" Callum asked, doing nothing to hide his disdain.

Ashford sighed. "Cal, I already told you to expect—"

"Yeah, but I don't get how you're okay with this. He's supposed to be your best buddy, and yet you're fine with him messing around with our sister? Letting her get beat up while he was—" Callum advanced, his arm barring across my chest. He slammed me against the nearest wall. "What the fuck were you doing while some thug was giving my sister a concussion?"

I had told myself I wouldn't react if Ashford or Callum were pissed off at me. I'd planned to accept it and let them get anything they needed off their chests.

But Callum could really be a little punk sometimes.

I grabbed his T-shirt in two fists and spun him, shoving him up against the wall. Switching our places. I kept my voice even, but I brought my nose an inch from his. "I don't blame you for being angry. But don't think for *one second* you're more furious at me than I am at myself. You have no clue how much I care about Grace."

"From where I stand, my sister deserves a hell of a lot more *care* than you've shown her."

I pushed back from him, turned away, and stalked into the kitchen. There, I grabbed a glass, nearly breaking it against the stone counter when I slammed it down and took the most expensive whiskey from my cabinet.

I'd taken one shot and was pouring another when Ashford walked in. "Callum's just upset. We all are."

"You think I blame you? I promised you I'd keep her safe." I nearly choked on the bitterness of those words. *As long as I'm around, I swear I'll do whatever it takes to keep her safe and sound.* I had failed. "Surprised you're not the one who shoved me up against the wall."

I took another glass from the cabinet and pushed it toward

Ashford. He poured himself a finger of whiskey. "Same reason I accepted you dating her. You're a good guy. One of the best, in fact. Not perfect, but last I checked, I had plenty of flaws myself. Including leaving Emma vulnerable in spite of my best efforts. It's what you do next that counts."

My first priority was to make Grace smile again. Make her feel safe again. Make her feel *loved*, because I was falling for her so fast it made my head spin. Seeing her injured, imagining losing her, had only convinced me of that.

But the flip side of that coin was much darker.

"Next? I plan to hunt down the piece of trash who hurt Grace and make him regret he was born."

"That's what I was hoping to hear."

TWENTY-EIGHT

Grace

I WOKE up from my nap in Dane's bed, and I saw a face I had *not* been expecting to see.

"Piper?"

"It's me."

I sat up carefully. "What are you doing here?"

"Your man flew me and your brothers out to see you. Emma's taking care of Maisie and Ollie while we're gone. How are you, sweetheart?" She was doing her best to stay cheerful, which Piper was skilled at even when things were awful. But I knew my friend, and she was shocked by the bruises and bandages on my face.

"I look worse than I feel." Though I didn't feel amazing, that was for sure. My nose and my ribs and head ached. "Seeing you makes everything better. Come here. I'm not going to shatter if you hug me."

"I know that, babe. Just hate seeing you like this." She sat beside me and held me close. Comfort spread through my body, making everything ache just a little less.

I couldn't believe Dane had flown my best friend here on zero notice to see me. Then again...of course he had. It was exactly the kind of thing he'd do, and I was so grateful for it.

I was less excited to see Ashford and Callum, just because I knew they'd be super intense about all this, but it was reassuring to know they were close.

"Do you feel like talking about what happened?"

Piper kept her arms around me as I explained it. I hadn't told her much about Nina Jamison, but Piper caught up fast.

"So this Vincent guy keeps showing up at Knightly Global hotels," she said.

"And the rehearsal dinner."

"Clearly something very shady going on. Dane has no idea what this could be about?"

"None. He thinks his brother could know something, but Kip hates him and won't tell him a thing."

"I guess the rich aren't immune to family drama," she joked. "Are you sure you want to get involved in that? I noticed you didn't object when I called Dane *your man*."

Her tone was teasing, but there was a kernel of sincerity to her question. And I felt my face heating in response. "You asked me yesterday what I really want. I'm pretty sure I want *him*."

Piper bit her lip, eyes shining with excitement. "Yeah? He's worth breaking your no-boyfriend vow?"

"It wasn't a vow." Okay, I'd been pretty dang serious about it. "But I think he's worth it."

She shrugged. "Don't expect me to argue. The man flew me to New York on a private jet. I'd tell you how much free food I ate, but a lady needs to keep some things to herself."

We both laughed. Then I grimaced. "Ow. My ribs. Don't be funny."

"Oops. Sorry. Tell me more about Mr. Hunky McHandsome instead."

So I did. I told her all about the shopping trip on our first afternoon. Visiting Dane's mom yesterday morning. Relaxing in Central Park. It was strange to think of how much had happened in such a short time.

Even with the terrible end to the evening last night, this was still the best trip I'd ever been on. Because of Dane.

Piper squeezed my hand. "He really does sound amazing. Good thing, because I wouldn't give you up for any less of a guy."

"Give me up? What do you mean?"

"Well, Dane's not going to hang around Silver Ridge forever, right? He lives *here*. His mom is here. So if you two really get serious..."

"Who knows what'll happen," I rushed to say, not wanting her to complete that thought. "I don't want to get ahead of myself."

But could I see myself moving to New York? Living in Dane's world instead of mine? Being away from Maisie and Piper and everyone else I considered family?

Dane had said he'd figure out the details of us dating, but what if his solution wasn't something I could live with?

"No, you're right," Piper said. "Forget I said that. I'm just happy you found a guy you can trust, because I know how rare that is."

"You don't think I'm moving *too* fast?"

Piper sighed, getting comfortable against the pillows as she considered my question. "I'm hardly the spokeswoman for falling in love. You know how I feel about that."

I nodded. Her ex-husband deserved a long walk off a mountaintop for the way he'd treated her.

"I have my son to think about," Piper went on, "and there are some things I can never risk again. I'm the founder of the Lonely Harts club for a reason."

"So we can commiserate over our terrible love lives and disappointments."

She laughed. "Exactly. But sweetheart, that doesn't mean *you* should hold yourself back. Trust is scary. But if you've found the real thing with Dane, then go for it. I don't want you to be lonely."

I heard the echoes of what she'd left unsaid.

I don't want you to be lonely just because I am.

✧

Spending time with Piper had been everything I needed. But I still had to deal with my brothers.

After a while, a soft knock came at the bedroom door. Callum opened it and looked in. "Everybody decent?"

"Nope," Piper said. "We're having a pillow fight in our undies in here."

"Thank you so much for that image." Callum stepped inside. I was surprised that Ashford wasn't with him, but they probably didn't want to overwhelm me or something like that.

When Callum got a good look at me, he cursed.

"It could've been a lot worse," I said testily.

"Is that supposed to make me feel better?"

"I thought you being here was all about making *me* feel better." Yes, I sounded petulant. But I was just giving back to Callum what he was dishing out to me.

"Excuse me if I'm not thrilled to see my little sister covered in bruises."

Callum was four years older than me, but the two of us had always been closest among our siblings. Growing up, we'd been united against the two oldest. Callum had a way of making even crappy situations seem fun. Aside from Piper, he knew me better than just about anybody.

But that also meant Callum and I bickered and argued for no reason at all sometimes. Callum had a unique way of driving me nuts, and I knew that I did the same to him.

I loved him fiercely. And if he had been the one in bed all bruised up after being attacked, then I would've been pretty pissed off at the world too. My brothers seemed to forget that I was just as protective of them as they were over me.

"Give me a hug already. I got one from Piper. Now it's your turn. Don't just stand there like a dumbass."

Smirking, Callum crossed the room and gently wrapped me

in his arms. "The firefighters send their love too. They want to send flowers as soon as I give them Dane's address."

"That's sweet. Could they not spread the gossip all over town that I was in the hospital?"

"Probably too late for that. Dixie may or may not be organizing a fundraiser for your medical bills and a parade for when you're back."

I doubted he was even exaggerating. But what could I do but laugh? I loved my neighbors in Silver Ridge. Just like I loved my brothers and my ridiculous roommates. Even when they were over the top.

"I bet her medical bills are covered by a certain billionaire," Piper pointed out.

Callum scowled as he grabbed an upholstered chair and dragged it closer to the bed. "Least he could do after letting her get hurt."

I was tempted to roll my eyes, but that would've been a lot for my headache. Usually Ashford was the grouchy one, not Callum. "Dane didn't *let me* get hurt. He had nothing to do with it, actually."

"But he didn't stop it."

"Dane is protective of me, sometimes annoyingly so, but he listens to me too. He respects what I think and what I feel."

"So do I!"

"And yet you're talking over me, once again!" I winced. I hadn't meant to raise my voice. I closed my eyes and took some deep breaths, ignoring the aches in my body as I calmed down. Callum stayed quiet for once. "I know that you and Ashford worry about me out of love. Probably something to do with how we lost Mom when we were kids. But there's a difference between caring about me and suffocating me, Cal. I'm twenty-eight years old, and you still see me as your baby sister."

He opened his mouth, probably to argue, but then thought better of it.

"Last night, I got hurt because I was trying to help someone.

A woman I didn't know. Was that stupid? Maybe. At first, I was angry at myself. I thought getting hurt was my fault."

Piper frowned, and Callum looked angry again, so I kept going before they could butt in.

"But I won't apologize for trying to stand up for another person. I was terrified, and I probably could've gone about it in a better way, but I didn't run from that situation. I stayed there and faced it." A tear slipped from my eye, and I wiped it away. I didn't want to get emotional right now, but maybe it was for the best. Just so Callum and Piper could see that this came from my heart. "I'm proud of myself."

"Then I'm proud of you too," Callum said softly. "I came here with certain assumptions. I should've waited to hear your side of it."

Piper squeezed my hand again. She was still sitting beside me on the bed, and she hadn't let go during my whole speech. It had felt so good to get all of that out. "Thank you. It means a lot to hear that."

"At least you got the guy's first name," Piper said, "which will help lead the police to tracking him down. And you said there were some security cameras that got certain angles of him too, right?"

"That's what the NYPD detective told Dane and me. I snapped some photos of him myself and recorded a video, but then the asshole took my phone after he—"

Wait. The photos on my phone.

Could I still have access to them?

"You don't have to talk about the attack if it's too much," Callum said. But I waved that away. He was reading my silence all wrong.

"I need my laptop."

Callum took off his baseball cap and ran his fingers through his hair. "Sis, you have a concussion. Aren't you supposed to avoid screens? And intense thinking?"

The doctor *had* said those things, but this was an emergency.

"My laptop's in the living room. Ask Dane to find it. He can look at the screen for me, but seriously, just *do what I ask*."

"Okay. Geez."

Callum returned with Dane and Ashford. "Hey, Gracie, how are you feeling?" Ashford asked.

"I'll give you all the updates later. First, I need my laptop. I have to see if I'm right."

Dane was carrying my computer under his arm. Piper got up so Dane could take her place right next to me. I recited my password, and he logged in. "What's this about?" he asked.

"Go to my cloud backup. My photos automatically get uploaded there from my phone." Same with videos. But I had no idea if the uploading had finished before Vincent took my phone and, most likely, trashed it.

Dane didn't make me wait long for an answer. A few taps of his finger, and he grinned. "Two photos and a video were uploaded to the cloud last night." He clicked a few more times. "Looks like you got a clear image of the man. This is going to make a huge difference in identifying Vincent and Lexi, *and* corroborating your testimony about the attack. We can send these to the detective as well as the private investigator. You did good."

"I did, didn't I?" I felt almost giddy with relief. Vincent, whoever he really was, was going to regret ever messing with me.

Dane's arm snaked carefully behind me, and he kissed me. Not just a quick peck, but a drawn-out moment of his lips caressing mine.

A throat cleared, probably Callum's, and Dane pulled back, smiling at me with a glint of humor in his eyes. He had kissed me in front of Piper and my brothers. He'd been kissing me in front of other people all weekend, including his family, but Ashford was his best friend. So the significance wasn't lost on me.

It felt like Dane had claimed me as his. And to my surprise, I was completely on board with that.

✧

I napped off and on for the rest of the afternoon, then managed to get to the dining room for some dinner. Callum made pasta, and Piper whipped up a salad. Dane had ordered more cheesecake along with the groceries we needed. I ate as much as I wanted of everything and soaked up the presence of so many of my favorite people.

Then after dinner, Dane ran a bath for me in his fancy marble-lined bathroom. He offered to get in with me, but I told him to go spend time with Piper and my brothers instead. I needed a little time to myself to decompress.

But when I emerged wearing a bathrobe, I was glad to find Dane sitting on the edge of the bed, waiting for me. He was in a simple white T-shirt and jeans, hair all tousled, and had no right to look that sexy when I was too injured to take advantage of it.

"Did everyone else go to bed?" I asked. The darkness outside the window told me it was getting late, though of course the city still buzzed below us with ambient noise.

"They were passing around my whiskey when I said good-night. Callum can drink."

I smiled. "Especially when it's the expensive stuff and someone else is paying. Was he being nicer to you?" I sat on the edge of the mattress, and Dane scooted closer, kissing my temple so gently I barely felt the touch of his lips.

"He's not scowling at me as much. Not that I care what Cal thinks, with all due respect."

"And you and Ashford? You're good?"

Dane nodded. "He and I talked a lot today. We're solid. But I don't want you worrying about that, okay?" He pulled a small gift bag from behind his back. He'd been keeping it out of sight. "Here. I have a present for you."

"You didn't have to—"

He gave me a scolding look, like he was saying, *You think I don't know that?*

I reached into the bag and pulled out a small box. It was a new phone. *Brand* new, the latest model that I never could've afforded. I'd bought my last one used, and it was such an old model it was practically a museum piece.

"Dane..."

"Don't make a fuss about me buying this for you. You agreed to let me pay for everything on this trip, and we're still on the trip."

I still wanted to protest a little bit. Simply because I didn't expect him to do things like this. He had no obligation to swoop in and fix things for me. Yet he kept doing it.

Except now, we were more than friends. More than a weekend fling. So I brushed aside any remaining discomfort and let myself get excited. "Thank you. This is beyond...anything." I tilted my chin, and he got the message, leaning in to kiss me.

Then he took the box from my hands and opened it. "I picked the powder blue to match the dress you wore to the rehearsal dinner. Because you looked so stunning in that. But if you prefer, we can switch it out for a different one."

"No, I love this one. I'll just have to get it set up."

"All taken care of. Your old number is transferred over. Same with anything that was on the cloud. You were great about backing that up, so you shouldn't have lost much."

"How did you manage all that?"

He shrugged. "I've got a guy. But fair warning. If you thought I was spoiling you already, you have no idea what you're in for."

I put my arms around his neck and thanked him again. For everything.

After putting on a T-shirt, I crawled under the covers. I didn't want to show it, but I was worn out and didn't feel so well anymore. I pushed my face into the pillow.

Then I felt warm fingers sliding through my hair. "Do you need a pain pill?"

"I took ibuprofen. I'll get through it."

The mattress compressed as Dane lay down behind me. "I knew guys in the Army who'd be whining nonstop in your shoes. You're tough."

"My brothers don't think so. But I told them I don't regret getting involved last night, even if it drew Vincent's attention. I think they're starting to get it." I'd had that conversation with Callum, and then a similar one with Ashford after we discovered the photos and video were in my cloud storage. Dane had sent the files to the NYPD detective, as well as Teller back in Silver Ridge.

Dane pressed a kiss to the back of my neck. "I know how strong you are. How *brave*. But I still can't stand seeing you hurt. It's..." His hand circled my wrist, not like he was trying to keep me in place, but like he needed to feel anchored himself. "It's intolerable to see the people I care about suffering and not be able to stop it."

I knew he was thinking of his mom. When Dane wanted to make something happen, he didn't hold back, but there were some things that nobody could control.

I pulled his arm forward so it draped over me, ignoring the slight twinge in my ribs. Taking his hand, I placed it over my heart. It beat against his palm. "You're making me feel better just by being here," I said.

"I'm not hurting you?"

"I promise, it's the opposite. I want you close."

Dane fitted his body against my back and held me. His legs tangled with mine beneath the covers. He'd stripped down to just his boxer briefs, and I felt the hard ridge of his erection as he kept pressing gentle kisses to the side of my face. "Sorry," he said, pulling back his hips. "Can't help it."

"I don't mind." I liked knowing how much he wanted me, even if I couldn't reciprocate right now. "I want to feel all of you. As much as I can."

He made a growly sound, tongue darting out to suck my earlobe. "You'll feel all of me again. As soon as you're better. I know the original plan was for us to head back to Silver Ridge on Monday, but I'd like you to stay here with me for a while. Flying with a concussion could make your symptoms worse."

The doctor had said something along those lines.

I did want to stay, at least for now. It would be hard to get my work done whether I was here or in Silver Ridge, given my concussion. Same with my volunteer work. If I had to do nothing and heal, I was fine doing it here. So long as I was with Dane.

"I'll stay for a while. But you don't need to get back to the ski resort? You said there was a lot to do there. The ski runs will be opening for the season soon."

"The staff in Silver Ridge is more than able to handle it. I'll do my part by phone and Zoom. But you're more important. I plan to be at your beck and call. You're going to get sick of me."

"Not likely. I'm pretty wild about you."

"Good," he said. "I'm pretty wild about you too."

But I did miss home. And I hoped I would never have to choose between Silver Ridge and the man I wanted to be with.

TWENTY-NINE

Grace

Day by day, I started to feel more like myself. Which was strange when you considered that I was living in a plush apartment in Manhattan with the hottest man ever.

A man who insisted on doing sweet things for me every single day.

Piper and my brothers stuck around for a couple of days, but then they had to head home. Callum especially wasn't thrilled that I would stay here in New York. But Dane promised to bring me back to Colorado as soon as I was well enough.

While I was here, I tried to make the most of it. I rested a ton the first few days, enough that I was dying of boredom. But once I felt ready, we took walks in Central Park and to Dane's favorite spots to eat almost every day. We visited Dane's mom again, and I went to see her with Margot when Dane had to go into the office. I got back to my bookkeeping work for my clients on my laptop, first with Dane and Margot's help, then on my own.

Dane even took me shopping for new glasses, since Vincent had broken my favorite ones. I tried to pay for them myself, but Dane insisted on ordering every pair of frames that caught my eye. I ended up with seven new pairs in various styles and colors to match whatever mood I might be in.

A few days later, I surprised him with a new cream-colored sweater, ordered online with my credit card. I promised to keep this one coffee-free.

And every night, I slipped into bed with him after eating the dessert Dane had surprised me with.

It was kind of amazing.

My only complaint was that almost two weeks had now passed, and we still hadn't had sex again. Dane kissed me and touched me all the time, and it was obvious how turned on he was. Yet he kept refusing to give either of us any relief. Me, because my ribs were still sore and I had lingering dizziness, nausea, and headaches. And him, because he said he didn't want an orgasm unless he gave me one too.

I mean, I wouldn't have been opposed to him putting on a sexy show for me or something. But when the man made up his mind, he was as stubborn as I was.

So I wasn't surprised when we were making out one evening, getting hot and heavy on his living room couch, and he stopped things when I rubbed my palm against his hardening cock through his jeans.

"I'm ready," I said.

"Are you hurting right now?"

"It's..." I flinched. "I'm hurting a little. I'm used to it."

"Then let's give it a couple more days."

"I thought you were going to spoil me. I want you to spoil me with your cock."

He smirked. "I will. When I'm sure you'll enjoy it as much as I do."

I grumbled under my breath about overprotective men. As I'd told my brothers, Dane always listened to me, which was crucial. But that didn't mean we always agreed. Why couldn't he just give up his sexual favors whenever I asked?

Okay, that sounded far more problematic when I spelled it out.

My getting better was a double-edged sword, though. Once I

was well enough to fly comfortably, it would be time for me to head home to Silver Ridge. At my last visit with the doctor, she'd said travel was safe. Just that it could make me feel worse.

I *wanted* to go home. I wanted to see my family and friends and get back to all the responsibilities I'd been letting slide while I was sick. I hadn't gone this long without seeing my niece since Maisie was a newborn, and video calls weren't cutting it. And it wasn't just that. The city was exciting, but I craved the mountains. Our little Main Street and my favorite hiking trails and Piper's coffee.

I was homesick.

But it sounded like the ski resort was running smoothly enough without Dane there. And other projects had been demanding his attention here. What if he didn't want to go back to Colorado with me?

How was this supposed to work between us?

Dane stretched out on the couch and pulled me to lay on top of him. "My private investigator called today," he said. "Warren. He has some news about the investigation into Vincent and Nina Jamison."

My heart rate jumped, and my fist tightened on Dane's shirt over his chest. "He found Vincent?"

"No, but he's got some progress to share. More than the NYPD has done."

Even with the clear images and video of Vincent that I'd provided, the detective assigned to my case hadn't made any progress in the last two weeks on finding my attacker. They hadn't been able to find Lexi either, the woman Vincent had been threatening. It was infuriating. Dane had been putting whatever pressure on the police that he could, but it hadn't made a difference so far. The detective kept telling us to be patient.

Dane was still convinced his brother knew more than he was sharing, but Kip and Bristol had left for their honeymoon only a couple of days after the wedding. I didn't know the exact date they would be back. Things were more tense than ever between

Dane and his father. It was something he didn't like talking about, but I could tell that it weighed on him.

"You're welcome to come with me tomorrow when I meet with Warren," Dane said.

I had made him promise to share everything he learned, and he'd been doing that. But I already had plans for tomorrow.

"Ayla's going to be in town. Ashford's sister-in-law. I'm supposed to have lunch with her."

"Right, I forgot about that. I could reschedule with Warren if you want."

Part of me wanted to be there for the update, just so I could get every scrap of information that could lead us to the man who hurt me. But it was also a relief, knowing I had Dane on my side. I wasn't in this by myself. As much as I wanted to be independent, I could also lean on him. I could trust him to handle certain things. Which was a big deal for me.

And he would share it all with me later, anyway.

"No. Go ahead and meet with him. I appreciate it. Everything you've been doing... I don't think I tell you enough how grateful I am."

He cupped my cheek, angling his head to meet my gaze. "You don't have to. I'm grateful for *you*.

"Then we can call it even."

"I'd rather not keep score at all." Tension flitted across his features before it vanished. And then he was kissing me again, helping me forget about anything except the two of us, right at that moment.

I met Ayla at a tiny Italian place. She was already there when I arrived, tucked into a table at the back so she would be less noticeable. She'd offered to have her driver pick me up from Dane's apartment earlier, but I'd wanted to take the subway and walk. It felt good to know I could find my way around this metropolis all by myself.

She jumped up when she saw me, opening her arms for a hug. "It is so good to see you! When I heard from Ashford that you were in the city, and I realized I was going to be here at the same time, it felt like Christmas came early."

Ayla's older sister, Lori, had been married to Ashford years ago. After Lori's death, Ayla and Ashford had been estranged for a long time. But they'd reconnected last summer, around the same time that Ashford got together with Emma.

Ayla and my brother had worked through a lot of things related to Lori's death. Now she was an important part of Maisie's life. My fellow aunt.

But Ayla was also one of the most famous pop stars in the world, which made it difficult for her to visit us in Silver Ridge as freely as she liked. Still, we had grown close in the last year and a half, and I was glad to call Ayla a friend. She was a world-famous celebrity, but she was also down-to-earth with a great sense of humor.

We both sat down and ordered some sparkling waters and appetizers. "I'm thrilled to see you too."

"Even if the reason for you being in town for so long absolutely sucks." She studied my face. Most of the bruises had faded, but I still had the bandage over the bridge of my nose to cover where it was healing. "It's up to you if we talk about that, or—"

"Second option, please." I was already anxious about Dane's meeting with the investigator and what he would learn. I wanted to focus on the good things in my life, and of course hear everything about how Ayla had been doing.

"Got it. So, what do you think of New York?" Ayla leaned forward with her elbows on the table. "Isn't it *amazing*?"

We talked about the city while we nibbled on antipasti. She said she appreciated that the paparazzi wasn't as bad in New York, but Los Angeles was her home base, and she didn't see that changing any time soon.

"And Mr. Dane Knightly?" she asked. "Is he as charming as his reputation claims?"

"More." Though it was bizarre that Ayla had heard of Dane's reputation on her own. Sometimes I forgot about the billionaire thing. "But he's also sweet and wonderful and pretty much my dream guy." No, that wasn't even true. Before, I didn't even dare to dream that I'd find a guy like Dane.

"Then why'd you frown when you said that?"

"Did I?" I hadn't even realized it.

Ayla tucked a lock of platinum-blond hair behind her ear. "You know, when you walked in, I thought there was something different about you. Like you take up more space than you used to."

I snorted, nearly choking on the burrata I'd just stuffed in my mouth. "Dane feeds me a lot of cheesecake."

She barked a laugh, making a few heads turn toward us and do double-takes. "Oh God, that is not what I meant. Though your curves are rocking, make no mistake." We both kept giggling. When we'd calmed down, she said, "I mean, your energy is bigger. You're more confident."

I set down my fork, considering. "I feel more confident. I like who I am with Dane. Someone who takes risks. Tries things that are exciting and different."

"New York is an ideal place for that."

"I do want to go home soon, though. I miss Silver Ridge so much."

"What about Dane?"

"That is a good question. A year ago, I would've said I could never trust a man enough to get this close to him. But I *really*, really like him."

Ayla smiled. "As someone who has trouble finding people she can trust, I know how significant it is for you to say that. I bet you two will work it all out. If there's trust, if there's *love*, then the rest of the details fall into place. At least, that's how it went for Ashford and Emma. Means the rest of us have some hope, right?"

I was nodding along before that four-letter word hit me. *Love.* The biggest risk of all.

A thread of fear snaked its way into my heart.

Thankfully, Ayla kept talking about Ashford and Emma, so I didn't have to dwell on my uncertainty.

My brother and his fiancée had finally set a date in February for their wedding. Ayla lamented that her schedule had been so difficult to work with, but she was excited to be going. "It's on my calendar," she said. "*Nothing* is going to keep me from being there."

"Except maybe a snowstorm. February in the mountains isn't the ideal time to hold a big event."

"Are you kidding? I love a winter wedding. So romantic. Also, don't talk about storms. Don't you dare jinx this. I already bought my dress and everything."

I laughed. "No, you're right. Positive thoughts. Maisie is going to be the cutest flower girl in history, and there's no way I would want you to miss that."

"Is Dane going to be there too?"

I took a sip of my water, trying to act nonchalant even though nerves swirled in my stomach. "I'm sure he's invited. Guess we'll have to see. What about you? Bringing a plus one?"

"Not planning on it. I'll be too busy with Aunt Ayla duties." She scowled. "Besides, I already expect your chief of police to complain about *me* being there, since he claims I'm a security risk. I don't want to subject anyone else to that."

I opened my mouth to say that Teller Landry wasn't so intolerable once you got to know him, but someone tapped my shoulder. It was the restaurant's hostess. She was holding a manila envelope. "Miss? Someone just dropped this off for you."

"For *me*?" I asked.

She nodded. "It was a bicycle messenger. He pointed you out. Said it was urgent." The hostess set the envelope on the table and shrugged, backing away.

"Don't open it," Ayla said sharply. "Are you sure that's for you?"

I turned the envelope over. It had *Grace O'Neal* scrawled on the front.

Ayla exhaled. "Okay. I thought it was...something else."

"You thought it was for you?"

She looked uncomfortable. "Some creep has been sending me things lately. An overzealous fan. It's just an annoyance. Never mind."

It sounded like more than an annoyance, but the envelope on the table demanded my attention. "Maybe this is from Dane. He's the only person who would know I'm at this restaurant." Except it was more Dane's style to show up himself. Or at the very least, text or call.

Unless something was wrong.

My hands trembled as I ripped open the envelope and pulled out the contents. Two sheets of glossy photo paper. A note was stuck to the front of the first photo.

He's not who you think he is.

I was in a daze as I removed the note and took a look at the photo beneath. It was a snapshot of Dane and a familiar redhead standing in front of an open doorway.

It didn't make sense.

"That's Dane, right?" Ayla asked. She tilted her head, trying to get a better look. "Who's he with?"

"Um...her name is Nina Jamison. But he told me he had never met her."

Ayla seemed confused, and I didn't blame her. She didn't know the entire saga around Nina and Vincent and the masquerade ball.

Why would Dane have lied to me about knowing Nina Jamison?

My hand reached out to flip the photo away and see the

second image. And bile rose up in my throat, my lunch threatening to come up.

In the second photo, Dane and Nina were *kissing*.

"I don't understand this," I stammered.

Ayla took the photos from my hands. Glanced at one, then the other. And then the note. "Okay, let's just take a moment. Because this whole thing is beyond shady. Maybe you should start from the beginning. Then we can figure out what this is about."

I nodded, trying to stay calm. But a voice I'd thought I had banished was whispering ugly things in my head.

You see what a fool you've been? You never should have trusted him.

THIRTY

WARREN CRENSHAW BUZZED me up to his Brooklyn office. I jogged up the stairs, and he met me at the door, reaching for my hand. "Knightly. It's been a while."

"I know. Too long. I really appreciate your help with this."

We went into the office. I said hello to his assistant, who sat in the tiny lobby area in front, and we went into the back room. Warren closed the door, gesturing for me to sit in the chair across from his.

"I was just thinking the other day of that jazz club we went to," I said.

He grinned. "You mean the one in Rome?"

"That's the one."

I had known Warren since my Army days, though he'd been a Marine. After leaving the service, he had worked in law enforcement for a while before becoming a private investigator. He was a useful man to know. Someone with a variety of skills and endless tricks up the sleeve of his trademark leather jacket. He had the hard edges and intense glare to intimidate even hardened criminals, yet the smarts and the subtlety to allow him to befriend almost anyone.

Also, he was a great guy with excellent taste in music. So there was that.

He whistled. "Rome. You're really taking me back. That was a memorable night."

"Certainly was. We should do it again sometime."

"Absolutely, but only if I can bring the wife. Sheila will kill me if I jet off to Italy without her. And maybe you've got someone special to bring along with you as well?" He gestured at the file on his desk.

I wasn't surprised he had figured that out. The guy was an investigator, after all.

"I do. Grace is very special. Exactly why your help on this is so important to me."

He flipped the file open. "Then let's get to it. I'm sure you wanna know what I found. Enough with the polite small talk."

"You know I hate small talk, and I'm rarely called polite. But yeah, let's hear it. I'd like to know whether I'm bringing home good news or bad."

"Listen to you, so domestic. I'll have to meet the woman who got Dane Knightly to settle down. A rare breed."

"About as rare as the woman who got Warren Crenshaw to put a ring on her finger."

He laughed deeply as he pushed the file across the desk. "Sheila will love to hear you say that."

I sat forward and looked at the top photo inside the folder. Immediately, rage flared bright and hot in my veins.

This was the man who'd given Grace a concussion and bruised her ribs. Who'd punched her *in the face*.

Vincent.

I had promised Ashford I would end this guy, someway or somehow, and I wanted that so badly. "Please tell me you have his full name," I said.

"Vincent Brady. This is his mugshot from his last arrest. Lengthy criminal history on this one. Larceny, fraud, and extortion. Plus a generous sprinkling of DV."

Domestic violence. "Since he likes hurting people who are weaker than him." I turned to the next page in the file, which detailed Vincent Brady's rap sheet.

"Ms. O'Neal's photos of him were key in identifying the man. They were nice and clear and head-on. I circulated those images with my network of informants, and that did the trick. Vincent has some mafia ties, but rumor is that he's gone into business for himself."

"What kind of business?"

Warren reached over to flip the papers in the file to another image. A woman with heavy makeup and blond curly hair. "Well, this is where Lexi Sanders comes in. Another identification my informants helped with. She has a criminal record as well. Petty theft, vandalism. And prostitution."

I looked up from the photo, frowning. "Lexi is a sex worker? Are you telling me that's how Vincent Brady is connected to her? He's a pimp?"

"But he's gone high class, or so the rumors say. Offering escorts to wealthy elites."

I cursed, sitting back in my chair. "Running escorts in Knightly Global hotels. *Shit.* Any indication that my brother is involved in this?"

"Not yet. But I'll keep digging. I'm not finished with show and tell, though. I've also got Nina Jamison's real name. It's Nina Badowski. She's also a known associate of Vincent Brady, and it's likely she's one of his escorts."

So much of this situation shifted into a new light. Nina had probably been at the ski resort to meet with Dirk Lancaster the night of the grand-opening party. He'd *hired her*. No wonder he'd been looking for that mask to identify her. He'd likely never met her in person beforehand.

An escort service running in *my* new hotel.

My fist clenched and released. I had no proof yet. But my brother had something to do with this. I was sure.

"Any idea where to find Brady?" I asked.

"It seems he's staying out of sight after the incident at your brother's wedding. He's probably left the city. If he turns up, you'll be the first to know. What you do with that information..." Warren spread his hands. "We can talk about options, but depending on what you want to do, we might have to continue that conversation somewhere more discreet."

I smirked. So Warren could already guess where my head was at. "What about Lexi Sanders or Nina Badowski?"

"I checked both of their last known addresses. Lexi's roommates said she'd cleared out a couple of weeks ago. But Nina has been missing for well over a month."

That fit with the conversation between Vincent and Lexi that Grace had overheard. "Nina hasn't been seen since she was in Silver Ridge," I said, remembering the conversation we'd had with Chief Landry weeks ago. "We also know from what he said to Lexi that Vincent was looking for Nina. If she works for him, that would make sense."

But why had Nina walked away from meeting Dirk Lancaster the night of the party in Silver Ridge? Why had she given her mask to Grace?

And assuming Vincent had broken in to Grace's house to steal it back, why the heck was that mask so important?

"We have to talk to Nina," I said. "She knows what all of this is really about."

"I'll keep working on it."

"Thanks for your help, man. I'll owe you."

"No kidding. Just wait until you see my bill." He closed the folder. "But we're not done yet. I've also got an update on the other matter. Grayden O'Neal."

"Oh?" I hadn't thought about Grace's eldest brother at all in the last couple of weeks.

"I had better luck finding *him*." Warren pulled out a sheet of paper and handed it to me. "Do you want me to make contact?"

"*No*. But...I'll let you know."

I hadn't even mentioned to Grace that I was looking for Grayden. Now, I wondered if this had been a mistake. When I'd asked Warren to put out feelers for Grayden, Grace and I had been in a very different place. The last couple weeks with her had shown me just how great we were together.

I was falling so hard for her.

But I'd fucked up with this Grayden situation. Gone behind her back. I just hoped Grace wouldn't be too pissed off.

✧

By the time I got home, carrying a chocolate-swirl cheesecake from our favorite bakery, I was aching to see my girl. Grace and I had been together so often the last couple weeks that I'd gotten used to it. She kept complaining that we hadn't been intimate, as if it was easy for me to tell her no. I *hated* telling Grace no.

I was going out of my mind with how badly I wanted to be inside her again. But I couldn't risk hurting her. Grace didn't like when I was protective because she thought that meant I viewed her as weak.

But it was the opposite. I liked to portray to the world that nothing ever got to me. But Grace *did*. She was my weakness.

I greeted the doorman on my way up. "Hey, George. How's it going?"

"Afternoon, Mr. Knightly. Ms. O'Neal is upstairs with a guest. Ms. Maxwell." Considering the other people who lived in this building, George didn't get starstruck often. He was a total professional. I couldn't count the number of times I had asked him to call me Dane, and it never stuck. But the look on his face told me that superstar Ayla Maxwell was a different story.

"Thanks," I said, making a mental note to ask Ayla to sign something and send it down to him.

I was glad that Grace was home already, and I tried not to be disappointed that we wouldn't be alone. Ayla was part of Grace and Ashford's family, and I hadn't met her yet. So I looked forward to that opportunity.

Maybe she liked chocolate-swirl cheesecake too.

I was whistling contentedly as I unlocked the apartment door and stepped inside. Quiet voices came from the living room, like the two women were whispering to one another. Then they went silent. Which seemed odd.

But I didn't think anything of it until I walked into the great room. "Hey, I brought dessert if anyone's interested."

My smile died a quick death when I saw their expressions.

"What's going on?" I crossed the room in a few quick strides. "Baby, did something happen?"

Grace was holding something in her hands, some sheets of paper, but I couldn't see more than that. Ayla stood up from the couch, smiling cautiously. "Dane, I'm Ayla. I'm going to take off. I was just waiting here until you got home. Unless you want me to stay, Grace?"

"No, I'm okay," she said softly. Grace looked pretty much as she had that morning, physically at least.

Whatever was happening here, I didn't like it, but if Grace wanted to be mysterious about it, I could wait a couple minutes. I set the cheesecake on a side table, along with my keys, while Ayla hugged Grace goodbye. Then she shook my hand. "Sorry to run like this. My driver is waiting outside. Maybe next time we can chat more."

"Sure. Sounds good." When Ayla was gone, I said, "You wanna tell me what this is about? Because all the anticipation is making me nervous."

Grace took a deep breath and looked into my eyes. "Someone delivered these to the restaurant while Ayla and I were having lunch." She held out the papers. I took them, flipping from one to the other.

What the *fuck* was this?

"It looks like you and Nina Jamison." Grace's voice was strangely flat.

"It isn't." I mean, the pictures were of me. But I had never in my life stood on this street corner kissing some redhead, much less Nina Jamison. Make that Nina Badowski. "These are fake."

But it looked bad. I realized that. And I could only imagine what Grace was thinking right now.

My heart hammered like a fist against my rib cage. For several agonizing seconds, she didn't say anything.

Then she nodded. "I know. But there were a couple minutes at first that my mind went to a pretty dark place." Her voice cracked on that last sentence, and I felt like that same crack had opened up in my chest.

"Fuck. C'mere." I picked her up and sat on the couch, cradling her in my lap.

"Ayla talked me through it. She said there are fake pictures of her online. People use AI and Photoshop and who knows what to make this stuff look real. I still needed to hear it from you, though."

"Then let me make it crystal clear. I have never met Nina in person. If I had, I would've told you."

"But who would do this?"

Someone who wanted to hurt Grace. And through her, hurt *me*.

Not only that. It was a threat. A message that they could get to Grace at any time, and that made my blood run ice cold. I wanted to seriously fuck up whoever was responsible.

But I was a lot more concerned about how Grace was feeling right now. "We'll find out. Are you okay?"

"Kind of. Not really." She tucked her head between my shoulder and neck.

Of course she wasn't. Those photos had played havoc with her trust issues. "What do you need?"

"Just to be with you. I knew you wouldn't lie to me."

Guilt ate at my insides. Because there *was* something I'd kept from her. I couldn't go another minute without giving her the truth.

"I wouldn't lie. But..." I cleared my throat. "There's something I need to tell you."

Her head lifted, worry on her pretty features.

"I asked Warren, my investigator, to track down your brother. Grayden."

THIRTY-ONE

Grace

I HAD BEEN on an emotional roller coaster today. And Dane was throwing me for yet another loop. "Your investigator was looking for Grayden?"

"Found him, to be exact. Warren gave me your brother's contact info today. I wanted to see if we could find him, just in case you decided you'd like to get back in touch with him. Since you mentioned it to me in Silver Ridge. But I got ahead of myself. I should have cleared it with you beforehand, and for that I'm sorry."

I was still stuck on the first part. My brain was having trouble processing it. "You found Grayden. Is he okay?"

Dane shifted to take his wallet from his back pocket. He unfolded a paper from inside and handed it to me. I pored over the words. There wasn't much. Two addresses, both in Seattle.

Grayden lived in *Seattle*.

A tear streaked down my cheek. "But he's okay," I repeated.

I hadn't seen or heard from Grayden in a decade. Over ten years. I'd been a teenager back then, still a kid. I'd wondered if he was dead. But he wasn't.

He was in Seattle, and I couldn't get my head around it.

"Grayden has no idea we were looking for him," Dane said.

"We haven't made contact with him. But yes, it does sound like he's okay. Warren didn't find anything to the contrary. Your brother is single, no kids." Dane brushed away my tears with his thumb. "Are you angry with me? You have every right to be."

"If I was angry, I'd tell you." I shook my head. "I'm feeling a lot of things. Too much. But not angry with you."

No. I just needed a minute to breathe.

This afternoon had been rough. The sheer terror of thinking I had been wrong about Dane. That had been like looking over the side of a cliff and feeling myself start to lose my footing. *Awful.*

Ayla had helped. She'd brought me back to reality. In a literal sense, because she had pointed out the subtle flaws in those pictures that pegged them as fake. Unfortunately, it was something she was experienced with.

But in the end, it wasn't Ayla who had convinced me. It was remembering something Piper had texted to me a couple of weeks back.

Trust yourself.

Ayla was right that I had changed. I was finally ready to trust my own instincts and believe what I knew to be true in my heart. Dane was a good man. Did that solve all our problems? No. But for a girl who'd been so terrified of another man betraying her, it was a pretty huge deal.

And now, this news about Grayden. He lived in Seattle. I had his address and his phone number. If I wanted, I could call him up right now.

Dane had done that.

He'd done that *for me.*

I put my arms around his neck, unable to stop from trembling. "Thank you."

"I overstepped."

"Yeah, but just take the win, Knightly. I'm giving it to you."

He chuckled and kissed my head.

"Ashford isn't going to like this, though," I said. "He wants nothing to do with Grayden."

"This isn't Ashford's choice. It's yours."

"He's your best friend. He's going to be pissed that you got involved."

"Ashford is important to me. But I choose *you*. Every time. That's not even a question for me. Hasn't been for a while."

A cascade of fluttery feelings went through me. I tipped my head to look up at him.

"I told Ashford weeks ago, even before we left Silver Ridge, that I liked you. He asked me, flat out, for my intentions. I told him that was up to you."

"But it's not really up to me."

"I disagree."

I scoffed, but I'd already dealt with too much today. Too many emotions. I didn't want to get into this. "Can I try that cheesecake you brought home? Dessert is exactly what I need."

I started to get up from his lap, but Dane held me tight. "Hold on. Not so fast. Tell me what you meant. Why isn't it up to you?"

"Because life is complicated."

"Can you be more specific?"

I didn't want to say it, but the words leapt from my mouth. This conversation was just pushing us toward the inevitable.

And Dane was *so damn pushy*.

"I'll have to go home soon, and you're probably going to stay here."

A line appeared between his brows. "You think I wouldn't go with you to Silver Ridge?"

"The ski resort is running fine without you. Your mom is here. Your life is here. Even if you come back to Silver Ridge for a few weeks or months, you're going to leave after a while. I like being with you, and I want to enjoy it, but eventually it's going to end. I *know* that."

I had been through so much in my life, and none of it had broken me all the way through. So I knew if and when things didn't work out with Dane, I would survive that too. Even if it meant a broken heart. I would keep going for my family. For Maisie.

But the thought of saying goodbye to him…it still gutted me.

Dane pulled me closer so my forehead rested against his. "We've already established I can be an idiot about holding things back sometimes. I'm not used to being completely open with anyone. I didn't want to rush this by saying it too soon."

"Saying what?"

"That I'm falling in love with you."

I couldn't move. Couldn't breathe. "Don't say that," I whispered. Because I struggled to believe this was really happening. This was a messed-up dream, and I was torn between wanting to wake up and wanting to stay here forever.

"I'm still doing it. Not telling you everything. Here's the truth. Since the minute you agreed to come to New York with me, I've been trying to figure out how I could keep you."

My pulse drummed in my throat. "Colorado is home for me. That's not going to change."

"Then I'll make it my home too."

"Just like that?" I asked incredulously.

"Yep. I'm a decisive guy. Also, let's be honest, I can afford to have what I want most of the time. Things that money can buy, anyway." His gray eyes slid away from me. "I've never told you why I really bought the resort in Silver Ridge."

"Why did you?"

"Part of it was envy, maybe, that Ashford had the kind of meaningful life there that doesn't have a price tag. And part of it was remembering trips to the mountains when I was a kid. How much it had meant to my mom. I just wanted to find something that truly mattered to *me*. Well, you're it. You're what I was looking for."

All I could do was blink at him. No one had ever said these kinds of things to me. "What about your mom? And Margot?"

"Leave those details to me. What you need to know is this. I'm in love with you. I'm in deep." He laughed softly. "It's a bit of a problem. It's been keeping me up at night, plotting ways to make you love me back."

This infuriating man. He'd pushed me into taking this trip with him. Pushed me into feeling things, *wanting* things, that I'd thought were impossible.

I had only just gotten used to the fact that I wanted to take a chance on him. I'd finally felt confident that I had my feet underneath me.

And now he was sweeping them out from under me. Once again.

My throat was thick, eyes tearing up again. "Don't do this to me, Dane. Not today. I can't take it."

"I'm sorry, gorgeous. I love you." He kissed a tear as it fell. "I love you." He kissed another, repeating those words again and again. Finally he asked, "What do you say?"

"That I think I'm falling for you too. And it *really* scares me. But it's also the best, most wonderful thing that's ever happened to me."

Dane wrapped his arms around my waist and pulled me close, kissing me breathless.

For the first time in two weeks, he wasn't being hesitant with me. His lips and tongue danced with mine, giving and taking. Making me feel exactly how much he craved me.

Then he pulled back, muttering, "Sorry. I wasn't thinking about your injuries."

I grabbed the collar of his shirt in my fist. "I have had a *day*, Dane Knightly. All I want is for my man to do filthy things to me. I don't think that's too much to ask."

"Are you hurting?"

"Not more than I can handle. You know I trust you. But I need you to trust that I know *myself*."

I thought for a moment he might deny me again. But instead, he tugged me roughly against him and claimed my mouth.

I straddled his lap, my hands seeking out his warm skin

beneath his shirt. My fingers traced his happy trail and ran through his chest hair.

Dane's masculinity was such a turn on. The strength in all those muscles. But in the past several weeks, his body had become a new comfort zone too. I'd never imagined that the very thing that excited me, got my heart racing, was also the place that I felt the safest. Right in his arms.

But I was beyond ready to have him inside me again. To have him push my limits, the way he had at the beginning of this trip. To feel the intense kind of pleasure that no one else had ever given me.

Dane broke our kiss long enough to yank his T-shirt off, then my own. I got rid of my bra myself and pressed my body against his, my hard nipples rubbing over his broad chest. Dane's eyes flashed with lust, and he grabbed my hips, thrusting himself against me. It was such a rough and dirty move, and I loved it. I felt how thick and hard he was despite the layers of clothes between us.

We really needed to do something about that.

He clearly had the same thought, because I was suddenly on my back on the couch, bouncing against the cushions. Dane unbuttoned my pants and pulled them down, then went to work on his own.

I went to take off my panties, but he shook his head. "No. Those are mine."

Then he grabbed the thin, lacy fabric in both hands and tore it apart. Holy crap. A jolt of pure desire throbbed between my legs.

"Is this filthy enough for you?" he asked.

"Definitely on the right track."

Dane shoved his boxer briefs down to his thighs. He fisted his cock and stroked it a few times, a predatory gleam in his eyes. Then he glanced to the side. "Fuck. Supplies are in the bedroom."

"I'm okay just like this if you are. We can go bare."

A groan rumbled from his chest. He brought his hand

between my legs and circled my clit a few times before dipping two fingers inside me. I gasped at the sudden sensation, but that quickly turned into a moan. It felt so good. And I still had my shredded panties on, which I had never realized would be so hot.

"I've been aching to get inside you again," he said, those gray irises as dark as gunmetal. "You have no idea how difficult it was to hold back."

"I thought we weren't doing that anymore." I arched my spine and wiggled my hips in invitation.

He grinned, incisors flashing. Holding firmly to my hip with one hand and his cock with the other, he pushed into me with one long, smooth thrust. "Oh, damn." His eyes closed for a moment and he gritted his teeth. "You better tell me if any of this is too much. Because I am dangerously close to losing control."

"I'm ready for you."

He grabbed my hands and pressed them above my head against the couch cushion. "Guess we'll see, won't we?"

He kept his upper body propped up, looking down at me as his hips pumped. Languidly at first, like he was testing me, before he picked up the pace and intensity. I had to wrap my legs around him just to hold on. The movement made me ache in my sore spots, but it just reminded me of how strong I was. I had been through so much, and I was still here. The fear that I'd held inside of me for too long was finally fading away.

I felt alive. *Free.*

"You're beautiful like this," he said. "But I can think of something even better." He pulled out of me and went down onto the floor instead, shoving the coffee table aside and sprawling right there on the rug in the sexiest display I had ever seen. He hadn't even bothered to take off his boxer briefs, leaving them down around his thighs. "Want you to ride me. Show me what you've got."

I got up, shoving my shredded panties off as I did, and straddled him, crying out as his cock filled me at this new angle. Dane held onto me and bucked upward. Still rough, but somehow a little more gentle on my head and sore ribs. Like Dane had somehow known exactly what I needed.

Our bodies moved together in a wild rhythm. Saying far more than we'd been able to express in words.

And then Dane said, "I love you, Grace," and my chest squeezed around my heart. I couldn't say that back to him, not yet, but I still felt it. I felt more for this man than I ever thought I could for anyone.

Love was a risk, but I had never known that stepping out into the open, facing the fear and taking that chance, could make me feel invincible.

"You gonna come for me?" he asked, low and sexy. I couldn't even answer. I was feeling too much. Everything crescendoed at once, the pleasure overtaking me. His name was on my lips as I cried out. Dane thrust his cock into me a few more times until he shouted, and I felt the hot pulse of him inside me. No barriers. I fell forward against his chest.

His heart beat against my cheek, thrumming just as fast as mine.

THIRTY-TWO

Dane

I'd never had sex like that before. Somehow uninhibited and completely connected at the same time.

Probably because I'd never been with a woman I was in love with.

The first time with Grace had been amazing, but my feelings for her had grown exponentially in the weeks since.

"We're going to have to do that as often as possible," I said, trying to catch my breath.

She giggled, snuggling against me, and I draped my arms over her back to keep her right there. I didn't want to move from the spot for as long as possible.

Grace was just...everything. I should've known she could handle far more than I had been giving her. And I didn't mean physically. I had kept things from her because of my own hangups. Facing a tense negotiation for a deal or hostiles in a war zone—those were things I could handle with barely a shift in my vital signs. But telling the woman I loved just how completely head over heels I was for her?

I'd been worried that she would get spooked. Run from me like she'd done the night of the masquerade party. But this time she hadn't, and *fuck* I was relieved.

All my life, I had pushed myself to accomplish great things. But Grace pushed me in entirely different ways. Winning her felt like the biggest accomplishment of them all. It didn't matter that she hadn't said she loved me. The declaration would come in time. I was still cocky enough to have zero doubts about that.

In all the ways that mattered, Grace was *mine*.

We both rinsed off in the shower, and then I ran a bath. It was big enough for the two of us, so I slid into the water first and pulled Grace between my legs and up against my chest when she got in.

We both relaxed, enjoying the heat and the closeness.

"I haven't told you what else I learned from Warren," I said.

I recounted the new info Warren had shared. Vincent and Lexi's identities, along with Nina's real last name. And the fact that they seemed to be involved in a high-class escort ring.

Grace turned to the side so she could meet my gaze. "Do you think that's why Nina was meeting with Dirk Lancaster at the grand-opening party?"

"That's my assumption. That she was his date for the night."

"But if they hadn't met yet, why did she decide to leave? Had she heard something bad about him?"

"That's possible. It's extremely concerning that this is going on at Knightly Global hotels. I think Kip is behind it. That's why he recognized Nina's name when I asked him about her. Jamison must be the alias she uses as an escort."

"But you think Kip would be involved in an escort business on the side? I thought he was too uptight for that."

"He's too uptight for a lot of things, but not if it's going to make money."

Kip had been so concerned about making his VIPs happy. The grand-opening party at the ski resort had been his idea in the first place. And then, after Nina stood up Dirk Lancaster, Kip had probably been fuming. Which explained why he had been harassing me afterward about providing a "personal touch" to the VIPs.

Personal touch indeed.

The whole thing was messed up, yet I couldn't put it past my brother. The only part that didn't make sense was that he would risk doing this under our father's nose. Dad would have an aneurysm if he found out that Kip was risking the Knightly name.

For whatever reason, Kip believed the risk was worth it.

"We have to find Nina," Grace said. "If she's in hiding from Vincent, then maybe she's trying to get away from this whole escort situation. We could help her."

"And she might have information to share that would expose the entire operation." Which was probably the very reason that Vincent wanted so badly to track her down.

Unless Vincent was trying to find her for a more specific reason. Which just reminded me of the mystery around Nina's red mask, and the fact that it had been stolen from Grace's bedroom.

"Warren is going to keep investigating," I said. "He's trying to locate all three of them. It sounds like Lexi took off, maybe for the same reasons as Nina. If we can locate either woman, then maybe they can tell us what we need to know. I'm also going to send Warren the fake photos you received today. Hopefully he can figure out who was behind that move as well."

"Do you think it's connected? The escort service and the fake photos today?"

"Maybe. If Kip's behind it, then I assume so. But whatever this is really about, sending that envelope to you today was like dropping a bomb. A declaration of war. They're trying to use you against me because it's obvious how much I care about you. And I am *not* going to let that go."

Thinking about it just made me furious again, and I kissed Grace's temple, taking comfort in knowing she was mine. Whoever had been trying to hurt us had only strengthened our connection.

I wasn't going to thank whoever was behind this, though. I wasn't in a forgiving mood.

"Kip will be back in New York any day now from his honeymoon. I'm going to confront him. And then I'm going to our father."

"Will he believe you?"

"I don't know. Unless I have some kind of proof, probably not. But it's what I have to do."

Either way, I didn't see how I could continue working for Knightly Global. After Mom had gotten sick and deteriorated so quickly, I had wanted to hold on to the only family I had left. Dad and Kip. As if reconciling with my brother, earning my father's approval, could somehow fix our family and bring my mom back to us. But that wasn't possible.

I loved my mom and would do my damnedest to take care of her, but I also had to do what was right for myself.

And that meant choosing Grace. Choosing *us*.

✧

We didn't bother to get dressed after the bath, just drying off and then tumbling into my bed. And of course, we wound up messy again. Making love all afternoon until we were exhausted. Though I was careful to be more gentle and pay attention to how she was doing. Grace was strong, and I trusted her to tell me what was too much, but I was never *not* going to put her welfare first.

Grace napped in my arms, while I stared at the ceiling, deep in thought. I was content though. How could I not be? I was naked in bed with the woman I loved. Hard to find fault with that.

I scowled when my phone rang on the nightstand, surprised to see Warren's name there. I hadn't expected to hear from him again already, especially because I hadn't sent him those fake photos yet.

Grace stirred, lifting her head. Her hair was frizzy and tangled from our latest lovemaking session. "Do you need to get that?"

"It's Warren, my investigator. I'll let him go to voicemail and call him back in an hour." Grace deserved some peace. Hell, so did

I. Besides, the more time Warren spent on my case, the more he could charge me. That was a bill I was happy to pay.

But Grace sat up, pulling on the sheet to cover herself. "No, it could be important. I want to know what else he's found."

"You're the boss." I smirked at her as I grabbed the phone. "Hey, Warr. You're on speaker with me and Grace."

"Grace, it's a pleasure to make your acquaintance. Dane's one arrogant asshole, but you've managed to wrap him around your finger. It's impressive."

I rolled my eyes and put my arm around her.

She laughed. "Um, hi Warren. Good to meet you too. Have you found something new for us?"

"I assume Dane updated you on everything we discussed at my office this morning?"

"Yes," Grace said.

"I had to go all the way to Brooklyn for it, too," I grumbled.

"The exercise is good for you. But trust me, I didn't know I'd have more for you so soon. In my line of work, sometimes information moves at a slow trickle. And sometimes it floods in all at once. I just got a hit on Nina Badowski. She used her debit card to get cash at a convenience store in Hart County, Colorado."

Grace jolted, spine going straight. "Hart County? That's where I'm from. Is Nina still in Silver Ridge?"

"No, she's in an unincorporated area in a remote part of the county. I was able to track her down to a motel. It's about, let me check...an hour from Silver Ridge. She's registered under another name, but the motel clerk confirmed what she looked like. Helped that I transferred a hundred bucks to the guy's Venmo account."

"So you don't think he'll tip Nina off?" I asked.

"Doubt it. I told him he'll get another Venmo transfer if he gives me a heads-up when she checks out. But she's been staying there a while. Pays in cash. This motel is cheap, but not free. I assume she avoided using credit cards to stay hidden, but she ran out of funds and got desperate enough to risk the debit card."

"How did you get access to her banking info at all?" Grace asked.

"Trade secrets, my dear. Dane, I'll send you the motel info. Let me know what else I can do for you. I could be on a flight to Colorado tomorrow."

"No," I said. "I need you at your desk. I'm going to send you some photos via courier. Grace received them anonymously today. They're deep fakes, made to look like I was meeting with Nina Badowski, along with a note. I want to know who sent them. It might not be connected to Vincent Brady and his attack on Grace, but it could be."

"Got it. I'll take a look."

"Talk soon." I ended the call, immediately reaching for Grace again. I needed her close, skin to skin, for as long as we had that luxury.

"So we're going back to Colorado?" she asked.

"What makes you say that?"

"We know where Nina is. Someone has to go meet with her and find out what she knows. I'm sure you're planning to go, and if you value your life, you'll bring me with you."

"I declare that I love you, and now you're threatening me?" I teased.

"If flying makes my concussion symptoms worse, I can handle it. Don't you dare leave me behind. You said in the past that we would make a good team."

"I remember."

"This whole mess involves me just as much as it involves you. I'm coming."

I nodded. "That's convenient, because I was going to insist you come with me anyway."

"You jerk. You made me think you were leaving me here!"

I kissed her, laughing. "I'm not going anywhere without you. If you think you're ready to travel, I'm on board with that. Let me see how soon the jet can be ready."

I called Margot and explained in general terms what was going on. That we needed to head back to Hart County as soon as possible.

After wrapping up the call, I set my phone aside again. "Margot said she'd work on it and get back to me in an hour. Best guess, I figure we'll leave late tonight or first thing in the morning."

"Then we'd better pack." Grace started to get up.

"Hold on a second. Not so fast." I pulled her against me so she'd feel my semi. My cock was just perking up, but with her naked in my lap, it wouldn't take long until I was hard and ready for the next round. "I can think of a better way to kill sixty minutes." I rolled her so her back hit the mattress, my body hovering over her. "I'd love to find out how many times I can make you come in an hour. If you feel up to it."

"If *you're* up to it, then bring it on."

THIRTY-THREE

Grace

THE JET LANDED in Colorado around noon the next day. Dane's Range Rover was waiting there at the private airport, freshly washed and gassed up. That was the amazing thing about having an assistant like Margot. Someone to make those little details happen, even when she was still thousands of miles away.

I couldn't believe how much had changed since I last set foot in my home state.

Dane reached across the center console to take my hand. "Good to be back?"

"It is." But even better to have him with me.

After so many weeks in New York, I was surprised to find myself already missing Margot, who I now counted as a friend. Not just because of her incredible admin skills, of course. I admired her dry sense of humor and no-nonsense attitude. I missed Dane's apartment too, even with its bland decor, just because I'd spent a lot of time with him there.

But as we drove across the border into Hart County, a feeling of completeness washed through me. As much as I had enjoyed NYC, this was where I belonged. With the mountains and broad expanses of sky and evergreens. Most of the fall color had faded, and there was a fine layer of snow coating the branches of the pine trees.

We wouldn't head to Silver Ridge until later, though. First we had to find Nina Badowski, and we had no idea how that would go. If she would be willing to talk to us at all.

Only a few trucks passed as we drove toward the address that Warren had provided for Nina's motel. Sun glittered on the recent snowfall. We were in a less populated area of the county, surrounded by national forest land and hiking trails, with hot springs not too far away.

"This is it," Dane said. He turned onto a short drive that ended in front of a one-story motor court straight out of the 1960s. A retro sign said *Spring Valley Motel*, and proclaimed below, *Vacancy*.

The parking lot was nearly deserted.

Dane pulled his SUV into a spot near the middle and switched off the engine. "Warren said she's in number 12."

That was at the far end. The curtain on that unit was pulled closed, no sign of activity.

"We know she's hiding here," Dane added, "and she must have a good reason. That could make her dangerous if she sees us as a threat."

"If you're trying to talk me out of going to the door with you, we already had that conversation."

On the flight, Dane and I had debated which of us should approach Nina first. Dane didn't want me going up to her door by myself. And I was afraid that she wouldn't open up to some strange guy. Maybe even less so if she recognized him as a member of the Knightly family.

"You agreed we would do this together," I said.

"I did, and I'm not going back on that. But we don't know what to expect. If I tell you to get out of there, there's not going to be time for long explanations. I need to know that you'll trust my assessment without question."

"I will." He had years of training as a soldier. Ashford had taught me plenty of self-defense, but the only time I had faced real violence was when Vincent had attacked me a couple of weeks ago. I wasn't looking for a repeat of those injuries.

Yet at the same time, I wasn't afraid, either. I could do this. I *needed* to do this. Whatever the true story turned out to be, I was convinced that Nina was a victim here. If she lashed out, it would only be in self-defense.

Dane reached over to touch my face. "I just can't let anything happen to you."

"Because you made some manly promise to my brothers?"

"No, because you're the best thing in my life. I would rather die than lose you."

"When you put it that way..." It was impossible to be annoyed at a man when he made declarations like that.

We got out of the car, closing the doors softly. Dane walked in front of me as we approached number 12. The curtains in the window didn't twitch.

The whole motel was so quiet. Unnervingly so.

But as we got closer, I heard the low murmur of voices along with music. A television.

Dane paused, keeping me behind him. "You ready?"

I nodded.

We stepped in front of the door together, so when Nina looked through the peephole, she would see us both. He started to reach out to knock.

Then I saw the scratches around the lock plate, and I grabbed his arm. "Dane, *look*." It was like my brain had flashed back in time by several weeks, to the night I had walked up to my house and realized someone had broken in.

"Fuck," he muttered. "Stay back, Grace. We need to call the police. If we don't have cell service, the front desk will have a landline."

But my safety was the least of my concerns at this moment. "Nina could be hurt!"

Dane rapped hard on the door. "Nina? You okay?" The door swung inward. It hadn't been latched.

Someone with red hair was sprawled on the carpet. A dark pool spread out beneath her.

No.

"Stay out of here," Dane barked. "Call 911." He lunged forward to check for vital signs. I couldn't move, my limbs frozen as I stood in the doorway.

There was no way Nina could lose that much blood and still be alive.

✧

"I'm Sheriff Owen Douglas." He held out his hand to Dane, then to me. "Thanks for waiting."

"Took long enough," Dane grumbled.

"I assume you have questions for us," I said.

We were in the tiny lobby of the Spring Valley Motel. The plastic chair I was sitting on was possibly the least comfortable in existence. Outside, the motel parking lot was crawling with sheriff's department vehicles. The front desk clerk had nearly gotten hysterical when he heard one of his guests had been attacked. I was pretty sure he was being interviewed by a deputy.

Nina was dead, and I felt sick wondering if there was some way we could've helped her. If we had gotten here yesterday instead of today...

I had no idea how long she'd been lying there, but Dane and I both guessed no more than several hours. She'd probably been killed overnight.

Sheriff Douglas nodded. "I do. A *lot* of questions. I trust you'll both be cooperative."

I had never met the sheriff of Hart County in person before, though of course I knew Douglas by reputation. I had voted for him in the last election. He was around Ashford and Dane's age, mid-thirties, wearing a white cowboy hat with his uniform.

My brother had spoken well of Sheriff Douglas in the past. Ashford had led some martial arts trainings for the department. But the deputies had kept us waiting in here for a while, even trying to separate us until Dane threatened to have his lawyer on the next flight out.

The sheriff dragged over one of the uncomfortable chairs. "I really should be questioning you separately." He held up a hand like he was trying to head off our protests. "*But,* I understand you've already raised objections to that. So I'll make an exception just to speed this along. Last I spoke to your brother, Miss O'Neal, Ashford mentioned you were staying in New York for a while. Yet here you are."

"We flew in today to find Nina Badowski."

"Do you know when exactly she was attacked, Sheriff?" Dane asked.

"We're in the process of determining that. It's one of the questions I have for you, in fact. Wasn't planning to start there, though."

"Grace and I have no idea. We weren't even in Colorado until a few hours ago. We came straight here. Found the door open and Nina on the floor inside."

"We explained that to the first officers on the scene after I called 911," I added.

Sheriff Douglas took off his hat, scratching at the buzzed hair beneath. "Yes, but I'm going to need to hear a lot more about why a rich New York businessman and a Silver Ridge local wound up here looking for a woman who turned out to be... Well, there's no way to put this delicately is there?"

"She had her throat cut," Dane said.

The sheriff squinted at him. "How do you know that?"

"How do you think? I have eyes." Dane had already told me that was what it looked like. But I suppressed another shudder and a wave of nausea. Dane's hand went to my thigh, a reassuring weight.

"A woman has been murdered," Douglas said. "I recommend cutting the sarcasm."

"We want to help," I interrupted. "But we already know who did this. His name is Vincent Brady."

"Did you see him here?"

"I haven't seen him since he attacked me in New York. But I'm sure it was him. We'll tell you everything we can."

I started with meeting Nina at the hotel's grand-opening party, though of course I hadn't known her name at the time. I shared how Nina had given me her mask. How Dirk Lancaster had mistaken me for her, and later Vincent approached me trying to find her.

Nina had disappeared that night. Whatever she'd been running from, she must've already known the danger by then. Why else would she hole up in this motel under a fake name?

Yet I didn't believe she'd wanted to put *me* in danger. The strap on my mask broke simply by chance. Nina made a snap decision to give me hers. She'd probably thought I might attract Dirk's and Vincent's attention, but then they'd forget about me once they realized I wasn't her. Even after the break-in at my house when the mask was stolen, Vincent left me alone.

Until, of course, I showed up in New York and saw him threatening Lexi. And got myself involved again.

I'd heard Vincent threaten Nina when he was talking to Lexi Sanders. Lexi was probably in extreme danger too, and I hoped she was staying hidden. But Nina had tried to hide, and Vincent had found her, just like Dane's investigator had.

Vincent had made it here first.

But what we still didn't know was *why*. Why Vincent would want to kill Nina to silence her. Why any of this was really happening.

Sheriff Douglas listened to all of it with a serious but impassive expression. "So Vincent Brady was searching for Nina, and so were you. Mr. Knightly's investigator tracked her down, and that's why you arrived today. To have a chat with her. But you haven't explained what you hoped she could tell you."

"That has to do with my father's company," Dane said. "Knightly Global. And a possible high-end escort business being run at my family's hotel properties."

The sheriff's stoic expression finally broke, revealing his shock. "Escorts?"

We answered the rest of Douglas's questions, but there wasn't much else we could add. There were so many gaps in what we knew. Finally, the sheriff fit his hat on his head and stood. "I would appreciate if neither of you leaves the county for the next week at least, in case I have more questions for you."

"Not a problem," Dane said. "We're planning to stay in Silver Ridge for a while."

"Chief Landry at Silver Ridge PD might also want to speak to you, since the break-in at Grace's home was his jurisdiction. I'll keep him updated on my side of things, and he can let you know."

After Sheriff Douglas left the motel lobby, Dane turned to me, his gruffness melting away. "How are you doing? This has been a lot."

"I'm pissed off. And I hate the thought that we might've stopped this. If Warren had found Nina sooner, or maybe if we'd tried to call her yesterday as soon as we figured out she was here, I could've told her Vincent had been looking for her."

Dane put his arm around me and rested his cheek against my temple. "She was in hiding, baby. She already knew. There was no way to predict if she would talk to us or if we could've made any difference at all."

I didn't want to accept that. I had to believe there would be some kind of resolution to all this. Some kind of *justice*.

"We passed a pizza place down the road," Dane said. "Let's get some food, and then we can head to Silver Ridge. I'm sure you're anxious to see your family."

"I am. I want to hug Maisie and I just... I just want to be with them. And you. I haven't even asked how *you're* doing."

"I'm alright. Next to you is the only place I want to be."

✧

I was too nauseous to be hungry, but food did seem like a good idea. At the very least so that we weren't jittery for the drive.

We passed beyond the police cordon and through a small crowd of curiosity seekers on our way out of the motel. Word was already spreading about a murder. Not a common occurrence anywhere in my home county.

The pizza place was a five-minute drive away. When we walked into the restaurant, with old-school country music playing from a jukebox and vintage skis and snowshoes decorating the walls, I did feel calmer. Like we had slipped out of a nightmare world and gone back to almost-normal life.

As soon as we sat down, Dane ordered us a couple of sodas. Which turned out to be perfect. The first few sips got my blood sugar back up and settled my stomach.

When the pizza arrived, though, my nausea returned. The image of Nina's hotel room surfaced again in my mind, and I pushed my plate away.

Dane frowned, seeming to look past me before his gaze returned to my face. "Grace—"

"I know I need to eat something, but I can't right now."

"No, it's not that." He was keeping his voice low, not even moving his lips much. "Don't turn around. There's a man who came into the restaurant about five minutes after us who's sitting at a table in the corner. He's fidgeting like he's nervous. And he keeps looking over here."

I stopped myself from glancing back, using the reflection in the decorative mirror behind Dane to scan the room. I spotted the guy he meant. Sandy blond hair, wire-rimmed glasses, a neatly trimmed beard. A gingham button-down shirt tucked into jeans. He didn't have the look of a local, especially someone living in a more rural part of Hart County.

Adrenaline roared through my veins again.

"I saw him outside the motel, too," Dane murmured. "The crowd that had gathered outside the police cordon. Know him?"

"Never seen him before." But the energy coursing through me wasn't fear. It was excitement. I leaned forward, elbows on the table. "What if he has information about Nina?" I whispered.

"Either that, or he's the one who killed her and he's looking for his next victim."

I scoffed, glancing at the guy in the mirror again. "Maybe we should talk to him."

"Nope. I'm going to pay, and then I'm getting you out of here. We've had enough surprises for one day."

"Wait. I have an idea."

Dane paused, waiting as he frowned.

Earlier, Nina's death had left me feeling defeated. But I couldn't just give up and walk away from this. I had been sitting still for the last couple of weeks, healing in a luxurious apartment with an incredible man taking care of me.

And during that same time, Nina had been all alone. Terrified. For her, the worst had happened. But I was still here.

I was finished with being passive. I had to *act*.

"I'll go down that hallway toward the restrooms," I said. "Maybe he'll try to follow me. If he does, you come up behind him and we'll confront him."

"Use you as bait? Absolutely *not*. You're still not healed, but even if you were, I'd still say no."

"We either go with my idea, or we head to his table right now and ask in front of the whole restaurant why he's staring. But given how anxious he is, that might scare him away."

"I'm not putting you in harm's way again. I'm planning to call Douglas and report it. Let the sheriff talk to the guy."

"Report *what*? That the guy's looking at us funny? Douglas

and his deputies are busy at the murder scene. This guy doesn't look like a killer. He wants to talk to us. This could be an easy way to get him alone so we can find out what he wants."

Dane groaned. "I never should've told you how brave you are. Shouldn't have encouraged you."

I smiled, knowing I'd won. "You're the guy who once compared me to a superhero."

"I did, didn't I?" Dane wiped his hand over his face. "Okay, we'll try it your way. But if the man makes any sudden moves toward you, I'm not going to mess around. I'm knocking him out, and we'll have to chat with him later when he wakes up. Assuming Sheriff Douglas doesn't have me in the county jail for assault."

"If that happens, I promise to bail you out."

THIRTY-FOUR

Dane

WARREN HAD BEEN RIGHT. Grace really did have me wrapped around her finger.

Grace and I had both seen something horrific today. But if I could've placed that burden entirely on me, I would have. My protective side wanted to bundle her up and hide her from any other harm that might come her way. Yet Grace had just told me herself what she truly needed. To figure out what the hell was going on and make sure it stopped.

I agreed with her reasoning. There was something weird going on with that guy in the corner who was watching us, and if the man had any kind of information on Nina or Vincent Brady, now was the time to find out before he disappeared like the other leads we'd had so far.

How this tied back to Knightly Global, to my brother... I didn't know yet. But I intended to find out.

My muscles tensed as Grace got up from the booth. She went straight for the hallway leading to the bathrooms near the back of the restaurant. I focused on eating and scrolling my phone, but I also kept the man in the corner in my peripheral vision.

The guy waited a minute, then two, drumming his fingers on his tabletop.

Then he got up, adjusted his wire-rimmed glasses, and walked toward the restrooms.

Fury surged in my body. Leaving a bunch of twenties on the table, more than enough to cover our tab and a generous tip, I got up to follow. I didn't actually think this man would attack Grace, at least not right away. But as for what the guy wanted, there was no telling.

The last time I hadn't been around when Grace needed help, she'd wound up in the hospital. I wasn't letting that happen again.

The hallway was long and narrow. I spotted the sign for the women's restroom at the far end near the back exit. The man stood and stared at the door to the ladies' room, shifting from foot to foot, like he was waiting for Grace to come out.

He glanced over at me as I came up fast. My hand clamped down on his shoulder. "You wanna tell me why you were following my girlfriend to the bathroom?"

His mouth opened like he might yell. So I hustled him quickly toward the rear exit door and pushed him through. Outside, I slammed him against the brick wall of the building. We were next to a dumpster, which hid us from the view of the parking lot.

"I can explain!"

"Then you'd better get going, because I already got one nasty surprise earlier today, and I'm not feeling very patient."

Grace pushed through the back door, standing at my shoulder. "Who are you?" she demanded.

The guy glanced from Grace to me and back again. "A reporter."

I tightened my grip on the man's shirt. "Some vulture looking for a tabloid story? That's supposed to make us *less* pissed off?"

"An investigative reporter," he rushed to say. "I was supposed to meet Nina Badowski this afternoon. She had information for me. But when I arrived, I found police surrounding the motel.

Since then I've learned you're the ones who found her body, I have to assume you might've been looking for the same info."

"Do you know who killed her?" Grace asked.

"I have theories. But nothing to prove them yet, and that's why I wanted to talk to you. I know you're Grace O'Neal. And he's Dane Knightly. You two are the only leads on this story I've got left."

Well, we had that in common, since this reporter was our only lead too. But I wasn't ready to back off and play nice just yet. "Then why follow Grace?" I demanded. "Why the secrecy? You could've come up to us in the restaurant and introduced yourself."

"You know what happened to Nina. You got a far more graphic warning than I did of what's at stake here. I have no idea who might be listening, but I don't want to end up like Nina did."

"Then why trust us at all?" Grace asked.

"Because I've been keeping track of this story for the last month." He nodded at Grace. "I know you were injured a few weeks ago at a Knightly Global property. And you, Mr. Knightly, barely get along with your family. Whatever's going on, it's clear you're on the outside of it. Someone *did* come to Hart County to silence Nina, but I'm sure it wasn't either of you, and it wasn't me. I'll tell you everything I know if you do the same."

I exchanged a look with Grace. She nodded, and I backed away, letting go of the man. "What's your name?" I asked.

"Norm Haber. Feel free to look me up. My photo and bio are online."

"We will," Grace assured him. "But I'd rather go somewhere else to talk. That dumpster really stinks."

✧

We chose a deserted picnic area near a hiking trail. Grace and I rode together, while Norm followed in his rental sedan.

"Norm Haber works for a major newspaper on the West Coast," she said on the way. "He matches the photos on his bio online. It seems like he is who he says he is."

"That's a decent start." But I still didn't know what to make of the reporter. It sounded like he had been investigating Knightly Global as part of this. Norm Haber was taking a risk by talking to me. I would be doing the same. But the *truth* was what mattered. If Kip was really working with Vincent Brady, I wasn't going to lift a finger to protect my brother. I had already made my choice.

Vincent had harmed Grace. He'd probably killed Nina. Anybody who was working with the man, related to me or not, was no friend of mine.

We sat at a picnic table. The trail was deserted, probably because the sky overhead was cloudy and gray, threatening snow. Grace zipped her puffer all the way to her neck, and she'd pulled a knit cap over her red and gold strands.

Norm set his phone on the picnic table in front of us. "Okay if I record this?"

Grace and I both nodded.

"So, Mr. Knightly," Norm began. "I want to take a step back, come at this story from the beginning. I'm curious about your decision to work for your father."

Grace shook her head. "No, you're going to answer *my* questions first."

Norm looked over at me like he thought I was going to contradict her. As if he assumed I wouldn't want her taking charge.

I just shrugged and bit back a smile.

I didn't want Grace in danger, but I enjoyed seeing her like this. Assertive. Telling this guy exactly how it would be.

"You said you've been working on this story for over a month," Grace said. "Did you contact Nina originally? Or did she contact you?"

"Nina got in touch with me," Norm answered with a sigh. "Said she had sensitive information for me that could implicate some rich and powerful people."

"A high-class escort ring," Grace supplied.

Norm looked surprised. "You were aware?"

"Not until a day or two ago. Dane had a private investigator looking into Nina. That's how we knew she was staying at the motel here in Hart County."

The reporter nodded. "Nina got in touch about a month and a half ago. Told me she could name names and provide proof. She told me she'd gotten access to the data through a client."

"Did she say who the client was?" Grace asked.

"No. She refused to give me too many details over the phone and wanted to remain anonymous in any future story. But she did say she had dirt on Knightly Global. That the company has ties to the escort ring."

Fuck. I'd already suspected my family was connected to this. But it still wasn't fun to get confirmation. "What did she want from you in exchange?" I said.

He shook his head. "Nothing. Just to expose her employers. If she'd wanted money, she could've used the info as blackmail or gone to a tabloid. I think she just wanted to eventually find a way out. But she was afraid of the escort ring's enforcer."

"Vincent Brady," Grace whispered.

"Yes. Brady's job was to keep a tight hold on the escorts. Given the sensitive information they had access to, the people at the top couldn't risk leaks getting out. Everything the women did was monitored, except when they were supposed to be with a client. It was hard enough for Nina just to get the burner phone that she used to communicate with me. That's why Nina and I planned our initial meeting carefully. The whole idea was to have her hand the proof to me right under Vincent's nose." He grimaced. "But I didn't make it."

Grace inhaled sharply. "The night of the hotel grand-opening party. Nina said her date stood her up. She meant *you*."

"But we assumed her client for that evening was Dirk Lancaster," I pointed out.

Norm explained how it was supposed to go down. Nina had arrived in Silver Ridge to be Dirk Lancaster's date for the night. Her red mask was supposed to identify her. But she had also planned to meet Norm.

"We weren't even going to talk," he said. "I was going to bump into her in the lobby, and she would hand off the data inconspicuously. Since it would be crowded, and she was already there to meet with a client, we figured the exchange would go unnoticed."

"Why not send it to you online?" Grace asked. "Or in the mail or something."

"And risk leaving a digital trail? Or having the package intercepted? She already didn't want to risk contacting a reporter in New York. She said her employers were powerful people with contacts all over the East Coast. These people were willing to kill to keep this stuff secret. As you both have seen."

Okay, fair point. This whole scenario was bizarre, like a plot dreamed up for a spy movie. But stranger things had happened. When it came to sex scandals, it wasn't that far-fetched to imagine that someone would kill to keep a witness quiet.

I put my hand over Grace's on the picnic bench, lacing our fingers.

Norm took off his glasses and rubbed his eyes. "The night of the grand opening in Silver Ridge, I was on my way to the ski resort when I skidded off the road on a patch of ice. Worst damn luck, and to cap it off, I had no cell service. I couldn't message Nina on her burner to explain why I was late."

"So she got scared," Grace said. "She assumed something was wrong. That maybe her employers had gotten to you and figured out her plan."

Norm nodded dejectedly. "Exactly. She decided to disappear. Right then."

"And she gave *me* her mask. To create a distraction. She knew

Dirk Lancaster would be looking for her, and so would Vincent Brady. She was lucky to slip away at all without Brady noticing."

I rubbed my jaw with my free hand. "But what about the data she'd wanted to turn over about the escort ring? What did she do with it? Could it have been on her burner phone? If she kept it with her, then her killer probably found it in her motel room."

Norm shook his head, leaning forward. "No, I don't think so. Listen. After the grand-opening party, Nina got rid of her burner. I couldn't reach her for a while. Had no idea what happened to her. I even called around to the local police in Hart County in the hopes of finding her, but I couldn't risk revealing my name. Otherwise I'd be revealing *her* as my source."

Grace's eyes widened. "So that was *you*. Police Chief Landry mentioned an anonymous call about a missing woman. That's how we figured out her name, at least the name she was using then. Nina Jamison."

"But then she *did* contact me again, about a week ago. She'd managed to get access to another phone, and she told me she was in hiding and hoped I could help her. She was running out of money. Didn't know where to turn. And she said she didn't have the data on the escort ring with her anymore, but she had an idea of where to find it. Because she'd *given it to someone else*."

Norm and I both looked at Grace. She sat back. "Wait, you mean *me*?"

"Did she give you anything else the night of the party?" Norm asked. "Anything besides the mask?"

Grace bit her lip, seeming to think. "No. Nothing. And I don't even have Nina's mask anymore. It was stolen."

"Hold on," Norm said. "*Stolen*? When did that happen?"

"About a week after the grand-opening party."

Grace told him about the break-in at her house. The three of us talked a while longer, trying to fit all these strange puzzle pieces together, but it wasn't easy.

Finally, we'd exhausted our theories. We exchanged numbers so we could keep in touch and share whatever we found.

"I'd like a more extensive interview with you on the subject of Knightly Global," Norm said.

"I'll consider it. But *you* need to talk to Sheriff Douglas. You have information on Nina's murder."

"I plan to come forward. I'm more concerned right now about Nina's killer coming after me. I have no idea how much they know. Whether they're aware she was in touch with a reporter. No offense, but I'm not telling *anyone* where I'm going. Not until I have enough to break this story wide open."

"Then maybe, after we're all convinced the danger has passed, I'll agree to an interview."

Not long after that, Norm took off in his sedan. Grace and I went to the Range Rover and got in. There was nothing else for us to do but head back toward Silver Ridge.

Hell, it had been a long day. I wanted to do something to make Grace feel better. Fuss over her. Take care of her, because the truth was, it made *me* feel better too.

I wanted us to take care of each other, and I was hoping she'd give that to me forever.

Yet at the current moment, Grace didn't seem like she wanted a pleasant distraction. She looked like a woman who meant serious business.

"What're you thinking about?" I asked as we pulled onto the road.

"Nina. Remembering when we met. She seemed upset and distracted. She didn't know what to do. I wish she'd asked me for help. Maybe I could have..." She trailed off.

"It's awful what happened to her. But I don't like the fact that she used you as a pawn."

"Nina was scared. The strap on my mask broke, and she decided to use it as an opportunity."

"Sure, but giving you the mask is one thing. If she knew how violent Vincent Brady is and she gave you sensitive information, she should've expected he might come after you."

"Nina didn't know if Vincent would stop her before she

could get away that night, and she couldn't let him find her with top-secret data about her employers. She probably just wanted to get rid of it and wasn't thinking too much about what would happen later."

"Yeah, but—"

Suddenly, Grace sucked in a breath, hand clapping over her mouth. "Wait a minute. *My purse.*"

"Did you leave it at the pizza place?" I slowed the SUV, about to make a U-turn.

Grace waved her hands. "No. That's not it. Not the purse I have today. Just...keep driving. We're going to Piper's house."

"Want to elaborate? I love you, and I'll do anything for you, but I gotta admit, I'm confused." I glanced over at her and was surprised to find Grace wasn't frowning anymore.

Instead, she was smiling.

"I think I know where Nina's top-secret information is."

THIRTY-FIVE
Grace

PIPER LIVED in a cottage a block away from Silver Linings Coffee. She opened her front door, all smiles, before I even had a chance to knock. "I had no idea you were heading back to Silver Ridge so soon. You must be feeling better, not that you let *me* know."

"I'm doing well." On our way here, I had messaged Piper to make sure she was home. But there was too much to explain to do it over the phone, and I was still trying to understand all of it myself. "I would've given you the heads-up sooner, but a lot has been going on."

"I bet." She smirked at Dane, who was right behind me. "Come in, but watch your feet. Emma and Maisie were over here earlier. The kids had a Lego party." We walked inside, dodging toys. "I lost the living room to the mess, and I'm trying to limit the spread, but you know Ollie. He's a force of nature. Do you want a drink?"

I had missed Piper like crazy, and I wanted to tell her everything that had happened. The good and the bad. But that would have to wait. At the moment, I had other priorities that were more pressing.

"This is going to sound strange, but do you have that purse

you loaned me the night of the hotel grand opening? The red clutch."

"Sure." She narrowed her eyes. "But—"

Piper's son came barreling into the entryway. "Hi, Miss Grace!" Ollie gushed. "Will you help me build my Lego city? I poured out all the pieces I have, and Mom said it's like a toy factory exploded in our living room!"

Piper looked at me with a silent lament, then turned back to her son. "Sweetheart, they just got here."

"But Mama—"

"I'd love to help you, Ollie," Dane cut in. "I happen to be a Lego aficionado."

Ollie eyed him suspiciously. "Who are *you*?"

Piper opened her mouth, probably to scold her eight-year-old about being rude to a guest, but Dane spoke first. "I'm Grace's boyfriend. Dane Knightly. She'll vouch for my character."

Piper's eyebrows shot toward her hairline. *Boyfriend*? she mouthed.

"Dane has my personal seal of approval," I said, pushing my boyfriend toward the living room Lego disaster. "Also, Maisie is a big fan of him. Dane gave Maisie that snow globe, remember?"

That was enough to convince Ollie. As soon as they were off in the living room, I grabbed Piper's hand and went toward her bedroom, which was at the back of the house. "Seriously, I will catch you up on what this is about. But I really need to see the purse I borrowed. It's urgent."

"Hey, if your boyfriend is going to entertain my kid for a while, I'll let you take your pick from my wardrobe. Anything you want."

"Just the red purse."

"I don't have many occasions to use my fancy stuff, so it's just been sitting here since you gave it back to me." Piper went to the closet and pulled out a plastic bin, removing the lid. There was the red clutch, right on top. Piper handed me the purse.

I held my breath as I opened the flap and looked inside.

Then my heart fell, all that anticipation fizzling out.

There was nothing but a keycard for the hotel inside. The one Dane had given me that night. *Shit.*

"Well, are you going to tell me what this is about? Did you find what you were looking for?"

I slumped down on the edge of Piper's bed. "It's not here. I can tell you, though." I owed her an explanation. Even if I'd been wrong. "You already know about Nina Jamison."

"Sure, the woman with the red mask who disappeared. You met her the night of the grand opening."

When Piper and my brothers had been in New York, I'd shared everything I knew about what led to Vincent attacking me. Which, at that time, wasn't all that much. Now, I told Piper the rest of what we knew. Including the fact that Nina had been murdered.

"That's horrifying. But what does that have to do with the purse?"

"We learned Nina had sensitive information she was going to turn over to a reporter. Something that could implicate Knightly Global in a high-class escort ring."

Piper whistled. "Dang."

"And I thought maybe Nina got spooked and passed that data over to *me* at the ski resort hotel. When we were in the bathroom, I almost forgot my purse. She handed it to me. Today, I remembered that and thought she might've slipped something inside. But there's just this hotel key. "

"She didn't give that to you?"

"No, that was Dane. After he invited me up to his hotel suite that night to sleep with him."

"Uh, he *what*?"

Had I not told my best friend that part? Oops.

I started to laugh, which felt good. It pushed away the disappointment a little. "I didn't even know who he was then, and I didn't go through with it. Obviously. Since you and I left together that night." I took the keycard out of the purse, feeling nostalgic. "But I was tempted."

"And now?" she asked. "Last time we spoke, you were still worried about moving too fast with Dane."

I slowly shook my head, staring at the keycard on my palm. "No more doubts about him. He's amazing. He told me he's in love with me, and he's willing to move to Silver Ridge to be with me."

She gasped, a delighted smile brightening her face. "Oh, Grace. What about how *you* feel? What did you tell him?"

"I—" The words evaporated from my head as I noticed what I held in my hand. Not just a single keycard for the ski resort. *Two.* There were two keycards here. They'd gotten stuck together. But where had the second come from?

"What's up?" Piper asked.

I separated the two cards, examining each one closely. There was a little square of plastic taped to the back of one, about the size of my thumbnail.

A tiny data storage card.

"Holy crap," I whispered. "I think this is it."

"What is *what*? I can't keep up with you today."

I pointed at the data storage card. "The secret info Nina wanted to give to the reporter. The reason she was murdered."

Piper inhaled. "Holy crap is right. People use these in digital cameras, don't they? I think I have a way to read this. We can see what's on it."

"Are you serious? Piper, I will love you forever."

She winked at me. "Save it for the amazing Mr. Knightly."

While Piper looked for her digital camera, I went to the living room and filled in Dane about what I'd found. A few minutes later, we were gathered around Piper. She'd managed to transfer the info from that tiny data storage card to her laptop.

"Take a look," she said.

The first document was a list of dozens of names. Kip Knightly and Dirk Lancaster were both on it.

"My brother's name is here," Dane murmured when he saw. He was sitting on the couch beside me, while Ollie continued to play on the floor, and Piper looked on curiously.

"Not clear yet what this list means," I said.

"True, but it's not good. Open the rest of the files."

The others were spreadsheets. Probably the books for the escort ring. Here I was, a bookkeeper, seeing the secret financials for a criminal organization. One that could implicate Dane's family and other powerful people. It would take time to go over all of this.

There was a lot of information here. Account numbers, transfers of money. Physical addresses.

"A lot of these are addresses of Knightly Global properties," Dane said. "Fucking hell."

"You're not having second thoughts, are you?" I whispered. "About sharing this with police."

"Absolutely not. We're going to expose the truth. Whatever happens, happens."

"Good." But anxiety tingled in the back of my mind like an itch I couldn't scratch. Nina had died for this information, and now my best friend had it on her computer. I didn't want Piper or Ollie to be in danger because of this.

I asked Piper to make a copy and send it to my email. Then I told her to delete any traces from her computer. As for the data storage card, I kept that as well. Dane and I agreed we would take a closer look at everything ourselves before turning it over to law enforcement.

I gave Piper and Ollie hugs on our way out the door. My friend was nervous about what all of this meant, and so was I. "Don't mention this to anyone," I said. "Not even Teller. Let Dane and me handle it."

"Okay, but if I get even the slightest hint that you're not safe..."

"Then you can join the long line of people determined to protect me," I teased.

I didn't need protection from hardships. I'd been through plenty and survived. But I also didn't resent the fact that Piper and my brothers and so many other people in my life cared about me. It was a privilege. I saw that now.

I had Dane beside me, though. A guy who wasn't just *my* superhero. He made me feel like a hero too.

We were going to figure this out. Together.

THIRTY-SIX

Dane

I PARKED the Range Rover with the valet, and Grace and I headed in to the lobby hand-in-hand. First time we'd been back to the hotel in weeks. And unlike before, we were together now.

I wanted to get her upstairs, snuggle with her in my bed—*our* bed—and sleep away everything that had happened today.

It would all be back tomorrow. A tangled mess that might finally destroy what was left of the Knightly family. I still wasn't sure how Kip was involved with Nina's murder or the escort ring. But when the news got out, it would cause a huge scandal. It was going to affect my mother's name and reputation, and Mom wouldn't even have a chance to speak for herself.

And my father? Was it possible *he* had something to do with any of this? I didn't want to believe that. But I had to acknowledge it was possible.

Maybe it was a blessing that Mom wouldn't know. There would be fallout for the company. Maybe for the ski resort too, since Knightly Global owned it. I had no idea what to expect. How far the Knightly name would fall.

For tonight, I just needed Grace in my arms. A reminder that some good might come from all of this.

So courageous, this woman. The best thing in my life.

Tobin stepped out from behind the reception desk. "Mr. Knightly, Ms. O'Neal. Welcome back."

I put my hand on Grace's lower shoulder and nodded hello to my hotel manager. "Working late again, I see."

"Thought I'd stick around after I got word you were returning. Your suite is ready."

"Thank you, Tobin."

"I have a new keycard for you."

"And one for Ms. O'Neal?" I asked. "She'll be staying. I want Grace to have full access to the hotel."

"Oh, yes. Of course."

While Tobin went to make another keycard for suite 701, I turned to Grace. "I know we haven't talked about living arrangements," I whispered. "I understand if you need your own space. But you're welcome here anytime you want." I bumped my nose against hers. "I love having you with me." In fact, it was so much worse than that. I craved having her near. Couldn't imagine going without her, now that I'd experienced living with her.

Grace's smile was sweet. "I love being with you too. I have a lot to catch up on now that we're back in Silver Ridge, but...I'm sure I'll be spending a lot of time here at the hotel."

Her answer made me happy, even though I wanted Grace here all the time. I was selfish like that. Always wanting more.

She'd blown me away today. How well she'd been handling everything the world kept throwing at us. Dealing with Norm Haber, finding that data storage card. Not to mention shaking off the shock of discovering Nina's gruesome death. Grace was incredible, an asset.

I'd told her once that we'd make a great team in business. Grace had a brilliant future ahead of her, and I would be lucky to be a part of it.

As soon as we get through this disaster my brother somehow pulled Knightly Global into, I thought with a sigh.

Tobin handed over the keycards we needed. Grace and I took the elevator to the top floor. We'd packed light when we left New

York to make things easy, just a duffel for each of us, which I carried. Margot was going to supervise packing up Grace's new wardrobe and everything else I needed for my move to Silver Ridge.

Upstairs, the lights in the entryway of my suite were on. A welcome basket waited on the table just inside. Grace stared at it.

"Do you think you'll keep living here at the hotel long-term?" she asked.

I set the bags down and pulled Grace to me, kissing the top of her head. "You don't like it?"

"It's beautiful, and I know it's convenient for you. But it's kind of impersonal. Doesn't really feel like a home. And it's still strange to me that the hotel staff comes and goes even when you're not around."

"I was thinking about buying a house, actually."

She looked up at me. "Really?"

"Yeah. I said I want to make Silver Ridge my home. I feel the same way you do about the hotel. It's fine for now, but I'd like something that feels more...permanent."

A place that Grace would want to live. *Permanently*. With me. A home we could share. But I didn't want to push her on that. I'd only told her yesterday that I loved her, and today had been beyond stressful.

I wanted it all with Grace. She'd said she loved being with me. Not quite an *I love you*, but not too bad either. We would get there.

"Are you hungry?" I asked. "I'm sure they stocked the fridge."

"No. Just want to get ready for bed."

"Okay." I pressed another kiss to her temple. "How about you shower and get changed. I'm going to the office to send some quick messages, and I'll join you in a few minutes."

"'K."

I stopped in the kitchen for a glass of water and a protein bar. Warren needed an update, and I wanted to see if he'd learned anything new on his end. But I was bracing myself for the other message I had to write. Figured I owed my father a warning about what might happen tomorrow. I wasn't keeping any of this a secret.

Tomorrow, after Grace and I took a closer look at Nina's files, we would send copies to Sheriff Douglas, Chief Landry, and the NYPD detective assigned to Grace's assault case. And then, to Norm Haber.

My father always harped about loyalty. He'd claimed I didn't respect our family. Well, if Dad felt that way, so be it. A warning about the impending scandal was all the loyalty I could muster.

But my steps faltered as I neared the door to the office. It was mostly closed, but light showed in the crack beneath and along the side. Could the staff have forgotten to turn it off earlier when they were cleaning? I'd left a laptop here while I was gone, but it was password-protected. There wasn't much else of value.

I reached out to push the door open. Then I blinked, caught off guard by what was waiting inside.

Ainsley Harcourt sat behind the desk. *My* desk.

"Ainsley? What the *hell* are you doing here?"

"Dane, we need to talk."

THIRTY-SEVEN

Grace

I WENT into Dane's bedroom and switched on the light. I was just about dead on my feet, and that California King bed looked extremely inviting.

Last time I'd been in Dane's hotel, I'd been staying in one of the other bedrooms. It was strange to be back here like this, not just sharing his bed, but actually as his girlfriend. His partner.

And he was going to buy a house here in Silver Ridge. I'd believed Dane before about his decision to move here, yet hearing those plans made it feel even more real.

It felt so good to be back in Silver Ridge, but even better to have Dane beside me and know that he would be a part of my life here.

Kind of terrifying, but wow. Really good.

Of course, the awfulness of that day's events weighed on my mind, sitting on the edges of every thought like a shadow. Even the shadows in Dane's bedroom seemed to shift like they were alive. Prickles of awareness raced up and down my spine, and I glanced around the room, feeling watched.

It was just the memory of what I'd seen earlier. The scene at Nina's motel. *Ugh.*

I pushed that image away with a shudder. We were safe in

Dane's suite now. I even heard the deep rumble of his voice. He was probably on the phone.

Everything is fine.

Or at least, it would be.

I went into the en suite and twisted the shower knob to let the water heat, thinking about what Dane had said. The house he planned to buy, and how he wanted me with him. He hadn't come out and said, *Move in with me*, but I knew Dane Knightly pretty well by now.

Did I want to move in with him?

It was fast, and I already knew Callum would throw a fit about it. But Ashford and Emma had moved in together quickly too. Just as friends at first, but Ashford had a thing for her by then. Everyone could see it, except maybe Emma.

But when you knew deep down something was right, why not go after it? I wanted to be happy. To have all the things I never thought I could have. I'd have to figure out some way to pay rent though. No way would I let Dane keep paying for everything. Though I had no doubt he would argue with me on that point.

We would figure it out.

Steam began to fill the shower. I started unbuttoning my shirt, but something made me stop. That same instinctual feeling from earlier. Like someone was watching me.

I glanced back at the bedroom. Dane hadn't come in.

But that feeling didn't fade.

I walked out into the bedroom. "Is someone there?" The door to the closet was cracked open. Somebody could be hiding in the darkness, looking out.

My heart raced. There was a heavy book on the dresser. I grabbed it, since I didn't see anything else to use as a weapon. I was probably just imagining things, but suddenly, being alone was the last thing I wanted. I would go to Dane's office and wait for him. Then we could shower and get ready for bed together.

Decision made, I glanced at the book in my hands, smirking when I realized what it was. *Advanced Techniques for QuickBooks.*

The very book I'd brought to Silver Linings Coffee on the day Dane and I had met. He must've bought it. He was ridiculous.

"Dane?" I called out, heading for the door to the hallway.

But a hand came down on my arm, tightening like a vise. A man had just stepped out of the shadows from behind me. I tried to swing the book, inhaling to scream. Then I felt the cold bite of metal against my throat. A knife.

"Don't move. Don't make another sound. Or you'll die exactly the way Nina did."

THIRTY-EIGHT

Dane

"How did you get in here?" I demanded.

Ainsley crossed her legs, leaning back casually. Like this was *her* office instead of the one in *my* private hotel suite.

Rather than answering my question, she said, "I came because your brother has gotten himself into some trouble. It's become a real issue. Not just for Knightly Global, but for my family as well." Ainsley picked up several glossy photos from the desk. I hadn't noticed them before. "Here," she said. "Take a look at what Kip has been up to."

"No, you showed up here. You're going to explain yourself."

"Just *look*." She held the photos out.

I exhaled. Dammit, I was way too tired for this.

Between her and her sister, Ainsley had always been the more reasonable one. Clever, but with a sense of humor. I'd considered her a friend.

But her showing up like this, unannounced? It didn't feel like a friendly visit. This was my turf, and yet I was on the defensive, and I didn't like it one bit. The fact that I'd known Ainsley almost all my life was the *sole* reason I hadn't thrown her out.

I knew a power move when I saw one. I just didn't know yet what Ainsley really wanted.

"Come on, Dane. We don't have all night."

Glaring, I snatched the photos from her hand and looked.

They were of Kip and Nina Badowski. Talking together. Kissing. These images were strikingly similar to the deep-fake photos that Grace had received of me with Nina. But something told me these ones were the real deal.

Kip, what have you done? I thought.

"Where did you get these?"

Ainsley waved her hand. "That's not important right now. I think we can agree Kip has shown a serious lack of discretion. He was seeing this woman, Nina Badowski. Paying for her services, to be more accurate."

Oh, hell. So he'd been a client of Nina's. Like Dirk Lancaster. Which explained both their names being on that list.

I tossed the photos back on the desk. "Was this before he got together with Bristol? Or after?"

"It's cute that you think the timing matters. But for what it's worth, it was before. He hasn't cheated on my sister. This couldn't have worked out better for her. In fact, to hear Bristol tell it, Kip has been very compliant."

"*Compliant*? That doesn't sound like Kip. Do you mean..." My mind worked fast, trying to put it together.

Then, suddenly, it clicked.

I muttered a curse. "Bristol is blackmailing Kip with these photos."

I had suspected their marriage was a business arrangement because I hadn't seen any kind of affection between them. But this was so much worse.

The corner of Ainsley's mouth twitched. "You guessed it. My sister has been busy."

Bristol had been the worst even when we were kids, but I'd never expected her to be such a snake. Then anger ignited in my chest as I thought through the full implications.

Bristol was blackmailing Kip...and using the photos to do it.

"Is your sister the one who sent those photos to Grace, but doctored to make it look like *I* was the one with Nina?"

Ainsley shrugged. "Bristol is awful, we all know that. I told her not to be so petty. But she's jealous of Grace."

"You *knew*?" I dug my fingers into my hair. "Do you have any idea what it was like for Grace to see those? To think I lied to her? I could've lost her over that bullshit."

I thought of the woman I loved in my bedroom right now, and all I wanted was to get Ainsley out of here. I didn't want Grace to hear any of this crap, not tonight. I could deal with my family's treachery tomorrow.

I pointed at the door. "I don't have the patience for this, Ains. Either tell me what you're really doing here, or get the hell out."

She stood up, placing her palms on the desk. "I wouldn't be here unless I had no other options. Kip's actions have had some unfortunate consequences, and I need to know whether you'll work with me on sorting all of this out and making it go away."

My blood ran cold. "Jesus. Are you talking about Nina's murder? Kip is responsible for that? Is that what you're saying?"

"In a way, yes. If he'd been smarter, none of this would've happened."

"Just say what you fucking mean," I seethed. "But know this. If you think I'm going to hush up the cold-blooded murder of an innocent woman for anyone, family or not, you're out of your mind."

"Then you need a reminder of what's at stake. Vincent, you can come in."

I whirled around to face the door.

And my entire world shifted into a nightmare.

Vincent Brady stood in the doorway with Grace in front of him. He held a knife to Grace's neck. Her amber eyes pleaded with me. Her lips shook as she tried to keep still. Immediately, I thought of the way Nina had died. Her throat had been cut, maybe with that same weapon.

My jaw clenched so hard that my teeth creaked, grinding together. "If you hurt her, I swear..."

"I don't want to hurt Grace," Ainsley said. "I happen to like her. But I'm a businesswoman, and I'll use whatever leverage I have."

I tried to project my determination through my gaze. *Hold on. I'm getting us out of this.*

"Leverage, huh?" I almost laughed as I finally understood, though I didn't take my eyes from the tip of the knife brushing Grace's neck. "You're the one running the escort ring. Is it just you, or is the rest of the Harcourt family in on it too?"

I was facing away from Ainsley, but I heard her come around to the side of the desk. Saw in my periphery as she leaned against it.

"Bristol works with me, though I often find myself questioning that decision. My father has no idea. He's like your dad. A dinosaur who wants to control his children by giving us bits and pieces of his legacy. I decided to break free of that. Start my own business, like you. But running escorts isn't really about cash. It's about information. Blackmail material that I can use to get what I really want."

"Dane is nothing like you," Grace said, then whimpered when the tip of Vincent's knife drew a drop of blood against her pale skin.

I took a few steps toward them, my fists clenching.

"*Dane,*" Ainsley said.

Vincent's mouth twisted. "Come any closer, and you won't like the result."

It took every ounce of willpower I could summon not to launch myself at the man. "I swear I'm going to kill you, Brady."

Vincent laughed and scraped the knife against Grace's skin again. She squeezed her eyes shut.

"Ainsley, if you want me to listen to your bullshit, then let Grace go. There's no discussion so long as that piece of trash is touching her."

Ainsley came into my field of vision, crossing her arms over her suit jacket. "You have nothing to bargain with. Zero leverage."

Yet we both knew that wasn't true. Otherwise, she would just make her demands instead of trying to get me on her side.

But I also had an additional bargaining chip.

"I have something you want. The information that Nina Badowski was planning to turn over to a reporter."

Grace's eyes flashed. "Dane, no."

Ainsley tapped her fingers against her arm, trying to hide the interest in her expression. "Is that right?"

Grace looked pissed. If at all possible, I wasn't going to turn over everything. But I had to get that murderer away from her.

"There are financials," I said. "And a list of names that includes Kip and Dirk Lancaster. I'm assuming that's a list of your clients?"

Now, I definitely had Ainsley's attention.

"Fine." She nodded at Vincent. "Grace will stay here, but I'll keep an eye on her myself. Probably smarter if Vincent is guarding you, anyway. So you don't do anything stupid."

The knife left Grace's throat, and I started breathing again. Vincent moved to my side, though he didn't get too close. Didn't want to risk me grabbing for it.

Ainsley crossed to Grace, held her by the shoulder, and made her sit in one of the chairs in front of my desk. Ainsley took the other. Grace kept her hand against the cut on her neck, eyes down on the carpet. Which bothered me. I hated seeing her so dejected. But at least Vincent wasn't touching her anymore.

"The information Nina stole," Ainsley said. "Where is it? I want every copy and a guarantee that you haven't shared it with anyone else."

"Don't do it, Dane," Grace countered.

Ainsley lifted her eyebrow, as if in challenge.

I sat against the edge of the desk, keeping Vincent in my peripheral vision. "You'll get it. But I have questions first."

Grace's head bowed. Her hair fell past her shoulders, hiding part of her face, and her hand rested on her knee, fingers spread.

We're getting out of this, I promised her silently. *And we'll make them pay.*

"And I can answer them," Ainsley said. "If I get your assurance that you'll make sure our fathers sign their partnership agreement. Harcourt Hotels merging with Knightly Global's resorts. I also want a guarantee that when you and Kip eventually get control of Knightly Global, you'll sell all of your shares to me. For fair market value, of course."

The picture became that much clearer. I assumed Ainsley and Bristol had originally operated the escort service out of Harcourt Hotels. Gathering blackmail material. Using powerful men's weaknesses to their advantage.

I almost couldn't blame them for it. *Almost.*

Then, Kip had gotten caught up in their net. He must've become a client, and Bristol and Ainsley blackmailed him into proposing to Bristol. Our families were already friends, so the engagement was believable. Neither of our fathers would object.

Maybe the Harcourt sisters had planted the idea for the hotel partnership in their father's mind too. While Kip had done the same within Knightly Global.

But this much was clear: Ainsley was really the one in charge. And what Ainsley truly wanted was to own a business empire, using any means to make it happen. The escort business was just a means to an end.

Ainsley wanted Knightly Global for herself.

"I can live with that," I said. "The only reason I joined the family company was for my mom anyway, and I'm just grateful she'll never understand how far Knightly Global has fallen."

"Then go ahead and ask your questions."

Grace still had her eyes on the carpet.

I love you, gorgeous. Just hold on.

I crossed my arms. "Is my hotel manager working for you? Tobin?"

Ainsley shrugged. "Of course. I made sure I had him in my pocket months before your grand opening."

Which meant Tobin had let her into my suite tonight. That rat. He was also probably behind the "glitch" that had prevented us from identifying Vincent and Nina when I first asked for the security camera footage from the night of the grand-opening masquerade.

So much for that raise I had wanted to give him. Unbelievable.

"And the break-in at Grace's house? Who did that?"

"Tobin too. He's been useful."

Though I'd been speaking to Ainsley, I still had my focus on Grace. She tapped her fingers against her knee. It distracted me for a moment. Was she trying to tell me something?

Then she pulled back her thumb. Tapped again.

Five fingers, then four.

Whatever Grace was trying to tell me, I didn't want Ainsley or Vincent to notice. "But why did Tobin take Nina's mask?" I asked, to keep the conversation going.

"By then, we knew Nina had vanished. We also knew she had access to sensitive information about my business. She'd been talking to Grace that night before she disappeared, so I had to make sure she hadn't turned over the stolen data. Tobin was looking for anything about Nina he could find. Guess he didn't look thoroughly enough."

Grace and I knew that wasn't quite accurate. She'd returned the borrowed red clutch to Piper, so of course Tobin hadn't found it. "But where exactly did Nina get that data in the first place?"

Ainsley laughed. "Oh, you'll love this. Kip gave it to her. Turns out he had more backbone than I expected. He was pissed off about the blackmail, so he stole our client list and some financials. He gave that info to Nina for safe-keeping."

"Why her?"

"Because the fool thought he was in love with her. He passed the documents to Nina and then told me and Bristol. He thought his act of rebellion would mean an insurance policy against us. But he basically signed Nina's death warrant."

Grace's fingers tapped again. She pulled back another finger. Going from four to three.

Oh, *shit*. She was counting down to something. What was Grace planning to do?

"We knew we had to find Nina before she shared that data with anyone," Ainsley went on, oblivious. "Vincent was tasked with locating her. He put pressure on anyone who knew Nina. You and Grace were never supposed to get involved."

Grace finally lifted her head, eyes narrowed with fury. "So Kip used Nina just as much as the rest of you. How can any of you live with yourselves?"

"Money is security," Ainsley said. "So I manage just fine."

The fingers on Grace's knee shifted to just two.

Dammit. Okay. So we were doing this. I had to be ready, and I had to make sure that Vincent and Ainsley didn't notice what Grace was up to.

I took a step forward, making Vincent's knife hand flinch in my direction.

"But you didn't expect Nina to go to a reporter," I said quickly. "Neither did Kip."

Ainsley's focus moved from Grace back to me. "When Nina disappeared, I expected she might be planning something along those lines. Didn't know for sure until you told me today. Want to share the reporter's name?"

"If you let Grace leave right now, I'll consider it."

Ainsley smirked. "You haven't even proved you have the stolen information."

"You're the one who's trying to add new terms to our deal. You haven't answered all of my questions yet. Why did Bristol send those fake photos of me and Nina to Grace?"

If Grace was surprised, she didn't react. She just tapped her fingers again. Still at two. But I was starting to sweat, wondering when she'd get to one and what would happen after.

Don't be reckless, baby.

"Like I said, Bristol can be petty. We knew that you were looking for Vincent and Lexi, that you were getting way too close to the truth about our business. Bristol thought it would throw you off balance or something. But mostly, she's just kind of a bitch."

I uncrossed my arms, forcing myself to appear relaxed, though every part of my body tensed in readiness for whatever Grace was about to do. "And then you must've found where Nina was hiding, and you ordered Vincent to kill her."

Grace's fingers shifted, another finger disappearing.

One.

Fuck.

Ainsley inclined her head. "I knew you had an investigator working for you, and I figured you might be close to finding Nina. It's a good thing we found her first. Vincent got to her just last night. When Tobin called me early this morning, letting me know you were on your way to Silver Ridge, I knew I needed to speak to you personally. So that we could get on the same page."

Grace's beautiful face had turned to stone. I could sense exactly what she was thinking. Ainsley had spoken so callously about ordering the death of an innocent woman.

"Then what is it that you want from me?" I asked. "Grace and I know about your business. We know you're responsible for Nina's murder. What did you come here tonight hoping to do?"

Ainsley spread her hands. "To call a truce between us. I won't harm you or Grace. Or rather, I won't have Vincent harm either one of you. You and Kip will deliver Knightly Global when it becomes time. Meanwhile, you let us run our escorts out of Knightly Global properties, including this resort. You don't interfere. You don't try to mess with me. And we can all be one big, happy family."

Grace's fingers tightened into a fist on her knee.

Zero.

With a primal scream, Grace launched herself at Ainsley. Their chairs both toppled. I heard something crash into the wall, but I had to trust that Grace could look after herself.

I grabbed Vincent's wrist to stop him from striking out with his knife, while at the same time I smashed my fist into the man's nose. Payback for what he'd done to Grace, and it was satisfying.

Vincent recovered fast, struggling with me for control of the knife. His leg swept out to knock me off my balance. I fell back against the desk. He tried to bring the knife down while I held his arm back, both of us shaking with the effort.

Blood dripped onto my shirt from Vincent's nose. "You're going to die for that."

"Not if I kill you first."

"I'm not the one with a knife pointed at his neck." Vincent grunted as he used his weight to drive the tip of the knife downward.

So I decided to let him.

Instead of pushing, I pulled down on Vincent's hands while I twisted rapidly to the side. The knife tip slammed into the wooden desktop, embedding there. Then I got my leg up between us and kicked out, shoving Vincent back.

Pain burned along the side of my neck, and wetness dribbled down to my shirt collar. That had been *way* too close.

I pulled the knife from the desk and levered myself upright. Ainsley was slumped on the floor over by the wall, and Grace crouched over her. Vincent looked from me to Grace, like he was trying to decide whether to grab her and make her a hostage. But that would mean turning his back on me if he wanted to reach her fast enough.

"Touch her and die," I growled.

With a bellow, Vincent rushed me. But I was ready for him.

I buried the knife in Vincent's chest, my other arm wrapping around his back like we were embracing. He struggled a moment, eyes going wide, before his bodyweight slumped. I stepped back, letting him go, and Vincent fell to his knees. Then he toppled to the side.

My blow had hit its mark, going straight to the man's heart.

Grace was crouched on the ground near Ainsley. She got up on wobbly legs. "Ainsley's out cold. Is Vincent..."

"He's not your problem." Vincent wasn't anyone's problem. Not anymore.

I crossed the room and pulled Grace into my arms. She was shaking. Then she pushed back from me and gasped. "Dane, your neck is bleeding."

"It's a scratch." I brushed her hair back from her face. Her glasses were askew, so I set them right. "Your head okay?"

"I'm good. If anyone got a concussion tonight, it's Ainsley."

"That countdown of yours. I can't believe you did something so reckless. But I'm glad you did."

"I'm glad you figured it out. Just..." She cringed. "Don't mention it to my brothers."

Was she kidding? I was going to tell all of Silver Ridge, hell, all of New York City too, that she'd saved both of us with that stunt. "I'll see what I can do."

"Today was a bit too much excitement for me."

I had to laugh. "Message received. I'll try to make our lives a little more boring in the future."

THIRTY-NINE

Dane

Ten Days Later

I did my best to deliver on my promise to Grace. But it didn't seem like *boring* was in the cards for us.

"Hot cocoa delivery!" I shouted, holding out a tray of insulated cups and bracing myself as a dozen kids descended. They were all in ski gear, with giant goggles and helmets obscuring their features but not hiding their smiles.

"Is there marshmallows, Uncle Dane?" Maisie asked, clasping her mittens together. "I really love marshmallows."

I leaned down and whispered, "I added extra to your cup. And Ollie's too." The kids were on a break from their ski lesson, and I'd offered to make the cocoa run.

Grace was on snack duty. She arrived minutes after me, carrying individually wrapped treats. "Who's hungry?" she asked. Grace was in full winter wear, with a white beanie pulled over her hair and her cheeks pink from the cold.

I wrapped an arm around her waist. "I'm hungry for something," I murmured, "and you're looking very sweet."

She smiled and shook her head at me. "I gave you some of *that* sugar just this morning. Don't get greedy."

"Then you should stop looking so good."

Only a week and a half had passed since Ainsley and Tobin's arrests and Vincent's death. Grace and I had been cooperating fully with law enforcement.

I'd also had an *extremely* awkward phone conversation with my father. It hadn't gone well.

Aside from that, I'd been helping Grace get back to the "regular" life she wanted. And since that included waking up next to her, sitting down for meals together with family and friends, and indulging in hot, uninhibited sex whenever we got the urge, then I was just thrilled to be a part of it.

She hadn't said she loved me yet, but I felt good about my chances.

Of course, now that we were back in Silver Ridge, there was a lot of small-town charm in our everyday life. *All* the small-town charm. In fact, I was proud to add to our town's offerings.

That was why I'd opened up the ski resort today for a locals-only community day. Free ski lessons, discounted lift tickets, and hot cocoa with obscene amounts of marshmallows. It had been Grace's idea, a way to give back to Silver Ridge and help me get to know its residents.

And I was thrilled to see that much of the town had turned out, including Ashford, Emma, and Piper. Even Callum and a slew of his buddies from Silver Ridge FD. Dixie Haines, Mayor Barker, and the other ladies from bingo were in the lift line, and Chief Landry and several of his officers had made appearances too.

The sun was bright despite the cold. We'd just gotten a heavy snow yesterday—perfect timing—which had blanketed everything like the promise of a clean slate.

Ashford lifted his chin as he walked toward me. My buddy and Emma had been snowboarding earlier, and I'd personally witnessed Ashford fall multiple times on his ass, much to his fiancée's delight. Ashford *hated* to be bad at things. To be fair, so did I. But we both enjoyed making our ladies laugh, so at least there was that.

Ashford reached me, and we watched the kids bound off with their instructor toward the bunny slopes. "A lot of people were surprised you and Grace weren't there last night," Ashford said.

I felt my smile freeze in place. "Can you blame us?" I glanced over at Grace, who was chatting out of earshot with Emma and Piper.

"No, man. Of course not. I'm happy you kept Grace away from it, and you know I've got your back. Just wanted to let you know in case some busybody brings it up."

Last night, Sheriff Douglas and Chief Landry held a town hall meeting to answer questions about Nina's murder and Vincent's death. National news of the larger scandal had broken in the last few days. Starting with an article by Norm Haber, which he'd published at lightning speed, probably so he wouldn't get scooped. Though I'd heard he was also working on a book.

The details were juicy. A high-class escort ring, a murder, and blackmail involving some of the wealthiest people on the East Coast, including the heir to Knightly Global... I'd ignored a slew of calls for interviews. More articles digging into my family would inevitably follow. I had no doubt documentary-makers and podcasters were busy trying to recreate the story with all its twists and turns and salacious moments. Plenty of people on Ainsley's client list, like Dirk Lancaster, had to explain themselves. I wanted nothing to do with that.

But for Grace and me, the mess wasn't anywhere near finished yet. No matter how much we wished the whole thing would go away.

"We were answering questions almost nonstop for days," I said. "I suggested we skip the town hall and let the authorities handle it, and I was surprised when Grace agreed."

Ashford chuckled. "Grace has never liked being told what to do."

"She does not, and I wouldn't have it any other way. Your

sister took out Ainsley Harcourt, the Heiress Madame." As Norm Haber had dubbed her in his article. "Grace is a badass."

Ashford muttered a curse. "Please don't remind me. Funny how you and Grace have been asking for privacy, yet everyone in Hart County knows all about how Grace risked her life to save the day."

My smile returned. Because I had spread that particular rumor myself. The town's residents adored Grace even more than before. Which was what she deserved.

Opinions on me were more mixed, since I was the New Yorker who'd brought such unsavory elements to their town. But the situation wasn't hopeless.

Tobin, my former traitorous hotel manager, had confessed to everything he knew about Ainsley, the escort ring, and his involvement in the break-in at Grace's house. Tobin had also confirmed that I had nothing to do with any of it.

Ainsley was going to be charged for the murder of Nina Badowski, since she'd ordered the hit. There were rumblings of other charges here and in New York, which would probably take months to sort out, including Bristol's role in everything. Kip and his new wife had returned from their honeymoon just in time for the truth to come out.

I had no idea what was going on with my brother. Whether he despised me even more, whether he'd be charged with a crime. Whether he still worked for Knightly Global at all.

My ever-resourceful assistant Margot had been doing her best to roll with the chaos, but even she didn't know those answers yet.

I expected the Harcourts would hire the best lawyers Manhattan had to offer to defend Ainsley, both there and in Colorado. But one thing was certain. I would use every bit of my money and influence to make sure Ainsley served prison time for Nina's murder. Same with Bristol.

Even if I'd been tempted to stay out of it, Grace wouldn't have let me. She'd already given me an earful about the subject. I'd assured her we were completely on the same page. There was no way I'd let either of the Harcourt sisters get away with their crimes.

"I'm just thankful Grace is okay," Ashford said. "Glad you're safe too, but my little sister..."

I nodded. I would never fully understand that big brother/baby sister bond, but I understood to the depths of my soul how special Grace was. "I get it. But I also want to make myself completely clear. I love Grace, and I would give everything for her. I mean *everything*. There was never a question of me walking away from that situation without Grace walking out right alongside me."

Ashford blew out a heavy breath, making white clouds appear in the frigid air. "I appreciate it. I asked for your intentions toward Grace once, and your answer was pretty vague. But I have the feeling I won't have to ask again."

A grin tugged at my lips. "I intend to make Grace very happy for the rest of our lives."

"Good answer." He scratched his beard. "I do have one other question for you, though."

"Hit me."

"Would you be my best man?"

I turned to stare at him. "Your best man? I assumed you would ask Callum."

He shrugged sheepishly. "Cal is my brother, and I love him. But you're my best friend."

I felt only the briefest hesitation. But I pulled him into a hug. "Then I'm there. I would be honored." I hadn't told Ashford yet about tracking down Grayden. Grace had asked me not to. I was leaving that to her, and I had to trust that Ashford would understand.

We had each other's backs. Someday, I hoped that Ashford would stand by my side when I married his sister. But the women we loved came first.

✧

I was all smiles as the day wore on. Helping out the staff, mingling with Silver Ridge residents, building a snowman with Grace and the kids during breaks in ski lessons. I even took Grace on a few easy runs, and while she was very much a beginner, she was getting the hang of it.

We reached the bottom of the run and snapped out of our skis just as my phone buzzed in my pocket.

Grace tugged off her helmet. "Someone calling you?"

I pulled out my phone. "Looks like a text."

"Let me guess, it's Dixie, demanding another hot toddy. We are probably going to have to cut her off."

I laughed, thinking of how Dixie had been tearing down the slopes. The woman claimed she didn't usually spend winter in Silver Ridge, preferring to head to the warmer climes of Florida, but she'd decided to stick around through Thanksgiving this year. I wanted her to make it safe and sound to the holiday and not take out anyone else either, so Grace was probably right.

But when I opened the text, it was from the assistant manager, Rhonda. She'd taken over for Tobin as the acting head manager until I made a final hiring decision. "Someone's in the lobby for me. And Rhonda added three exclamation points, so I assume it's urgent." I gave Grace a quick kiss. "I'll be back. Watch out for Dixie. Love you."

"I value my life, so yes, I'll be watching for Dixie. Hurry back."

I left my skis in a rack, still grinning as I headed into the lobby.

Then I saw who was waiting for me near the reception desk, and I stopped in my tracks. "Dad." I glanced over at Rhonda, and she mouthed, *Sorry*.

No wonder she hadn't mentioned who was here. My father

had probably asked her not to. He was *my* boss and the ultimate owner of the ski resort.

"Son. Is there someplace private we could speak?"

I had to assume Dad had made the trip all the way to Silver Ridge to chew me out in person. Nothing to do but get this over with. "Sure."

I led him to Tobin's former office, which Rhonda had been using as acting manager. But she was at the front desk for the moment, and I had no intention of taking my father up to the hotel room I shared with Grace. We had moved our things out of the top-floor suite after it became a crime scene. We'd been staying in a mountain view room on the fifth floor instead.

"I didn't know you were coming."

"I decided it would be better to do this unannounced."

"Okay." I pointed at a chair, but my father didn't sit. So I didn't either. I waited for the verbal evisceration to begin. For my betrayal of our family, for the damage I'd done to Knightly Global. Though I'd only been the messenger.

But that wasn't what happened.

"First, uh..." My father trailed off, his face slack with uncertainty. Something I'd never seen in my life. "I'd like to apologize for the way I reacted when we last spoke on the phone."

Shit. An apology? This had never happened before either.

"When you first broke the news about what Kip had done, the blackmail, the murder, all of it... I was very shocked and upset."

"Understandable." I dug my hands into my pockets, not sure of what to do with myself.

My father clasped his hands behind his back. "Kip has decided to take a leave of absence from the company. He's also going to seek an annulment from Bristol Harcourt, though I'll let the lawyers sort that out."

"Makes sense." But I wanted to go back to the part about this leave of absence. "Did Kip admit to his role in everything?"

My father nodded. "He's cooperating with the NYPD, even against his own lawyers' advice. Says he's deeply remorseful about what happened to..." Dad cleared his throat. "That woman he was seeing."

I sighed. "Nina Badowski. The woman died because of Kip. Maybe not directly, but I still consider him responsible. The least you can do is say her name."

My father blinked, some of his pride returning. Here was the infuriating man who had disowned me. Who had never seen me as good enough for our precious family name.

But then he said, "You're exactly right. Kip does feel responsible for Nina's death, and he told me he's committed to doing what's necessary to get his life back on track. To atone. Including making his own apologies to you and to Grace, for the fact that she got caught up in it."

I would believe that when I heard it, but it was something. Hell, I hadn't expected to hear these words coming from my father at all.

"Thank you for letting me know," I said sincerely. "But I don't see why you made the trip all the way here. You could've done this over the phone."

"I came here in person in the hopes of mending our relationship. I know we've disagreed in the past—"

I snorted. "Dad, that's an understatement."

"So it is." Was that the hint of a smile on Dennis Knightly's face? "When you joined the company, you did it for your mother. Not because you truly wanted to work for me. You bought this ski resort and practically moved in because you wanted to get away from our family."

My hackles rose, though what he was saying was true. "I'll buy the resort from you, if that's what you want. You won't have to deal with this project anymore, since it's beneath you. You won't have to deal with *me* anymore."

"No, that is the last thing I want," he cut in. Dad rubbed a hand over his face and sank into a chair. "I'm here to beg for your forgiveness. And ask for your help. Knightly Global has suffered a serious blow. I've been a fool. Failed to see what was in front of me."

I sat in the chair beside him, resting my elbows on my knees. "I came to Silver Ridge hoping to find what I was missing," I said. "And I did. I found Grace. She's the woman I want to spend my life with. I also found a place that feels like home, and it's partly because Grace is here. But that's not the only reason. Being here reminds me of the best times growing up. Vacations to the mountains. The times we were happy. When we were a family."

Dad looked at me. *Really* looked at me. "Those memories are very special to me as well. If you'll stay on with Knightly Global, then we can consider Silver Ridge a satellite office. You can work from here." That hint of a smile snuck into his expression again. "Though it's up to you to discuss the matter with Margot."

I huffed a laugh. "Yeah, I think Margot is meant for the city, through and through. We can make it work though. If you're serious about this. If you'll treat me as a partner and not as an annoyance. I don't mean my job title. I couldn't care less what it says on the plaque outside my office. I need to know you'll respect what I bring to the company."

"You've got my full support. And my respect. You've always had my respect, even if I've been an idiot about showing it."

"Thank you." Though part of me still wondered if my dad had been replaced with a clone or something.

"I hope you're willing to get started right now," he said. "Because we have a lot to discuss."

I sent off a quick text to Grace, letting her know I would be busy for a while, but that all was well. I sent off a similar text to Rhonda at the front desk, though without the heart emojis.

Dad gave me a quick-and-dirty picture of how bad things were. How the board was losing confidence. How investors were threatening to pull out. But after a couple of hours, we had a strategy prepared. I would hold a teleconference with the board as soon as possible to answer their questions and concerns. And assure them that I wasn't leaving the company.

Hard as it was to believe, especially for me, I was going to stay on with Knightly Global. It had to be different this time. But I was optimistic that it would.

My father leaned back in his seat. "I was hoping we could have dinner tonight. With Grace. I'd very much like to meet the woman you love."

Geez, was he kidding? "You already met her, Dad. In New York. Did you forget?"

"I remember," he snapped. "But I'd like to make a better impression. Do you need me to spell it out? I probably came across as an ass the first time, and I want my future daughter-in-law to like me."

I almost laughed and made a quip about his *other* experience with daughters-in-law, but my father's sense of humor only stretched so far. "She's not your future daughter-in-law just yet. I'm working on that. But dinner would be great. You can meet Grace's whole family." That was going to be interesting. But the O'Neals were as good as my family too, so Dad had better get used to it.

But there was one more thing I had to address before we were finished.

"Dad, we haven't talked about Mom. We've never really talked about her diagnosis or her treatment. Her future. I know it's not easy to discuss, and we don't have to hash it all out now."

"You think I'm not doing what's best for her?"

"I don't think that," I said softly. "I just want to be involved. I love Mom too."

His expression was pained, and for a brief moment, I glimpsed the agony he felt. Dad had never let me see it before.

"What I'd really like," I added, "is to be able to bring Mom out here to Silver Ridge. I think she'd love it, whether it's a short visit or a longer stay. I realize it depends on what the doctors say, and a bunch of other factors, but I'm asking for you to at least consider it."

He thought for a while. And then he nodded. "It's been horrible. Watching her slip away when she's still there in front of me. Your mother is the love of my life. I would do anything for her."

I put my hand on my dad's shoulder. "I know the feeling."

FORTY

Grace

Dennis Knightly, sitting on the floor of Ashford's apartment in his custom suit and building Lego sets with Ollie and Maisie.

Not how I'd ever dreamed today would end.

But after a fun-filled day of sunshine, ski lessons, and hot cocoa, my closest family and friends had taken over Emma and Ashford's place for dinner. Including Dane's father, who actually seemed to be making an effort.

Considering that Callum and his firefighter buddies were here and getting as rowdy as usual, it was pretty dang hilarious. Manhattan meets Silver Ridge.

But the very best part? The wide grin on Dane's face as we stood in the kitchen, drinking beer and relaxing.

We were full of pizza and caesar salad, a little tipsy from the growlers of IPA someone had brought from Hearthstone Brewing. For the first time in well over a week, the world felt like it was right-side-up. Better, in fact, than it had ever been before.

I loved being here with our family and friends, but I also couldn't wait to get Dane alone later, when that grin would be just for me.

Emma squeezed in beside me and clinked her beer glass

against mine. "Dane's father paid for dinner *and* extra orders of cinnamon twists. Maisie's a fan."

It was noisy enough in the apartment that there wasn't much risk of us being overheard. "Free food means he's got the volunteer firefighter vote too. If Dennis springs for high-end bottles of whiskey later, he'll be *in*."

Emma didn't look convinced. "Unless you don't like him. He'll be on the outs around here unless he gets the Grace O'Neal seal of approval."

"That's not actually a thing."

"Wanna bet?"

To be honest, I'd been less than polite when Dennis had first appeared this afternoon. While he and Dane had been talking in the hotel manager's office, I'd been biting my nails, wondering how bad it would be. But then Dane had brought his father outside to where we were all gathered, and Dennis apologized to me for everything I'd been through.

"What about Dane?" I'd asked, pursing my lips. "Did you apologize to your son?"

Dane had placed a hand on my hip and tugged me against him. "At ease, O'Neal," he'd murmured in my ear. "I'll give you all the details later, but we're good." By then, we had a crowd gathered, everyone curious to meet the head of Knightly Global and ask nosy questions. I let them have at it. Though I'd been very civil about it.

"If Dane's okay with his father, then I'm okay with him," I said to Emma. "But you're exaggerating how much pull I have in this town."

"When I moved here, people were welcoming. But if you'd decided I was bad news? Yikes." Emma made a face. "You didn't want me dating Ashford at first, and for a few days there, I was sweating it."

I laughed. "Like I could've kept Ashford away from you. I *wouldn't* have, of course. I'm thrilled you'll be my sister-in-law soon. Officially."

"Speaking of the wedding." Her teeth tugged on her lower lip. "I've been meaning to ask, but you were in New York, and then things were so crazy."

"Ask what?"

"If you'd be my maid of honor."

"*Me*?"

"You're like a sister to me, and you've become one of my closest friends. You've done so much for Ashford and Maisie. It feels right. Plus, I hear Dane will be best man. Would you be up for joining the fun?"

"Oh my gosh, *yes*." I hugged her, tears stinging my eyes.

My life wasn't boring anymore. But it was so incredibly rich. And I wasn't referring to money. I was in a relationship with an amazing guy—who also happened to be smoking hot—and we had our families around us. It sounded like Dane's father was on board with Izzy coming to visit, which would be huge for Dane and his mom both.

It could really be like this, I thought to myself. *I could feel this happy every day.*

We still had to deal with unwanted media attention related to the scandal and the legal cases against Ainsley and Bristol. And things were still tense between Dane and his brother. But I could see the light at the end of it.

There was only one thing still occupying the back of my mind. Well, two things. The first was that I still hadn't told Dane I loved him. Every time I thought about it, the words got stuck.

The second thing was even more complicated. I had to make a decision. But I had to tell my brothers first, and they were *not* going to be thrilled when they heard.

After Maisie's bedtime, things quieted down. Callum's roommates headed off to a bar, and Piper took Ollie home. Dane was in the living room talking to his father. So I went looking for my brothers.

I found Callum, Ashford, and Emma up on the roof, bundled

up against the cold. They had several lawn chairs up here, so I took an empty one.

"There's something I wanted to talk to you guys about."

"What's wrong, Grace?" Ashford asked. Going to worst-case scenarios the way he tended to do, though less often since Emma came into his life.

Callum frowned, crossing his thick arms over his Silver Ridge FD sweatshirt.

"Nothing's wrong. Not exactly." I pulled the folded piece of paper from my back pocket. I'd been carrying it around for over a week, ever since Dane had given it to me. I figured it was better to just spit this out, rather than trying to build up to it. "I know where Grayden is."

Callum cursed and grabbed the paper, while Ashford went completely still.

"He lives in Seattle," Callum read. "What the fuck? How did you find this out?"

"Dane hired a private investigator to track Grayden down."

Ashford's eyes flashed. "He *what*?"

"Don't you dare be mad at him. Dane did it for me because I wanted to find Grayden. I haven't contacted him yet. He doesn't even know I was looking for him."

"Are you going to contact him?" Callum asked.

"I haven't decided for sure. I wanted to discuss it with you. *All* of you," I said, nodding at Emma, because she was part of this family too. "I'd like to, though. I'd..." Tears burned at my eyes, itched in my nose. "I want him to know I miss him. That no matter what, we're still family."

"I don't miss him." Ashford stood. "Do what you feel is right, Grace, but I can't be a part of this."

Emma reached for him. "Ashford—"

He took her hand and kissed it. "Let's go back inside. It's getting cold."

It was clear that Ashford wouldn't discuss the subject any further, so I didn't try to argue. After he and Emma had gone, I turned to Callum. He was still looking at the print-out with Grayden's info on it.

"Do you feel the same as Ashford?" I asked.

"I dunno, G. This is tough. The soldier in me wants nothing to do with Grayden. He dishonored himself. Dishonored *us*."

"We don't even know what really happened," I pointed out, but Callum kept going.

"Then there's the part of me that worshipped the ground our oldest brother walked on. It's good to know he's alive, at least. But talking to him, letting him be in our lives again... I just don't know."

"Will you hate me if I get in touch with him? Will Ashford hate me?"

Callum glanced up, brows knitting. "Geez, Grace. No. We could never hate you. Ashford will calm down. And I'm fine with whatever you decide. Just be careful. Don't be surprised if Grayden disappoints you."

I already knew that was a possibility. But by trusting Dane, I'd proven that the risk of putting myself out there was worth it.

Grayden had been a good man once. Maybe he still was. I owed it to us all to find out.

✧

"I told Ashford and Callum about finding Grayden."

Dane brushed the hair back from my face. "And?"

We were lying in bed in our hotel room. Dane's father had taken a room on a different floor, and he had a flight out first thing tomorrow morning. We'd already said our goodbyes. Dane had shared with me everything that he and his father had discussed. His dad's apology, and the possible beginnings of a better relationship between them. I hoped so.

But we hadn't talked about my conversation with my own family yet. Not because I hadn't wanted to share. I had just been focused on Dane, which to me was a luxury. After so many years of being the baby sibling, who everybody always looked out for, I longed for someone of my own to take care of. I'd tried to take care of Ashford and Maisie. Heck, I'd tried to take care of the whole town in some ways. But Dane was truly *mine*.

I still felt uncertain about the issue of my oldest brother. But I had zero doubts about Dane's support. I owed him so much.

"Ashford reacted the way I expected."

"I can talk to him tomorrow."

"No, it's fine. I told him not to be mad at you, and I don't think he is." I thought of my brother's reaction, and it dawned on me. "Ashford's afraid of getting hurt again. Callum is probably the same. He was less adamant about it, but he's not ready to talk to Grayden yet either." Ashford and Callum were both fearless in many ways. But when it came to our family's history, they had both been through a lot and still struggled to talk about it. Funny to think that, for some things, I was the strong one.

Dane cuddled me against him, stroking up and down my back over my T-shirt. "What about you? Have you decided whether to contact him?"

I had known I wanted this for a while. So why wait any longer?

I sat up, glancing at the clock. "It's almost midnight. Almost eleven in Seattle. Do you think it's too late to call?"

"If I were Grayden, I would want to hear from you anytime, any day."

I grabbed my phone and the paper with Grayden's number. My hand shook as I dialed. "Do you want me to stay?" Dane asked.

"Please. I need you here."

He snuggled in close to me. As I listened to the line ring, my heart jackrabbited against my ribs.

"Hello?"

I gasped. That was my brother's voice. My response was trapped in my throat.

"Hello? Uh, it looked like a Colorado number calling?"

Now, I heard the anxious hope in Grayden's voice. The same thing I felt. "It's me. Grace."

There was a pause. "*Gracie*? Oh my God."

We didn't talk for long. Just enough to establish that we were both healthy and doing okay. Same with Ashford and Callum. Grayden peppered me with questions, wanting to know everything—how I'd found him, what I did for work, if he had nieces or nephews—but we both agreed we should set up a time to talk later, when it wasn't almost the middle of the night.

Dane sat close to me the whole time, silent but giving me strength through his presence.

Finally, we said goodbye and ended the call. I stared at the phone in my hand for a long while.

"How do you feel?" Dane asked.

"Kind of overwhelmed. But grateful. So grateful for you." I lifted my eyes. "This is the best gift you could ever have given me. I love you so much. I've loved you for weeks, but I was afraid to say it."

"I love you too. With everything I am."

Then I dissolved into tears and folded myself into his arms.

Epilogue

Grace

"Merry Christmas, baby," Dane murmured in my ear. "I have one more present for you."

"Is it in your pants?" I whispered back.

He burst out laughing, making everyone else in the living room turn and stare. "Nothing to see here," he said, then lowered his voice again. "Actually, it's out in the car."

I'd already had the best Christmas ever. Last night, we'd taken over Piper's house for a raucous Christmas Eve, almost too many people joining the celebration to fit. Especially when you added the kids and Stella the dog. Dane and I had brought the champagne and the cheeseboard. Yum.

This morning, I'd woken up next to Dane, and we spent a luxurious half an hour in a bubble bath, kissing and caressing each other until we both were so turned on we couldn't stand it anymore.

We hadn't even made it to the bed, Dane taking me up against the dresser beside a full-length mirror. I hadn't been able to take my eyes off of us as he'd thrust inside me, filling me so perfectly with every stroke. A Christmas gift to us both.

Then an hour later, we met my family at Ashford's apartment for Christmas breakfast and opening gifts around the tree. Dane was still a mediocre cook, but Callum had taught him how to make a mean pancake. On our last visit to NYC, Dane had bought some kind of rare maple syrup from Canada that was like liquid gold. This morning, he'd passed around the bottle at the breakfast table and brought out French butter, too. Maisie ate six pancakes before Ashford made her stop.

And then, when we were all gathered around the tree, Dane surprised me with a necklace. It had a pendant of the letter G crusted in tiny diamonds. Gorgeous and completely over the top, something I would never dream of asking for. Which somehow made the gift even better.

For Dane, I'd ordered a simple, masculine leather cuff branded with our names and the date we met, the day I'd bumped into him and spilled hot coffee down his front. Mortifying in the moment, yet a memory that never failed to make me smile. And still a running joke between us.

I had more than I could ever have imagined. So much love and laughter and happiness every day. What more could I ask for?

I'd had several more conversations with Grayden in the last couple of months, thanks to Dane tracking him down. My oldest brother wasn't planning to visit Silver Ridge just yet, not until Ashford and Callum were willing to see him, but I hoped we would get there.

Even work was better than ever. Dane had invested in my bookkeeping business, which helped me hire employees and expand my base of clients. He interacted with all kinds of people as a representative of Knightly Global, and he loved referring new clients to me.

I appreciated everything Dane did for me, and I did my best to show my love in turn in every way I could. But the man was making me look bad. I hadn't bought anything else for him to open.

I'll make him a nice dinner, I decided. *Followed by a massage and an epic blowjob.*

We'd been back in suite 701 since the beginning of the month, after some renovations. Dane's office looked completely different than it had when Ainsley and Vincent showed up on that fateful night. But neither of us had wanted their actions to dictate where we lived. And there was no question that we wanted to spend every night together.

Besides, I had been tired of living in a hotel room with no kitchen. Dane offered to move with me to the firefighter house, but I declined. Would've been funny, though. Seeing my billionaire boyfriend battle for space with four other guys and sharing one bathroom. Except I would've had to deal with that too, so yeah, no thanks.

One afternoon, I'd asked Dane if he would rather move back to New York. As much as it would pain me to be away from my family and friends, I would've done it. I adored Silver Ridge, but Dane meant even more to me. He assured me that he really did want to stay in Colorado.

I still didn't want to live in a hotel forever. He'd mentioned buying a house, and it seemed like he was making up his mind about that. Yet being with Dane meant that, no matter where we slept, we were home.

As for the Harcourt sisters, they'd both pled guilty to numerous charges and would soon be calling prison cells home. I thought of them very little these days, and that was how I liked it.

We hung out at Ashford's a while longer, enjoying a lazy Christmas morning. Emma told me the latest on the wedding plans. The big day was coming up in February, less than two months away, and it promised to be unforgettable. I looked forward to seeing Ayla there, since I hadn't seen her in person since New York.

Maisie roped Dane into playing with some of her new toys, while I helped clean up the kitchen and grabbed another cup of coffee. After lots of hugs with Emma and my brothers and my niece, Dane and I finally went out to his SUV.

He opened the passenger door for me, giving me a quick kiss before I got in. I glanced eagerly around, playing with the pendant on my new necklace. "Where's my other present?"

"So greedy. Be patient."

I stuck my tongue out at him.

Dane rounded the car and got in. Once he was in the driver's seat, he reached over and opened the glove compartment, pulling out a small rectangular box wrapped in silver paper with a gold bow.

I smiled as Dane set it in my lap. Maybe I *was* getting a little greedy, but I blamed him. Always spoiling me. But when I picked up the package, studying its shape and feeling how light it was, the smile slipped from my face.

Oh lordy. Was this what I thought it was?

I glanced up at him, my eyes probably wide as saucers. He laughed. "Relax. It's not that."

My shoulders lowered. I wanted everything with Dane, but an engagement was a step more than I was ready for. And like he so often did, he'd read that on my face.

"Go ahead and open it."

I untied the bow and lifted the lid. A key lay inside. It looked like a house key. Nervous excitement surged into my chest again. "What's this?"

Dane started the engine and put the car in gear. "Well, I have a confession. Your real present isn't really here in the car. I fudged the truth. The key is only a small part of it."

"What did you do?"

He grinned. "Patience. I'm driving you there right now."

After the first few turns, I had no idea where Dane was heading. We were driving away from Main Street and the central commercial district. Driving toward the foothills.

Then I really started to wonder. But when Dane took a

certain street and a familiar house appeared up the block, my mind turned into a whirlwind.

No. Way.

He pulled into the driveway of an adorable, one-story bungalow with cheerful yellow siding and a tiny porch. Snow dusted the rooftop and lawn. But in the summer, I knew the grass would fill in, and the back window of the house would overlook fields of wildflowers leading up toward the hills.

Dane switched off the SUV and nodded at the key he had given me. "Have you guessed it yet?"

"You didn't," I said breathlessly.

He smirked. "Oh yes, I did."

"You bought this house? *My* old house?" This was the place I had used to rent. The house that I had loved and improved with such care before the landlord broke our oral agreement and I got forced out. "How did you even know?" I had never mentioned this place to Dane. I'd moved out of it before I had even met him.

"Callum told me. Said how heartbroken you were when you had to leave it. So I worked out a deal with the new owner. Made her an offer she couldn't refuse."

"That's ominous."

Dane laughed. "Nah, just offered her a tidy profit and covered her moving expenses. We closed last week, and she's all moved out."

I still couldn't get my head around it. "You talked about buying a place, but I figured you meant a fancy custom home up in the hills. This place is tiny. I adore it, but it's much smaller than your apartment back in New York. Smaller than your hotel suite."

His hand cupped the back of my neck. "Technically, I didn't buy it for me. I bought it for *you*. There's some more paperwork we need to do, but the house will be in your name. I'd love to live here with you, if you ask me, and the square footage doesn't matter to me. I just care that you like it. You can do whatever you want with this place. Even make it an investment and rent it out. It's yours."

This. Man.

"I…I don't know what to say. Except thank you. And I love you."

"Anything for you," he said simply. And for Dane, it really was that simple. He leaned over to kiss me, and I held his face, opening up to the strokes of his tongue and then returning them with equal passion. I tried to put everything I was feeling into that kiss. How much I loved him. How I would do anything for him too.

If Dane wanted to live here with me, my dream guy in this adorable house, then I was all in.

But seriously, I had to come up with an epic Christmas present for him next year. I had some catching up to do.

"So you thought I was proposing when you first saw that gift box, huh?" he asked after we both had to take a breath.

I felt a blush spread up my neck and into my cheeks. "I want that someday. Don't get me wrong. But…"

"Not yet," he finished for me. His fingers caressed my cheek. He wore the cuff I'd given him on his wrist, and for a second, I imagined a ring on his finger too, declaring that he was mine. I was certainly his. Even if I wanted to wait to get engaged, there was no question where I belonged.

"I'm not going to rush you into anything," he said. "Even though I am pretty pushy."

"You are. And you called *me* greedy."

Dane's nose nudged mine. "But I'm not hoping for that much, am I? I just want you to spend forever with me."

"For a start." I smiled, my lips brushing against his.

"Exactly. Forever will do. For a start."

✧

Ayla Maxwell, Two Months Later

I had just arrived in Silver Ridge for the big wedding weekend, and Ashford was *stressed.*

Emma groaned. "I love my fiancé, but he has been getting on my last nerve. He thinks this storm will interfere with the wedding."

I sat at the table and grabbed a cellophane bag and some ribbon. "I checked the forecast before I left LA. I thought it wasn't that bad."

"It's not," Grace cut in. "The storm will bring just enough snow to make all the trees around the Last Refuge Inn look beautiful. The wedding will be perfect. Ashford is just a worry wart."

That was definitely true.

"How about you go relax for a while," I said to Emma. "Let Grace and me take care of the rest of the favors."

It took some more convincing to get Emma to let us take over. But Grace and I finished assembling the wedding favors, and then I took my favorite little girl in the world out for an afternoon adventure.

Maisie and I skipped along together, holding hands. I was wearing a baseball cap and sunglasses, though I still got some curious looks. The Silver Ridge locals were used to me by now. Tourists could be another story. The ski resort drew plenty of them, and the media attention around my family here had inspired some of my fans to visit in the hopes of seeing me. But it still wasn't as much of an issue as the paparazzi who liked to follow me on a daily basis in LA.

I thought of that creepy anonymous envelope I'd received several months back and suppressed a chill. Whoever had sent it, they'd left me alone since. Better to put it out of my mind.

"Where should we go first? The park?" I asked.

Maisie tapped her chin, a tiny replica of her dad. "How about Silver Linings?"

"You goof. We went to the coffee shop this morning. I seem to remember you eating a cinnamon roll as big as your head."

"But I didn't get to have a muffin," she said reasonably.

I cracked up. "You're determined to get as many treats out of me as possible this weekend, aren't you?"

"Is it working?"

Of course it was working.

After not being in her life for so many years, I tended to give Maisie anything and everything she wanted. Maybe it was just my deprived inner child coming out. I wanted to give Maisie all the things my sister and I didn't have growing up. Well, a loving father was number one on that list, and thankfully Ashford had that covered. But I was determined to fill in any other possible gaps.

Was I overcompensating? Possibly. But I didn't tend to do things halfway. I rarely took no for an answer. Especially when it was a territorial man standing in my way. That was why I hadn't given up on reconnecting with Ashford and Maisie, even though my brother-in-law had tried to avoid me for years.

Ugh, speaking of territorial men.

"There's Uncle Teller!" Maisie said, waving at the police SUV as it rolled slowly by. Police Chief Landry sat in the driver's seat, arm draped casually over the steering wheel. He smiled and waved back, but his mouth twisted a moment after.

I couldn't tell where exactly he was looking because of his sunglasses. But I had the feeling that frown was aimed at me.

From the moment we'd met last year, Chief Landry had made it clear he didn't like me. "*So you're who all that fuss is about*?" he'd asked, his tone dripping with disdain. As if I'd wanted those reporters to mob Ashford and Emma's building. As if I hadn't been desperate for a break from the constant attention. The chief had wanted to make sure I knew he wasn't impressed with me. And every time we'd crossed paths since, he'd barely been civil.

Well, I wasn't so impressed with that man either. Even if he was a close friend of the O'Neal family and enough of a presence in Maisie's life to warrant an uncle title.

Teller made me nervous. It wasn't just the fact that he was a military man, like my father had been, because Ashford and Callum had been in the Army too. Same with Dane. It wasn't those intense-looking scars on the chief's face, either.

Nope, it was the constant scowl he wore around me. But damned if I was going to show how much he unnerved me.

Maisie wasn't looking at me. So I lifted my hand. Extended my middle finger. And scratched my head with it, keeping that finger way up high so he couldn't miss it.

There.

Now Chief Landry knew exactly what I thought of him too.

Find out what happens when Ayla and Teller are stranded together in STORMSWEPT COLORADO! An opposites-attract, forced proximity romance.

A Note from Hannah

While I adore writing about Silver Ridge, Colorado, I was so thrilled to take Grace and Dane on a jaunt to NYC! Especially that shopping trip. (Perhaps some imaginary wish fulfillment on my part.)

I also wanted to continue developing the backstory of the O'Neal family, which will unfold throughout the series. If you're curious about Grayden O'Neal, rest assured, he will get his own story!

But next in the series, it's Teller and Ayla's book, Stormswept Colorado. These two had instant sparks in book 1, but it wasn't the good kind. *Whoops*. They can't stand each other. They also couldn't be more different, not just in age but in life experience. Yet when Ayla's stranded in a snowstorm—and a stalker fan won't leave her alone—Chief Landry will be there for her. Neither of them has any idea what they're in for.

Many thanks as always to my ARC readers, and to my fans who keep reading and enjoying my stories. It means so much to me to be able to share them with you.

Until next time—
Hannah

More from Hannah Shield

Hart County

Starcrossed Colorado (Ashford & Emma)

Moonlit Colorado (Dane & Grace)

Stormswept Colorado (Teller & Ayla)

Sunkissed Colorado (Callum & Zandra)

Homeward Colorado (Grayden & Piper)

✧

Last Refuge Protectors

Hard Knock Hero (Aiden & Jessi)

Bent Winged Angel (Trace & Scarlett)

Home Town Knight (Owen & Genevieve)

Second Chance Savior (River & Charlotte)

Iron Willed Warrior (Cole & Brynn)

✧

West Oaks Heroes

The Six Night Truce (Janie & Sean)

The Five Minute Mistake (Madison & Nash)

The Four Day Fakeout (Jake & Harper)

The Three Week Deal (Matteo & Angela)

The Two Last Moments (Danny & Lark)

The One for Forever (Rex & Quinn)

✧

Bennett Security

Hands Off (Aurora & Devon)

Head First (Lana & Max)

Hard Wired (Sylvie & Dominic)

Hold Tight (Faith & Tanner)

Hung Up (Danica & Noah)

Have Mercy (Ruby & Chase)

About the Author

Hannah Shield writes spicy, suspenseful romance with pulse-pounding action, fun & flirty banter, and tons of heart. She lives in the Colorado mountains with her family.

Visit her website at www.hannahshield.com.

www.ingramcontent.com/pod-product-compliance
Lightning Source LLC
LaVergne TN
LVHW041106080826
845145LV00007B/1695

* 9 7 8 1 9 5 7 9 8 2 3 8 0 *